A Cup

of

*R*EDEMPTION

CAROLE BUMPUS

Carole Bumpus

SwP

SHE WRITES PRESS

*This book is dedicated to the memory of Marcelle Zabé,
the real woman who was my inspiration and muse.
And to her daughter, Josiane Selvage,
my dear friend and confidante,
whose very life exudes the courageous, strong, and joyful character
of her French mother.*

*I am deeply indebted to these two women and to their entire family,
who allowed me the privilege to base my novel on a fictionalized version
of their lives.*

$\mathscr{L}$ist of $\mathscr{C}$haracters

Å

Sophie Zabél Sullivan (Primary character)

Jerome Sullivan (Tertiary character) – Sophie's husband

Marcelle Pourrette Zabél (Primary character) – Sophie's mother

Jules Zabél (Secondary character) – Marcelle's husband and Sophie's father

Kate Barrington (Primary character) – friend and confidante to both Sophie and Marcelle

Matt Barrington (Tertiary character) – Kate's husband and dearest friend

Thierry Pourrette (Secondary character) – Sophie's oldest brother (of 3)

Christian Pourrette (Secondary character) – Thierry's son

Jeannine Pourrette (Tertiary character) –Thierry's wife

Julien Zabél (Secondary character) – Sophie's 3rd brother

Michela (Marucci) Zabél (Tertiary character) – Julien's wife

Gérard Pourrette (Secondary character) – Sophie's 2nd brother

Jacqueline Pourrette (Tertiary character) – Gérard's wife

Honorine Pourrette (Secondary character) – Marcelle's mother

Raymond Pourrette (Secondary character) – Honorine Pourrette's husband

Tomas (Tertiary character) – Marcelle's step-father ... or was he?

Marie-Anne Tetiau (Tertiary character) – Marcelle's grandmother

Pierre Tetiau (Tertiary character) – Marcelle's grandfather

Aunt Suzanne (Tertiary character) – sister/aunt to Marcelle in Paris

Madeleine (Tertiary character) – Tante Suzanne's daughter, cousin to Sophie

Micheline Thionet or Mimi (Secondary character) – friend to both Sophie and Marcelle

Genéviève (tertiary character) – Marcelle's friend and roommate during wartime in Paris (WWII)

André (tertiary character) – Marcelle's lover during WWII and Gérard's father

Christophe (tertiary character) – first love to Sophie (father forbid her from seeing him)

Sophie-Marie Chirade (Secondary character) – best friend to Marcelle from Mainsat; goes by the name Marie (namesake to Sophie)

Ambrose Yieux (possible father to Thierry) – from Saint Brieuc, Brittany

PROLOGUE

$\mathcal{S}$earch for $\mathcal{M}$e. $\mathcal{S}$earch for $\mathcal{P}$ourrette

(Retrouve mes origines, ma famille paternelle.
Cherche qui etait mon père)

$\overset{.}{\underset{.}{\text{A}}}$

October 2001

HE AUTUMNAL BREEZE SWEPT over the French village cemetery of Evaux-les-Bains and cut through the tombstones where the three adults remained before their mother's grave. No one spoke. No one cried. Sophie swallowed hard. *Grief,* she thought, *is a private matter.* She knew how to contain her emotions, as did her brothers. Their mother, Marcelle, had taught them well.

A blue silk scarf slid off Sophie's head and onto her shoulders. Her short brown curls, touched faintly with grey, appeared to have sprouted wings as the wind buffeted her bird-like body. She felt her brothers sway on either side of her as swirling dry leaves lifted up and around them. Thierry, the oldest, breathed in hard, touched his chest, and then gasped. At sixty-six, he already had heart problems. Sophie feared their mother's death would push him over the edge. She looked up at him, his face tense and taut as a mask. *Has he ever forgiven Maman for abandoning him?* Over fifty years of explanations should have helped, but had they? *Does anyone ever get over being abandoned?*

She turned toward Julien. Her youngest brother stood tall. He had taken their mother's death in stride, although his experience with her had been altogether different. He'd always known their mother's love. Sophie, too, had been held in her mother's embrace. *No,* she shook her head, *the loss of Maman will hit Thierry the hardest.* She reached over to squeeze Thierry's hand, but it was stuffed tight into a ball in his pocket.

"Are you all right, Thierry?" Sophie whispered.

He cleared his throat, and something incoherent slipped out. She didn't catch it; she didn't ask again. Pain seemed to eke out through the seams of his old leather coat. She longed to wrap her arms around him but instead clutched her wool cape closer to her. Her small frame began to shake. Every part of her wanted to wail, to howl. *Why now, Maman? Why now?*

Once again, she swallowed her anguish. Repression was her ally. The trees creaked and whined with the wind. Dust rose from the open grave. Her scarf took liberties and fled from her shoulders. After the heartbreaking suicide of Gérard, their brother, fifteen years ago, Sophie had closed down. Even when her father's death followed three years later, she deigned not to weep. *Why would I?* She stifled a sob. But with the loss of their beloved mother? These two dear brothers were all she had left of her immediate family. She gritted her teeth, and once again, held tough. *Thank God for antidépressseurs!*

Julien scooped up Sophie's scarf, knocked off a dried leaf, and handed it back to her. A smile crossed Sophie's lips; her shoulders relaxed. Tying her scarf about her neck, she skillfully executed a French knot as thoughts of her mother softened. Her mother's death had come so suddenly. Although she was eighty-two, her mother had been in excellent health, or so she had said.

"Do you think her doctor expected this?" Sophie asked her

brothers. She thought of the last call she had made from her home in California to her mother's doctor in Fontanières. Had she misunderstood his words? A pall of guilt pressed down on her.

"He never mentioned anything to me, Sophie," Julien replied. They both looked at Thierry; he remained mute.

"Thirty years ago I promised *Maman* I would be here for her. Did I fail her?" Sophie's voice was barely audible.

"If so, then we all failed her," Julien said. "We live here in France and still didn't know the seriousness of her illness. Besides, that was a promise you made when you married Jerome and moved to the States. *Maman* knew you would be here when you could, and we all knew you left to get away from Papa . . ."

As if openly bidden, an image of their father's scowling face floated through her mind. Shards of rage followed and then spread down through her body. She shuddered, blinked her eyes, and focused on the grave once more.

When Julien had called her to come immediately to France, the realization that her mother's life was ending was startling. It was only a few short weeks after the Twin Towers had fallen in New York, so it had been a wild flight from the States to reach her mother's bedside in time. She shook her head again as her nerves strained at the memory. But the crowning blow came when she arrived at the hospital, just in time to say goodbye. Her mother died within minutes—as if she had been awaiting her arrival. With her last breath she hoarsely whispered, "*Retrouve mes origines, ma famille paternelle. Cherche qui était mon père.*" Stunned and shaken, Sophie started to pull back when her mother firmly grabbed her sleeve and said, "China," before she passed.

Sophie stewed over her mother's final request: She understood her mother's desire to search for Pourrette. Her mother had never known her own father who was lost after WWI, but she carried his name forward. Sophie's two oldest brothers, Thierry, a product of rape, and Gérard, the love child of a failed World War II affair, had also carried the same surname. Perhaps *Maman* wanted to remove the stigma that had followed her all her days. Sophie's father had never failed to point out the *bâtards* in her mother's family. But why the mention of China? Was that where her mother's father, Pourrette, had gone?

As she was only slightly aware of the workmen who shuffled quietly to the open grave, Sophie paid them little heed as they went about completing the interment. The lacquered coffin reflected a hint of sunlight just as it was lowered into the crypt. The concrete lid, which was scraped into place, startled her. She grabbed her stomach. The finality was even more painful than she expected. Funny, she didn't remember feeling anything when her father died. In fact, it had been years now and she had yet to cry for him. But this was her *maman.* She choked back her tears.

Staring straight ahead, yet seeing only a blur, her eyes rested on the black granite grave marker before her. The names etched in gold read: *Famille Fermier/Pourrette* (the Fermier and Pourrette Families). She knew the Fermiers were Thierry's in-laws, but where was *her* family's surname? Where was the name Zabél? Her father had been buried here. She shrunk back with disbelief.

Sophie felt like whimpering. She clamped a hand over her mouth to keep from verbalizing her thoughts. *Mon Dieu, what a mess! Three generations of Pourrettes who don't know who they are or where they came from . . . So, Maman, where do I begin?*

"Ashes to ashes; dust to dust . . ." Those words, those final words, spoken only thirty minutes before, reverberated through her head. Father Laurent had been kind enough, but Sophie had winced at his eulogy. Those dutiful prayers had been spoken by a priest for a woman he probably had never met. That very priest, who blessed and commended her beloved *Maman*'s body to heaven, probably didn't have a clue *who* her mother was!

Well now, *that* was the mystery, wasn't it? Her own mother, Marcelle Pourrette Zabél, hadn't known who she was either! She hadn't known her father; her mother had basically abandoned her . . . had she ever found anything to link her to any person, place, or piece of God's green earth? And now that she was gone, her mother's last words haunted her: *Sophie, search for me. Search for Pourrette.*

CHAPTER ONE

A Flood of Memories

USK WAS FALLING as Sophie drove the few kilometers to her mother's house in Fontanières. After the funeral, she, Julien, and Thierry had gone back to Thierry's farm for the reception. The house had been filled with friends and family awaiting their arrival, but once they had pulled into the farmyard, Thierry had climbed out of the car and immediately bolted around back. Julien and Sophie looked at each other.

"This is going to be a difficult time for him," Sophie said as they both made their entrance into the celebration of their mother's life.

Yes, it had been a long day, and Sophie needed time alone. She pulled her car up in front of her mother's house and turned off the engine. Her tired eyes rested on the house before her. She sighed. She loved this little cracker-box of a house. It represented the only place she knew her mother to be happy. It was snuggled comfortably off the main road yet was in the center of the village. The lace curtains on the two front windows reminded Sophie of eyelashes on welcoming eyes. The dilapidated wooden benches in front of the small fenced yard were now in shadows; withered sunflowers and weeds leaned back for support. They, too, reminded her of the hours she had spent sitting and sipping wine with her mother as they laughed, told stories, and caught up.

Sophie took a deep breath. Her arms slackened as her hands slid off the steering wheel. For once she allowed herself to reflect on the true enigma of her mother. Subtly hidden within the bravado and cheerfulness her mother had put forth lurked a deep core of sadness—a sadness that Sophie believed had permeated her mother's every waking moment. Rare were the times when her mother had openly revealed her past or her darkest secrets, but they were there.

And where was my father when I visited? Sophie could almost hear the sound of the TV blaring in the background. He rarely joined in on family time unless Sophie brought Jerome, her husband. In fact, her marriage to Jerome was the only thing in her life that her father seemed proud of. Sophie looked back at the forlorn little house—the only house her parents had ever owned. To this day, she had no earthly idea what secret weapon her mother had wielded to force her father to move here. It was so unlike her. *Maman,* who had been so quiet and reserved in her father's company, had never attempted to rock his boat. His voluminous rages kept her silent. So how did this happen? Their marriage had never held a moment of happiness. So, when they moved here to Fontanières, far away from his roots and those filthy iron mines he had worked in in Ste. Barbe, what did she have on him?

Sophie pondered that question as she reached for her purse. Of course, *she* knew why *Maman* wanted to move here. She wanted to be near Thierry. And why not? After World War II, she had been forced to leave him behind, and she had missed out on much of her eldest son's life.

Sophie climbed out of the car and looked around the empty streets. A feeling of desolation engulfed her. Not far from here, her parents had met during the war. Barely nine months and a day later, she, Sophie, was born. So, why had her father abandoned young Thierry here in the Auvergne while he moved the rest of the family to Ste. Barbe in the Lorraine? No wonder Thierry had been unconvinced of their mother's love.

She slammed the car door. *No one talked; no one explained a thing.* Again, niggling thoughts of her father came to mind, but she didn't have the energy to think about him now. She shook her head in despair and trundled off through the garden gate. How her father had figured into any of this old drama was yet to be determined—and that wouldn't be done tonight.

Fumbling in her purse she found the key. She took three steps to cross the yard, inserted the key in the lock, and set her shoulder against the front door. She pushed hard and the stubborn old door, swollen from rains and time, creaked open. Sophie smiled. She had helped her parents make this purchase. Actually, it was because of her husband's generous nature, as he had put up the money. She was proud of him.

Ruminating over these tidbits of history, she flipped on the light and walked through the living room. Tossing her purse on the table, she picked up the phone and dialed her husband in California.

"Honey? Oh, did I wake you?" Sophie said, cupping the phone against her chin. She silently counted on her fingers the number of hours between the time zones of California and central France. Nine hours. *Why do I always forget that?*

Jerome was recovering from hip surgery when they received the call about her mother. He was unable to go but, graciously, insisted she leave right away. Sophie had no choice. Blessedly, she never questioned his love for her during their twenty-eight years of marriage and had always been able to count on him. In fact, he had been the only man, beside her brothers, she had ever counted on.

"No, it's okay. I'm just happy to hear from you. How did the funeral go, my dear?" He yawned into the receiver.

"It went as well as could be expected, although I'm so tired I can barely think." She reached for her purse and splashed its contents onto the table to find her cigarettes. Realizing she had given them up years ago, she inwardly moaned, *Oh, a cigarette would taste so good right now.* "How are you feeling, love?" she asked, changing the subject.

"Ahh, much better. I'm still a bit groggy, but better. I think the pain medication is finally kicking in. How long will you be staying, Soph?"

"I don't know. I know there will be legal papers to handle tomorrow, and then I should probably decide what to do with *Maman's* house before I head back. If the doctor gives you the okay, maybe you could come over and join me." Her voice lifted in hopes of cheering him.

Sophie paused as she thought of the many times she and Jerome had travelled back and forth to France to visit her family. "It's funny," she said, almost to herself, "you never learned to speak French."

"What, my dear?" he asked. "What are you talking about?"

"Oh, I'm sorry, Jerome. I'm just really tired. I'm beginning to talk nonsense. That's so like me, *mais oui?* I'm so glad you're feeling better, but I'm exhausted. If you don't mind, I'll talk to you at length tomorrow."

"Talk to you tomorrow, love."

Sophie hung up the phone. Funny how a conversation she'd recently had with her friend, Kate, surfaced just now. It was Kate who had asked her why Jerome had never learned French. Sophie enjoyed that about Kate. She was straightforward and wasn't afraid to ask questions. This was a trait she found appealing about Americans, but she, herself, even after moving to the States to marry Jerome nearly thirty years before, had not picked up the habit. She found Kate an easy woman to be around and one whom she had warmed to immediately. Why, once their mutual hairdresser had introduced them, they had become inseparable. And over the past six months, Kate had become the easiest friend to confide in. Plus, it didn't hurt that Kate had become fond of her mother. They both enjoyed talking about food. Oh, those lengthy yet delightful coffee conversations the three of them had had together—talking, drinking coffee, sampling desserts, sharing stories and recipes. What else would have compelled the three of them to decide to tour through France together?

Thinking of food, Sophie walked into her mother's kitchen and pulled on the light chain that hung over the wooden table. The blue ceiling light, which swung back and forth, swirled in the air, forming eerie shadows across the walls. Sophie's eyes scanned the mottled and badly worn kitchen counter. *Just a bit of leftover wine,* she thought. *Surely there is at least a bottle or two here, somewhere.* Opening the cupboard doors, her hands glided along the chipped edges of the handles as if searching for her mother's last handhold. *Ah, ha,* she said to herself. One bottle tucked in the back of the cupboard still had some dregs left. She jerked open the middle drawer, grabbed out the corkscrew, and noted the name of a California winery, Wente, embossed on the handle; it was one she had frequented with her mother. Memories crowded every corner.

Mais oui! But, of course, that was how it all began—over a glass of champagne and dinner with Kate. She pulled the cork free and searched for a clean glass. Sorrow flooded Sophie as she continued her thoughts. *Kate and I were supposed to be traveling with Maman— now.* For months they had been discussing their plans to take her mother to Vannes, her mother's birthplace in Brittany—just one last time. *But 9/11 happened, we postponed the trip, and now, Maman, you are gone!* Sophie choked as her grief welled up in her throat. She gulped at the wine. *Egad! How long has this been around?* She gasped. *Vintage. It will have to do.* She swilled down another gulp.

Yes, that was it, she thought as her eyes watered. *Maman had opened up to Kate about her childhood in Brittany; she told her about being abandoned by her mother and about the rape which gave her, at the age of sixteen, my brother, Thierry. Why on earth, after all these years of silence, was she so open with a stranger?*

Sophie fussed about the kitchen, poking through the cupboards and peering into the fridge, all in hopes of finding a scrap of something to eat. *I should have eaten more at the wake.* She had no idea what she would find, as her mother's death had come only hours after her own arrival from the States. There had been so much to take care of for the funeral that she barely remembered how long she had been there. Tucked back in the corner of the refrigerator was a blue crock of eggs. A small container of boleti mushrooms was hidden on a shelf in the door along with a scrap of brie and some butter. "*Une omelette aux champignons*," she chirped.

With omelet essentials in hand, she closed the refrigerator door with her foot and let the cheese, mushrooms, and butter tumble onto the counter. Hanging onto the eggs, she pulled out the omelet pan—the very one her mother had taught her how to use—and set it on the stove to heat. Oh, the laughter they used to share as her mother patiently taught her and Julien how to break an egg and make an omelet. And then the *crêpes* . . . "*Crêpes*," she laughed out loud. The fun the families had together during *Chandeleur,* the Festival of Lights. She couldn't recall the reason for the religious holiday, but the laughter rang through the air each time they were given turns to flip the *crêpes* high in the air. The goal was to catch it back on the paddle without dropping the *crêpe* or sticking it to the ceiling. *Wait!* She stopped to think. *That's it! We held a gold coin in one hand, while tossing the crêpe with the other, all in order to win good fortune or money.* "Not an easy task when you are laughing," she chortled out loud. While adding a knob of butter to sauté the mushrooms, she quickly broke two eggs into a bowl, added a dash of water, and lightly whisked them together. She cocked her head and listened for the very moment the mushrooms had finished sizzling, and then she poured the eggs into the pan.

Quickly tilting the pan back and forth, her thoughts again drifted back to the first conversations her mother had had with Kate. Kate knew enough French, but of course, Sophie still had to translate many of her mother's words. It was during those translations she became painfully aware of the depth of information her mother was revealing. And Kate hadn't wanted to miss a single word. She had been honestly captivated by her mother's story.

Anguish shot through her and surprised her with its force. Sophie shook her head in disbelief and choked down another swallow of bad wine. She minced the chunk of brie, dumped it into the egg mixture, and deftly lifted one edge of the omelet, folding it over. Within moments she slid the omelet onto a plate and called it good. Sophie picked up a fork and her glass of wine and sat down at the kitchen table. She inhaled the eggs almost before they cooled.

It was through Kate that I began to truly listen to Maman's story, she thought, wiping her mouth with the back of her hand. She should call Kate tomorrow and tell her what had happened. Again, grief and disappointment shot through Sophie.

Leaning back, Sophie looked around the kitchen—from the old splotched cupboards, to the dinged-up counter, to her mother's chipped green recipe box, to the very table where she sat. She ran her fingers over the surface of the tablecloth and caressed the shape of the cracked dinner plate. *This was where the most intimate of conversations with Maman took place,* she reminisced, *yet, in all those years, I never dared to ask her a single personal question.* Nor had Sophie revealed her own secrets. For the past forty years, she had been suffering from the same recurring nightmare and had not breathed a word about it to her mother. Somehow she knew her father was involved, but even after he died, she couldn't bring herself to tell her mother. Her eyes filled with tears as images of the nightmare came into focus. Always, just beyond her bed, she sensed a man standing near the doorway. Separated only by a gauze-like curtain that moved gently and ethereally, she could never make out who was standing there. Always, she would rise up in bed to call out, yet terror would set in. Sensations of the almost-mystical moved with the curtain, yet pangs of foreboding persisted. *Was it Papa?* She let out a wail, grabbed up her empty glass, and rushed out of the kitchen. Suddenly, she stopped.

China? Maman, you said the word China *before you died. Did you mean 'china cabinet'?* She spun around and walked directly to the china hutch, where only a few pieces of fine hand-painted gold-rimmed plates remained—few because she had so few in the first place. Sophie swung open the upper glass doors, where she remembered a treasure trove used to reside. Yes, when she was little, she used to dream of having something as fine as this. But when the time came and her mother offered her the cabinet, she lived half a world away.

As for the dishes? She couldn't bear the memories of those ghastly family dinners. What had they called them? *Diner avec une vache enragée.* Dining with a mad cow! *Mon Dieu!* Back then, her mother was a paragon of sanguine expectation. She was always hoping that they, as a family, could have a pleasant meal together. But no matter what, her father would sabotage every one of her efforts. Not a single word was uttered or a note of laughter was allowed to escape into the air in his presence. There they were—Julien, Gérard, and Sophie herself—sitting in stark silence with their parents, choking down every morsel their mother had lovingly prepared. Unfortunately, all they wanted to do was flee from their father's glare. Time and again, nervousness would set in —oh, it was so like them—and she and her brothers would find themselves breaking into fits of laughter, which would quickly end with them getting spanked and sent to bed. No, she had no desire to eat off those plates again. She poked through the wild array of contents from her purse and pulled her glasses free of the mire. Slipping them onto her nose, she peered more closely into the cabinet.

She didn't know what she was looking for, but she peeked into the blue-glass vase and deep into the bottle-green pitcher. Nothing. She opened the silverware drawer and rummaged through the tarnished pieces. She stooped to look into the cabinets below, where some of her mother's old serving bowls greeted her. She got on her hands and knees and ran her fingers lovingly along the old blue crock her mother had used to make bread. A new flood of emotions caught her off guard. She reeled back on her haunches and then . . . *Wait. What is that?* In the back of the hutch, a glimpse of something white caught her attention. She stuck her hand behind a wooden salad bowl and pulled out an envelope. Lifting it into the light, Sophie could see her name written carefully across the front in her mother's meticulous handwriting. Her hands began to tremble. She recognized her mother's blue stationery. Tears began to flow down her cheeks as she wrested the envelope open. She pulled the two onionskin sheets free and hurried to the sofa to turn up the light. She shifted her glasses up before wiping her eyes with her sleeve and then began reading:

My dearest Sophie,

When you find this letter, it will be after I'm gone. I had hoped that I could tell you some of these things in person; alas, I am out of time. Please do not be sad for me. You children and my darling grandchildren have given me a most gratifying life.

Ma chérie, I have two requests. Thierry's son, Christian, has asked that I help him find his grandfather. He convinced me to break my silence. He expressed his concern about his father's bouts with depression and feared he would take his life, like Gérard. He will need your help in searching for this family. It may be an uncomfortable affair, though he now has their names.

For my second request: After our lengthy talks with Kate last winter, and with Christian more recently, I realize the importance of seeking the identity of my own father. I know that may surprise you. Actually, I started this process thirty years ago when I wrote to find out details of my father from my Tante Suzanne in Paris. Unfortunately, she passed away about that time. I grieved for her, as she was the last family member to know the truth about my father. It is possible that she left word with her daughter, your Cousin Madeleine, so, in addition to helping Christian, I would like you to find out what happened to my father—Pourrette. You might begin by contacting Madeleine and see if she was given any information. Christian may also be able to help, but I think he has his hands full. Your brother, Julien, may also be helpful, although his allegiance has always been colored by his love for his father.

So why now, I know you are asking. Why after all of this time? Well, my dear, for the same reasons Christian needs to find his grandfather. The pain of having no father—even the memory of one —has rent my soul and affected me all my days. Unfortunately, the ridicule I endured blinded me to the pain and suffering your brothers also must have felt. My heart breaks for my sons, and if I cannot alleviate their pain before my death, perhaps I can provide some salve in the form of knowledge for their children. As Christian pointed out, that could be my final gift: my redemption. You see, Sophie, it's not just what we know that guides us through life, but also what we don't know that can rise like a specter and impact our every waking moment.

Now, where to begin? The attic. For years now, I have not been able to climb those steep steps, so I have failed to pull things together for you. Among your father's and my collective boxes, you should be able to find some of my own individual things. You'll find mine marked and separate from the others. In them you will find papers and legal documents, and hidden below you should find some old letters, address books, and journals dating from just after WWII.

Don't be dismayed if you don't have the earlier journals. Most of those I've left in the care of my dear friend, Sophie Marie Chirade. You might remember me mentioning her, although never in front of your father. She lives nearby, her number is in the address book, and I would ask you to contact her soon. She, too, is in poor health. She will be expecting you. She has promised to give you the earlier journals to help you piece my life story together. Maybe with this information, along with help from your cousin, Madeleine, you will be able to find enough clues to lead you to my father's family.

One of the reasons I was hoping to visit Vannes with you and Kate was to check the records at the town hall. Take Kate with you. I think she has good instincts. Also, I contacted your good friend and mine, Mimi Thionet, to help in the research of my father's records in Brittany. She still works near the hall of records in Vannes, so she may be able to assist.

Please know that as my strength is waning, my mind is clear and I know what a tremendous weight I am placing on you. Sophie, if anyone in the family can manage this, it is you. Please know that I love and trust you, my darling daughter, and I know that you will do your best.

My deepest love and gratitude, Maman

Sophie slid down on the sofa, scrunching a crocheted pillow behind her head. What did she make of this letter? She was still so jet-lagged—yet she felt relief to have some direction. When she had first heard her mother's last words, she had felt like she was free-floating. She looked at the last paragraph again and then crushed the letter close to her heart. No longer was she feeling the need to run from her mother's challenge. She felt the love and gratitude her mother had expressed in her final letter.

Gripping the letter tightly to her, she stood and walked to the stairs to climb up to her mother's bedroom. She needed some sleep, and tomorrow . . . tomorrow, she thought, she would call Kate. But on the fifth step, she spun on her heels and descended down the stairs to the phone. She dialed Kate's number in the States and sat back down on the sofa. *I have to tell Kate about Maman's death and her final letter. She must come to France to help me. She's the only friend I can turn to; the only one I trust.*

CHAPTER TWO

$\mathscr{F}$loating $\mathscr{I}$sland

$\mathrm{\overset{|}{A}}$

$\mathscr{K}$ATE FELT WRUNG OUT after she hung up the phone. She poured herself a cup of reheated coffee and slumped into her kitchen chair. Burying her head into her folded arms, she began to cry; her body shook with anguish as the conversation with Sophie began to sink in. She was devastated. She had fully embraced her friendship with Sophie, but there had also been a connection with Marcelle. Her story had resonated with Kate, but she hesitated to pinpoint the source. She chalked up this new response to the recent loss of her own mother. Marcelle did remind Kate of her, but at this moment, her heart simply ached for both Marcelle and Sophie.

And she had really been looking forward to traveling throughout France with those two. Damn! Kate realized she had pinned more than a few hopes on their trip. She had loved learning French cooking at the elbow of this mother/daughter duo, but to travel with them to collect more recipes and stories— that would have been a dream come true. Kate sat up and sighed. Obviously, something more was at stake for her, but again, she didn't want to face it.

Time evaporated; her coffee turned cold. Wandering into the bathroom, she splashed water on her reddened face and stared at her image through swollen eyes. *Looks as if I've been through a car wash—without a car. What's with me?* She had to get a grip. She had a schedule to keep, groceries to buy. She pawed at her frosted blonde hair, cajoling a few wisps back into place. She paused. She may be a tad overweight, but at least she liked her own face. And her husband, Matt, loved her deep blue eyes and her smile. She fell in love with him the day he said, "Even from far away, I can hear your smile." Such a romantic, that one. She was lucky in love, at least this time around.

Kate headed into her home office and closed the door. She was alone in the house, but who knew for how long. Always some brash upstart kid of theirs could barge in. Her brass nameplate, loose on its screws, clanked in place on the door: one more reminder of things coming undone. She, Kate Barrington, a disgruntled former therapist, had discarded her family practice in favor of finding an occupation that held less stress. Her husband had encouraged the change. He knew how unhappy she had become. After years of working with court-ordered families and women who had suffered abuse, she had reached the conclusion that change for families could not be affected under duress. "Families are doing the best they can, and applying additional pressure isn't helpful," she had said boldly, as she stormed out the agency door. Yes, that had been Kate's excuse for her departure a year ago.

But, in retrospect, she knew the real reason she had left. It hadn't been her role as therapist that had gotten her down. It had been her role as a mother. *Lousy* is how she would describe herself in non-clinical terms. This feeling of self-loathing hadn't come on suddenly—it had been a slow, accumulative effect. Two of her own children hadn't launched well and kept returning as if on bungee cords. She had one grandchild whom she adored, although he, too, was arriving on her doorstep with increased indifference. Then, there were her husband's two grown children who resided on the opposite coast, and when they visited, they seemed, in their glassy-glow-outward-show of things, to have a silent pact of acceptance of her—but barely. Even after all these years.

Okay, it probably had been insane for them to marry with four teenagers between them at the time, but hadn't they, as a couple, leaped over most of the hurdles? *Lord, I'm the one who needs therapy!* Kate knew that the net result was that if she wasn't preparing a meal for them, bailing them out of heaps of trouble, or handing them money, she felt invisible. And that was only part of what put her over the edge. She decided that if she couldn't be a decent mother to any of her own children, then how in God's name could she pawn herself off as a legitimate family therapist? So, after resigning her position at the agency, she had turned on her heel to search for other ways to fill her time and passion . . . which she thought she had found. French cooking! My gawd! What was going to become of her? She had more degrees than a gal has a right to, yet she remained totally adrift. What was she waiting for?

She slipped into her office chair, swiveled up to the desk to search for her passport, took a sip from her cold coffee, and began fiddling with her computer. An image suddenly popped up on the screen of her dear friend Sophie sitting next to Marcelle. Kate had taken the photo right in her own kitchen. The expressions on their faces were joyous, and she could almost hear their jubilant banter. Always, wild laughter ensued when those two got going. Kate sat back in her chair. This photo had been taken the first afternoon Marcelle and Sophie had come to teach her about French cuisine. That had been the day she learned to make Marcelle's Floating Island dessert, and the beginning of a friendship began to fill a void that Kate had not realized was there.

Meeting Sophie had been serendipity, one of those glorious

chance crossings. Kate had been chatting with her hairdresser, Carolyn, about her desire to take cooking lessons—French cooking lessons—and Carolyn mentioned that she had a French client who might be able to help. A few days later, Sophie called.

"Al-lo, Kate? This is Sophie Sull-i-vahn," the voice chirped lightly over the phone, a French accent prominent with every syllable. "You don't know me, but Carolyn . . . Yes, yes, Carolyn," she chortled, indicating their shared hairdresser, "said that you are a Francophile of sorts, and that you are interested in learning to prepare French foods, *oui*? Yes? Well, I would love to help! I am from France. You can tell, *n'est-ce pas?*" She tittered this time. "Could you and your husband come over for dinner tonight? Is it possible? He's out of town? Ah well, then, you won't want to be alone. *Oui*? Ah, good! I will invite my French friends along with my mother who is visiting for six months from France, and we will have a grand party. You can meet us all, and we will all share our favorite recipes with you. Would that work for you?"

That evening, as Kate anguished her way across town to Sophie and Jerome Sullivan's home, she found herself trembling at what she was embarking on. Yes, she had accepted Sophie's invitation for dinner, but she realized she had no clue what to ask these newfound acquaintances—French ones at that. As she drove through town, niggling feelings of panic began to surface. *What am I doing?* she asked herself. *I only know rudimentary French, and what if they don't speak English?"*

Pulling up to the given address, she parked her car in front of a small white ranch-styled house. Yellow roses were blooming in the front yard, and potted geraniums had also failed to notice winter. A small white sign near the front door proclaimed, "*Attention: chien bizarre!*" She laughed out loud at this touch of what she hoped was French humor and prayed no wild dogs were actually inside. Her panic began to drain away. Feigning confidence, she got out of the car, strode to the front door, and rang the doorbell.

Immediately she could hear a wild frenzy of barking behind the door. *Gawd*, she thought, *should I run?* An elderly gentleman ushered her quickly into the house and slammed the door behind her, as a welcoming committee of five tiny fur balls continued loudly yapping. *Ah, the chiens bizarres!* Over the din, she thought the man had introduced himself as Sophie's father, but she wasn't certain. She heard laughter from the back of the house and then rapid French commands calling to the dogs. The gentleman waved her toward the kitchen as he busily herded the noisy crew to a back room. Continuing down a dark hallway, she followed the tantalizing aroma of roasting meat. *Mmm, lamb*, she thought. A petite woman, barely five feet tall, wearing a brightly colored blouse and black skirt, turned from the sink to greet Kate. With hands dripping wet, Sophie introduced herself.

"*Bonsoir, mon amie*," she trilled, as she embraced her before planting kisses on both her cheeks. Obviously, she knew no strangers. The tightened coils in Kate's neck began to relax.

Sophie, somewhat shorter than Kate, stood grinning up at her and her hair. They both broke out laughing. Their matching hairdos were a clear indication they shared the same hairdresser. As Sophie moved quickly about her kitchen, images of Betty Boop floated through Kate's mind, not that Sophie was from that era. In fact, Kate figured they both were baby boomers. But, there was something in her demure yet coquettish moves that elicited the image.

"May I help?" Kate asked.

"No. No. You can sit over there, Kate," she said, her still-wet finger indicating an empty barstool. "I'm almost done," she said, filling the room once more with her heavy accent. She placed a bowl of mixed nuts on the bar in front of Kate along with a small tray with fresh butter-filled radishes sprinkled lightly with *fleur de sel*.

"Is this a French recipe?" Kate asked.

"Oh, but of course. They're yummy! Try one." Kate picked up a radish and bit into it.

"Mmm. You're right. They're soft, yet crunchy, savory, and salty at the same time. Delicious!"

"I can see we are going to get along just fine," Sophie said.

Having quieted the dogs, the elderly gentleman joined them in the kitchen. "I figure you couldn't hear a word I was saying in that hallway, so I decided I better set the record straight, my dear. I'm Sophie's husband, Jerome." Smiling proudly, he thrust his hand out and shook Kate's hand heartily. Sophie handed him a bottle of champagne and seated herself across from Kate. With pomp and a bit of flourish, Jerome opened the champagne, poured three flutes, and slid onto a bar stool next to his wife. He scooped up a handful of nuts and popped them into his mouth just as the other two were lifting their glasses in a toast.

"Tchin-tchin," Sophie said, as three glasses clinked together.

"Tchin-tchin?" asked Kate. "Is that French?"

"I don't think so . . . but, whatever. It's what we've always said," Sophie said with a wave of her hand.

"This is quite a nice treat," Kate said. She held the glass to her face as the bubbles softly exploded against her nose.

"Oh, my, Kate. This will be your second French lesson for the evening. The French *always* begin a gathering with champagne," Sophie said.

"Always?"

"Always!" replied Jerome. "That's the best part of being married to a French woman!"

"The *best* part?" echoed Sophie. "This is the *best* part?" She grinned coyly up at her husband.

"So, what's your story? How did you two meet?" Kate ventured. Jerome put his arm around his wife and pulled her closer. She melted automatically into his side.

"Well, Kate, that's a very interesting story. You see, I'm a native-born Californian," Jerome began with bravado, a shock of white hair rising above him like a rooster's comb, "and when we met . . ."

Sophie giggled as they both rushed to talk first. "We met," Sophie interrupted, "exactly twenty-eight years ago. Right, Jerry?"

As if a recording had been switched on, their story rolled off their tongues in tandem. "We met on an airport shuttle at JFK," Jerome stated. "I was returning from France after completing a contract there in solar energy . . ."

"And I," Sophie interrupted, "was returning to France after an international conference in New York."

"In economics, right, my dear?" He didn't wait for her answer. "So, our paths were literally crossing. We had little time to connect, yet . . ."

"Yet, we *deed*," Sophie grinned, as she completed his sentence.

"It was quite amazing that it happened at all, because I knew no French," he stated. "Even though I worked in France, I never learned a single word of French, whatsoever," he proclaimed.

"*Steel* doesn't," Sophie giggled, "and I knew four languages, but knew no English at that time."

"I know a little French myself, but I'm not fluent," Kate responded. "So, how in the world were you two able to communicate?"

"Somehow we were able to exchange our names and our business cards, and the rest? The rest is a whole other story in itself." They beamed at each other over their champagne and clinked glasses in honor of their capricious love.

"Wow! How romantic," Kate exclaimed. "What are the chances of finding love in such an unlikely place? That couldn't have been easy."

Sophie said, "I'm not saying it was easy, but it has always been quite magical." She winked at Kate.

"Do you remember the first time you saw Sophie, Jerome?" Kate pushed.

"Oh my, yes!" He settled himself more firmly on his barstool, tossed a couple of nuts into his mouth, and continued. "I would have to say, I heard her before I saw her. It was her laughter, a most infectious chortle. I simply had to see who on that grim shuttle bus was having such a good time. I squeezed my way through the other passengers until I was close enough to start up a conversation . . ."

"But then he couldn't because he realized that I was speaking French . . ."

"And he didn't know French," Kate put in.

"*Mais oui!* Being a scientist for solar energy, he was used to *tout le monde* knowing English, but I immediately loved his eyes. For me, it was love at first sight . . ."

"And I was smitten by your charm, my dear. You were so young and so very lovely. And for an old man, I must confess, I fell head over heels for her. I simply couldn't leave until we had at least exchanged business cards. I don't know what I thought would happen, but as it turned out, you wrote the next week, right?"

"Right! And then you asked your boss, an Italian, no less, to translate my letters and send letters of response. Gino kept up the romance, that's for sure!"

"Sounds like a scene out of *Cyrano de Bergerac* . . ." Kate commented.

"*Mais oui, mon ami.* Cyrano, of course, was a fellow Frenchman! Also he was a dramatist and certainly a romantic. What could be a better comparison?" Sophie responded with a flourish and the toss of her hand.

Just then, the doorbell rang. The sound of muffled barking erupted down the hall. Two couples opened the front door and strode into the Sullivan home, obviously familiar guests. Jerome popped the cork on another bottle of champagne, and the evening grew lively. In the midst of the conversations, both French and English, Sophie disappeared into a back bedroom and came out with her mother. Marcelle, who had been resting, came to life at the sound of her native language being spoken. She knew a smattering of English but was most at home with French. As she was introduced to Kate, she drew her green sweater about her bosom and leaned her cheek up to be kissed. Adjusting to this new tradition, Kate bent down and kissed both Marcelle's cheeks. Marcelle was a short woman—a fireplug of a woman. To say that her height of four foot eight equaled that of her girth would be an error, though it came close. But her every move was complete animation and life: her deep brown eyes sparkled, the wiry curls on her slightly greying head bobbed, and her face, which appeared to have been etched with hard times and hard work, continuously broke into a smile before she erupted with laughter. Clearly, she was enjoying herself and her daughter's guests.

Once they were seated for dinner, red Bordeaux was poured, and Sophie entered the dining room holding a platter. "For our new friend, Kate, who is here to learn all things French! We have French-style roast leg of lamb, French-style *haricot vert*, or green beans, roasted vegetables with French herbs, and, of course, a must for all Frenchmen, couscous!"

"*Mais oui,*" responded each of the French women around the table.

"But, of course," echoed their American husbands in English.

As Jerome, with great panache, began to slice the lamb, Sophie settled down at the table next to her mother and Kate. "You see, the French culture is comprised of many influences. France used to have many international territories, so it stands to reason those influences—foods, spices, traditions—would become part of our own. Couscous is an Algerian accoutrement, but it has become a huge staple in the French family diet. *C'est vrai?*"

"Yes, it's true, my dear," responded Jerome as he passed the sliced lamb around to their guests.

What followed for the next four hours was one course after

another of delicious French cuisine. A new bottle of wine was opened with each course, and the conversation flowed equally well. As far as Kate could tell, this meal had no end. It was well after ten o'clock, a weeknight for these working people, but no one noticed.

As the cheese board was accompanied with a basket of baguette slices, Marcelle leaned close to Kate and said, "So, you are interested in learning how to prepare our cuisine, *n'est-ce pas?*" Marcelle peered over the top of her wine glass as she spoke.

"*Oui,* madame, I would love to learn what makes your cuisine world-famous; your *haute cuisine,*" Kate said.

"Our *haute cuisine?*" Marcelle bit into her cheese and bread. A twinkle flitted through her dark eyes.

"*Oui,* but more than *haute cuisine* I would prefer learning the fine art of traditional French cooking."

"Well, madame, our traditional cooking is rarely considered fine, but we certainly keep a respectable *cuisine pauvre.*"

Kate was brought up short with this French term. Her face turned quizzically toward Sophie.

"Kate, *cuisine pauvre* means *poor kitchen* and refers to traditional peasant cooking. These are the recipes that have been handed down through the many, many generations, and this is the type of cooking *Maman* taught me. As a matter of fact, we continue to use her recipes every day. Like this evening!" Sophie popped up from the table, disappeared into the kitchen, and then reappeared at the table.

"And for our finale," Sophie announced, "we have as the pièce de résistance, *Maman's* Floating Island dessert." Sophie winked at her mother as everyone swooned. Kate's eyes grew wide as what looked like a bowl of white cotton was placed before her. She picked up her spoon and with the first bite discovered the delicate sweet flavor of meringue and orange, which melted onto her tongue like a soft cloud. Delectable!

Soon, it was time to go home. The lively chatter and the enthusiastic energy had made Kate's head swim. Or, perhaps, it was the wine. She chided herself for not having written down a single recipe, but then everyone was making their way to the front door.

"I can't thank you enough, Sophie," Kate effused. "This evening was delightful. What a gift!"

"Oh, Kate, you are so welcome," Sophie said as she escorted her to her car. "Perhaps, if you still want recipes from French families, you could start with my mother. I'm sure she would enjoy that—talking about French recipes and telling her old stories. She will be leaving for France in a few weeks, just in case you want to include her."

"I'd love it," Kate replied. "And I would love to begin with her recipe for her exquisite Floating Island!"

Later that week, Kate invited Sophie and Marcelle to her house. She was nervous as she futzed about her kitchen putting the finishing touches on a lavender lemon tart and laying out the ingredients she had been told would be needed to prepare the Floating Island dessert. The doorbell rang. With Sophie in her wake, Marcelle strode through the living room and into the kitchen with remarkable confidence and a sense of belonging.

"You have a beautiful home, Kate," Marcelle said, her eyes darting around the interior of her kitchen. She walked over to the window, where Kate's collection of Provençal santons was displayed. She picked up one of the dolls and flicked a piece of dust off the fedora of an old man carrying his gift of *crottins* of goat cheese in a petite basket.

"All gifts to the saints," Marcelle murmured. She set it down and picked up the old woman, who carried a sheaf of lavender. "Lovely," she said quietly.

"Yes, this *is* a lovely home," Sophie said as she, too, walked around the kitchen island to join her mother.

"Would you like a little tour before we get started?" Kate asked.

Both turned toward her, their faces lit up. Marcelle practically bowled Kate over as she made her way out to the living and dining rooms. She went directly over to the china cabinet and peeked in.

"Sophie, do you recognize these tea cups? I believe I have something similar," she exclaimed, as she eyed the antique collection.

"These were handed down to me from my great-aunt," Kate said. "I believe they are French." Small pink roses graced the white cups, and a dainty gold border surrounded every dish.

"Don't I, Sophie?" Marcelle asked. "Or did I give those to you?"

"Yes, you do, *Maman*, but they are probably tucked back in your own china cabinet. I certainly don't have them—yet," Sophie joked.

Marcelle continued to waltz around the dining room table, lightly touching the back of the chairs and caressing the damask table runner. Sophie walked directly to an array of paintings Kate had displayed on the wall.

"These, too, are from France, aren't they? I recognize the lavender hills of St. Remy, Provençe, right?"

Kate blanched. The décor throughout her home was a display of all things French: Country French furniture, antique plates and cups from a favorite French aunt, oil paintings and little santons from Provençe . . . She was seeing her own environment through their eyes, and . . . She gulped, then grinned. "What can I say?" she stammered. "I'm a Francophile!"

Marcelle moved over to her, gently patted her hand, and said, "*C'est compréhensible*, madame." She then spotted a pitcher from Brittany. "Quimper!" she burst forth. "Quimper is near where I grew up. In Vannes! Have you visited there?"

Kate shook her head no. "I'm afraid I haven't, madame."

"I'll have to tell you all about it, as that is the place I learned to cook. Maybe we could go there together some day, *n'est ce pas,* Sophie?"

"That's a grand idea, but I would expect we should get started here first, don't you?" Sophie encouraged. They returned to the kitchen.

With a little help from Sophie, Marcelle slid onto a chair at the kitchen table. This appeared difficult, as her feet did not touch the floor, but Sophie sat beside her, and the lively French banter floated through the air like birdsong.

The three had mutually decided to start with the lavender-lemon tart and coffee before beginning Kate's first culinary lesson, so while Kate poured their coffee and cut the tart, she found herself observing both women. Even though Marcelle and Sophie were basically strangers to her, they were settling in easily.

Balancing the cups of coffee along with the dessert on a tray, Kate joined the mother and daughter at the table.

Marcelle smiled up at her, relaxed, and sat back as her pumps, which had been dangling off her toes, slid to the floor with a thunk. Her brown eyes sparkled as she picked up her cup and sipped her coffee.

"I'm curious, madame," Kate said as she picked up her fork. "What foods did you prepare as a young wife in France? Did you prepare the Floating Island back then?"

"What foods did I prepare? In France?" Marcelle echoed the question. She threw her head back and laughed, her deeply resonant voice filling the room. But then she sat back in her chair as her eyes lighted on the birds fluttering outside the sliding glass door. Kate was surprised at her laughter but followed her gaze to see what had caught her attention. The California hills, just beyond her backyard, were vibrant green from recent winter rains, and the birds were having a heyday. She imagined Marcelle's mind fluttering too, back through the cobwebs of her past. Through the glass table top Marcelle's shoeless feet swung under the chair, back and forth, to and fro. Marcelle stretched her back, picked up her fork, and sampled the lemon tart.

"Mmm, *très bon*, madame." She swallowed. "Maybe I should get *your* recipe." She paused. "Well, to answer your question," she began, her rich voice rising, "I never had to diet." She tossed her head back and laughed again as she licked lemon curd off her lips. She pulled her large brown sweater about herself as Sophie tittered at the old family joke. Clearly Marcelle Zabél had stories to tell.

"It was during World War II, you see," Marcelle began again, "and we had to forage in the fields for every potato, every carrot, even for an onion or two. We had a chicken once in a while, or a bit of rabbit. You know, some of the foods I learned to cook back in '43, I still prepare today, like *pâté de pomme de terre*. You wanted recipes, *oui*? I'll be sure to give you that one."

Kate nodded. "I would love that."

"Potatoes and cabbages were our mainstays, of course, but we were lucky to have anything at all," Marcelle continued. "Sometimes, when the Germans confiscated our food, we were forced to sneak into the night in search of even one potato. It was perilous, mind you. We hoped no land mines had been laid during the day and that no German caught us outdoors after curfew.

Kate had not been prepared for this turn in the conversation and looked for help from Sophie, who merely shrugged and waved a limp hand into the air. "*C'est la guerre*, as they say," she laughed. "And, it is her story." She patted her mother's hand once again, reassuring her, or perhaps herself.

This is not the story I expected, Kate thought, *but wherever Marcelle is willing to go, I'm willing to follow.*

"*Oui*, it is my story! But, even when I close my eyes now—what—sixty years later, I can still *feel* the fear pour through my body." She shuddered involuntarily as she clutched her sweater more closely about her. Her eyes drifted beyond the back windows to the finches, which were raising a ruckus in the bird feeder. A wild frenzy of chirping and tweeting brought a soft smile to Marcelle's lips before she continued on.

"I remember German soldiers barking orders to search our farm yet again." She paused. "Sometimes at night, I imagine I can still hear their *botte militaire,* or jack boots, crunch . . . crunch . . . crunching across the gravel in the farmyard." She gulped down her coffee, grounding herself into the present. Kate wondered if she should stop her from continuing, but Marcelle seemed determined to go on.

"We were fearful for so many reasons, but especially because we were harboring *le Maquis* in our midst. Do you know about *le Maquis,* madame?"

"No, I don't believe so," Kate replied, fiddling with her coffee cup.

"Well, *le Maquis* were the freedom fighters, like the French Resistance, in our rural area of central France. They were a loose-knit organization but, at the time, those young renegades were our only hope. I suppose that was why I fell in love with one of them . . . and married him." She chuckled and speared another forkful of tart. Kate let out her breath and took a sip of her own coffee. The air had lightened with Marcelle's laugh.

"War," announced Marcelle, "has a way of working on people and creating interesting bedfellows, you might say." She laughed again and winked at her daughter, who was obviously a product of this union. Sophie smiled as Marcelle raced on.

"*Voyez-vous,* France was not only at war with Germany, but also with Italy. But our greatest enemy was our own Vichy government. That's another long story," she said with a toss of her hand, "and our biggest fears, madame, arose from the fact that we never knew who we could trust. Both sides within our borders, the Vichy and the Germans, were turning neighbor against neighbor. It was horrible! No one felt safe." Her wrinkled hand lifted again and lightly touched her brow as her face furrowed at the recollection.

"And we knew there were people in nearby villages who were against us for having *le Maquis* around. It put everyone at risk, you see, and too many of us had known of family or friends who had simply disappeared or were later found shot at the side of a road. You can't know the fear we lived with," she uttered with a shake of her head.

Sophie and Kate took a collective breath and then gobbled down bites of tart.

"How did you know what was happening? Could newspapers report any of this at the time?" Kate asked.

"Everything was pretty much propaganda, but I do remember reading a quote years later by Jean-Paul Sartre. He, like me, lived in Paris at the beginning of World War II. Someone had asked him a similar question, and he replied: "How can the people of free countries be made to realize what life was like under the Occupation?" It is impossible for me to explain what it was *really* like, but, if you are interested, I'll try," she said as determination rose in her voice. Her fingers ran around and around the handle of the cup.

Kate was entranced and nodded for her to go on.

"One time in particular, the Germans had been told that *le Maquis* were operating out of the village near our farm. The soldiers went door-to-door questioning everyone, but they were not getting answers. We were terrified! Many of the villagers knew that my new husband, Jules, had been living at the farm along with several other *Maquis*. We felt it was only a matter of time before they would be found. I tried to put it out of my mind. It was hard not knowing what the future would hold for us." She brushed an errant lock of greying hair from her face. "We all knew only too well if the *Maquis* were found, they would be shot on the spot and we would be sent to Poland in cattle cars. War was like that!" She paused and took a deep breath, and as she lifted the coffee cup to her lips, the cup hung midair.

"I'll never forget the story of Oradour-sur-Glane. Do you know this story?"

"No, madame, I'm sorry. I don't," Kate replied. "I don't seem to know very much about your war."

"Well," Marcelle said, as she set her cup back on her saucer, "it was one of the saddest stories ever. It broke my heart then, as it does to this day." She looked into her cup, which was almost empty, but saw nothing before her. She had entered the world of her past.

"A German doctor had been sent to the village of Oradour-sur-Glane, a village to the southwest of us, having been summoned by the family of a woman who was having difficulty delivering her child. When he neared the village, the *Maquis* surrounded his jeep, and without understanding his mission, they gunned him down. Once the Germans heard of the doctor's death, they returned to Oradour, where they rounded up the village women and children and herded them into the local church. They taunted them and tried scaring them to get information about the *Maquis*. The Germans were certain someone would talk, but no one did. Infuriated, they barricaded the doors of the church, and if anyone, even a child, attempted to leave, they were shot in the feet or legs with machine guns. Then, the soldiers doused the church with petrol and set the building on fire. In the meantime, all of the men and boys were marched into a nearby barn, and there they met the same fate. All but a few died. They died in order to protect *le Maquis*."

Kate gasped and turned to Sophie for confirmation. But her expression, like Kate's, was one of surprise.

"Well, we were devastated when we heard this and fearful that our day would also come. I still shudder when I think of it. It could have been us . . . it could have been us!" She sat there shaking her head, trying to clear it of the painful memory.

Tears sprang into Kate's eyes. Wiping them away, she looked over at Sophie again, who was wrapping her arms about her mother.

"I can't imagine how difficult that must have been for you," Kate mumbled lamely.

"*Difficile? Mais oui,*" she said with a forced laugh as she gently pulled away from Sophie. "I would say so. It was hard enough for families to make ends meet, but our everyday lives were filled with devastation for more than five endless years. Our only hope was for the allies to bring help to us, and we knew that could only happen if brave people like my husband, people in *le Maquis,* could help."

"You are so right, *Maman,*" Sophie soothed.

Without breaking stride, Marcelle smiled and said, "Shall we prepare the Floating Island? It is quite easy. Nothing like this delicious tart. Now, to begin with," Marcelle said, pushing back from the table and scooting her feet back into her shoes, "the French name for this dessert is *oeufs à la neige.* We will begin with two cups of milk and the peeling of one orange. Are you ready, Kate?"

Kate spun into action and produced the measured amount of milk and orange peeling. Sophie had prepared her well. Marcelle picked up a small copper pan and began to heat the milk with the rind, bringing it to a boil. In the meantime, she had Sophie beat the egg whites until they were stiff. Slowly Marcelle added confectioners' sugar and lemon juice into the mix while Sophie continued beating the whites. Kate stood by taking notes.

"Now, Kate, take a tablespoon and scoop out the beaten egg whites and mold them into the shape of large eggs." Kate put down her pad of paper and pen, and gently Marcelle guided Kate's hands as she patted and shaped the foamy masses. Marcelle reduced the heat on the milk to a simmer and had Kate place the "egg shapes" into the liquid to cook and expand. They blossomed, they ballooned, and within moments, Marcelle scooped the whites out of the pan with a slotted spoon and laid them to drain on a clean dish towel.

"Voilà!" she said with a flourish.

"Voilà," Sophie and Kate echoed.

As they continued to work in a slightly awkward but synchronized fashion, Kate thought back on the story Marcelle had just told. She thought her first question about foods Marcelle prepared as a young wife had been a simple one. She felt so naive. She really didn't know anything about World War II in France. Even Sophie had looked surprised. It seemed her mother had revealed a most spectacular tale, and to a stranger, no less.

"Madame Zabél, you mentioned being from Brittany. When were you born?" Her question must have floated out of the blue, but Marcelle immediately stepped back from the stove and stood tall. The deep lines in her face smoothed as her rich voice lifted.

"I came into the world with a bang!" she resounded. "Gunshots, shouts of wild rejoicing, cries of joy and great jubilation echoed through the streets of Vannes," she said with her hands taking flight. A new sparkle danced through her eyes. She stopped talking for a moment and picked up a wooden spoon and began to blend the egg yolks in a bowl, adding granulated sugar, vanilla, and a pinch of salt. Slowly she poured the hot milk over the yolks, stirring rapidly now with a wire whisk.

"Now, Kate, watch this carefully as you stir." She handed her the whisk. "Be careful not to let the custard curdle."

Curdle? Kate thought, *I'm not certain what that looks like.*

"Kate, do you have a fine-mesh strainer?" Sophie asked. Without lifting her eyes from her job, Kate pointed to the drawer that housed such items. Sophie dug down through the panoply of utensils and came out with a winner.

Marcelle continued her story. "Music played in the streets for the first time in four years. People danced, sang, hugged, and cried. It was quite a wild affair, I was told. Not just for my birth, of course," she laughed, "and not just for Brittany, but for all of France. You see, I was born on November 11, 1918 . . . Armistice Day, the last day of World War I." Her voice held a triumphant lilt.

"My *grand-mère* often told me the celebration was just for me and that they even thought of naming me Victory." She laughed again at the old family tale, which rolled off her tongue as being so familiar.

"*Grand-mère* used to tell me many things about that time. You see, she was the one who raised me." Marcelle closed her eyes for a moment as if reflecting back more than her eighty years.

"'What did people do during the war, *Grand-mère?*' I used to ask her. I must have been seven when we first started this game. 'Well, *ma chérie*, it was a difficult time. The men who marched off as soldiers in November 1914 expected to return home in time to eat their Christmas goose. Everyone was surprised when the war lasted four long years. No men were left to handle the fishing boats,' she would say, waving her hand in the direction of the nearby sea, 'and, no men were around to bring in the few crops that grew. War was not a time for choice, Marcelle, only a time for survival.'

"'So, what happened after the war?' I would ask her," Marcelle continued, "and always I received the same response: 'The losses of men left mothers, fathers, young wives . . . all weeping in the still of the night or filing into the church to pray to their saints. Your mother was among them, you know. Many a day, the only sound to be heard was the *chink . . . chink . . . chink . . .* of the masons chiseling the names into stone on the village war memorial for those who had died.'

"'Was my father's name among them?' I would ask." Marcelle stopped. "But no answer ever came my way."

Kate's head jerked up and she looked at Sophie, almost willing her to give her some clue of where to go with this, but Sophie was studiously staring at the strainer.

Marcelle took the strainer from her daughter's hands and

began straining the custard into a glass serving dish. "Now we'll chill this. And when it is cold, arrange the egg whites on top. Decorate each egg white with something colorful, like a maraschino cherry or candied fruit."

"Oh, oh, Kate, you can also weave a web of golden spun sugar across the surface, if you choose," Sophie exclaimed a little too enthusiastically.

"Thank you. This is beautiful—or will be when it's done," Kate said. "Now, would you care for a bit more tart, Marcelle? Sophie? A refill on your coffee?" Kate needed to sit down.

Both nodded assent, and they traipsed back to the table with new wedges of tart in one hand and slopping coffee with the other. Somehow, a strange but sweet new bond had formed unwittingly between the three of them: an acceptance and an understanding that one could share anything. And from that moment on, they did just that.

❦

Crimped up from sitting so long at her desk, Kate staggered from her office chair to a standing position. She let her legs acclimate before moving slowly toward the kitchen once more. *Getting old has its drawbacks,* she muttered to no one in particular. She poured herself more coffee and grabbed up a sticky day-old donut. Swiveling back into her chair again, she tucked her feet underneath, bit into the donut and took a quick sip. *I can't believe she's gone.* What had there been about Marcelle that had not let her go? Even Kate's husband was curious about the draw, but she had resisted putting her finger on it. *Is it her openness? Her honesty?* Kate licked her fingers, then cradled her coffee to warm her hands before perusing her file drawers for her passport. She was surprised to see her husband at the door.

"Are you in there?" Matt asked, as he poked his head into her office. He had just returned from work in Silicon Valley. "I thought you had flown the coop, my little chickadee." His blonde hair stuck up in wild disarray. The removal of his favorite hat was not always kind to his looks, but his demeanor remained sweet. Kate turned toward him and smiled at her wild-haired guy but remained at her desk. Her legs had gone numb again, and she was grateful her husband hadn't requested she move.

He lumbered into the room with two lattes from Starbucks, kissed Kate, and placed one cup on Kate's desk beside her half-eaten donut. He plunked down on her settee.

"Thanks, honey. This beats the dead coffee I was drinking. I missed our morning chat today. Early meetings again?"

"Sorry about that! I missed you too!" He reached out and touched her knee.

An early-morning ritual had been part of their lives since they married over fifteen years before: Two steaming cups of coffee and two drowsy-headed friends commiserating for an hour before facing the day ahead.

"So, what's up?" he asked, as he settled back into place. Kate swiveled around to face him.

She told him of Sophie's call and the sad news of Marcelle's death, and then she said, "Sophie wants me to use my ticket to fly to France to help her with her mother's affairs."

"All right, Miss Marple, what's that mean? What's going on?" Matt asked jokingly. "You have been consumed by Sophie's mother for months now. I know you've been looking forward to traveling to France, but how does that make sense now that Marcelle has passed away?"

"I'm not sure either," Kate said as her eyes dropped toward her lap. "I don't know why, but I find myself thinking about Marcelle and her life story night and day. And now, I feel I have to go to France to help Sophie."

"I hate to be the one to point this out to you, but I think you're too close to her story."

"What do you mean I'm too close?" Kate's face flushed with exasperation. Matt held up his hand as if to calm troubled waters.

"I'm not the psychologist here," he continued, sipping his coffee, "but there is something about her life that you relate to." He hesitated. "Maybe I'm overstepping my bounds here, but is this about Lisa?"

Kate's head snapped up at the mention of her daughter's name, but at first she didn't answer. Instead, she reached over and took his hand.

"You're probably right. This may be about my need to find some answers about my relationship with her. I've been thinking back over these conversations with Marcelle and . . ." Kate paused. "I was so hoping to go to France to find out."

"What makes you think the answers are there?" he asked.

Just then the phone rang. Kate answered on the second ring. "It's for you," she said, handing him the phone. Matt quickly eased out of her office, and Kate made an effort to stand. She dropped her feet to the floor, stood precariously on one foot and then the other. She placed some notes about Marcelle in the top drawer and picked up her latte, cup, and saucer but then heard a thunk. Looking down, she spied her missing passport, sticky with donut residue, but not the worse for wear. *This will not be the journey the three of us planned, but perhaps I can help Sophie fulfill her mother's dying wish . . . and, perhaps, find ways to resolve the trauma with my daughter.*

CHAPTER THREE

Treasure Found

A

*S*OPHIE AWOKE FEELING DRUGGED from yesterday's funeral and the discovery of too many mysteries involving her family. She longed to turn over and go back to sleep, but she remembered her mother's final letter and forced herself from the comfort of the duvet. Padding down to the kitchen, she put a pot of coffee on the stove and opened the refrigerator for some nourishment. Nope, she had finished that off last night. *Un petit déjeuner would be nice, though,* she thought, but she wasn't in the mood to venture out to the market. Still a bit dazed from so little sleep, she walked to the sink, where last night's dishes stared up at her. She turned on the hot water. Her eyes rested on two scraggly brown sunflowers outside the window as her mind floated on the small clouds of steam that arose around her. She had so much to do and so much to think about, but right now some mindless chore would calm her nerves. She plunged her hands into the hot water.

Once the coffee finished perking, she poured herself a cup and started up the stairs to the attic. Sophie thought of the phone call she had placed the night before to Kate. She had practically begged Kate to come to France. And Kate had agreed, hadn't she? Just knowing that her friend would be arriving soon gave Sophie strength. Still, another wave of anguish hit her as she reached the last step. She faltered, spilled her coffee, regained her footing, then ducked her head just in time to miss a low-hung beam at the top of the stairwell. Sophie felt overwhelmed by the written requests her mother had laid out, and she had so many unanswered questions . . . But she thought, *All right, Maman, you've brought me this far.*

She fumbled in the dark for the light cord. The bulb flickered on. It was dim, but the room became illuminated in a thin cast of greenish light. Stacked along the walls were dozens of faded cardboard boxes covered with dust and cobwebs. Each box, she was sure, contained letters and papers from as far back as—well, who knew? She stood in the center of the room and gulped down most of her coffee. She placed the cup on a low shelf and blew a thick layer of dust from the first box. She opened it and began digging through.

Hot dusty hours passed as Sophie coughed and cried her way through the boxes. Her mother had been right. If there were family documents to be found, this attic was the place. Sophie's *bulletin de naissance* lay at her feet. There it was, a thin sheet of paper, brown and brittle with age, stating:

Bulletin de Naissance
État-Civil
Sophie Juliette Paule Zabél,
Née de Jules Charles Zabél, cultivateur
et Marcelle Margueritte Pourrette, épouse
à la Mairie de Mainsat-Creuse

Staring at her birth announcement, for a moment she once again questioned her own legitimacy. Was this a family habit?

Both her older brothers were born out of wedlock and bore the Pourrette name, so what about her? Wasn't that one of the pressing questions she had wanted to ask her mother? Her relationship with her father had been so rocky, and because she was born barely nine months after their wedding, she often wondered if she, too, was a product of one of her mother's liaisons. She shook her head, shocked at her own thoughts. How dare she even think like this? She had just buried her mother the day before. Fortunately, her outbursts of anger had never been aimed at her mother. Never.

Sophie shoved her thoughts aside and picked up Julien's records along with her father's. Strangely, the most questionable records—those of her mother's birth and the births of her two older brothers—were suspiciously missing. Financial records, employment records, and an odd lawsuit filed against her father from the iron mines he had worked for fifty years of his life were all in order and had been carefully filed away. Even another old recipe box with her mother's careful handwriting reached out and touched her heart. She gently ran her fingers across the script, muttered a prayer of forgiveness from her mother and . . . She paused.

What Sophie truly wanted to know—what felt so pressing that she could barely breathe—was not her mother's identity, but the identity of that elusive man she kept seeing in her nightmares. It was always the same—someone standing over her as she lie sleeping. But she could never decide if she was asleep or awake. The shadows that crossed the walls at night always seemed so real, as if they had substance. Sophie rocked back on her heels and then stood to walk around in the cramped space. She tried to breathe in deeply, but with all the dust, she came up short and began to cough, to choke.

She gasped for breath again, and finally it came. An incident that had to do with her father's uncle—a real drunken derelict, if there ever was one, had attempted to rape her when she was fourteen. But the person who had made nocturnal appearances over the past forty-plus years was not that man. She held a somewhat fragmented memory of the attempted rape, but it was always accompanied by a stench—an odor of an old man who never bathed, smoked too much, drank too much, and reeked to high heaven. Without fail, the odor of run-down nursing homes always elicited the same painful memory. But this nightly apparition of her nightmares always brought with it its own pungent, almost metallic smell. And what followed was a sense of impending pain just about to pounce upon her. Her greatest fear had been that this was a buried memory of her father. Was that possible? Could she have so significantly blocked something from her mind that she had no conscious memory of it? Sophie kicked at the floor, and a thin cloud of dust rose into the air. She had finally mustered enough nerve to ask her mother about the dream, but she had waited too long. Her therapist had told her that suppressed memories open up once one feels emotionally ready, stable. But, *mon Dieu*, when on earth would that be? Up to this point, only antidepressants had allowed her to sleep, but she had spent years staggering from one day to the next in a semi-drug-induced fog. Had another rape occurred? And if so, by whom? She stared long and hard at the remaining unopened boxes. Could there be an answer in there for her?

She shivered and drew her sweater closer to her body. She walked over to her coffee cup and finished off the cold residue. To even have brazen thoughts such as these shook her to the bone. She rarely allowed her thoughts to stray down such dark paths. Oh, she had learned the hard way. When she was much younger, too many of those dark paths had ended with her attempts at suicide— but now she needed to center on her mother's request. She took a deep breath and settled back on her haunches. *Haven't forty years of counseling helped?* she asked the crossbeams around her.

Okay now, what should I be focusing on? Ah, qui est Maman? Qui est Pourrette? Who is Mama? Who is Pourrette? Maman's maiden name was Pourrette, but she was never told who her father was. Why was there such a mystery? Sophie had been told many times that *Maman's Grand-mère* Tetiau had raised her, but her mother didn't carry that surname. On one occasion, while talking with her mother, she had ventured a guess that her mother's mother had remarried, and she, therefore, must be carrying her stepfather's surname. Sophie remembered with pain how her mother had become so angry with her, which was rare, and told her under no circumstances would she would ever divulge "that beast's" last name. *Oh, poor Maman,* she thought sadly. Too many bitter memories. Too few, sweet.

Why weren't any of these names written down in their family missal? And if her mother knew they weren't up here, why did she tell her to search here? Sophie shoved her hand into her sweater pocket and pulled out her mother's final letter. She carefully unfolded it and took another look.

Hmmmh! She wrote that there are letters, address books, and journals from after World War II. Sophie's head began to spin and her vision blurred as tears stung her eyes. Dodging a spider web, she took another look around. She had to get a grip on this, as once these papers were dispersed, she would never again have the chance to find the truth. *And what had happened to the letter found in Gérard's pocket after his suicide? Didn't it contain his own father's name?* Sophie shook her head to clear her mind. *Where is that letter now?* Tears continued to track down her dusty cheeks as she thought of her beloved brothers. *And,* she thought, *if family was so important, Maman, why did you leave Thierry behind after the War?* Sophie was exhausted. Her mind was spiraling. Too little sleep and too many unanswered questions.

Dust motes now danced through the golden shafts of light that filtered in through the east-facing dormer. Another section of boxes Sophie had not noticed earlier became illuminated. She picked her way carefully through the boxes and over to the other side of the room. The boxes bathed in iridescent light were marked with her mother's name, *Marcelle.*

Was this a trick, or was it magic? Her mother believed in magic, but she didn't. This was merely sunshine flowing through the only window—nothing more. She got down on her knees and pulled another box toward her. She could see that there was twine tied around and around the box. She looked on the floor to see if scissors could possibly have been left behind. This was not likely, so she stood and crossed the room, where a glint of light had caught her eye. On the shelf next to her coffee cup was a pocketknife. *Surprising!* She picked it up and headed back to cut the cord on her mother's things.

Just like her mother had described, the box had more official papers—this time she found the deed to the house in her mother's name. This surprised her, but she put it aside and plowed even deeper. Surely, this would be where she would find her mother's birth certificate and possibly her older brothers'. That would certainly speed things up in her search, but she came up empty-handed. Now, she sat firmly on the dusty floor and took the documents and letters out of the box and began reading each one. *Maman, you must have saved these for a reason.* Sophie recognized the names on letters from some of her mother's old friends in Ste. Barbe. She assumed they had all passed away, but she put them aside to look at later. There were school papers from not only Sophie's and her brothers' days at school but from her mother's days as well. Sophie scanned one of her old math tests, one on which she had done well. Tears welled in her eyes. All these years, her mother had kept these little mementos. Sophie wiped her eyes with her sleeve. A smudge of grime streaked across her cheek and over her nose. Just as she started to put the math page down, she recognized that her last name, Zabél, had been spelled with only one *l.* She laughed at that old family joke. Their real name should have been written with two *l*'s, as in *Zabélle*, but the clerk at the recording office had made the error, and it was carried to all of the children. One more matter of questionable identity.

She riffled through more school papers but found nothing worthy of merit. She picked up a stack of her mother's school papers, which were tied with a ribbon. Her mother had always said she loved school and had always wished that she had furthered her education. The handwriting was in French, but some of the side notes were in her old Breton language. She looked for her mother's maiden name on these papers, hoping to find a new clue. But there in bold box print was, Marcelle POURRETTE. Nothing new. Nothing new.

A yellowed onionskin sheaf of pages floated out of the pile. Sophie started to shove them back into the box when she caught a glimpse of her own name: *Sophie Juliette Paule Zabél.* Embossed in faded royal blue script was the name of Ste. Barbe's only hospital, *Hôpital de San Gabriel.* Sophie searched for a date on the paperwork. On the final page, alongside her father's signature, was the date September 24, 1959. She must have turned fifteen a few weeks before. What were these documents? She perused the medical jargon but couldn't make out the treatment she had received. She couldn't remember what had taken place. Was this when she fell off her bicycle? Why would her mother keep these old forms anyway? Hospitals were a financial burden on their father, so they rarely went. Oh, the price they had all paid! Sophie set the pages to the side along with the deed and letters from the old neighbors.

At the bottom of the box, she found a packet of some of her father's mining papers. She found it odd that they were hidden in her mother's box. But along with the packet were the journals her mother had promised that were dated from the time the family arrived in Ste. Barbe shortly after WWII. *These may contain some clues*, she thought. She placed those aside also. Sophie knew she had missed something but couldn't figure out what. After she stacked the deed, a few letters, the mining papers, her medical papers, and the journals on the floor beside her, she spotted another box in the distant corner. The slope of the roofline made it difficult for her to walk upright, so she bent at the waist and crept forward.

Here was one of the last remaining boxes, and Sophie was surprised to find it filled with some of her father's baskets, a craft he had taken great pride in and had taught her when she was young. She lifted the carefully woven baskets out of the box and held them up, one by one, admiring his work. She recognized the yellow grasses, once deep green in color, that they found together in the back field near their *coron,* the mining housing. She brushed her hair back from her face. A smile crossed her lips. She reached deep into the box. Along the side were some of her father's personal papers. She flipped through a stack but found nothing that caught her attention. More mining paperwork. She ran a final cursory hand around the bottom of the box, and her fingers lit upon two small packets of letters. She held them to the light and tried to make out the names and postmarks. Within the first packet, there must have been twenty letters tied together with a hank of weaver's twine. The letters were from over forty years ago. Sophie's hands shook. The envelopes were well-worn from being opened, almost to the point of disintegration. A scent of old roses—old women—wafted from the yellowed sheets. Her father's name was scrawled across the front of the envelope with their old address in Ste. Barbe. Within the envelopes she found letters, lurid love letters requesting her father to do . . . the most embarrassing of things. She blanched, but opened one, two more. *Why did he keep these? Who were they from? Was he hoping Maman would find them?* These questions entered her mind like shards of glass. Her head ached. Again, she held the letters up, one by one, to catch the light. The name Clarissa met her eyes. *Clarissa who? Who was this wanton woman, and what did she want with my father?* Could this have been her father's second cousin? Sophie had known her father had been involved in a lasting affair, but she never knew the woman's name. She always had found that difficult to understand since they lived in such a tiny hamlet. But gossip, she knew only too well, was never told directly to you, especially if you were the subject. The last envelope in the pack had the Fontanières address. *Right here! How bold could this woman be?* She wrapped the envelopes back up in the twine much like her father had and started to place them back in the box. She needed time to think about this. She set them back on the floor.

The second packet in her lap now caught her attention. She got up and went toward the window. Immediately she recognized her mother's handwriting. The unmistakable lilt and scroll of her penmanship was all too familiar. The letters were postmarked '46, '47, '50 . . . and were addressed to Thierry Pourrette in Mainsat— the same village where she, Sophie, had been born. There must have been twenty of them tied again with—how odd—a hank of weaver's twine. Her father's twine. There were fifteen letters over fifty years old, and all of them were unopened. *Unopened.* Sophie decided that there was no time like the present, and, with the help of the pocketknife, she sliced open the first envelope. She read through the first letter and gasped. Right then the doorbell rang. Sophie plucked up the letters, the medical papers, and the recipe box and raced down the stairs.

Her younger brother, Julien, was standing at the door. He was heading back to the Lorraine and dropped by with some fresh croissants and slices of leftover ham and cheese from the wake. Even though her youngest brother seemed to be coping well, he said that Thierry was struggling as if under the weight of wet cement.

Sophie walked into the kitchen with Julien following close behind her. She headed toward the coffee pot as he placed the food on the counter.

"He's still asleep," Julien told Sophie as he lifted the croissants out of a cloth bag, "which is unusual for Thierry." He shook his head. "Knowing only the life of a farmer, he has always been an early riser."

"Would you care for some coffee before you go?" Sophie asked her younger brother. He nodded his head and immediately sat down at the kitchen table.

"I knew he would have trouble losing our mother," Sophie said as she poured a fresh cup of coffee and replenished her own. She joined her brother at the table. "But I think I have something to cheer him up." Sophie showed Julien one of the letters written by their mother to Thierry when he was a young boy.

"What? What do you make of it?" Julien asked, as he bent over the letter. He held the pages gingerly in his hand, read them, then turned them over and over and returned them to Sophie. "I don't understand. The letter was written to Thierry over fifty years ago by *Maman*, and she's pleading with him to come live with us in Ste. Barbe."

"Yes, it is clearly a letter of a broken-hearted mother wanting her son back," Sophie said softly.

"And it says on the envelope, 'return to sender.' These letters were never opened or read by Thierry."

"Exactly, and that handwriting is not our brother's. In all his years, he will never be able to print that concisely. Obviously, it's not our mother's . . ."

"Well," said Julien, draining his coffee cup and rising to leave, "once Thierry gets up and over here, I'm sure he will feel whole again. I can't imagine why *Maman* didn't give him these letters years ago. She was so distraught that she could never get close to him—could never prove her love for him."

Sophie nodded. "I know. That absolutely breaks my heart, too, but Julien . . ." she hesitated, looked down into her lap where the other letters rested, and then looked up at her brother who was now towering over her chair. "I didn't find the letters in *Maman's* box. I found them *hidden* at the bottom of Papa's personal box." Her eyebrows arched in the telling. She watched his face to see if he understood her meaning.

"Papa's? Are you sure?" Julien sat back down.

"Oh, yes, I'm certain it was Papa's. There were *two* packets of letters tied with this same weaver's twine, stuck down at the very bottom of his box of old baskets," Sophie said pointedly. "You know. The baskets he was so fond of making."

"Oh, yeah. I remember . . .Two packets? Is this another quiz?"

"No. No quiz," she said, as she slowly produced the love letters written to their father. Julien took these letters with even more trepidation. He eased one envelope slowly from within the twine. He read their father's name written on the front, turned it over, and withdrew two sheets of stationery from within. The scent of stale roses once again wafted into the air from the brittle pages and penetrated the room. Once again, Sophie could see how the letter had been folded and refolded, probably ten thousand times, and she grimaced as the thought took root. She watched for her brother's reaction. He had always been the closest child to their father, so perhaps he would have a better understanding. Or a better explanation. She didn't dare attempt one as her mind automatically thought the worst.

"What do you make of it, Julien?" she asked, once he finished and placed the letter back into the reeking envelope.

"Oh, my Papa," he sang to the tune of the same name. "Whatever have you gotten yourself into this time?" He opened the letter once again and read aloud from the beginning:

"*Mon cher, mon dear, dear amour. Patiently I await your return—to our home—to our bed . . .*" He grinned over the top of the letter at Sophie and shrugged his shoulders.

"I'm sorry, Sophie. I don't know what to make of it. We always knew he had had a long-term love. I remember when our parents decided to move down here to Fontanières—*Maman* decided that she could no longer handle his affair, even when he promised her that it was over. But, you know our Papa. I think this woman was an addiction for him. Even when our parents came to visit me years after they moved from Ste. Barbe, he would leave *Maman* at our house and disappear for days at a time. She was so humiliated, but she tried not to let on. At least she doesn't have to put up with his nonsense, lies, or guff anymore." He stood once again. "I've got to get home. And it's a long, long drive, so I better get moving. How long are you going to be here, Soph?" he asked as he pulled Sophie to her feet to kiss her good-bye.

"I'm not certain. I have a number of things to do before I fly back to the States. Plus my friend, Kate, may be coming to help me, so . . ." He kissed her *adieu*, and she closed the door after him.

After refilling her cup once again, she returned to the living room. The mere mention of Kate's name conjured thoughts of the first cooking lesson her mother had given Kate, and this jangled into motion what Sophie now remembered as the shift, the change she had felt, which had opened up her mother in a way so atypical to her closed demeanor. Her mother had begun a litany of tales Sophie had never before heard, and she had revealed to Kate family secrets unequal to any Sophie had ever known. Sophie stifled the discomfort those thoughts brought and picked up the stack of letters and legal documents and the recipe box she had thrown on the sofa table when she had answered Julien's knock.

Sophie spent the rest of the morning huddled in her bathrobe reading one page after another of her mother's journals, crying, then sorting through legal papers and reading through more letters. Thierry arrived later that afternoon looking as if he had just crawled out of bed. His dark curly hair was punked out on top, and he looked ten years older than he had the previous day. Being under strict orders to deliver his wife's *potée auvergnate* to Sophie, he had no choice but to visit. Sophie hadn't realized how hungry she was before he arrived, but she never could resist Jeannine's delicious sausage and chestnut-stuffed chicken dish. What a treat! The succulent and savory aroma filled the small house and thankfully expunged the air of dead roses. Sophie's mouth watered as she set the platter on the kitchen counter and made a fresh pot of coffee.

"Oh, and a bottle of wine, too," Thierry said, slowly withdrawing it from deep within a pocket.

"How marvelous," she said as she turned to hug her brother. "Your wife certainly likes to spoil me, doesn't she? Is she joining us? Do you want to eat with me, drink with me, or do you just want some coffee?" she asked.

Thierry mumbled something about coffee, pulled up a kitchen chair, and sat down with a dull thud. "I can't believe she's gone, Soph. I just can't believe it." Tears spilled down his leathery cheeks and splashed onto the dusty vinyl tablecloth. Where the spatters appeared, a spot of aging yellow took its place. He dropped his head close to where she had placed his coffee. Sophie reached over to move his cup but instead placed both her hands on top of his massive arms as waves of internal sobs racked his body. She reached up and touched his curly dark hair. Little tufts of white hair jutted out from over his ears, and once he raised his head, she could see how much he looked like their mother. Like never before.

"Oh, Thierry," she breathed quietly. "*Mon cher frère*," Sophie, too, burst into tears, stumbled from the table, and moved to his side. Dropping to her knee beside his chair, she wrapped her arms about him as they both wept. For the first time in their lives, time gentled and came to a standstill.

She had no idea how long she had remained on her knees, but she was aware of the warmth of his skin and the smell of the farm on his old leather jacket.

"Thierry, have I ever told you of the first time I met you?" she murmured. She looked up into his face.

Like a small boy between sobs, he nodded his head in the affirmative, but she proceeded to tell him the story anyway.

"I remember it," she began, "as if it were yesterday. I was about ten years old, so that would have made you eighteen. Our parents had bought their first car, and we—our parents, Julien, Gérard, and I—had driven all the way from the Lorraine to the Auvergne— a very long drive. I remember feeling strange about meeting a brother I didn't know." She grinned up at him and swiped away her tears. "The lengthy trip was a real adventure for us, but somehow I mostly remember the tension that seemed . . . well, really heavy."

"I can imagine," he said, as a brief burst of nose-blowing was followed by a simple snuffle. He wiped his eyes with his handkerchief and stuffed it into his jacket pocket.

"When we arrived at the farm where you lived," she continued, "you weren't there. We were told by the family you lived with that you were working in a nearby field. So we went there to meet you. As I recall, it was only a short drive to the top of a knoll, where we clamored out of the car. I don't know why I remember this so vividly, but it was a hot summer day, beautiful and clear, with a bright blue sky. It seemed we could see forever, with rich green valleys and pastures spread out below us. And there you were, the most beautiful man I had ever seen in my life, working all alone in the wheat fields. You were tall with curly dark hair and broad sun-bronzed shoulders. I remember how the sunlight shimmered off your body." Thierry squirmed a bit in his seat, yet he listened. He pulled his handkerchief back out of his pocket, then stuffed it back in again. Clearly he was uncomfortable, but she continued without hesitation.

"Even though the wheat field was probably small, it seemed to me to have no end. And there you were—working hard at making stacks of the freshly cut wheat. As you wielded the scythe, I remember your sway was calm and regular, wide and precise. And

I still remember the noise of the scythe cutting against the tall dry stalks that held the clusters of wheat. *Whooof. Whooof. Whooof.*

"You looked up from your work as we walked toward you, but you didn't know us. I doubt you expected us. I just remember the look of fear on your face and your dark brown eyes—the same as *Maman's*—wide with anxiety. And then you recognized *Maman.*" Sophie stopped and got up off her knee.

"I remember *Maman* rushed to hug you, but you withdrew. Thinking back on it now, Thierry, I understand why. It had been too many years." Sophie moved to the other side of the table and sat down. "I probably didn't even talk with you during that first visit." She took a sip of her lukewarm coffee. "But I've probably made up for it since, right?" She smiled into his eyes. "Once we left, I remember being surprised at how the air felt against my skin, thick as honey yet electrically charged. I looked around expecting to see an electrical storm following us, but the sky was clear. But, oh my, how our *Maman* cried. Most of the way home she continued, and it was a very long trip."

Thierry pulled back from the table and walked to the sink. "Sophie, do you remember a friend of *Maman's* named Sophie Marie Chirade?" Water splashed wildly in and then out of his cup and onto the front of his flannel shirt and leather jacket. His wet hand dabbed at the spots but only enlarged the stain.

Sophie's hand had been playing across the worn tablecloth; she'd been poking her forefinger into another tiny fissure that had formed when she heard Marie's name. Suddenly, she sat up and took in her brother's words. She hadn't shared with Thierry the search her mother had requested, as she still questioned his fragile state, but the mention of the name brought her to attention. *Maman* had mentioned Madame Chirade in her letter.

"Vaguely," she answered. "Wasn't she a friend of *Maman's* during World War II?"

"Yes. Madame Chirade called me this afternoon. She told me

she first met *Maman* shortly after *Maman* and Gérard came down from Paris. I'm not so sure of the date. Probably around '43." He turned around, his eyes scanning the room for a dry dishtowel, his hands still dripping wet. "But after the folks moved to Ste. Barbe, I suppose they lost track of each other. I figured *Maman* struck up their old friendship once she returned to live here in Fontanières many years later. Anyway, when Madame Chirade heard about *Maman*'s death . . . she said she waited until after the funeral before she called me." Picking up a cloth napkin, he turned back to the sink and dried off his cup. "She said she's been ill so she was unable to come to *Maman*'s funeral. But if we ever want to talk with her about *Maman*, we should give her a call. I wrote down her number here somewhere." He pawed at the front pocket of his now-damp blue flannel shirt and through his jacket pockets. Sophie spun around in her seat and stared up at her brother's back and broad shoulders. He turned and handed her a torn stub of paper, which had a number scribbled across its face.

"What did you think, Thierry? How did she sound?"

"Well," he shrugged, "she sounded fine. I don't know. I haven't talked to her before, so I don't know how far gone she is. But as I was driving over here, I got to thinking that she might be the only one still alive who knew our *Maman* during the War." He turned the spigot on again, and a rush of cold water splashed into a dirty bowl in his hands. "She sounded like her mind was pretty sharp, and I thought if you wanted to find out information, about . . . anything about our family, maybe our *Maman* confided in her and . . ."

Sophie wondered whether she should share her search with Thierry. He would have to know sooner or later. Finally she stood up, handed Thierry her empty cup, and opened one drawer after another in search of a tea towel. "I think we should give her a call and go talk with her. You're right. If we wait too long, all of *Maman*'s connections will be gone."

"Ah, Sophie," he hemmed and hawed, "I'm maybe not the one to go with you. I just thought if you went for the both of us, maybe she would open up to you."

"Well, then, I'll give her a call," Sophie said as she slipped her arms around his waist and gave him a quick hug.

As Thierry started for the door, Sophie said, "By the way, I have something for you." Sophie picked up the packet of letters she had left in the living room and placed them in his hands. On the front of every letter in beautiful script—the script she knew he would recognize as their mother's—was his name. Sophie studied him, waiting to see what he would do next. Thierry glanced down at the letters cradled in his hand for a long time, but he made no move to open the envelopes or explore their contents. Instead, he stuffed the bundle into his pocket, mumbled his thanks, and walked out the front door. After Thierry disappeared, Sophie sagged in the doorway, wondering if she had done the right thing. Thank goodness Kate was arriving in a few days. She desperately needed someone to lean on.

CHAPTER FOUR

A Meeting with
Madame Chirade

AIR FRANCE 7400 BUMPED onto the tarmac, lifted up, then landed more securely back onto the ground before rolling to a halt. Kate's flight from San Francisco to Paris had been flawless, but her flight to Lyons had been a white-knuckler. She was more than just a little happy to see her good friend waving wildly through the glass doors as she passed through to the baggage claim room. Sophie rushed toward her with her arms out and kissed her on both cheeks. Kate had made it, and their odyssey was about to begin.

Outside, the October wind howled around the two women as they shoved Kate's luggage into the back of Sophie's red Citroën. Over the din of the airplanes' roar of the Lyons airport, Sophie shouted and then signaled for Kate to hop into the car. Before Sophie could start the engine, Kate grabbed her hand and said, "Sophie, I just want you to know how very sad and sorry I am about your mother's passing. I can't believe she's gone. I'm so grateful I got to know her."

"Thank you, Kate," Sophie blinked rapidly. "I can't believe she's gone either."

Kate looked more closely at Sophie. Dark circles hung around her eyes, and deep crevices she had never noticed before cut through her friend's face. "How are you doing, Sophie? How are you really doing?"

"As if I'm on remote control," Sophie laughed. "I try to think about what to do next, yet I can't focus on what steps to take. That's why I'm glad you were able to come. Truly." She turned the key in the ignition, and the car roared to life.

"Nice car, Sophie," Kate said as she settled back into her seat.

"It's a rental. Yes, it's bright, but it should handle our needs."

"That it should! Upward and onward."

Kate stripped off her black coat and scarf. She had taken the State Department's orders literally following the 9/11 attacks—*Do not dress like an American*—and she wore her darkest colors for the trip. She glanced once again at Sophie, who was wearing a wild array of colorful combinations with geometrical designs prancing across her coat and scarf and down her hose. Kate laughed out loud and said, "I see I didn't dress for the occasion."

"Ah, no problem, Kate. We'll turn you into a Frenchwoman soon enough!" Sophie grinned. "Now, are you ready for a trip down memory lane?"

"More than ready, mademoiselle."

"Madame," Sophie corrected.

"*Mais, oui!*" Kate tittered in acknowledgement. "Already I've forgotten my French. Oh, la, la!"

As Sophie shifted the car into gear, her on-board computer automatically engaged and a syrupy-sweet woman's voice began speaking French. To Kate, the intrusion felt as if a stranger had taken up residence and had become an impertinent backseat driver.

"So, who is your other passenger?" Kate asked.

"I call her Justine. She knows only French, has a mind of her own, and has an insatiable appetite for chewing up instructions, but she's been a decent companion." Just then, Justine began chastising Sophie for not turning *à gauche ou à droite* (left or right). Sophie grinned sheepishly.

"I'm certain you two will figure it out." Kate settled into the passenger seat. "I'm just glad to be here, Sophie."

"I am, too, Kate. You know that *Maman* requested you to come help me, right?"

"No," Kate raised an eyebrow, "I missed that piece."

"She took to you, too. Why else would she have told you all our secrets?" Sophie laughed.

"Sophie, that was a surprise for me, as well."

"Oh, Kate, I'm *so* glad you are here!" Sophie reached over and squeezed Kate's hand. "I don't think I would be able to handle all this alone. Last night I spoke with Madame Sophie Marie Chirade, one of *Maman's* oldest friends. I told her that *Maman* had left me a final letter instructing me to contact her."

"Was Madame Chirade receptive?"

Sophie nodded.

"Well, that's wonderful! Maybe this is the break you need."

Just at that moment, the wind, which had been buffeting Sophie's car with clouds of dust, brought Kate to attention as she looked out the window. Winter had not set in as of yet, and although she had missed the brilliant autumnal colors of weeks past, the muted browns and rusts of dried leaves and withered vines were a subtle background to the bright green nests of parasitic mistletoe. Those seemed to be leap-frogging from one leafless tree to another along the highway as Sophie careened ahead. Kate's mind, too, was whirling. She realized she had missed what Sophie was saying, catching only the tail end.

". . . *Mais oui*, I do believe our time with Madame Chirade will be well spent and a great place to begin. So I hope you aren't too jet-lagged, as the only time we can visit her is on our way back to my mother's today. She is preparing lunch for us. Will you be all right with that?"

Kate nodded her assent and answered, "Why not?" Sophie took a deep breath and patted a list that lay on the seat between the two of them. "I've made up some questions to ask Madame Chirade about *Maman*. If you think of anything to ask, please feel free. *So, what is most pressing?* Sophie asked herself. *Questions about Thierry? Or, perhaps, Gérard?* A large knot formed in her stomach, as she wondered if her own identity might be tied to the answers she would be receiving. She had felt certain about her family before, but now the truth felt like sand slipping through her fingers.

Kate, noticing the look of consternation on her friend's face, reached across the seat and patted Sophie's hand. "I'm here with you, Sophie. If you need a break during your conversation, just say so. These mysteries don't need to be resolved in one afternoon." Sophie let out a breath she didn't realize she had been holding; she smiled.

After a couple of hours' drive and a short snooze for Kate, they pulled up in front of a two-story grey stone house. "This house," Sophie said to Kate, "is very old, well over seven hundred years old, and is built in the age-old style of stone stacked upon stone." A red corrugated roof that sagged low over the doorway, the victim of some long-ago windstorm, matched the hue of the window and door framing. The red was a welcome contrast to the grim-colored stone. The freshest appeal came from the splash of plastic pink petunias and magenta-flushed geraniums that hung in pots mounted along the second-story windows.

Sophie Marie Chirade stepped out onto the porch and waited for the two women. A withered hand patted a stray white curl back into place while the other hand smoothed the blue checked apron over her wraithlike body. Her illness was ebbing, she told herself, and her strength was increasing. As she watched Sophie and Kate approach, a smile enveloped her face. Marie would make it through this day one way or another. It was too important.

"Sophie, it has been years," she said with a slight rasp to her voice. "You look so much like your mother. I see it there in your smile," Marie grasped Sophie's shoulders with a strength that surprised even her and placed a kiss on each cheek in greeting.

"*Merci*," Sophie said as she stepped aside. "And this is my dear friend, Kate. Kate Barrington. She knows a smattering of French."

Kate extended her hand. "Very pleased to meet you, Madame Chirade."

"How delightful to meet you, too, and I know a smattering of English," Marie chirped as she ushered them inside. "And please, call me Marie."

The moment the front door opened, the pungent aroma of cabbage and savory pork immediately swept past Sophie. "Mmmm. It smells delicious in here, and oh, so familiar. What are you cooking?" Sophie asked. The two women edged into the small hallway behind Marie.

"A local specialty, *potage auvergnate*. Since you consented to stay for lunch, I thought I would prepare something nice, local, and something I used to make with your mother. Basically, it's just cabbage soup with chunks of pork. It's easy to make. Of course, during the war, we would pretend to have pork, but surely your mother prepared this for you in the past, *oui?*"

"*Oui!* But I guess I never realized where the recipe came from. Now that *Maman* has gone, I am beginning to realize how little I know about . . ." She stopped short.

"I know what you are going to say," Marie interjected, "but I, for one, am simply overjoyed to be able to fill in those parts of your mother's life—if that would be helpful." Marie led Sophie and Kate into her overcrowded living room. The room held two overstuffed chairs in diminished shades of green chintz, which sat across from a rose-colored taffeta sofa. An ottoman and coffee table were also thrown into the mix, and movement in the small room was difficult.

Sophie began again, "You're right. I mostly remember *Maman*'s wonderful soups. For us, it was always comfort food. For her, it was a blessing to be able to stretch a meal. Come to think of it," she said wistfully, "she always gave credit to living here in the Auvergne. And, to you, Marie."

"Oh, that's sweet, Sophie. How I miss her already. Did you know your mother was like a sister to me all these years? Did you know that I've known *you* since you were born? Before, even."

"No, I didn't know much about my mother's past, and that's why I've come—to ask you some questions about her," Sophie stammered. "I'm trying to understand what her life was like during the War and before . . ."

Marie waved her hand for them to sit but found her little dog on the sofa noisily snoring away.

"Froufrou, stop that racket and get off the sofa." She lightly swatted the dog to make room for her guests. The black-and-white ShihTzu looked drowsily up from her spot, rolled her large black eyes, yawned, and jumped to the floor. Sophie patted her head before she slid out of her woolen cape and laid it on the back of the sofa. Kate, still feeling a chill, left her jacket on.

"I've been expecting you, Sophie," Marie said. "I have a great deal to tell you—and to show you. But before you are seated, could you both help me with the tray? We must begin with a little nourishment," Marie said. She slowly turned and headed for the kitchen, clutching the edges of her apron with an arthritic grip.

"You know, your mother was one of a kind—a strong and courageous woman—the best friend I ever had. Even my dear husband, Jacques, God bless him," she crossed herself, "could never be closer to me than your mother."

"But all those years we lived in Ste. Barbe," asked Sophie, as she followed Marie, "did you stay in contact?" She was searching through her memory for Marie's name in some recollection. She knew her mother had mentioned her, but for some reason it was always whispered and Marie's name never came up when her father was around, so . . . Already she was feeling disoriented. Kate got to her feet and followed behind.

"Ah, *mais oui.* We always leaned on each other throughout the years."

The three headed into the kitchen. A white hutch, which displayed pink-flowered china, stood against one wall with a formidable-sized cast-iron stove shoved up next to it. Along the opposite wall sat a *maie,* a wooden bread trough, that had been made into a table and was set for their *déjeuner.* Next to the sink and elegantly laid out on the cracked linoleum counter was a porcelain tray with three crystal wine glasses along with a pink-flowered plate layered with savory crackers.

"Oh my, these lovely plates are like the ones my great-aunt gave me," said Kate. "Remember these, Sophie? Your mother said she had some dishes similar to these."

"Exactly like these," Marie said. "We purchased them together after the War. It was one of the few extravagances we made together." Marie reached into her refrigerator and brought out a bottle of sweet Grenache wine.

"Would you do the honors, Sophie?" She handed her the bottle along with a corkscrew.

"I would be pleased to, Marie. Oh, this *is* a marvelous wine. Is this from Banyuls-sur-Mer?"

"Do you approve?" Marie asked.

"*Mais oui,* Marie. This is a special treat. Thank you," Sophie purred.

As Sophie removed the cork and filled the three glasses, Marie lifted the lid on the bubbling pot to check the *potée.* Once again, the acrid yet pleasant aroma ascended through the room, whetting

Kate's and Sophie's appetites even further. Neither had eaten much breakfast, and hunger pangs were gnawing from within.

"Oh, this smells absolutely divine, Marie," murmured Kate.

"Marie, Kate loves to learn new recipes, especially our *pauvre cuisine*. That's how *Maman* and I became good friends with her— over a stove, right Kate?"

Kate's blue eyes sparkled. She started to nod her head when, suddenly, it hit her that Marcelle was really gone. Kate dropped her head.

"*Mais oui*, my dears. I would be happy to share the recipe, Kate," Marie said kindly.

Eyeing the crackers on the plate, Sophie placed the glasses on the tray and made her way back into the living room. Kate grabbed up the bottle and followed. Sophie, surprised to see Froufrou was back on the sofa again, yelped with laughter and almost dropped the tray. Regaining control, she placed the tray on the coffee table before scooping Froufrou into her arms and sitting down. Laughing, Kate put the wine alongside the tray and sat down next to Sophie.

"What happened?" Marie asked, as she ambled toward her chair.

"I was just startled by Froufrou. But, you see, she's letting me sit with her, and we're both quite comfortable." Sophie stroked the dog's head as Froufrou nuzzled closer.

"I believe she's now a permanent fixture," Marie smiled, and she eased slowly into her chair. "What would you like to know?"

Sophie stood and handed the wine glasses around before sitting down again. "Oh, so many things, Madame . . . Marie. *Maman* told us many stories about her childhood in Brittany, but not much after she left Vannes. When did you first meet her?"

"Tchin-tchin, *mes chères*. To blessed friendships," Marie said as she held up her glass in a toast. Sophie and Kate raised their glasses.

"Well, let me think," Marie said, after she had sipped her wine. "Your mother had been living in the Auvergne for a short while before I actually met her. It was probably back in '43. I was immediately drawn to her. Must have been her spunk," she laughed and took another sip of wine.

"Funny," Kate said, "that's exactly how I would have described Marcelle."

Sophie smiled.

"Anyway, the family she stayed with here in the Auvergne—they never treated her well, so I guess that was why we became such good friends. Now, this was well over sixty years ago, so I may have some of this mixed up." She lifted the wine glass to her lips but set it down without drinking. A shadow crossed her face. "As you can imagine, Sophie, Kate, war has a way of foisting people onto each other who, under ordinary circumstances, would never have crossed the street to say a single pleasant *bon jour*. But choice was not an option.

"My husband was part of the *Maquis*. Do you know about the *Maquis*?" Both women nodded their heads in the affirmative. "At the time, we lived on my in-laws farm about five kilometers from where your mother lived. I, too, became active in the secret organization by providing meals, washing clothes, writing letters for the men, hiding documents, and handling the radio . . . anything to help out."

Marie reached for the crackers but stopped. Kate handed her the crackers, then slid back in place.

Marie chewed a cracker slowly, and then said, "We were also busy working the fields. Most people had one ox to help with the plowing of the wheat or oat fields, but we had a tractor in addition to our truck. In spite of our good luck, it was difficult to get fuel. Many times the vehicles sat in silence." She exhaled deeply as if the memory wore her down.

"During the best of times, we grew wonderful vegetables, but during war time we grew only potatoes, lentils, beans, and carrots, plus corn and beets for our cattle. Oh, and then there were those horrible *topinambour*."

"*Topinambour?*" Kate asked.

"Those bitter vegetables my mother called Swedes and hated so!" Sophie let out a laugh. "*Maman* detested those things because she said other than carrots, that's all she ate in Paris. They're like turnips."

"Very similar in flavor," replied Marie. "We also had a small orchard that, in spite of the Germans helping themselves, produced delicious apples, pears, and cherries. And we also made use of the walnuts and chestnuts. Chestnut flour is quite good, you know." Marie laughed. "I remember your mother telling me that in Paris, she and her roommate tried to make chestnut flour, but they never had enough chestnuts at one time . . . Oh, but you asked, how did I meet your mother? I'm sorry, Sophie, I get distracted easily. Please bear with me."

Sophie nodded for her to continue but kept a watchful eye on her. She knew Marie had not been well before the funeral, and she was concerned these conversations might be taking a toll. Oh, but the verbal collage Marie was creating of her mother was such a gift. She caught her in mid-sentence.

". . . and once when I was walking from one farm to another carrying a basket filled with fruit, vegetables, and, of course, hidden messages, I first met her. I immediately liked her, as she had a ready smile. And unlike so many from that area, she never complained and was always willing to work hard. Most of all, I remember her ability to laugh. Her eyes would sparkle with such light, and the sound of her laughter was like rare music. I doubt if she ever knew this, but everyone wanted to be near her. She was that ray of sunshine that penetrated the darkness of war." Marie peered over her glasses at Sophie.

"People feel that way about you, too, Sophie," Kate said quietly. "Honestly, Marie, they do."

"I can imagine that's true. You are so like your mother." Marie's glasses slid halfway down her nose, and a kindly smile lit her face. Sophie waved away their observations, but her cheeks flushed with pleasure.

"I'm sorry, Sophie. I've strayed off the topic once again. I was talking about your mother's laughter. Yes, her laughter was especially a gift during those dark times. There were no festivals, no celebrations of any grand sort. And rarely did we acknowledge the saints' days. The people still went to church, even though German soldiers might attend too. That, of course, only infuriated us as we already felt so violated."

"I remember *Maman* mentioning that no Frenchman or woman would do anything to let the Germans think they were having fun," Sophie added.

"That's true. Sometimes we would have a ball or a dance, but we hid this activity from the Germans. We French were in mourning. Because many were not able to gather with their own families during those war years, we got together with those we worked with side by side. I believe that was how my bond became so strong with your mother. We were always facing life-and-death situations together. We desperately wanted to get rid of the occupiers."

Marie put her wine glass down, shifted her frail body in her chair, and attempted to find comfort. "Not long after your mother and I met, we realized we shared many of the . . . well, the same life experiences. We both had become pregnant outside of marriage. Fortunately for me, I was able to marry Jacques, the father of my son Frederic, but I could understand much of what your mother experienced. To have gone through her pregnancy alone . . . I was always so amazed at her strength."

Kate remained silent but nodded her head. Yes, she could understand, too.

Sophie hesitated, then said, "Not just one pregnancy, Marie, but two. She went through two of them alone."

"Yes, *ma cher,* she told me. She told me how she had been . . . well, attacked when she was sixteen, and then gave birth to Thierry in Paris. But she also told me André was at least nearby when she gave birth to Gérard."

"André? Who is André?" asked Sophie.

Marie paused.

"Marie, is André the name of Gérard's father?" Sophie asked, her voice rising. "I never knew." She appeared shaken. Suddenly, she got up and poured herself more wine before offering more to Kate. It was clear that Marie wasn't drinking much of her own.

"All we knew," continued Sophie, sitting back down, "was that Gérard was her love child, born from the one man she truly loved. Of course, I knew none of these details until after my father passed away."

A shadow passed over Marie's face, and she let out a cough.

"Well, Sophie, I'll do my best to tell you more. But I believe that he, André, was separated from his wife when your mother first met him and became pregnant. He could not obtain a divorce. There was something about his wife's mental health . . . All I know is your mother suffered from loneliness most of her life, if you understand what I mean."

"*Mon Dieu,* do I! My mother's move to Ste. Barbe was sadly not an improvement to her life."

Marie stood to check on the potée as Sophie again topped off her glass. She noticed Kate had barely touched hers, while she had swilled down a goodly amount. She was drinking in this newfound information at the same rate as the wine. She knew it was already taking a toll, yet her body was not relaxing, and cold was seeping into her bones. She pulled the afghan, which had been flung onto the sofa, over her legs.

"Are you doing all right, Sophie?" Kate asked while observing her friend's movements.

Sophie's laugh sounded mechanical. "I don't know. I feel like

I'm hearing about my life for the first time—not just my mother's. I'm almost panicked at what will come next."

Just then, Marie returned with a small plate of hors d'oeuvres —olives, almonds, radishes, and more snack crackers. She eased herself slowly into her chair once again.

"Now, where were we?" she asked. "I guess I was telling you that your mother and I shared a great deal, and the bond that formed lasted until her death."

"Marie," Sophie began, "how did my mother meet my father? Of course, they have told me before, but I was wondering how you remember this."

"Oh, *ma pauvre fille*, I would be happy to share that story." She wiggled around in her chair once again. "Sorry. Old age has made sitting a little painful for me. Such a nuisance. Now, your mother was living with the Amberts on their farm. Thierry was eight, I believe, and Gérard was around a year old, I believe. The Amberts had been slipping food to the *Maquis*, who would sneak into the farmyard at night. The *Maquis* hid out in old sheds and in haylofts, and they even slept in haystacks at night if they weren't on night patrol. During the day, they worked for the local farmers or moved about the countryside out of sight of the Germans. They were all young . . . late teens, early twenties, and inexperienced.

"It was about this time that Jules, your father, lumbered into the kitchen where your mother was busy feeding the baby and helping with dinner. I happened to be there, too, so I remember he was quite tall . . . almost had to duck to clear his head . . . and his demeanor was quiet but intense. His dark brown hair was slicked back and tucked under a black beret. *Chercher une querelle avec un allemand.* Always one to seek a German quarrel. I remember his light blue eyes swept the kitchen with wariness and fell upon your mother. I never knew him to show much facial expression except that one moment when he first met your mother. Immediately, they found themselves captive, one to the other, but not a word was exchanged." Marie looked up at Sophie. Sophie smiled, and Marie continued.

"He was gaunt, thin beyond words, and had come to the farmhouse for food. Your mother, who was quite short, looked dwarfed next to him. A slight smile broke across his face as he was introduced, but he stayed aloof. I never remember him able to relax, but under the circumstances of war, that would have been difficult.

"Before your mother arrived at the Ambert farm, Jules worked for several local farmers doing odd jobs, but he never hung around long. He stayed just ahead of the enemy while awaiting orders. But after he met your mother, he came to the Ambert's farm regularly. He helped out, then he vanished into the night. His life as a *Maquis* was always secretive, so, unlike the rest of us, when the Germans came near the farm, he had to disappear. Your mother trained your brothers not to mention his name. Gérard, who was such a happy baby, enjoyed the game, but Thierry never took to him; he felt protective of your mother. Nevertheless, your mother fell in love with him. Love comes at the most inopportune times, doesn't it? But I remember feeling happy for her, as I think she really fell for him.

"And my father? Did he fall in love with her?" Sophie asked, leaning forward in her seat.

Just then, a timer went off in the kitchen. "I believe our *déjeuner* is ready," Marie said, avoiding the question. She stood and moved slowly toward the kitchen.

Sophie looked at Kate, shrugged, picked up the tray, and followed. Marie lifted the lid on the stew and, once again, the pleasant aroma, rich with the fragrances of garlic and salt pork, filled the room. Swimming in the thick broth were turnips, potatoes, carrots, leeks, and cabbage—a full and hearty meal. She ladled three bowls full and set them on the table.

"Why, Marie, I do believe you've prepared enough food for an army," Kate joked.

"I think Marie knew how hungry we were, Kate," Sophie said.

Marie kindly smiled as Sophie assisted Marie in opening a bottle of red wine.

"Sophie, Kate, it has been such a long time since I had guests here. I can't thank you both enough for coming." Tears shimmered in Marie's eyes.

"It's our pleasure, Marie." Sophie felt a lump in her throat. She changed the subject. "Your son, does he live nearby?"

Marie paused. "No. He died fighting in Algeria . . ."

Sophie grasped Marie's hand.

"My, that seems so long ago now," Marie said with a wave of her other hand. "Unfortunately, we never seem to end wars, do we? If only we would leave wars in the hands of women . . ."

Sophie lifted her glass. "To a time without war and to our hostess. Tchin-tchin!" Together, the three joined in the toast. Sophie's and Kate's heads dropped toward their bowls as they began to devour the *potée*.

"Mmmm. I didn't think it could be possible, but the food tastes even better than it smells," Kate said as she quickly finished her bowl.

"*C'est vrai*," Sophie said as she helped herself to more. She had been so hungry that she could not even think. And with that wine? "Would you care for more, Kate? Marie?"

Kate accepted another portion, but Marie had taken only a few bites. She quietly sat back and enjoyed her guests.

"This is so unlike me, Marie," Sophie said, wiping her chin. "I usually am the one to eat like a bird. This is so delicious."

"Yes, Marie! I'm usually the one to eat copious amounts," Kate said, patting her stomach.

Their conversation remained light . . . about the weather, about farm prices, about what would become of farming now that France was biting down on another bullet of belt-tightening. Nothing more about family until after they had finished lunch. Marie brought out a coffee cake, cut it, and turned to prepare coffee. Sophie poked the tines of her fork into the warm cinnamon-laced cake. She let the sticky goodness cross her tongue, and she swooned.

Marie smiled but sat back down, a determined look etched on her face.

"Sophie, I made a promise to your mother that I was to tell you or your brothers all I know about her. And she left her journals with me to give to you."

"Oh, that's right," Sophie said, placing her fork back on her plate. "*Maman* wrote me a letter before she died, and she mentioned her earlier journals."

Marie stood up and retrieved several small cracked leather-bound books from her kitchen counter. "Yes, she wanted me to give these to you."

Sophie picked up one of the journals, which had been laid gently before her. Tears freely flowed down her cheeks. She didn't know what to think. She opened the journal and quietly traced her finger over her mother's script. Here was her mother's story—one she possibly had never heard.

"If *Maman* wrote these for us children, why didn't she give them to us?" Sophie asked, swiping the tears back with her napkin.

"She gave them to me years ago, before your father passed away. She wanted to make sure her history was not lost, if you understand my meaning."

Sophie nodded. Unfortunately, she did.

"Sorry to keep asking, but, about my father," Sophie ventured, "did he ever fall in love with my mother?" She pressed for more. "Is there something more you can tell me?"

"Let's continue our conversation in the living room, shall we?" Marie stood up slowly once again, and Froufrou, who had been camped out on Sophie's feet, woke with a yelp. Once in the living room, Marie seemed even more unsteady. She grabbed the back of her chair.

"Marie, why don't we help you to bed?" Kate suggested,

placing her hand gently on the elderly woman's elbow.

"Yes, I'm afraid our visit is taking a toll on you," Sophie said, taking Marie's other elbow. "We'll continue this conversation again another time." Marie started to resist, then turned and, without a word, headed to her bedroom.

"I'm so sorry. My strength isn't what I had hoped," Marie said as she began to undress. She looked at Sophie, the expression on her face inscrutable. "I do want to tell you about your father. Truly, I do." The dog hopped up onto the bed with her mistress and settled in.

After Sophie and Kate helped Marie into bed, Sophie said, "You just rest, and I'll give you a call later to see how you are doing." Kate patted her arm, but Marie's eyes were already closed. Before leaving the house, Kate and Sophie washed the plates, cleaned up the kitchen, and turned off the coffee. Sophie picked up the precious journals, and the two headed to the car.

Once in the driver's seat, Sophie sighed. "Why, oh why is it that when the topic of my father arises, people avoid the discussion?" She looked at Kate. "Let's get you back to *Maman's* house. You must be exhausted." Sophie started the engine.

Even before Marie heard Sophie's car pull away, her eyes opened. It was clear Sophie needed to understand her father's feelings for Marcelle. Unfortunately, Marie knew too much about Jules, yet, even after sixty years, she was afraid to reveal his falsehearted deceit. *If I had not been so fearful of Jules's death threat, I could have told Marcelle of André's wartime visit. I could have saved her from a life of misery.* Despair and remorse brought fresh tears that coursed down the furrows of her wrinkled cheeks and dampened her pillowcase. She turned out the light but continued to be immobilized by her thoughts. *Is this something I should share with Sophie? Do I owe her that ugly part of her father's history?*

CHAPTER FIVE

$\mathcal{U}$nfit for $\mathcal{C}$hildhood

$\underset{A}{\mathsf{I}}$

$\mathcal{K}$ ATE AWOKE WITH A JERK. She was soaked to the skin with perspiration and couldn't make out her surroundings. Jet lag encompassed her as if she were wrapped in a cocoon, but slowly she noticed a thin stream of light eking under the doorway. She lifted her head slightly. The light, she determined, was from the hallway of Marcelle's home. She relaxed back onto the pillow. How long had she been sleeping? She turned to see the clock, but it wasn't visible. Slipping further into the bedclothes, her mind drifted back over her dream. She wished Matt were here to soothe her. He had been supportive of her coming to France but had no clue to her motives. How could he, when she didn't know either?

Her old therapist notions were playing over and over in her mind. *Was Marcelle seeking redemption? And what about her own search? Was she also seeking redemption?* Perhaps Matt had been right. Perhaps her trip to France was not about Marcelle, but about Lisa, the daughter she had given up for adoption. She swallowed hard. Just then, Kate heard a sob. Was that her? She clapped a hand over her mouth, but then a second sob echoed up the stairway. Kate tossed her coverlet back and her toes searched the cold floor for her slippers. *Dang things—never where you can find them.* She grabbed her robe, wrapped it quickly around herself, and was out the door and down the stairs before she realized what she was doing.

Sophie, wrapped in a large green comforter, sat on her mother's sofa surrounded by the journals Marie had given her. The moment she heard Kate clatter down to her, she quickly wiped her nose with the back of her hand and swiped away her tears.

"Are you all right, Sophie? Is there anything I can do?" Kate knelt down beside her.

Sophie blew her nose and pointed to a journal in her lap. It took a few moments for her to compose herself, but then she patted a space on the sofa next to her. "Here, hop in here. It's still chilly. We can share this comforter. I was just reading one of *Maman*'s earliest writings—when she was still a kid. This one," she said, picking up an age-worn green journal. "She writes in here that her stepfather used to come into her room and . . . touch her." Sophie closed her eyes.

"Touch her? Abuse her?" Kate leaned closer to her friend. Not only was the room cold, but this revelation sent chills through her body. She shivered.

"I'd say so. I guess it began once she moved to Paris to live with her mother. When her grandfather passed away, her grandmother couldn't afford to keep her, so she was forced to move to Paris to live with her mother and stepfather. She was around nine years old." Sophie blew her nose and shook her head. "She always hated it; she missed her grandmother so much."

"I didn't realize there was a stepfather, Sophie. I don't recall her mentioning him."

"Long ago I remember *Maman* mentioning him, but she would never utter her stepfather's surname."

"So, it was definitely not Pourrette, I take it."

"Nope. She carried the Pourrette name from birth, so that wouldn't make sense. And the topic of her stepfather was never again broached." Another tear leaked down her cheek. "You see, I had no idea that *Maman* was . . . was . . ."

"Molested? Do you think that's what happened?" Kate picked up another journal and flipped through the pages. "This one was written several years later. How long did you say she lived with her mother?"

"She returned permanently to her grandmother's when she was fourteen or fifteen. Why do you ask?"

"After years of working with women who have been sexually abused, I've learned that pedophiles rarely remain at the stage of simply touching. Usually they escalate, and that might be the reason she finally ran back to Vannes for good. Did she ever tell you why she moved back in with her grandmother?"

"Not specifically, so I suppose she . . ." Sophie moaned. "*Mon Dieu*, this is now beginning to make sense. That was when *Maman* ended up dropping out of school and began work. Oh, *Maman!* No wonder you gave me no choice but to finish school. That was one of her unrealized dreams."

Sophie's head dropped into her hands as she sunk further into the comforter. Silently, she began to cry; her body shook uncontrollably.

"Maybe this is too exhausting, Sophie," Kate said softly. "Perhaps you should try to get some sleep. We can talk about this later in the morning . . ."

"No. No. I can't sleep now. I simply can't." She pushed the comforter to the floor. *My nightmares,* she thought. *They're getting stronger now that I've returned to France.* "I can't sleep yet, Kate," Sophie said. "You go ahead . . ."

"No, no. I'm fine. Should I fix some coffee then? Marcelle made certain that you received these journals, so she must have wanted you to learn something here." Kate scootched off the sofa. "And, when I return, would you mind translating some of these entries for me?"

"Not at all," Sophie said, "but I'll get the coffee." She disappeared into the kitchen, and as Kate sat back down, only the sounds of the clock ticking could be heard. Shortly, Sophie returned with two cups of coffee.

"I'll start with this earliest one," Sophie said, picking up the green journal again, "so you can meet *Maman* when she was nine."

Paris, 1927

Nimbly running up the apartment house stairs, Marcelle tripped a light fantastic. One more bedeviled week of school was over. In Vannes, she had always liked school, but this new Parisian school? Well, hate was not too strong a word. Everything was different. Everyone was different. She hated the teachers who made fun of her Breton dialect. She hated them when she was forced to recite before her class in "perfect French." Yes, she had learned to speak French in her Vannais schools, but she never spoke anything but Breton at home. She was uncomfortable with it and was now forced to speak only French. Had she moved to a foreign land? And, once outside the classroom, she especially hated her classmates who never missed an opportunity to make fun of her for being a tomboy. She had no sanctuary. At least there was no school tomorrow. Her only break. What a relief!

She bounced up a few more steps when a wave of despair enveloped her. She missed her *grand-mère* and longed for the warmth of her arms around her. Early memories of comfort flooded through her. Why hadn't she soaked up her grandmother's loving like a sponge? Yes, she knew she was too old for these thoughts. She plunked down on the top step outside their apartment door, and her thoughts drifted back over the months she had lived in Paris. *Mama's kind enough and seems to like me, but she always works late. How will I ever get to know her? Oh, I miss Grand-mère so,* she inwardly wailed.

Pulling her bony knees to her chest, she wrapped her arms about them. Sitting on the top step, she rocked back and forth, the step squeaking in cadence with her movements. Even this reminded her of her grandmother's rocking chair. Back—squeak—forth—squeak; back—squeak—forth—squeak. Comfort came close in this rhythmic motion.

Blinking back tears, she peered over her knees. Across the street, a shadowy figure stood—a man half-hidden by the foliage of a plane tree. Her neck jerked higher to see more clearly. Did she recognize him? She didn't know who he was, but she had seen him on a number of occasions in the park; she remembered him because he had a distinctive limp. Strange! But there he was, observing her, and so close to home. *Who is he?*

Suddenly, her head snapped back. She remembered Tomas, her stepfather, might be home early today. Panic seized her. He might be lying in wait. Revulsion swept through her; she stopped rocking. Carefully, she slipped off her shoes. Thoughts of the man across the street disappeared from her mind. She focused on getting in the front door, down the hall, and to her room before Tomas knew she was home. She would lock the bedroom door and wait for her mother's return from work. The thought of Tomas's hand sliding up her legs once again and under her—no—no . . . She shook her head; she would run away before he got a chance to do that again. She trembled.

Silently, she pushed the door open, making certain the lock did not clack into place. Smelling cigarette smoke, she determined he was only a short distance away. Cautiously, she tiptoed down the hallway, avoiding the creaking floorboards. She scooped up her beloved cat, Kiki, as she swept past. Somehow, she determined, she would find money and disappear after nightfall.

"What's that?" Marcelle wondered. Endless hours had passed

while she stayed hidden in her room. With only her cat to keep her company, she watched the light from the afternoon sun disappear outside her window and the sky turn from deep blue to black. One more night her mother was late. She listened carefully. The front door slammed. She could hear her mother's footsteps move through the hallway to the kitchen. She breathed a sigh of relief. The muffled voices of her mother and Tomas could be heard. Then, "Where is she, Tomas?" her mother yelled. She stormed down the hallway toward Marcelle's bedroom. "Have you tried her door?"

"Of course he tried my door," Marcelle whispered to her cat, but she had lodged a chest in front of it. He knew she was there, but blessedly, he hadn't tried hard this time. She jumped off her bed and heaved the chest back into place. Tomas had often threatened her if she told anyone, and . . . She knew he was evil and would do whatever he promised. She couldn't say a thing to her mother anyway, since he was always nearby. "Don't even think your mother will believe you," he had taunted.

"What's going on in there, Marcelle?" her mother asked as she opened the door. She stepped into the room and looked about her.

"Nothing. I'm just reading."

"There's nothing on the stove to eat. I had to work late again, and then I find that neither of you have thought about supper. What am I going to do with you?" her mother hollered.

"I'm sorry! I'll help you, *Maman*. I just got caught up in this book," she lied. "I'm terribly sorry. Time got away from me." She looked up into her mother's face and was once again startled by her beauty. She could only hope one day that she would be as lovely— those dark, shiny curls, her heart-shaped face, her full red lips . . . Even when her *maman* lost her temper, her rosy cheeks made her hazel eyes look so beautiful. Marcelle never tired of gazing at her. She longed to be closer to her but knew that was not to be.

Tomas's face suddenly appeared over her mother's shoulder.

He leered at her in the way that she had come to despise. She determined she would leave that very night.

After a simple dinner of toasted bread with her favorite *saindoux*, she feigned sleep and slipped off to bed. Later, she could hear his voice and then his groans reverberating through the thin wall, which separated her room from theirs. She wrapped her pillow around her head. She waited for silence. Loathing ripped through her body. His moans were exactly the same as the ones he made with her . . .

She waited. Once snores replaced all other sound, she stole from her room. Stealthily, she moved back down the hallway. She almost stepped on Kiki. Marcelle crouched down and lovingly held her cat, not knowing if this would be the last time she could. She stood, stole two francs from her mother's handbag, and slipped out the door. Never had she been out this late before. As she ran toward the train station, she realized she had forgotten her coat. She stopped and then continued on. Shivering against the chill, she stood on her tiptoes to see into the ticket booth. The ticket agent, seeing her distress, came out of his booth and put his long grey sweater around her shoulders. He asked her where she was heading at that time of night.

"To *ma grand-mère's*, monsieur," she stammered. "To Vannes— for good!"

"Ah, *ma petite*, then it will be a one-way ticket to Vannes, *n'est-ce pas?*" he asked. She nodded her head and was on her way.

❦

Kate silently handed Sophie another journal, and Sophie continued to read.

Fall, 1934

"Who's there?" Marcelle called out. Her grandmother had passed away several months before, so Marcelle, at sixteen, was forced to fend for herself. She had gone to work at a family-owned dairy in a northern Breton village, where she sold milk products from an in-house store. She was given room and board but little else for her efforts. Her room, an eight-foot square, was in the attic, high above the store and directly above the owner's apartments. Her hopes and dreams of becoming a teacher had, for the time being, come to an end.

"Who's there?" she called out again. Stumbling could be heard on the wooden staircase. The footsteps fell at an uneven cadence and were punctuated with a dull thud as the wall reverberated from the force of an unsteady gait.

"Who's there?" she shrieked in panic, and then the door to her room burst open. Pieces of the doorjamb splintered into an explosion of wood fragments, which were hurled through the air. She covered her head with her arms and cowered on the bed. Her room was small—just big enough for a narrow bed and a makeshift bureau which held her only belongings. But her privacy, her most precious possession, now lay splintered, along with the door, on the floor. Memories of her stepfather's onslaught of abuse pitched her against the opposing wall.

It didn't take long for Ambrose, the farmer's oldest son, to cross through the doorway and fill the room with his drunken and menacing bulk. She saw the look in his bloodshot eyes and recognized the leer she had faced time and again with her stepfather. Once again, no one came to her rescue.

Within a few months' time, Marcelle was asked to leave her job, her only home, and find her own way. The family clearly would not tolerate housing a wanton and pregnant wretch such as herself. The memories of the last encounter would reverberate in her head throughout her life.

"Who do you think you are?" shrieked Ambrose's mother. She was highly offended when Marcelle suggested her son was the baby's father.

"You may think that you can bring this family down to your level, but you have another think coming," the woman's voice shrilled.

The back door to the dairy slammed shut, and Marcelle was left standing in the cold. She picked up her parcel of clothing from the snowbank where it had been thrown and, with tears streaming down her face, she made her way to the nearest road. Thoughts raced through her head. She had hoped to rise above her own mother's experience and shame, but her greatest fears had become a reality; shortly after turning seventeen, she found herself pregnant and unmarried.

As she walked along the road, the evening Angelus rang out from the Catholic church across the valley. Six PM. It was already dark, almost Christmas and she had nowhere to go. Surprisingly, the sounding of the bells brought a sense of familiarity. As a child, the bells were a signal for routine, for safety, and for comfort. It meant a time for prayers, a time for *Grand-père* to return from work, and a time for their evening meal. And, the pealing of the bells reminded her of the mythological City of Ys, the very stories her beloved grandfather had always told. Dahut was a mythological character in Brittany who became pregnant as a young girl and was cast out to the sea, where she became a mermaid. *Am I doomed to live out the same story as Dahut? Have I not just been cast into the sea because of pregnancy?* "Oh, *mon grand-père,* I swore to you I would never follow in my mother's footsteps," she said to the heavens above. She couldn't believe her misfortune.

༄༅

Kate returned from the kitchen with more coffee for the two of them, and after Sophie stood to stretch, she picked up another journal. She and Kate shifted back onto the sofa.

As Sophie began to sip her coffee, she wondered, *How is it Maman never told me about being molested, but told me of her rape . . .*

when she knew perfectly well I had been moles—raped too? Even in the privacy of her own thoughts, Sophie hedged her own reality. Immediately her nightmares loomed before her—like a vulture ready to pounce, no longer waiting for her to sleep. *Was it because of my rape?* After forty years, why didn't she have answers?

"What happened to her?" Kate asked, breaking into Sophie's thoughts. Tears had filled Kate's eyes, too, as she thought of her own daughter, Lisa, but she quickly swiped them away. Marcelle's journal had struck a heavy chord. "How did she survive?"

"All I know," Sophie mumbled, "is that six months later, Thierry was born on the first of July, 1935, in a convent in Paris. Five years later, while *Maman* was working at the Citroën factory, the war came." Sophie sorted through the journals and opened one from that period.

⋄⋄⋄

Marcelle bolted upright in bed. "Genéviève," she screamed, "what is that sound?" Her head felt as if it might explode. Too much wine from the night before. She couldn't shake the ringing in her ears. She looked at the bedside clock. 1:00 AM. She couldn't think. The sound continued to whine and reverberate, echoing between the buildings and along the streets below her Paris *pensione* (apartment).

"Gené, where are you?" She looked toward the empty bed and tried to see, but there was no light anywhere. Suddenly, the apartment door slammed shut as Genéviève flew into their room. "Of course, when I go to the bathroom, the Germans attack! They've finally attacked! Can you believe that? They said they would, and now . . . We need to go. We need to get to the basement shelter. I heard bombs going off, I'm sure of it." She quickly pulled a long coat over her pajamas, grabbed her purse and cigarettes, and then kicked off her slippers and pulled on her shoes.

Marcelle, blinking, tried to focus. She still was not connecting

• 84 •

with the reason the sirens continued to wail. Slowly she slid out from under the duvet and dropped to the floor to hunt for her shoes. Geneviève, who was now dressed and ready to run, screamed at her over the din.

"Wake up! We have to go now! Where are the gas masks? What did we do with them? Did we leave them back at the factory?"

Finally alert, Marcelle pulled her coat over her nightgown. "Those relics? Do you really think World War I masks can possibly protect us?" Not pausing for an answer, she moved through the dark like lightning and grabbed the gas masks from the top shelf of the closet. She would check out these so-called protective devices down below.

The two raced down three flights of steps, stumbling into the throngs of neighbors heading to the shelter. The halls were dark, and as they descended, the reality began to seep in.

"This must really be it!" Geneviève whimpered. "Looks like the *Drôle de Guerre* (Phony War) is finally over."

As each one fled out of the dark stairwell, the dim light was startling, but welcome. Lanterns, which were strewn throughout the basement, radiated a luminescent glow through the dank room. The residents, only slightly familiar with this room, much less each other, sank onto their haunches along the damp walls. Match after match was struck as cigarettes were nervously lit, as if on cue.

Marcelle covered her nose with the sleeve of her coat. The putrid smell of centuries of dampness and mold now commingled with clouds of blue cigarette smoke. Despite all the people in the room, the space was unusually quiet. Heads were cocked to the side to catch any outside sound. Bombs? Could bombs be exploding nearby? The siren continued to blare as they slipped into their own thoughts.

How is my Thierry? Is he frightened? Is he safe? Marcelle's anxiety rose as the sound of bombers roared overhead. Her son, only months before his fifth birthday, was still living in another *arrondissement* (district), as were all the children of single factory workers of Citroën. The nurses' home was the only place he had known since his birth. Marcelle felt fortunate to have child care, but the grave drawback was that she lived kilometers away from him and saw him only on weekends. As painful as that was for her to accept, the promise she had made to Thierry to remain together was tossed aside for economic security.

And how secure were they all feeling right at that moment? Marcelle looked around and for the first time noticed other women crying into their coats. Were they longing for their children too?

When did this all begin? When would it end? The newspapers had been constantly talking of war, so was this really it?

"All right, Marcelle. Help me out with this," Geneviève's loud whisper jarred her thoughts. "Do you think this is the real thing?"

"Well, didn't France and England declare war on Germany back in September, last year?" Marcelle asked. "Isn't that when the *Drôle de Guerre* began—nine months ago?"

"Why, we could have had another baby in that time," Geneviève giggled, but she fell silent. Both were single mothers, so having another baby was no joking matter.

Geneviève nervously tapped another cigarette out of her pack, offering one to Marcelle. "The Communist Party. That was when the Party was banned in France. Remember?"

Taking the cigarette, Marcelle rolled it back and forth between her fingers, waiting for a light. "Yes, that was when us factory workers lost many of our rights, but with war looming, we had no choice . . . Plus, who else provides child care?" The match flared as she leaned forward with her cigarette.

"And, just when we learned to make cars, they converted the plant to making weapons!" Gené paused and inhaled. "I hate to think of us having to use those weapons, but maybe this moment was what we were working toward. Do you think we're ready?" Geneviève blew out a puff of smoke.

"Us? Or do you mean France?"

"France, silly." She whispered now. "With all of the reports we've heard on the radio about the treatment of Jews and . . . I don't know. Do you think we're ready to stand up to the Germans?" Geneviève suddenly took short, staccato puffs.

Marcelle turned and looked at her roommate and, for the first time, wondered if Gené was Jewish. It hadn't dawned on her before, but if that was true, it would be a real concern for her. Everyone knew Jews were being scapegoated.

"Sure, no problem. Since World War I, we've always had the upper hand. We have nothing to worry about." In the dim light, Marcelle peered at the cracked gas mask lying in her lap. She wondered if it worked and what its use was in the first place. She had failed to listen to instructions at the factory, and she guessed she had failed to realize her own roommate's fears of being Jewish.

"I hope so," she heard Geneviève reply. "At least we have the Maginot Line. Surely, our forces are prepared now." Her head jerked upward. "What's that sound?"

A disembodied voice from the dark replied, "That's anti-aircraft fire. We're fighting back all right."

"I can't stand closed-up places," Geneviève whimpered, squirming around and hoping to see where the voice had come from.

"Blitzkrieg," rasped a grizzled elderly man seated near the girls. He leaned close, his breath rancid with wine. "The air tactics you're hearing are called *blitzkrieg*. They're going to come at us by air. Not by land. Don't you girls listen to the radio?" he hissed. He slid closer to them. "Got an extra cigarette?"

Reluctantly, Geneviève offered him her pack, eyeing the man as he scooped out a couple, stuffed one in his pocket, and lit up another.

"I hate to admit this," he slurred, "but until I heard the radio reports, I thought maybe we were safe. Now? It may be too late."

Both women reeled from his words, along with the reek of his bad breath.

"That can't be true," said Geneviève with a resolute air. As soon as the words left her lips, her body began to shake.

⁕

Sophie got up, went to the bathroom, and then poured herself more coffee. She offered more to Kate, but Kate declined. Kate's head was heavy from fatigue. She stood and walked over to the window. It was almost dawn, and a rosy light formed a backdrop to the dark silhouette of trees. She turned back to Sophie, who was sitting pensively on the couch. "Did you know any of this before?" Kate asked.

"Not really." Sophie shook her head, her dark brown curls bobbing with her movements. "At least, not this kind of detail. She always joked about her life and said such things as, 'Well, we could still get a good Margaux.' But I doubt she could afford wine like that at any time." Sophie pressed both hands against her head. "I didn't even know she had written these journals." She reached for another one, unable to break the connection with her mother.

"Well, then, let's read on," Kate said, returning to the sofa.

June, 1940

Stepping outside the front door of her *pensione*, Marcelle breathed in deeply. Two weeks had passed since the first air raid. There had been several more, but she had suffered nothing more than a lack of sleep. *Out of sight, out of mind.* The air was thick with the smell of lilacs and the exquisite promise of summer. The soft blue sky could be seen through gauze-like clouds. Laughter spilled out of an upper-story window, along with the music from

· 88 ·

a tinny radio belting out a new Piaf tune. Birds sang along as if there were no tomorrow. It was Sunday, and a fine day to be off work. Marcelle laughed at herself, as she felt like a young kid again. *Not hardly,* she giggled, *I'm already twenty-one.*

At a fast clip, she walked toward the *Métro.* She was looking forward to spending the day with her son. He was getting so big now, with dark, wavy ringlets caressing his head and the biggest brown eyes she had ever seen. *He will love this day.* Such a gentle soul, he enjoyed sitting on the bank of the Seine. She could hear the church bells ringing throughout Paris as she disappeared into the dark tunnel of the subway.

An hour later, as Marcelle walked along the streets with Thierry, she thought back over the past few weeks. She still found it hard to believe that war had been declared, even though she saw refugees flow in from the North. Somehow, she had managed to block out thoughts of war; even Genéviève hadn't seemed distressed. The air raid now seemed like a bad dream. And, perhaps, she had misread her roommate's religion. She was a secretive one, and Marcelle never pressed.

Thierry pointed with his small finger up in the air. They both were surprised to see anti-aircraft guns perched on top of the Arc de Triomphe. Nearby, some of their favorite statues had been surrounded with sandbags. Other than that, only an occasional man in uniform reminded them of the possibilities of war. Was there war or wasn't there? It was too impossible to fathom.

As they walked along the Avenue des Champs-Élysées, the sidewalk cafés were overflowing with fellow Parisians drinking café au lait and gossiping. Voices were raised with exuberance at anecdotes and stories found in *Le Figaro,* the daily newspaper. Unrestrained laughter echoed through the streets. No one seemed to take anything seriously. How could they? Look around! Today, their beloved Paris was shimmering in the sunlight, and the normally murky Seine flowed like a scarf of blue silk. Why not rejoice?

Marcelle purchased *Le Figaro* while Thierry handed several sticky francs to the tobacconist for a small paper cone filled with candy. As he carefully unwrapped the sweets, she opened the paper and read, "War is competing with eternal Paris. But springtime in our fair city, with war looming on the horizon, is like a lovely woman being forced to accept the attentions of a man she despises." Oh, didn't she know what that was like! Her eyes scanned for notices of ration cards available at city hall. Only bread tickets at first. Yes, she knew that. She looked for the date when full rationing would follow. She read the recipes on how best to use leftovers. She chuckled. Leftovers? What was that? The article described stuffing an artichoke. If only she had an artichoke. She laughed out loud now and grabbed up Thierry's hand. He smiled up at her, not knowing the joke, as they walked into a *marché* to purchase a few items for their picnic.

Running along the Seine's edge, Thierry skipped stones and poked his bare toes into the cool water. In spite of his quiet manner, he rarely showed fear around water and ventured onto a small rock a few feet from shore. Marcelle drank him in with her eyes. She couldn't get enough of him and begrudged the fact they were forced to live apart. Again she thought of the promise she had made to herself—and to Sainte Anne-d'Auray—to never be apart from her son. How she hated to admit that her dream of becoming someone other than her mother was not to be.

Marcelle looked around. The noise level along the river seemed pastoral. She hadn't paid much attention until now, but the lack of noise for this city was, indeed, odd. Then she remembered that many of the city buses and trucks had been requisitioned to the Front. That would account for it. She sat down on the grass again and watched her son at play.

Placing a blanket on the grass, they shared a baguette, a small wedge of Gruyère, and a peach. It was in the quiet of their picnic she regaled Thierry with the same tales her grandfather had spun for her: The story of Dahut and the mythological City of Ys. The sunlight burnished their cheeks as they lay nestled together with the myths of Breton gods rising with the soft, undulating breeze. *Moments like these,* she thought, *should last forever.*

That evening, long after Thierry was returned to the nurses' home and Marcelle was back at her *pensione,* the Germans attacked both French and British boats along the *quais* of Dunkirk. Although Marcelle was unaware, this was the beginning of the end of France as she had known it.

Later that week, as Marcelle and Gené walked to the *Métro,* they both chattered wildly, neither one paying attention to the other. Marcelle talked of food. She was always hungry, and since they were to be paid that day, her thoughts were of picking up vegetables for the evening's dinner. "Meat is out of the question, but my mouth is watering for a potage of springtime vegetables —all simmered together into a nice *mélange* of herbs," she chattered.

Gené, who had been on a date the night before, had only thoughts and words about this new man in her life. But when they least expected it, feelings of anxiety fell on them like pollen from the blossoming trees. They had read the news about the bombings in Dunkirk, and as they dressed that morning, they listened to a French-language correspondent on a German radio station announce to Parisians, "You were right to take advantage of your last peaceful Sunday." They had looked at each other and laughed. "Propaganda," tossed Marcelle. "That's all this is about. More propaganda."

But just as they turned onto St. Germaine Boulevard, a cacophony erupted, and they were jolted by the sights and sounds. It was as if a moving farmyard was sweeping past them. The flotsam and jetsam of dazed and disheveled refugee peasants passed them by. Seeming not to see anything before them, people moved along not knowing where they were heading, just walking, walking. Beaten-down women with exhaustion etched into their eyes carried infants swaddled in mud and blood-spattered blankets. Terrified-looking children with tear-streaked faces held hands or led puppies on a string. Older children pushed baby carriages loaded down with bedding, pots, and pans. Teens pulled small wagons with wailing toddlers clamoring to get out or get in. Horses, oxen, and cattle were harnessed to farm wagons, carriages, cars, and drays. The elderly, with eyes glazed and faces hardened, perched on top of these conveyances clutching babies, valises, chickens in parrot cages, or each other.

Horses whinnied, children cried, horns honked, dogs barked, but the ever-grinding wheels of this odd parade creaked by.

"Where are the men?" Marcelle asked an old woman who appeared to be observing the parade.

"You don't know?" Her voice cracked with emotion as tears flowed down her wizened cheeks. "There are no men. There are no soldiers. They were either captured or killed. And that mighty line of defense for France?"

"The Maginot Line?" asked Marcelle.

"It didn't hold!"

"What do you mean it didn't hold?" Gené gasped.

"The enemy came by plane. Mademoiselles, the only French soldiers you are apt to see are running ahead of the Germans because the Germans are at our back door," she spit out. Marcelle gaped at the woman.

"Were you there? Is that what you've seen? The Germans are entering France?"

The old woman nodded sadly and said, "What we've seen will haunt us for a lifetime, mademoiselles. Our homes were destroyed; our husbands and sons killed. We've stepped past the dead bodies of innocent children strafed by German airplanes . . . Oh, I've lived too long. Too long. I can't go on." She slumped down on the sidewalk and began to cry piteously.

Gené pulled Marcelle aside. "I know we should do something, but what can we do? And our jobs. We are late for work."

Marcelle leaned down to comfort the old woman, but the woman pushed her away. "Your friend is correct. You need to save yourselves," she said.

At lunchtime that day, Marcelle and her friends filed out of the factory and across the street to lunch along the Seine. Midday was a mixture of sunlight, intense blue skies, and dense clouds, but Marcelle couldn't shake the images from that morning. She looked around for vestiges of the refugees but saw nothing. The air, which was warm with summer and held the possibility of rain, seemed the only threat. Marcelle watched as preschool children frolicked noisily along the river with their caretakers, as housewives hung wash outside their *pensione* windows. An old man tugged at an errant weed from his begonia patch.

Just then, the sound of thunder split the air around them. Sirens began to blare—air raid sirens. Unbeknownst to Marcelle, high above those billowing clouds were more than two hundred German bombers heading for Paris, with both the Renault and Citroën factories as their primary targets. For months now, Marcelle knew their production lines had been manufacturing war products, but now the Germans were coming to take them out.

Marcelle looked into the sky. Having seen the remnants of war that morning, she panicked. She jumped up, gathered her lunch box, and headed for the *Métro*. Most of her friends, lackadaisical at best, joked that they would probably never see an enemy plane. Instead, they casually ambled after her into the *Métro* tunnels. They had no way of knowing that more than a thousand bombs were to be dropped during that attack. When they all emerged into the light of day, they were stunned to see numerous Citröen buildings, their workplace, seriously damaged and ablaze, with glass and debris littering the connecting streets. A wail went up, and Marcelle turned toward the cries on rue Poussin. The concrete shelter, which had been crowded with women and the preschool children she had seen playing along the Seine, was crushed. No one survived.

Marcelle froze. She feared for her son; she had no way of contacting him. She was afraid to step forward. She and her coworkers watched for a few minutes before they darted across the street. Returning to their own buildings, some found their work place hardly damaged and were told to go back to work, as if nothing had taken place. Within less than twenty-four hours, production of shells for the 75-millimeter cannons was up and running.

"I was so frightened hearing the bombs exploding," Marcelle said to Geneviève, "but I can't imagine what it must have been like for our children." Once Marcelle was able to call about Thierry, she, thankfully, was told there had been no bombing in his area. Geneviève nodded. She had also been told that her daughter, older than Thierry, was to be moved with all the older school children away from Paris.

"Even though I don't want Ann-Marie to leave Paris, I want her to be safe—and far away from here."

That evening, as the two women made their way home after work, Marcelle thought about the prospect of having Thierry sent out of town. Of course, she wanted him safe, but . . . While stepping over shards of glass that had been strewn around for blocks, Marcelle leaned down and peeled brown paper away from one piece of glass.

"What is that?" Geneviève asked, peering into Marcelle's hand.

"Not sure. Isn't this the same paper we put on our windows to protect us against blasts?" asked Marcelle.

"Looks like we wasted our time with *that* project! Look at

those apartment houses. Only half of them are left standing!" Gené waved her arm wildly.

One of the buildings had several walls stripped away while the rest were intact, as if it were a doll house, open on one side for the entire world to see. Beds remained made and in place. Chairs continued to act as clothes horses. Bathrooms appeared to have been popped in like an afterthought, but now with toilets dangling out over the street.

"You know what seems curious—almost eerie?" Marcelle asked Geneviève. Her friend stared at her. How could she guess?

"There's no panic," Marcelle said. "Only outrage. People are simply upset that this has caused such a mess!"

"That's the French for you! Almost like these things couldn't possibly be happening. Hmm! Let's stop at the *marché* before going home. *J'ai faim!* When we get home you can prepare your *grand-mère's* potage. But no topinambour!"

"That seems so long ago, doesn't it?"

Before work the following day, Marcelle purchased *Le Figaro* from the local *tobacconist*, only to have it confirmed that her work at the Citröen factory had been the prime target for the bombers the day before. She shivered. *Would they be back?* She noticed people listening to a radio, so she sidled up close beside them.

"What can one believe?" a young woman asked of no one in particular. They all knew the Germans had been broadcasting propaganda for weeks now. "So, tell me, how are we to know what information is accurate?" she asked again. Within moments, she received a myriad of responses. *Yes, typical French,* thought Marcelle. *You ask ten people in a room the same question and you receive at least fifteen answers plus hours of discussion in the interim.* She laughed to herself, but hurried away from the radio toward the Metro. Paris had been taken off guard, and she prayed that they could right themselves, and quickly. Anxiety riddled her every move, but she headed to work all the same.

The sun was streaming through the lace curtains, finally filling Marcelle's living room with the promise of warmth that had been missing all night long. Kate shivered and stood to stretch her legs. Sophie stood, shivered, and wrapped her arms around her. She stopped to whack the furnace thermostat.

"I need to have Thierry check this furnace. Maybe he has some good ideas. Do you want any more coffee? Or do you want to get some sleep?"

"I doubt I could sleep," Kate said, hopping up and down to keep warm. "You know, I had wondered how your mom managed once she gave birth to Thierry—she was pretty young."

Kate slumped back into the covers. She had had it easy when she gave birth as a single mother to Lisa. No, she didn't have family around either, but she was older by a few years. And she could call on family if necessary. At that time, the Vietnam War was raging in the wings, but she was far away from any action. Feelings of guilt washed over her.

"What are you thinking about?" asked Sophie as she came back into the room. She handed Kate a cup of rewarmed coffee and a hardened croissant and nestled in near her.

Kate pushed down her thoughts of Lisa once again. "I was thinking of what your mother told us about her time in Paris. She made it sound like a simple inconvenience. No big deal! So, what do you think it *was* like?" Kate asked. "I mean, living in Paris once the Germans arrived? Did your mother mention that?"

Sophie sheepishly grinned and retrieved another journal. She plunked down next to Kate, then sat with her hands resting in her lap. She didn't know what to think. It felt like she was reading about someone she had never met. She opened her mother's journal and again traced her finger over her writing. This seemed to be a habit she had just picked up. Perhaps, she hoped, through touch, she could transcend into her mother's past. She had never wanted to understand her mother more than now. Taking a sip of coffee, she mulled over the words, swallowed, and began to read.

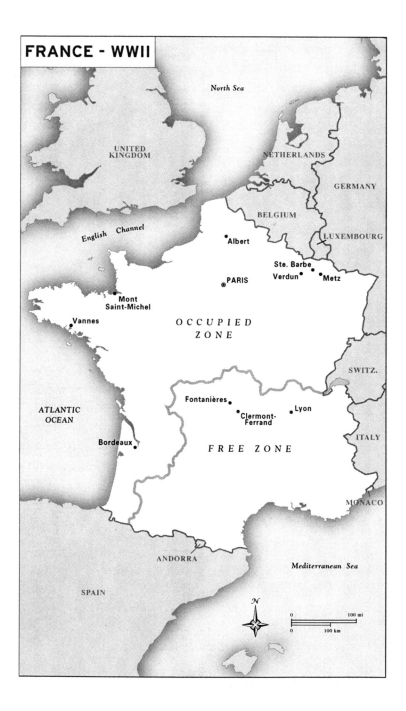

FRANCE - WWII

North Sea

UNITED
KINGDOM

NETHERLANDS

GERMANY

BELGIUM

English Channel

LUXEMBOURG

•Albert

Ste. Barbe•
Verdun• •Metz

⊚PARIS

•Mont
Saint-Michel

OCCUPIED
ZONE

•Vannes

SWITZ.

ATLANTIC
OCEAN

Fontanières•

•Lyon

•Clermont-
Ferrand

Bordeaux•

FREE ZONE

ITALY

MONACO

ANDORRA

Mediterranean Sea

SPAIN

𝒩

0   100 mi
0   100 km

CHAPTER SIX

$\mathcal{T}$he $\mathcal{E}$xodus of $\mathcal{P}$aris

(*L'Exode de Paris*)

T WAS ALREADY 11:30 AM. Marcelle and Gené had packed their bags, only one per person, and had been waiting for the train to take them to Bordeaux. They had been waiting since five thirty that morning. In fact, their entire Citroën crew had congregated outside the Gare d'Austerlitz station. Citroën was rebuilding its factory in Bordeaux. Standing on one leg, then the other, sitting on their belongings, shifting back and forth, all were waiting. Unfor-tunately, they were not alone. Thousands surrounded them, all waiting for the same train.

When Marcelle awakened that day, it had been another beautiful June morning. The cool air that swept into the small open window held the scent of jasmine, and the promise of early summer was within arm's reach. She crawled out of bed and inhaled the sweet fragrance. It was impossible to imagine Paris had entered into this nightmare. *How could it possibly be? Paris has never looked lovelier!*

By midday, the heat had become unbearable, and there was

nowhere to go. As the sun beat down, the hopeful passengers began shedding their jackets, their hats, their sweaters, and the many layers they wore, as they could not pack them all.

Gené, not able to stand still, insisted on checking for the train, again. Marcelle folded her jacket in quarters, placed it atop her valise, and sat down. Her job was to hold their place in line. Time and time again, Gené returned with no new information, "*Le train qui a été retardé!*" Well, Marcelle knew the train was delayed! Every fifteen minutes, the stationmaster had been screeching, "We apologize for the delay!" But after several hours, she noticed no new announcements were made.

Through the din, families clustered together. Haggard mothers chastised their errant toddlers while desperately clutching crying babies along with belongings to their chests. Marcelle thought of Thierry but prayed that she could arrange a better life for him in Bordeaux. Right now, he wouldn't have to face this madness. He was much too sensitive to endure such noise.

A young woman's piercing voice jolted her to her senses. She looked up. The woman was begging for help. As a teacher from a nearby girls' school, she had arrived with one hundred orphaned young girls, and she was desperate to get them on board the first train leaving Paris.

"They must be saved," she kept crying out. "They have to go first! They have no one left!"

"Are they Jewish?" Marcelle heard someone ask.

"Does it matter?" the teacher asked. She shrugged her shoulders and shook her head. After much deliberation, the stationmaster, frantically, escorted the young girls inside the station as hundreds more pressed forward to join them. The teacher sat, despondently, weeping on someone's forgotten luggage.

"I will never see them again," she cried. "I don't even know where they are going."

Placing her hand on the sobbing woman's shoulder, Marcelle asked, "What about you? Are you not going with them?"

"They won't take me on board; I have no pass. I have no idea what I'll do now. There must be children left in the City to teach—somewhere."

Before Marcelle could respond, the teacher stood up. Tears streamed down her face as she disappeared into the crowd.

The day turned into evening, and the only train finally came, loaded up and left the station. Hundreds, thousands who had been patiently waiting had been left forlornly behind. Marcelle and Gené picked up their bags and returned to their *pensione*. They now had no other choice. The next day, they would begin to walk to Bordeaux.

On June 11, Marcelle and Gené were no longer witnesses to the parade of the masses; they were now participants. They entered *l'Exode de Paris* (the Exodus of Paris). As they walked, stores and restaurants closed their doors, put away sidewalk tables, and rang down shutters. It was hard to imagine everyone locking up and leaving everything they owned behind. But then, everything was hard to imagine.

Their walk was made more difficult as commandeered cars, trucks, and taxis forced them off the road and into the ditches. There was hardly any room to move. And the noise! Horns blared, babies cried, dogs barked, and mothers shouted. Bicycles, motorcycles, wagons, and carts, all were heaped with people and their belongings as they inched along together down the roadway. Like the week before, when Marcelle and Gené stood on the corner watching the Dunkirk refugees, now they, too, were fleeing. At least, they told themselves, they had jobs waiting in Bordeaux.

"I can't believe we are a part of this . . . this river of humanity," Marcelle said, wiping her brow.

After days of walking, standing in food lines, and begging for water, they moved toward the city of Tours. Out of nowhere, planes were heard overhead. They were swooping down and strafing them as they scrambled off the road. Everyone ran screaming in opposite directions, while Marcelle and Gené found themselves pressed up against a stucco wall.

"Surely our world is coming to an end," sobbed Gené.

"Would you look at that?" someone shouted. Their heads snapped in that direction.

"Would you look at that?" he yelled again. "*Mon Dieu*!! Those aren't German planes! They're Italian!"

Like wounded animals, the sound of wailing erupted around them. Life's overwhelm was taking its toll. They had to get out of there and to Bordeaux, fast.

⸺ ⟨⟩ ⸻

Sophie sighed. "The day after my mother left Paris, the city was declared 'open,' and the Germans marched in, unopposed. *Maman* once told me that the Parisians who were left behind felt demoralized, angry, and betrayed. 'They have sold us out like rabbits!' she used to say, for there was no one left to protect them —or to protect my brother, Thierry."

"She was truly a brave woman, wasn't she, Sophie? I'm not certain I could have managed as well."

"That she was. Some of this I've known before, but it hurts my heart to never have realized all that she endured." She wrestled a Kleenex free and blew her nose long and hard.

After a few moments, she asked Kate, "Now, where was I?" She stuffed her Kleenex inside her robe and snuffled slightly.

"I can't imagine walking to Bordeaux. How far is that?" Kate unconsciously rubbed her lower back at the thought of Marcelle's journey.

"Hundreds and hundreds of kilometers," Sophie replied. "Somehow, I got the impression they boarded a train in Tours and continued on to Bordeaux. Anyway, I believe it was within a matter of days of the Germans taking hold of Paris, and even though the French harbored great resentment, Parisians found they still had to work for them in order to make a living. So I believe many, like my mother, returned to Paris, as there was no hope of working in Bordeaux. And, of course, my mother came back for Thierry. She called those times back in Paris *le temps des autruches,* or the time of the ostriches. They couldn't stomach working for the Germans, but they had to work nonetheless."

Paris, August 1941

One warm, sensuous evening in late August, Marcelle exited the *Métro* after work and headed to the *marché.* The humidity wrapped about her like a soft blanket, and as she looked up, she was surprised to catch sight of the first star. A year had passed since the exodus, and she had always looked to the stars in hopes of making a wish to shorten the war. Her life had become an endless drone of events: work, standing in interminable lines, and more work. On rare occasions, she would see a movie, but her real joy was her weekly foray to visit her son.

It had been a particularly strenuous workday, and usually she had no energy for anything or anyone. But for some reason, she started up a conversation with a young man in the line leading to the *marché.* As they both eased through the queue toward the food bins, they found that what they had come for was long gone. Just as they both reached for the last onion, their hands met. Electricity shot through Marcelle's body as they stood with their hands wrapped around each other's. Marcelle threw her head back, and her low, resonant laughter filled the now-empty aisles of the store. The young man released his grip as they both headed to check out. There was no more food left in the store. He handed the clerk his last ticket as the lowly onion was wrapped and handed to Marcelle. *L'amour des oignons!* Yes, it was a love of onions—or simply the need for food—that brought the two together.

"My name is André," he said softly, as the doors slammed closed behind them.

"*Excusez-moi?*" she said, standing on her tiptoes. "What did you say?"

"I said my name is André—André Mathieux," he said, as he laughed. The deep blue of his eyes disappeared into the crinkled edges of his smile. His wavy blonde hair flopped down over one eye as he leaned down to speak to her. His smile was lit from within. He was tall, about six foot one, with a slender build. His face, his handsome face, was definitely not the rounded fleshy face of a Breton. No, his features were finely chiseled and angular. His lips were full, and as Marcelle gazed up at him, she resisted the impulse to touch their softness.

"So, now that I've purchased your dinner, mademoiselle," he said with a mischievous smile, "would you do me the honor of telling me your name?"

"*Pardonnez-moi*, monsieur?" she stammered.

"André, *s'il vous plaît*," he said again.

"Forgive me, my name is Marcelle Pourette," she said.

"So, Marcelle Pourette, can you prepare a *soupe à l'oignon pour deux?*" he asked.

"*Mais oui!*" she exclaimed. An uncharacteristic burst of confidence flowed through her. "Monsieur, this onion could be the meal for many—not just two!"

"Ah," he said, leaning down low to peer into her eyes, "but, I would love for it to be for just us two. Your place, or mine?" he asked her boldly.

She stammered something about her waiting roommate, and then he said, "Mine, then. It's not far, and I believe I have a chunk of hardened bread and even some cheese to grate over the top. It will be a feast! Will you come?"

"My roommate . . . she may be expecting me . . ." her voice began to waver.

"You can call her from the call box outside my *pensione*. I enjoyed our earlier conversation, and I would love to have your company for a few hours tonight. That is possible, *n'est-ce pas?*"

Marcelle didn't know what had come over her. She barely remembered their earlier conversation, as she was still caught up in the electricity she had felt when their hands encircled the onion. At that moment, the war, for once, was far away. Only these two existed.

She turned to walk alongside André. She felt as if she were floating next to him, although she could have been on tiptoe. He towered well over her petite frame. For a few minutes, she imagined herself to be as beautiful as her mother had been. As she crushed the wrapped onion close to her heart, all she could think of was this man's face—his sweet, handsome face. This man, who only thirty minutes before had been a total stranger.

"So, where are you from, Marcelle Pourette?" he asked.

"From Brittany, the land that extends into the sea," she quipped.

"So, dear woman from the land that extends into the sea," he asked as he walked backward with a twinkle in his blue eyes, "what makes women from Brittany so beautiful?"

"Oh, la, la, that's easy, monsieur . . . André . . . there is an old Breton proverb that can explain that. *Dounoc'h eo kaloun ar merc'hed 'vit ar mor douna euz ar bed,* she repeated to him in Breton. She laughed at the perplexed expression on his face.

"It means that the heart of a woman is deeper than the deepest sea. It means that if you capture her heart, she will be yours forever. And, what is more beautiful than that?"

"*C'est vrai, ma petite* Marcelle. So, in that case, do you believe in love at first sight?" he said as he caught up her hand and they strode down the avenue together.

They fell in love, and the darkness that had permeated their lives lifted. No matter that the war continued unabated; no matter that she was the mother of one young son or that he was separated from his wife due to her mental illness. The frenetic passion they shared became one of the few reasons they got up each morning and the only reason they tumbled into bed together each night . . . each day . . . each night. Under the best of circumstances, a love affair can have no rhyme or reason. But during a time of war, a love affair can sometimes be the *only* rhyme—the *only* reason to continue on. Realizing their good fortune, they held tightly to each other and rejoiced.

Marcelle continued to work every day, as did André, who taught at a local boys' high school academy. He was fortunate to have work, as many mid-level children, like Gené's daughter, had been sent away from the City during the initial bombings. Marcelle could see that André's love of books and his interest in learning were two ingredients that had been missing in her own life. With his passion at hand, she, too, warmed herself at the flame.

And his love of children? Did that include Thierry? Yes, indeed, and that was the magical measure. Thierry, at first, was resistant to sharing his mother, but, by the time he felt sheltered in their light, Marcelle was once again pregnant. Nine months later, she delivered another beautiful baby boy. She named him Gérard— Gérard Pourrette—with the promise of giving him his father's last name in due time. The family that Marcelle had always dreamed of having was finally becoming a reality. She had never been happier in all her life. The year was 1942. She would be turning twenty-four this year.

Unfortunately, life for all Parisians became more and more difficult. Rumors were said that the Vichy, not the Germans, were rounding up Jewish families and sending them away. But where? Plus air raids became more prevalent as the allies began bombing the city. Time after time, Marcelle and Gené ran for the *Métro* to hide, and many times they were forced to witness the resulting devastation. Marcelle could only pray that her two sons were safe and well cared for while she was away. She knew that Thierry had nightmares about the images he had seen before, but now? He was getting to be so old. And it broke her heart that she was often away from her sons when those fearful attacks took place.

Soon, a new evacuation order was called for: more children were to be sent to the countryside for their safety. This meant Thierry was to be sent by train south of the *ligne de démarcation*, to the free zone. Marcelle breathed a sigh of relief, as Thierry would, at least, be safe and also would be able to sleep at night. Still, she was terrified of sending him away, as it had been over two years since Gené had received any word from her daughter.

Marcelle and Thierry stood on the same platform of the Gare d'Austerlitz, where Marcelle had attempted to leave during *l'exode*. Was there no end to this war? Memories of children being passed overhead and away from their parents flooded through her mind. She remembered the teacher who wept piteously when forced to leave her class of orphans at the station. She blinked back her own tears.

She looked down on her seven-year-old son. Thierry stood limply beside her, all his belongings packed into one small valise. She had attempted to learn of Thierry's possible destination, but no one had information. Hundreds of other mothers, like her, crowded the train platform holding the hands of their children. Putting on their bravest faces, they all attempted to remain cheerful, only to break down once the trains had left. For as long as Marcelle lived, she would never forget how Thierry had sobbed into her skirt, willing her not to send him away. Again and again, she promised him she would come to him as soon as possible.

⌒◌⌒

By 1943, the bombing had become an every-night occurrence. Marcelle could not sleep or eat, for fear consumed her. She could barely work. The war, which had seemed to disappear once she met André, was now baying at their door. Once she learned of Thierry's whereabouts, she requested from the authorities an evacuation pass, an *ausweis* or *laissez-passer*, to enable her to travel to the free zone with Gérard. She could not continue without Thierry, and she needed her beloved baby to be safe.

Marcelle and André made plans to leave Paris together. It took months for the *laissez-passer* to arrive, and when they did, the passes were for only Marcelle and the baby. She continued her vigil, yet nothing appeared for André.

She begged him to check with the authorities, but there was something, a hesitation in his response or maybe an unexpressed reluctance to leave that she couldn't put her finger on. His wife was still in a mental ward, so no divorce had been sought. It still would be difficult to get a divorce through the Church. Funny, she had never asked him if he was Catholic. Could he be Jewish? Fearing both question and answer, she prayed to Ste. Anne to give her direction.

About this time, Gené disappeared. Some told Marcelle she had been taken away by the Nazis, but other coworkers said she simply walked out the back door of the factory. Marcelle never knew what happened. Here was her best friend, her roommate, and the one who had been with her through the birth of her two sons, and Marcelle had no idea who she was or what she was running from. Marcelle pushed harder to leave Paris.

When her evacuation date arrived, André encouraged her to go ahead. He said he would follow her as soon as possible. She was beside herself with worry. As far as she knew, his pass may never have been requested. She feared the worst—that his activities with the Résistance had been discovered or that he was, indeed, Jewish, and in order to protect her and their son, he had said nothing. That was the insidious side of war: secrets withheld from the closest of people.

On that last bleak morning as the train slowly pulled out of Gare d'Austerlitz, the place of tears, she remembered seeing André's face skirt past the window. She wondered if this would be the last time she would ever see him . . .

Sophie sat up and dabbed her eyes with the corner of the comforter. She reached to the floor and picked up her empty coffee cup and sat contemplating the sediment at the bottom.

"*Maman,*" she said out loud, "however did you find the strength to leave the only man you truly loved and who truly loved you? I had no idea what you gave up for us kids."

Kate stayed silent. No platitudes would help. Sophie closed the journal. She was exhausted and needed to sleep.

Finally, Kate spoke. "I swear, Sophie, the more I learn about your mother, the more I'm convinced that she is owed a measure of . . . of . . ."

"Of redemption?" Sophie asked, as she moved toward the kitchen to put their cups in the sink. "I feel the same way, and believe me, I am determined to find her some."

$\mathscr{D}$ining with $\mathscr{M}$ad $\mathscr{C}$ow
(*Diner avec la Vache Enragée*)

$\overset{\text{\tiny\^{}}}{A}$

*T*HE FOLLOWING DAY, Sophie and Kate loaded their luggage in the car and headed north to the Lorraine. It was a lengthy drive, but Sophie was more than motivated. After devouring her mother's journals, she was compelled to capture the history where she and her family had grown up: Ste. Barbe. A place she had been avoiding since she left nearly thirty years before. Sophie drove straight to her brother, Julien's.

Julien and his wife lived in a small village near Metz, in the heart of the Lorraine. Sophie and Kate arrived just as the sun was setting. "I hope we haven't missed cocktail hour," she laughed as she and Kate climbed out of her car. After the long drive, she could do with a drink.

Julien opened the door before Sophie knocked. He swooped her into his arms and gave her a welcome as if they hadn't seen each other in years. Once Sophie got her breath, she said, "Julien, this is my good friend Kate. She has come to help me with my discoveries." Julien leaned forward and kissed Kate on both cheeks, then stepped back.

At that moment, Michela, Julien's wife, peeked around the corner. Michela was a petite woman, shy even, but she sported a thatch of candy apple red hair. She had the body of a dancer, lithe and spare of weight, so her shyness didn't match up with her brightly colored hair.

Sophie squeezed Michela to her. "New play coming up?" Sophie asked her sister-in-law, as she reached up and fluffed Michela's hair.

Michela turned a quizzical expression and then a smile spread across her face. "Yes, how did you know?"

As the talk turned to the new play Michela was performing in, the three women made their way to the kitchen while Julien was relegated to dragging in luggage from the car.

Once Julien appeared in the kitchen a few minutes later, Michela had already opened and poured the champagne and was moving them into the comfort of the living room. The four formally toasted Kate and Sophie's safe arrival as Sophie kicked off her shoes and nestled down on the sofa next to her brother. Michela floated into her favorite chair opposite them as Kate joined the circle.

Brother and sister relaxed easily into each other's company, and by sitting back, Kate could see how closely they resembled one another—and their mother. When they turned their heads to laugh, threw their hands in the air, waved their arms about, or subtly winked, Kate recognized Marcelle. She missed Marcelle more than she expected.

As for the two siblings, they reconnected like a well-practiced comedy team. Even though they were in weekly contact by phone or Internet, each time they came together, they reveled in each other's company. Michela added a bit to the conversation, smiled, and headed into the kitchen to finish dinner.

"*Coquille St. Jacques*," she finally announced. "In honor of my sister-in-law, Sophie, and her friend, Kate," she grinned."

"Ah, *ma chère*, my favorite, too!" Julien jumped up and gave her a quick peck on her cheek. He then pulled Sophie to her feet.

"She prepares the freshest sea scallops," Sophie exclaimed to Kate. "They're incredible!" She smacked her lips together as they followed the tantalizing aroma to the dining room. Julien slowed to open another bottle of white wine, and they all sat down at the table.

"So, what is your secret with your sea scallops, Michela?" Kate asked as she dipped her finger into the delicate sauce surrounding the scallops.

"Plenty of butter and freshly grated orange peel," was her reply. "It's probably the most French of all my cooking, as I usually follow my Italian heritage."

"Oh, you are in for some heavenly treats here, Kate," Sophie said kindly. "Our entire family has enjoyed your family's treasure trove of recipes, Michela."

The conversation continued with light banter, regarding talk of politics and gossip from old Ste. Barbe. Plus jokes—many, many jokes. As Julien finished one joke, he started a new one. Tears streamed down the women's faces as Julien continued center stage. Clearly the role of family clown was one in which he resonated.

After the dinner plates were cleared away, Julien opened yet another bottle of wine and Michela reappeared from the kitchen with a plate of local cheeses from the nearby Vosges Mountains.

"What have we here, Michela?" Kate asked her. "This looks delicious!"

"For tonight's cheese selection, I've found a kindly cow's milk, a vacherin," Michela, said with a dramatic flair, "and, along with this fine cheese, may I present an array of thinly-sliced prosciutto and fresh fruit."

"Ah, a vacherin, huh," Julien blew out. "That reminds me of a story about our father, right, Sophie?"

"That our Papa was a cow? What are you talking about?" Sophie was already giggling when she realized which story Julien was referring to. He was mocking their papa's nightly rages, referring to them as *diner avec une vache enragée,* or dining with mad cow. She was surprised her brother had broken over the line of comedy to this more serious subject, and in front of her friend.

After Michela and Kate had retired for the evening, Sophie sat alone with Julien in the dimly lit living room. They each quietly sipped one of the remaining thimblefuls of their father's eau-de-vie, lapsing into past memories. This was the last of the bottles their father had made, as France had come to its senses and retired all the family licenses to make and bottle eau-de-vie. No longer was the privilege handed down to the sons in the family. And, it was a good thing, as the aged liqueur could almost raise their father back from the dead!

"Julien," Sophie said, "I invited Kate to France to help me sort out both *Maman's* and Papa's stories. She met *Maman* in California and was instrumental in getting *Maman* to open up about her life. I need more help with my investigation, but, well . . . I've been holding back on telling her some of the details about Ste. Barbe." She paused. "But *Maman* was so open with her . . ."

Julien shot Sophie a puzzled look. "Do you have to tell her anything?"

"I do, but I'm not certain how much to tell her about those miserable years we had growing up with Papa. In fact, I'm surprised you brought up the mad cow thing tonight."

"Remember, I am younger than you. Maybe what you remember was before my time," Julien said, clearly uncomfortable.

"No, Julien, you were definitely there. With your comment about the mad cow, I know you remember our father's nightly routine . . . Oh, Julien, the sound was unmistakable: that *swish-*

swish-swish of our father's corduroy work pants, the sound of his heavy boots hitting the back steps, the rancor in his voice as he swore at our neighbors. Why, I remember we—you, Gérard, and me—would look at each other and race for the stairs."

Julien nodded his head slowly as she continued on.

"Just the mere cadence of Papa's footfalls taught us to detect his mood. '*Soupe au lait* is home,' Gérard used to say."

"What? What did he say?" Julien almost choked on the liqueur.

"'*Soupe au lait* is home.' The milk, which can sour at a second's notice, has arrived at our door. You remember."

"Gérard was a clever one, though. I remember one time when . . ."

"I remember," Sophie interrupted, "that most nights were no different than any other. Don't change the subject. We would grab our books and race up the stairs to take cover. Even the thought of him catching us reading sent us flying. You remember that, don't you?"

Julien looked stunned, or swacked, but said nothing. He took another sip of eau-de-vie. Sophie got up, left the room, but returned fairly soon with a stack of old journals.

"Please, Julien," Sophie pleaded. "I'm not making this up." She took a deep breath and let it out slowly. "All right, maybe you don't remember, but Papa didn't believe in reading books. The newspaper was the only written word he read, and even then, he was certain it was filled with political trash. If there was anything against the Communist Party, he would hit the roof. When he came home, it was like a large boulder had been dropped into a shallow stream. Every particle of living matter in our house was flushed from its bearings and sent skittering in opposite directions. And no one went toward that back door . . ."

Julien nodded in agreement. He figured this discussion was bound to happen. Maybe now was the best time to open it up.

"After *Maman* died," Sophie continued, "I climbed up to the attic, where some of these journals were kept. I showed you the letters I found about Papa, remember?"

Julien nodded his head. He hated heading into the past, especially when it involved his father.

"These journals were given to a friend of *Maman's*, a Madame Marie Chirade, for safe keeping," she said. "Anyway, Marie was able to give me these. Our mother wrote them during World War II."

"Why safe keeping? What was the mystery?"

"Maybe *Maman* thought Papa would destroy them, or ridicule her for what she had written."

"Or, destroy her *because* of what she had written . . ." Julien said, his face darkening.

"Ah, you do remember." Sophie pulled back, arching an eyebrow. "Actually, she left these journals for us, for after she passed away. I've read most of them, and I found some she wrote during our time in Ste. Barbe. She actually took time to write down her feelings during those horrible nights with Papa!"

"Probably once he stormed out!"

"Julien, when I first read these pages, our past came back like it was yesterday. Listen to this." Before he had a chance to protest, Sophie had opened one of the journals and had begun to read aloud.

Autumn, 1954

I watch my children's ascent as they scramble to their rooms. With great sadness and trepidation, I turn in the kitchen to check on the pan of water heating on the stove. It has to be heated to the correct temperature. My man expects that much.

His wizened and angular face, with those deep-set blue eyes, always enters the room before he does. Coated in sweat and the inevitable greenish-yellow dust from the iron mines, his face glowers. He heaves a final epithet at the neighbor as he enters the kitchen and slams the back door behind him. The house reverberates on impact. My children know to take cover.

As he strides across our kitchen, I find myself reaching out to touch him. Maybe this will be the day he won't slap me away. I so long for a simple, gentle touch. What would I do without the tenderness of my children?

Sophie looked up at her brother, tears brimming. She swiped them away, and continued reading.

Snatching up the cloth and towel I had carefully lain out, he begins his wash up, his evening ritual.

My intention is to stand out of his line of fire, yet I don't dare leave the room. His ire only follows me, hounds and berates me. No matter what imagined transgression flits through his mind, the anger he holds seethes from his every pore. It awakens with him every morning and lies down with him every night; there is no room for the likes of me. That quiet, seemingly shy man I fell in love with during the war never accompanied me back to Ste. Barbe. Often, I wonder if I knew him at all.

Stripping away his heavy blue jacket, then his work shirt, he drops them in a pile at his feet. He stands in his *marcel*—those once-white, now-dingy yellow undershirts he wears every day, the ones stained with iron ore and daily sweat that never get clean enough for him. He takes up the pan of warmed water and begins to wash what grit and grime he can from his face and hands, and then the cloth moves up and down his sinewy, gaunt frame.

I'm not a bad cook, but as I stare at his thin back, I feel guilty because he is never interested in my food. My children snicker about how thin their father is, saying, "The skin from his belly can touch the skin of his back." They giggle. Whenever I encourage him to eat, I face his harangue—"I'm not hungry because I'm too disgusted with you"—and then he does not speak to me for weeks at a time. Weeks, mind you! How can that be? The thought makes me limp. It takes energy to hold anger . . . but then he's always had plenty of energy, hasn't he?

As he bends over the sink tonight, I slip near him to retrieve his soiled clothes. I notice the blue of his veins stands out from his pasty white skin; it is so much lighter than my own. His once-straight back now is rounded. The years of working the iron mines have taken their toll.

My heart saddens for him. The muscles in his back flinch as he splashes cold water over his shoulders, and then he turns to face me. I yearn to see his smile—even that V-shaped smile of his that stretches across his thin lips. Instead, he snarls; he always snarls. At least in that, I know what to expect.

"What are you staring at, woman?" he bellows. "Get my goddamn dinner on the table. And where are those damn kids, anyway? I'm hungry. Now," he stomps his foot as he roars.

No matter how quickly the children arrive in the kitchen, it is never fast enough. I call them, and then turn to the stove to remove the pot-au-feu from the oven. I can smell the slightly acrid odor of the overcooked vegetables; the pot-au-feu has been baking too long. I gulp. I can expect this will add to the evening's bone of contention—the only bone we can afford. Because he insists we sit down as a family, we are often forced to wait for hours, never knowing when or if he will arrive.

In one or two strides he moves through the kitchen, and I hear his bones collide with the wooden chair as he sits down at the table. With one flick of his finger, he turns on the radio. Even though the politics of the broadcast will invariably increase his rage, he rarely sits without the news blasting through the small room.

Sophie always arrives first. She nods at her father and eases into her place next to him. Sheepishly, the two boys, Julien and

Gérard, quietly slip into the room and into their chairs. No one wants to be singled out or noticed, for their father's normal response is to yell at them or backhand them.

I see this man has taught them, without his realizing it, that rage has no depth, that kindness can be as fleeting and as thin as a butterfly's wings, that pain can leap across the table at them like a frog's tongue, and that silence can weigh more than a thousand kilos. Never will he recognize that his behavior will force them all to flee from our house, forever. Guilt washes over me. Their only purpose to remain in our home is solely to stand between myself and the man they call Papa. (My heart aches to even write this.)

Sophie looked up at Julien once again. Tears were making a steady stream down both sides of his face. He made no effort to discourage them. He simply cried. As difficult as it was to continue, she did so.

I bend low to ease the stew from the oven. I can count on his not helping, so I quickly wipe my tears on the pot holder. I heft the stoneware tureen, which is filled with a small scrap of hard salt pork, a bit of leftover beef, and the now-burnt vegetables, out of the oven and onto the table. The sausage that is called for in the recipe was not added, as the week's check was unusually small. Or so he tells me. But he tends to notice the omission of ingredients and blames me for my inept cooking. I prepare myself. My eyes mist over, as I attempt to keep from crying. To my children, I must appear as if I am not offended, but I, too, have nowhere to hide. Guilt once again overwhelms me. The only life I have created for my children is in the ring closest to the eye of a storm. Eventually, and it is one of the few things we all can count on, the storm will come to rest on each one of us, one at a time. There is no rhyme or reason to it. It is just how he is. We constantly sit in dread.

After the main course is eaten, or likely just stirred around the plates, I hand my husband the basket of sliced baguette with our worn-out wooden cheese board. I have only a few scraps of cheese for tonight's meal. I send up a prayer that Sophie, bless her, will not make a fuss. She detests eating cheese with her bread, as it always makes her gag. Foolishly I think, *Why can't she be like other French girls?* But there's nothing like blaming the victim.

Clenching my teeth, I silently will my children to behave. Even though I know there is rarely an answered prayer, I hope this night's tirade will take no victims. I lean toward young Julien to urge him to hold his tongue and not crack jokes that will send the two others into fits of laughter. *Why is it that he always performs these antics during their father's radio show?* I especially pray that Gérard will show respect toward his father, not that he owes his father as much. That is one thing Jules has never showered on him, my son. Yes, my son. My body is exhausted from being taut with anxiety for years.

I believe in the sacred vows of marriage; I believe in the importance of family. And I will implore my children to walk within happiness instead of beside it, not as their father has always done. Ste. Anne, I implore you to help me to be an example to do the same.

Tonight, it isn't the cheese, the pot-au-feu, the possibility of jokes, or the insubordination of Gérard. It isn't the gagging reflex from Sophie as she attempts to eat her cheese and bread. But it is Sophie's turn all the same. It is her shoes! Jules notices where she has left them—only a matter of centimeters from their normal position by the back door, but then, that is all it takes to set him off.

He lunges at Sophie and lifts her off her chair by one arm. He moves her frail body through the room like lightning and forces her to her knees and with his gnarled hand on the back of her head, he plants her nose squarely on top of her shoes. And then, as if steering a car, he eases her shoes into their proper place.

"Now, can you see where they belong?" he rages above her. Sophie knows not to cry out, but tears bleed from my eyes all the same. I sit in my chair tonight, weak with the knowledge that I have taught my beautiful young daughter not only to hold her tongue but to also hold onto her fear. She is so bottled up now that her fear is destined to create its own inner rage. One day, my daughter will seek her own outlet—that I can be certain! Again, I pray to you, St. Anne d'Auray, to protect her.

⁓⁘⁓

Julien put his arms about his sister, and together they cried. Without further discussion, Sophie got up from the sofa, announced that she would be driving to Ste. Barbe in the morning, and headed off to bed.

CHAPTER EIGHT

Rinsing Sanity Back
into Her Life

A

S SOPHIE DROVE UP the highway the following morning, she had been so busy filling Julien in about their mother's journals and her visits with Kate to Madame Chirade's that she was surprised when she realized they were almost in Ste. Barbe. Had Ste. Barbe changed that much, or was she tuning out? She was grateful Julien was accompanying them, because coming home to Ste. Barbe was always difficult for her. Stinging memories of her father flooded through her. She shivered. Leaving had been easy. Hadn't her mother convinced her to marry after high school? Terrified she would have a baby out of wedlock, her mother told her to marry and break free of the dissonant trauma her father imposed. Too bad she never loved her first husband. Sophie's shoulders shuttered once again. Even today, the thoughts of her life in Ste. Barbe forced her nerves into a vibrating jangle. She was in no hurry to return. Anguish knotted her stomach; more painful memories bubbled into her throat. But she knew she must forge ahead.

The wind and rain had picked up as she was driving, and the thought of seeing their grimy little town once more was almost more than she could handle. It had never been a pretty town—not really—no iron mining towns are. What she expected to see, as if it hadn't been indelibly imprinted on her mind already, was how the dark grey silt, which had sifted over the town throughout a hundred years of mining, gave the town the same tinge of slag.

"Nothing glamorous here," Sophie said to Kate, who was sitting in the backseat. "No reason for us to hang around long." The weather reflected her mood, and she knew that the rain would make the buildings appear even more dismal, weeping dark rivulets down their outer walls. *What a sad, pathetic place this is!* Clenching her fists and her jaw at the same time, she willed herself to hold it together.

"Kate, Julien," she said with a note of cheerfulness she did not feel, "we're almost here." Julien looked at her like she was losing it but said nothing. He came here regularly, as his wife's family still lived here. Even after all these years, he still had friends who lived here. He didn't give the place much thought one way or another, but he could tell from the pitch in his sister's voice that she was struggling hard to be here.

"After World War II was over," Sophie said, "our family moved from central France back to our father's home area, where he had a job waiting for him, Kate." Sophie turned toward Julien.

"I'm just filling Kate in on some of our history and also trying to put it all into its proper perspective." She pulled up to a stop sign. "I've realized over the last few days, Julien, what I thought was real or true may not have been. So I'm doing a backtracking of the facts. Can you just go along with me on this?"

Julien looked back at Kate and shrugged, "Fine! What more do you want tracked down? History of our mother or our father?" He glanced sideways at his sister to see the color drain away from her face. She was clutching the steering wheel as if it would escape.

"Don't answer that last question. We'll do whatever you want," he said more softly.

"Thank you," she said. Her voice was full of misery, but she continued on.

"After the war, our father worked here at the local iron mine, which was fortunate, as jobs were few and far between. Our grandfather had worked the mines, along with many of his brothers, so it was natural for Papa to bring our family to Ste. Barbe to live. Right?"

"Right. What are you getting at?"

"I'm wondering why our father, who mistreated our mother so, brought us back here in the first place."

Julien cringed. He swallowed his pride and said, "Economics! Jobs! Where else would he go?"

"I'm just questioning his real motives to return. We know that he had a longtime lover here—I've already explained this to Kate—so, I'm just wondering if he came back for her." Kate slid deep into her seat and remained silent.

"Now that sounds pretty cynical, even for you, Sophie. That lover could have been in his later years. We don't know much about her, do we?" Julien looked out the window. He was steamed.

Sophie drove into Ste. Barbe from the south, turned at the corner, and headed down the familiar block of Rue de la Poste. She slowed in front of their old *coron*, the same dilapidated row housing where the two had grown up. Just like she had envisioned, the drizzle that was continuing to fall was like a pall over the old street. Nothing had changed. Just as Sophie pulled up to the curb, Julien hopped out of the car.

"What are you doing, Julien? Are you insane?"

"Just checking things out," Julien said. "Let me show you around, Kate. This is where so many of our memories took place," he opened the door for Kate and began walking down the block. He was describing something to Kate, Sophie could tell, but she made no move to open her window or to join them.

Sophie could catch a little of what Julien was saying, as his voice carried. He was pointing out their house and the house of Jean-Pierre, their favorite cousin, only two doors from their own. Out of the corner of her eye, she caught movement from the upstairs window of the unit where they used to live. From her old bedroom, the lace curtains parted and a gaunt-faced woman peered out. *Could that be Germaine?*

"Oh, how vividly I remember living there . . . here," she groaned to herself. *Une expérience cauchemardesque, that's what it was. A complete nightmare . . .*

Sophie could no longer ignore the memory of seeing her father and his lover once when she was eight years old, although she had spent many years trying to forget it. Now, as she sat staring at the house, the memory came back in piercing detail.

⁂

The day had started off innocently enough. Sophie had bounced off the top step and onto the sidewalk in front of #72 Rue de la Poste, just missing landing on her mother's foot, as her *Maman* stood waving *adieu* to her father. He was leaving for work. As Papa turned the corner, Sophie, too, wished him a good day. He had turned, shifted his leather lunch satchel higher on his shoulder, and glared in her direction, but kept going.

The springtime morning was crystal clear, and warmth wrapped it in sunshine. She wasn't about to let her father's sour mood change hers. It was another saints' day, and school was out for the day. Sophie flicked her dark hair back from her face. She had grand plans for her day off.

Hardly able to contain herself, she couldn't wait to get to her friend Mimi's. Today was the day they were planning to . . . She couldn't even let the thoughts float free, not with her mother so near. She clamped her fist over her mouth to keep her secret hidden.

"Sophie, have you cleaned your room yet?" her mother asked.

"Sure, *Maman*, I've done all my chores."

"Did you clean up after your brothers, too?"

This sounded like a trick question, but before Sophie could answer, she heard a low-pitched cackle from across the street. Germaine, *la bonne bavarde*, the biggest gossip in all of Ste. Barbe, stepped forward from where she hovered near her front step. She prowled Rue de la Poste like a carnivore after any bit of carrion for future gossip. She laid claim to any family squabbles or tidbits of rumor, all for the pure pleasure of passing it along. As her broom swept the street clean before her *coron*, she waited. Her neighbors knew she never slept.

"You gonna believe your little missy, Marcelle? You gonna believe *anything* your daughter has to say?" she hissed. A gleam of light caught in her devilish eyes. "Surely she's the fruit which has fallen from *your* tree, right Marcelle? Just like Gérard?"

Sophie's eyes widened. Could *la bavarde* read her thoughts?

Normally hidden in the shadows, like a viper lying in wait, Germaine eased into the street. As she started toward them, Marcelle waved her hand and disappeared into the house, leaving Sophie blinking into the sunlight.

What had the old *bavarde* meant about her mother's tree? Did she already know about Sophie's secret? She knew the mean old bag meant her mother harm, but she never understood why. It was the tone of Germaine's voice she could read like a book. She had learned that from her father.

Placing her hand deep into her pocket, she fingered the few coins she had collected from her chores along with a few 1/10 pennies she happened upon in the back of her mother's drawer. She had carefully wrapped the coins in her handkerchief, so no jingling could be heard. Clasping the coins in her right hand, she wondered if the *bavarde* was, indeed, a *sorcière*!

Before she could move along, Julien came tumbling out the

front door and landed in front of her. Her six-year-old brother could be such a pest.

"You wanna go to the store, Soph?" he asked. "Maybe we could get some pennies from *Maman* and we could go . . ."

Fearing that her already absconded funds would come to light, she pushed past him, fully aware that he was about to follow. She moved down the block, hoping their cousin, Jean-Pierre, would take him off her hands. And he did just that.

She continued down Rue de la Poste then, hopped and skipped along the broken sidewalk to Rue du Luxembourg.

Crossing a rutted dirt road, she skipped toward the corner where most of the neighborhood stores were located: the shoe and fabric stores, the grocery, the *tabác*, and her favorite local hangout, the café. Before reaching the corner, she slipped behind the shoe store. There she opened a side door to a dank stairwell, which led up the steep wooden steps to Mimi's grandmother's apartment.

Immediately, she was rocked by a sickly odor descending from above. *Mon Dieu! What is that awful smell?* Standing on the stairs while attempting not to gag, the door opened from above, and Mimi's bright face beamed down on her.

"Are you coming up? What took you so long?" she asked, as she bounded down the stairs to grab her friend's hand and drag her up the steps. White goose feathers hovered in their midst and clung to them on their ascent. Mimi's pigtails had been turned from blonde to white before they reached the uppermost landing.

"I had to get rid of my little brother," Sophie said as she looked around the sparse apartment. Standing in the kitchen, she noticed the unmade bed by the stove, where Mimi's uncle Jo-Jo slept. She could see into the bedroom, which Mimi shared with her grandmother. The bed was carefully made, but white downy feathers covered literally every level space in the two rooms.

"What's happening?" Sophie asked. "And what is your *grand-mère* cooking?" She knew Mimi's Polish grandmother was especially poor. She was a widow and raised her own geese, rabbits, chickens, and even turkeys for barter, but Sophie couldn't detect what the awful smell was.

"Oh, that's beef lung. *Grand-mère* was given a nice lung in exchange for all these goose feathers.

"Do you like lung?" Sophie squinched her nose up in disgust.

"It's okay, I guess. But then, I eat anything." Mimi flipped her pigtails behind her.

"I've got an explosive idea," Sophie said in a loud whisper. "Today's the day we are going to learn to—to smoke!" She jumped back and shrieked with delight. "Do you have any money for cigarettes?"

Mimi cast her eyes around. She knew her grandmother rarely had cash. The sting of poverty came when you least expected it. She shook her head and shrugged her small shoulders.

"That's okay, Mimi. I probably have enough. Do you have matches?"

Mimi lifted the lid on a wooden box and held up four matches. She stared at them, then put two back. She knew the importance of matches. There was nothing she hated more than waking up cold and having no way to get heat. She shuddered and handed the matches to Sophie.

"*Vite, vite*," Mimi said. The two bounded down the stairs and into the sunshine. Hand-in-hand, they skipped to the corner, giggling and laughing along the way. Sophie stopped.

"Let's circle around the stores before we go straight to the *tabác*. Okay? We'll fool everyone that way."

She grabbed Mimi's hand, and the two turned the corner and skipped back along Rue du Luxembourg. In no time at all, they were back again, nearing the *tabác* and the café. They could see the older kids goofing around inside. Checking to see if anyone was watching, they quickly disappeared into the *bureau de tabac*. The proprietor, Madame Falan, stood with her back to them. Her graying hair was worn low in a bun on the nape of her neck.

"She's such a sweet old lady. Do you think we should do this?" Mimi whispered to Sophie.

"Sure. We're here now. Are you ready?" She nervously fidgeted with the handkerchief stuffed into her pocket; sweaty fingers wadded the cloth around the coins again and again. Finally, Madame Falan turned toward them. A smile was always present on her tired yet kindly face. As Madame Falan bent over the counter, her half glasses slipped down her nose.

Sophie steadied herself and looked into her face. Before she could speak, Madame Falan asked, "Have you come for Monique, Sophie? If so, you've just missed her. She mentioned that she was teaching you to ride a bike. Is that why you've come?"

Sophie swayed as her courage began to ebb, and then she stepped forward. "*Non. Je voudrais deux cigarettes, s'il vous plaît, madame?*" Madame's eyes seemed to enlarge as her glasses magnified her surprise. She stared down at the two small girls before her and asked if the cigarettes were for them.

"*Oh, non madame, c'est pour mon papa,*" Sophie squeaked. She pushed all the little coins out of her handkerchief and onto the counter.

"*Deux, seulement?* You want only *two* cigarettes?" Madame Falan asked them, cocking her head to the side. Skepticism now clouded her countenance.

Sophie had never considered this ahead of time, but, of course, her father would never buy just two at a time. He would buy a full pack. She blanched.

"I assume you will want his brand then, right girls? Gauloise? I'm surprised he didn't pick them up before. He was in here thirty minutes ago." The two girls looked at her in surprise, but shook their heads wildly in confirmation.

"*Oui*, madame," they chirped together. "Gauloise."

"Now, does your father also need matches?"

"*Non*, madame," Mimi said, patting her pocket. Suddenly, she dropped her hand to her side. Quickly, Sophie began to loudly count out her pennies as Madame Falan turned to hand her two cigarettes. Her large hand rested on top of Sophie's.

"You two be careful to get these safely to your papa, Sophie," she said. Mimi smiled broadly as Sophie stuffed the cigarettes into her pocket. They backed out of the store.

"I thought your father was at work, Sophie," Mimi whispered loudly.

"He must have been on an errand or something. Now, let's get going." With the cigarettes hidden in her pocket, Sophie surveyed the people around them, praying she didn't see anyone familiar. So far, so good!

Attempting nonchalance, they entered an alley, which led to the end of the vegetable gardens and onto a path that wound past the six-foot-tall walled *vespasienne.* Heading to ford the nearby stream, Sophie suddenly began dramatically spitting. "Tuh! Tuh! Tuh!" she spat.

"What's wrong, Sophie," Mimi asked. "Swallow a bug?"

"No," she spit again. "You know what that *vespasienne* is used for, don't you?" Sophie's tiny finger pointed at the wall, her voice shrill with outrage.

Mimi shook her head; her pigtails were awhirl. Just then, a man came out from behind the wall, smiled smugly, zipped his fly, and sauntered past the girls. Mimi's light blue eyes bulged. "What was he doing?" she whimpered.

"That's what I'm talking about! Oh, it's horrible! And, the smell!" She pinched her nose. "And look where their pee goes— right into our favorite stream!" Their faces contorted with disgust as they leaped over the water and raced into the adjoining field. Weeds towered above them as they zipped toward their favorite rock. Mimi stood on tiptoe to see if anyone had followed them. No. Again, they were in luck. They crouched down where they were certain of invisibility and took out their two cigarettes and two matches.

"One match for you; one match for me," Mimi said. "Now, who lights the cigarettes? Do you know what to do?"

Sophie nodded her head. She had seen her father smoke ten thousand times before. She took her match and bent her head low behind the stone and had Mimi lean close to her. "All right now, I'll light my cigarette and then yours. Just suck in once I light it."

The first match blew out with the wind. The second lasted long enough for Mimi to get a puff, and then they touched the cigarettes together. Finally, they were able to produce a little smoke. They both sucked in deeply, and immediately, Sophie convulsed into a bout of coughing. The cigarettes tasted horrible! How could they have guessed the Gauloise would taste so nasty? Sophie was certain she was seeing double.

Mimi began gagging and lost her breakfast in the bushes. Once she got back her breath, she asked, "Why are we doing this, Sophie?" She wiped her mouth clean with her sleeve.

"Because it's *verboten*," she said, as she spit out the German word. Her father never tolerated any German being spoken, and no German products were allowed to cross their threshold. Just spitting out the word made this adventure even more thrilling. She grinned broadly, wiped her eyes with her sleeve, and stubbed out her barely smoked cigarette. Debating whether to keep the cigarette or not, she stuffed it into her pocket for later.

The two girls opted for separate paths back into town so no one would be the wiser. They were to meet up in a few minutes at the café. Mimi headed across the field in the opposite direction of the *vespasienne*, and Sophie chose a detour back through the field. She followed the stream along the back of the dairy.

As she scooted along, spitting loose tobacco leaves from her tongue, she heard movement in the field. She panicked! Had someone seen them smoking? Were her brothers or cousins spying on them? How could she ever explain this to her father? Thoughts of his whippings caused her to stumble; her foot slipped into the stream.

Then, she heard a woman's laugh—a bawdy deep-throated sound that rose up through the stalks of weeds and lingered in the morning air. Sophie stood stark still. She had never heard laughter like that before. The woman laughed again, and the sound was followed by a man's distinctive low yet grating guffaw. It was familiar. Too familiar! Sophie's ears perked up. That's Papa! She had almost missed it, as he so seldom laughed at home, but it was indistinguishable: like gravel sliding down a rain pipe.

What was he doing here? What was he doing with this woman? She crept closer to see if she could . . . There, she witnessed her bare-naked father writhing on the ground lying on top of . . . Who was she? Sophie took off running back along the stream. When she arrived back at the café, she was out of breath and terrified. She swore to herself if she survived this ordeal, she would never, ever smoke again. And as for her father? She never told a soul what she had seen, but from that day forward, she never trusted the man she called Papa.

꽃

Revulsion washed over Sophie as she sat in the car. *Of all the memories to surface, why this one?*

"Sophie! Sophie," Julien had been rapping on the window to get his sister's attention. "Come out and walk with us a few moments. The rain has stopped. It's lovely."

Sophie, still rattled, stepped out of the car and linked arms with both her brother and Kate. Had that really been her father in the fields? She shook her head to clear her mind and joined in with her brother as they repeated an old jingle they had made up as children: "Polish, French, Polish; Belgium, Italian, and once again, Italian . . ." They laughed together as they crossed the street.

"French, Italian, Polish, Russian, and last but never least, French."

"What's that about?" Kate asked them.

"Oh, that's how we used to keep track of our diverse neighborhood. Miners and their families came from all Europe for work," Sophie replied.

"And that is why we have a varied and rich cuisine, right Soph?" Julien said, licking his lips.

"Ah, yes, that's right. Remember we mentioned Michela's family coming from Italy? Her father moved here from Italy to work in the mines, and then he married into an Italian family here and raised his family.

They continued past Percevals chicken farm and passed the old ballroom and adjoining café.

Sophie slowed. "I remember peeking in here to see if Jean-Pierre's father was here. He was always so kind to me—to us. I loved that man, didn't you, Julien?"

Julien nodded his head and shoved his hands into his pockets. They continued on down the block together, turned the corner, and then Sophie led them toward the old *lavoir*. "Kate, this was where our mother spent many of her hours washing our laundry."

"Oh, brother! You want to show Kate this?" Julien asked.

Kate's eyes lit up. "I remember your mother telling us about the *lavoirs* in Vannes, right Sophie? Somehow, she made them sound magical, but this place . . ." Her voice dropped.

"Doesn't look like any magic happened here," Julien completed her sentence. The broken-down, abysmal-looking building made of hand-cut stone and hewn timbers revealed centuries of masonry and woodworking tradition. This had been the central gathering place for the women of their neighborhood. It had been an important part of their communal life, but for their mother, this had been the only place she used to chat and laugh with other miners' wives.

"You know, Julien, I can almost see *Maman* wearing that same old maroon-plaid dress she wore, bent over the trough, scrubbing and rinsing our father's dingy work clothes."

"Yes," Julien said sadly. "No matter how hard she scrubbed, Papa was never satisfied, as it was impossible to get the grime rinsed free."

A light rain began to fall again. Sophie shook her head in dismay. As hard as her mother tried, she could never please their father . . . so maybe this was the only place she was allowed to be herself. She must have known of their father's infidelity. And now that Sophie was aware of her mother's love affair with André, she questioned why she chose a path that led her to a hideous, loveless marriage. Had she chosen marriage as the means to legitimize her children?

As Sophie stood in the drizzle, a vision came to her of her mother standing up, straightening her back, wiping a strand of dark hair from her eyes, and throwing her head back and laughing —laughing so hard she grabbed hold of the stone wall to gain support. *This must have been the place,* Sophie determined. *This must have been the very place where she came to rinse sanity back into her life.* Sophie's eyes flickered once, twice, and then the vision was gone.

CHAPTER NINE

The Day of Our Father's Rage

S OPHIE SHIFTED INTO DRIVE and raced down Main Street, screeched into a U-turn, and headed back toward the highway to Julien's. Kate snapped her seat belt into place. St. Barbe must have been inhabited by too many ghosts for Sophie, and Sophie was now determined to leave them behind as quickly as possible.

The three had dropped by Julien's mother-in-law's house for coffee, but once Sophie began quizzing her about their papa, Julien steered her back out the door. Sophie was enraged.

"How am I going to get any answers about Papa if you cut me off?" Sophie asked, pressing her foot to the gas.

"Were you really expecting answers, Soph? I'm married to her daughter!"

"Julien, whenever I ask people about Papa and his past, they are still too frightened to talk—and he's been dead for years. Even when I mentioned his name to Marie, *Maman's* old friend near Fontanières, she came unraveled."

Kate sat quietly in the backseat but nervously eyed the road ahead. Sophie didn't seem aware that she was getting dangerously close to the truck ahead of her.

"Of course, I know," Julien said. "I have to deal with Papa's past on a regular basis. That's what I get for living so close to our hometown. At least you've been able to get away."

"Yes, but never far enough." Sophie swerved into another lane, averting an oncoming car. Kate slunk deeper into her seat.

"But, Sophie, at least you got away!" Julien's voice rose. "I've been stuck right here to deal with all . . . all of the fallout between *Maman* and Papa. Whenever they would come back here for visits, Papa would disappear for days, leaving *Maman* here while he went . . . Well, we all knew where he went, but it was so . . . so . . ."

"Painful," Sophie cut in. "I'm sure, Julien. But the truth is, I don't know what is true, and I'm continually haunted by many things Papa did. And, I can never forgive him for how hard he was on Gérard. Remember the day of our father's rage?"

Like a name from a familiar book title, Sophie rolled the words off her tongue. Then she waited. Sensing the import of her words, Kate leaned forward in her seat. Sophie was alluding to a particular day in their family's past, and there was no question this was momentous.

"What are you talking about, Sophie?" Julien was feeling like he was losing his mind. He didn't want to return to the past. It hadn't been good the first time around, so why would he want to go back now?

"Oh, you remember, all right," said Sophie, giving him a sidelong glance.

Julien looked down at his hands. How could he forget? He still had his own nightmares about how his father had erupted that day and how their family had disintegrated—disintegrated because of his father's rage. Julien opened his mouth to respond then thought of Kate, sitting in the back. Warily, he peered over his shoulder at her. Her attention was focused on the hillsides outside the window. He remained mute.

"Why, Julien," Sophie railed on, "all we could do was stand there and take Papa's anger. This might surprise you, but *Maman* wrote about this incident in one of her journals."

"No wonder she hid her journals at a friend's for safekeeping!" he mumbled.

"Don't worry about Kate. I've told her about this, too, so it's no secret. Open the glove compartment and take out the maroon journal. Turn to the page I've marked with a withered flower."

Julien stared at the glove compartment, willing it to disappear before he had to do as his sister commanded. He knew he was reacting foolishly, but he had an awful feeling about where this conversation was headed. Was she right? Was he fearful of learning something? After a few moments' hesitation, he reached into the glove compartment and began sorting through the thin, somewhat tattered volumes. He, too, took some time touching the jacket covers and looking over his mother's words. It was like his mother was no longer gone. He shuddered. Why was Sophie airing all their family's laundry? He felt tears burn the back of his eyes. From his earliest memories, he knew his mother to be the soul of their family. She was the buttress against all that was evil; only now did he realize how much he missed her. He gulped.

Sophie, too, breathed in deeply and then let it out. She was finding it difficult to get enough air, and Julien was not forthcoming. She rolled the window down. *What was going on with him?* Almost without thinking, she blurted out an introduction to their mother's entry. "Kate, our father's fits of anger had been accelerating for some time. So we were doing our best to stay out of his way. I remember it was a Sunday, right Julien?" Sophie didn't wait for an answer. "I remember we were all home from school. Gérard had broached the subject of becoming a mechanic's apprentice instead of continuing on with his formal education. Do you remember, Julien? Do you? Our mother was terribly upset because she wanted him to go to college." Sophie's voice ricocheted through the small car.

"When was this, Sophie?" Julien asked. "I can't seem to find the right journal." His fingers had become numb as he thumbed through one journal after another.

"Now, let me think. Gérard would have been fourteen at the time, so that would have made you nine or ten."

"Okay," said Julien, calculating the ages. "That would have been around 1956." He was surprised his hands had begun to shake.

"It says the date on the proper page." Sophie blew out another deep breath. "Our mother always knew Gérard was bright. We thought him clever, but she could see he had potential, so she told him no when he suggested dropping out of school."

"I'm beginning to remember . . ." Julien stuttered. A wave of guilt crested and then washed over him. All his life, he was the only family member who had never faced his father's ire. He had been the loved son, the son who could do no wrong. On the other hand, Gérard, according to their father, could do no right. Even at a young age, Julien had learned the safety of aligning himself within his father's shadow. But it was on this day—this very day Sophie was insisting on dredging up—that he realized the why of it all. Again, a wave of angst rolled over him, and sweat broke across his forehead. Why had he never reached out to Gérard? Why had he preferred to huddle in the safety of his father's protection?

"So, Kate, our brother Gérard, being a normal teenager, was hitting his stride. He resisted our mother's decision. He wanted his own independence and to get away from our family. He wanted to find a job and move out. And who's to blame him?" She turned sharply at the corner leading up to Julien's street. Kate grabbed for the armrest and hung on.

"Our father had always treated him miserably," Sophie continued. An image of Gérard shielding himself from their father flashed through Sophie's mind, his sweet, gentle countenance suddenly clouded by yet one more moment of harassment. Nowhere to run, nowhere to hide. "Gérard's only chance of survival was to get away from the wave of venom that flowed from our father." She shook her head as her voice slipped an octave lower. Kate leaned closer to hear.

"Julien, this was the most devastating event to happen to our family. Nothing could ever be taken back, and nothing would ever be the same after that day."

"Why don't we wait until you and I can talk about this," Julien said, his jaw clenched. "We're almost home."

Sophie shot him a look, then she shrugged and kept quiet.

Once she pulled up to Julien's house, Julien disappeared into the kitchen to put on a pot of coffee with Sophie hard on his heels. Eager to get some breathing room of her own, Kate went straight up to her room, where she placed a call to her husband. She was afraid she had intruded on Sophie and her brother, and she needed Matt as a sounding board. He was always helpful when she felt she was adrift in unfamiliar waters. And she felt she was neck-deep at that moment and going down.

"How are you, love?" Matt said as he answered. "How's it going? Are you ready to come home yet?"

"Actually, I'm doing . . ." she exhaled. "Well, I *am* feeling a bit homesick. Yes, to think of it, that's exactly it. I just needed to hear your voice." Over the next twenty minutes, Matt calmed her down and gentled her waters.

"Hang in there, darling," Matt said. "Sounds like Sophie is going through a lot right now, and I'm sure you're providing just the support and strength she needs."

Kate took a deep breath and exhaled. "I hope so. Thank you, sweetheart."

She caught up on the household dramas, and just as they were about to hang up, Matt said, "By the way, Kate, Melody is trying to reach you. She seemed pretty concerned about you."

Kate fiddled with the edge of her pillowcase. She had not talked to her sister in weeks, which was unusual. "Oh. Okay. Thanks. I'll give her a call."

After exchanging a loving farewell, Kate hung up. She had been thinking of putting in another call to her daughter Lisa, but she stopped herself. Instead, she laid down on the bed to think, but typical of her reactions to stress, she fell asleep.

Back in the kitchen, Sophie was perched at the table, listening to Julien.

"*Maman* always took Gérard's side," Julien said, getting cups from the cupboard.

"Someone had to, Julien. You know that! Someone had to protect him," Sophie's anger was rising once again. "And until that day, we didn't know why."

"I was only nine or ten, so I don't know if I remember many details . . ."

"You've got to remember, Julien. Just think back." Sophie rose from the kitchen chair, hysteria now overtaking her. "One of my nightmares is about this very day! The day I truly lost faith in Papa! Oh, Julien, sometimes I swear I'm going crazy! You've got to help me sort through this! You're the only stable one left in our family." She latched onto his arm and looked up at him.

"*Mon Dieu*, Sophie, I'm sorry I've . . . well, I'm sorry I haven't been the brother that you've needed." Julien set the cups of coffee on the table. His hands were shaking, but he pulled his sister to his chest and held her as her body shook. Internally, he was questioning his own stability. Tears covered his shirt—both hers and his. What was happening?

"Ah, *ma soeur*," Julien finally said, wiping his face, "I have a difficult time returning to bad memories. But, as resistant as I am about this, we will work through this together." He led her back to her chair and helped her sit down.

"I'm sorry I've been obstinate about this. I do remember," Julien said, sitting next to her. "How could I forget our Papa's lifetime of hatred and loathing, of his ugly treatment of everyone and everything in his life, especially of dear *Maman* and Gérard? And I too have nightmares about the pain he created in the living room that day so many years ago. Yes, Sophie, I do remember." He sighed.

Together, the two sat side by side in order to face the memory of the devil who resided with them on that fateful day.

༄

"Stay out of this, *putain.*" Jules hissed the insult *whore* at Marcelle once again. She stepped back. His body had become taut, his jaw clenched, his neck stretched out of the loose-fitting collar of his shirt, as he, like a serpent, was poised to strike.

Sophie grabbed Julien by his arm, and they quickly darted for the stairs. As they cowered on the darkened steps, Julien's small body shook violently beside her. Sophie wrapped one arm around him and scooted him closer. They had witnessed their father's anger often, but this time . . . This time, they knew it was different. The air crackled about them.

Marcelle slumped forward once she slid onto a dining room chair. Even though Jules had not physically hit her, he may as well have. She began to sob.

"Don't you see, I want more for my son," she cried. "He is too smart to work on cars. He should start *lycée* so he can go on to *université.*"

Jules pulled his fist back as if to strike, his arm rigid yet vibrating with the anger that coursed through his body.

"My son?" he seethed. "My son?" At once an almost inhuman keening erupted from him, a noise that was more animal than man. "EEEIIIIEEEEEYEE!" he screamed.

Gérard was paralyzed with fear. Standing between his parents, he didn't know where to run. What was this about? He had never thought of continuing his education. He would complete *collège* (junior high) at age fifteen, and he hadn't dared to dream beyond that.

"I'll be fine as an auto mechanic," he said, shushing his mother. He wanted to be out from under his father's wrath, but in his gut, he felt torn. Should he leave home, or should he stay to protect *Maman?*

He turned slowly to face his father, his own anger rising. "Don't ever call her that, Papa! She is no whore! She doesn't deserve that!" His voice cracked. He licked his full but dry lips, yet stood tall. His eyes were almost level with his father's.

"You have no idea what I'm talking about, do you, boy!" Jules spat. "She deserves to be called that and more." He stepped forward in one move and knocked Gérard to the floor.

"That's it," Marcelle said. "*J'ai fini!* I'm done."

"*Fini?* I'm the one who is finished with you. You think I should work my ass off so your *bâtard* can go on beyond junior high? Well, *putain*, you have another think coming!"

He took another step forward, towering over her. "This charade has gone on long enough. You want your son to go farther than I have? You want him to have more? Then have his *real* father pay his way! Make that happen!" His eyes were yellow slits of glowering hatred.

Gérard, who had remained on the floor, rose on one elbow. His blue eyes were wide with horror as he cried, "What are you saying, Papa?" His voice cracked with emotion as his eyes flashed from his father to his mother and back again. "What are you saying? Answer me! Are you not my . . ." He rose to his feet.

Jules spun around, ready to take him on, his fist balled again and raised midair. Jumping from her chair, Marcelle grabbed Jules's arm just as he swung, and his hand caught her in the side of the head. She crashed down beside a chair and slid across the floor. Sophie and Julien raced out of the stairwell screaming as they encircled their fallen mother.

"You leave our *Maman* alone," Julien squealed. "Leave her alone."

Gérard spun his father around. "What are you saying?" he yelled in his father's face. "Tell me!"

"You're a smart boy, right? Can't you figure it out? I'm *not* your father. I have never been your father, and I'm not going to pretend to be ever again. Just ask this whore of a mother, for once."

Marcelle curled up on the floor, sobbing. Her reddened hands covered her tear-blotched face, and the sounds the children knew only too well reverberated through the room.

"*Maman.*" Gérard stooped down to his mother. He gently pulled her hands away from her face. "Dear *Maman*, what is he saying? Is it true?" His voice shook. Anger and fear surged through him.

"*Oui, mon fils, c'est vrai,*" Marcelle whispered. Gérard leaned in closer, as her voice was inaudible. "*C'est vrai.* It is true."

Gérard rocked back on his knees. It was as if she had slapped him. "Is that why he has always hated me? Do you mean to throw me out like you did Thierry?"

At first, Marcelle's head reeled back as his words assaulted her. Sophie and Julien wrapped their frail arms about her. But just as she reached out to Gérard, he jumped up and raced from the house. The back door slammed behind him as his feet clattered down the well-worn steps. He fled into the nearby fields.

Marcelle struggled to her feet, throwing her younger children aside. She flew out the back door after her son. She was frightened that she would lose him—lose him, too. When she finally discovered him, he was crouched down beside the creek behind the *vespasienne*. His sobs were silent but uncontrollable. Marcelle knelt down, pulled him into her arms, and tried to console him. She rocked back and forth, holding him close. She could feel the heat from his body seep into her own as they sat alone. Not a word was spoken, and the only sounds heard that afternoon were the water cascading off the stones of the brook and the muffled cries of a mother with her son.

Minutes passed. Perhaps hours. Softly, Marcelle began to speak. "I have wanted to tell you, *mon fils*, but . . . well, I didn't know where to begin."

"And Thierry? Do we have the same father?" He spat out the words, as if they burned his mouth. "Is that why his last name is Pourrette—like your maiden name? Is that my name too? Who am I, anyway? Who is my father?" The questions gushed from him, echoing the cadence of the nearby stream.

Marcelle leaned back against the *vespasienne*. She had known this day would come sooner or later, but no matter how often she had played this scenario over in her mind, she had never found the words that would serve her son well.

"Your father is not Thierry's father. I was raped when I was sixteen, and because I had no family to speak of, I made my way to Paris, where Thierry was born in a Catholic convent. I stayed in Paris, where I was able to provide for him by working at Citröen."

"But what about me? What about my father?" he cried.

"Gérard, your father was the only man I ever truly loved—and the only one who truly loved me. But, the war, *mon cher*, brought us together in Paris, and then we, like a loosely-woven cloth, were rent apart and forced to go our separate ways. He was to join me after the war, but . . . but I never heard from him again. I fear the Germans took him away because of his work in the Résistance. I never knew what happened for certain. War, my dear Gérard, has many casualties, and our love became nothing more than collateral damage."

She turned and cradled his face in her hands and looked straight into his dark blue eyes. "But your father is with me every time I see your face, every time I see you smile. And like you, he had an intense love of books and learning. He was a professor in a boys' *lycée*. And he loved you so very much. That's why I've been pushing hard for you to continue your education. You are the embodiment of his spirit."

Gérard sat listening to the tenor of his mother's voice. The words, still too raw to take in whole, lodged inside him and knotted in his gut. He had little energy to digest it. His body remained tight, not yielding to her softness or warmth.

"Have you ever wondered why I've always protected you from your father? From Jules?" She leaned closer to him.

Gérard formed no words. He could barely nod his head as tears splashed down his reddened cheeks.

"Even though he legally adopted you and gave you his name, he never accepted you because you were my son from a love affair in which he could never compete. I'm so very sorry, Gérard. I'm so, so sorry!"

"So, I'm nothing more than one of your sins?" Gérard's words lanced into her body and made permanent purchase in her heart.

She stared down at her dry, wrinkled hands. "Is that what you think, *mon cher*? Is that how I've treated you?" A lengthy pause followed.

"No, *Maman*. No, I know you've always loved me—that you have always treated me differently than the others. Until now, I didn't know why," he said as he turned to burrow in closer. "It finally makes sense now."

Together, they sat for another hour, holding on to each other, crying, talking, and crying once again. Years of pain washed down the stream that day, but unfortunately, not all of it was released. Life for these two—for their entire family—would never be the same after that day.

⚛

Sophie's mouth was dry. She walked over to the sink to rinse out her coffee cup, filled it with water, and leaned against the sink as she drank it down in one gulp.

"I know I've put you into an awkward position," she said to Julien. She swiped the back of her hand across her mouth. "Kate, too, for that matter. I know you didn't want me to involve her, but she's the only one who isn't a family member who can give me perspective. But I also need your help. When did you say Michela is due home?"

"She won't be home for a few hours," Julien said. He felt completely drained. He walked to the refrigerator, pulled out a bottle of champagne, popped the cork, and poured two flutes of the foamy essence. He turned and encouraged Sophie to join him back at the table.

Drying her cup, she took the glass and toasted, "To *Maman*! God love you, dear *Maman*! Tchin-tchin!" Sophie sat down opposite Julien and took a sip. "Thank you, Julien. There is so much I need to sort out, and talking with you helps."

"Tell me more, Sophie," Julien said, gently.

"I have a list of things, and probably none of them have anything to do with *Maman*." She looked up from her glass just as her brother flinched at her first words.

He cleared his throat. "I guess I knew that, Sophie. I know you want to search for our Papa's illustrious past, but what do you expect to gain?"

"I want to know if he kept his promises to *Maman*. Did he really go back for Thierry, like he said? Did he adopt Gérard? I somehow don't believe so. I want to know who his lover was, and I want to know . . ." Sophie gulped down her champagne, "and, I want to know if he sexually abused me when I was young . . ."

Julien gasped. He put his glass down and looked at her. "You think he did, Sophie?" His soulful eyes hardened. "Why do you think that?"

"Julien," Sophie swallowed, "for years now, I've had these other nightmares . . ." She closed her eyes and felt a tingle at the back of her neck. "There's a man who looks like Papa—standing in white light, yet back in the shadows. It's like he's behind a gauze curtain, preparing to come into my room. Before I can make out who he is, I wake up, but because I am so terrified in the dream, I . . . I just need to know who this mystery man is and what he has done." She paused and then slumped in her chair.

"Sophie," Julien said, reaching across the table and taking both her hands, "how will you find out?" He could feel his own heart racing; what was that about?

"I need to return to the hall of records in Ste. Barbe. The records might give me information about *Maman* and about Gérard's situation. And then I have this paper." She pulled the tattered hospital record from her sweater pocket, the one she had found in their mother's attic. She handed it to Julien.

"What is this?" he asked. After reading some of the details, he looked at the date and then placed it back on the table between them. "What does this mean?"

"I don't know for certain, but it states that I was in the hospital on that particular day and time."

"But I don't understand. Do you remember being in the hospital? How old were you?" He picked the paper up again and read the date.

"I was fifteen. At first I was thinking it might be nothing—like I fell off my bike or something—but then I remembered that we never went to the hospital unless it was an absolute emergency."

"Right," Julien tossed his head with distain "We never had insurance or money for such things. Even if we showed up with a broken arm," Julien said, as he lifted his left arm part way into the air. "Remember when I fell out of the tree and we were so scared Papa would find out?"

Sophie nodded. "Yes, we lived our entire childhood in sheer panic or terror, didn't we?" She laughed, yet she felt like crying. "Ah, but we survived it, too."

Julien took a sip of champagne and smiled. "We survived because *Maman* made it worthwhile."

"Yes, she always turned every trauma into a game—once Papa had gone to work. What fun she gave us kids! Remember when she made the Ping-Pong table out of our dining room table?" Sophie smiled at the memory. Julien fingered the wrinkled hospital bill, then placed it on the worn cotton tablecloth.

"I'm sorry, Soph. Do you think your nightmare is about something that happened at the hospital?"

"Possibly. I don't know if you remember this, Julien," Sophie began, "but when I was around fourteen, Papa took me over to Pont-à-Meuse. I think it was one of the rare times he allowed me to ride in our car. Of course, he left me at *Grand-père's* and then disappeared. Anyway, it was on one of those nights that I fell asleep awaiting his return. It must have been well after midnight when I woke up in great-uncle Tobias's bed."

"That old escargot?" Julien growled. He pushed back forcefully from the table, stood, and began to pace. "He was such a detestable man! Ptuy. Ptuy. Always saying such foul things, always embarrassing *Maman . . .*"

"Right. That old escargot," Sophie said. She shuddered and wrapped her arms around herself. "Anyway, I awakened to . . . I remember he had poured some wine into my glass earlier—not the watered-down kind—and we had laughed a good bit. I might have been drunk because he had taken all my clothes off and was . . . and I think it was his hand in my . . ." She glanced at Julien and then looked away. She bumbled ahead.

"When I awakened, I guess you would say he was . . . molesting me. Oh, Julien, I was so frightened." Simply by saying what had happened, she began reliving the past. She started to shake. She stood and stumbled toward the kitchen window and gazed blindly outside, the tumultuous scene playing out again and again in her mind.

Sophie remembered the roughness of his hands as she tried to roll out from underneath him and onto the floor, her skin bruising from his grasp. Somehow, she had gotten away because the next thing she could remember was wildly searching for her clothes. She was crying so hard that she couldn't see anything in his darkened bedroom, so she grabbed one of his old shirts and pulled it on before racing into the kitchen. The smell of stale tobacco smoke mixed with the reek of an old man's sweat had seeped into every thread of that shirt, and to this day, that smell . . . Sophie took a deep breath and slowly let it out. She dropped her head to the kitchen counter and began to sob.

"I'm so sorry, Sophie. So very sorry," Julien said, moving to her side and putting his arm around her. "Did you ever tell Papa about it?"

Sophie stood and placed a palm on each of her inflamed cheeks. "After *grand-mère* cleaned me up, she asked me not to worry Papa. Uncle Tobias was her brother, and Papa never got along with his stepmother." She turned around to face Julien. "So I didn't tell him. I also never visited there again, either."

Julien rubbed his temples. "Do you think this incident has something to do with this hospital bill?" The crumpled paper hung limply from his fingers.

"Actually, I don't know. It wasn't until after I was an adult that I remembered the memory myself. But this billing says I was in the hospital at that age. It could have been when I attempted suicide, after Gérard left . . ." She paused. "Or it may have followed after this . . . molestation."

Again, Julien flinched at the rawness of the discussion. "So, your nightmares," he stammered. His head was spinning. "You mentioned gauze curtains. Like in a hospital? Do you think your nightmares lead back to this incident and Ste. Barbe's hospital?" After leading her to the table, he slumped into the chair opposite her. "And what does this have to do with Papa?"

"That's what I'm determined to find out. I have to go back to that hospital, uncover the mystery behind this billing . . . Julien, I've had these nightmares for over forty years now, and they are increasing in intensity. I have to know why I'm so fearful of Papa in my dream. Unless you can think of something."

Julien thought for a moment and shook his head. Inwardly, he was terrified of even thinking. Was Sophie saying that she had also been sexually molested by Papa? Julien's old theory about what one doesn't know can't hurt you was now hurting. He drained the rest of his champagne in one gulp.

Sophie looked at her watch, then turned to look out of the kitchen window. The sky had grown dark, and she suddenly realized she had left Kate upstairs for quite some time. She, too, gulped down her champagne.

"I need to get upstairs and check on Kate." She stood up, then turned toward her brother. "Thank you, mon frère. Thank you for listening to me."

Julien walked over to his sister and gave her a long hug before she pushed off and disappeared up the stairway.

"Weren't you going to prepare your world-famous watercress ravioli?" she tossed over her shoulder. Before she reached the top of the staircase, she could hear the crash and bang of pots and pans coming out of the cupboards. He was at it.

"Tell Kate I would be happy for her assistance, if she's interested in learning the recipe," Julien called after her.

⁘

Upstairs, Sophie tiptoed to the room where Kate was staying. "Kate, Kate, are you awake?" Sophie asked, gently tapping on the door.

"Come in, Sophie," Kate yawned as she shook herself awake.

"Sorry, I didn't mean to wake you," Sophie said, as she slipped into the room.

"It's all right. I need to get up anyway or I'll be up all night," Kate said. "Come. Sit."

Sophie sat on the edge of the bed next to Kate and gave her a tentative smile. "I wanted to apologize for springing my intense family dramas on you today—especially when you had no means of escape."

Kate sat up and laughed. "No problem, Sophie. As a therapist, that's always a workplace hazard. And all families need time to work through their issues alone, too. Were you able to open up to Julien?" Kate scooted against the headboard and pulled the quilt up under her arms.

"Actually, that's what I've been doing. I finally told him about my nightmares. Remember the hospital bill I've been carrying with me? Well, I think that paper is a clue to my depression.

"That's monumental! How was Julien with this discussion?"

"That's a funny thing," Sophie said as her finger outlined a square on the patchwork quilt. "He was really struggling to be there for me, but . . . well, he did his best. He's a good brother, and I feel a lot better about opening up to him."

"I'm glad to hear that," Kate said as she swung her legs out of the covers and stood on the cold floor. She bounced back into the bed again. "Whoo. It's colder out there than I expected."

"I'll turn up the heat. But when you're ready, Julien invited you to help him with his world-famous watercress ravioli. He's getting things started, so maybe in twenty minutes or so? Oh, and the champagne awaits," Sophie said as she walked back to the door.

"I have to make a quick phone call to my sister before I come down, but then I'll be right there."

"Take your time," Sophie said. "Julien's a slow cook. Everything has to be chopped just so before he even sets the water to boil."

"Oh, and Sophie," Kate said. Sophie paused on the landing. "I'm glad you were able to open up to your brother."

"Me, too, Kate," she said, "me, too." And with that, Sophie disappeared down the stairs.

$\mathcal{L}$onging for $\mathcal{F}$rance $\mathcal{A}$gain

A

FTER SOPHIE LEFT, Kate sat in bed and looked at her surroundings. She hadn't noticed before, but now she realized this must have been Julien's teenage daughter's room. How had she overlooked this? "Teenager" shrieked from every corner. Goth black fabric swagged across the windows, closing out all light, while matching folds of black swept to the ceiling to drape loosely above the bed. Classic posters of teen idols plastered the walls and stared down at her from the ceiling. Plastic CD cases were stacked twenty high and outlined the room, making access to the closet nearly impossible. A red guitar with a broken neck had two strings climbing up the walnut bureau and intertwining with the phone cord of an old pink princess-style phone. *My goodness! Do they have these, too?* Kate thought. How old was this girl? Who was this "princess"? Kate pulled on her slippers and got up to look around.

Her own house used to be filled with teens morphing in and out of dark phases of angst. They left their straw-blonde hair to childhood and adopted the hairstyles of the other-worldly, all in the hopes of being different and, therefore, fitting in. Hair-dying fiascos of all kinds happened in the privacy of their family bathroom. Kate laughed out loud. She remembered the morning she enrolled her daughter into a new high school. Kate had married Matt that summer and had moved with her kids to a new city. While Kate was adjusting to a new marriage and going to graduate school, she needed to help her children acclimate to a stepfather, a new home, new friends, and new schools. Not a kind thing to do to her twelve-year-old son, Ian, much less her sixteen-year-old daughter, Addy.

The night before Addy registered for high school, Kate helped her dye her hair from light blonde to jet-black. At the time, she had not realized that her daughter's plan for her first day of school was to make a grand entrance by punking-out her jet-black hair and then allowing the locks to droop down into her eyes, leaving the woeful impression of a giant tarantula nested atop her head. Kate remembered walking casually through the hallways with her daughter, pretending that everything here was normal; and this, indeed, became the new "normal."

Yes, jet-black, blue, green, and, come to think of it, candy apple red hair graced the halls of their home and the corridors of the local schools. Sometimes punked into spikes, sometimes shaved and shorn into Mohawks or into straightedge *x*'s that stretched across the top of her children's heads. Yes, all the bases had been covered.

Reminiscing about her teenaged children, Kate's thoughts drifted to the daughter she had given up for adoption. To Lisa. How had *her* childhood gone? Had she chosen to rebel like her half brother and half sister? Had she been able to adjust to being adopted? Had she flung herself into the midst of teenage angst while questioning her identity? *Couldn't blame her, if she did.*

Kate picked up her cell phone, suddenly eager to connect with her sister. She dialed Melody's number, closed her eyes, and waited for her to answer.

"Melody, how are you?" Kate asked. Her sister was the one person she could share her deepest thoughts with, despite that they lived half a continent apart. Melody was three years older, but, according to Kate, was half a century wiser. She lived in the Midwest and was a minister, and she carried compassion around with her as her only necessary tool. But since Lisa had come back into her life, Kate had put distance between them. Melody had been encouraging Kate to come visit her, but instead, she had run to France. *What was she running from?*

"How are *you?*" Melody asked, after their preliminary greetings. "What are you doing in France, Katie?" Skepticism was sprinkled between her words.

"Ah, dear sister, you know me. I was longing for France again."

"Again?" Melody asked. "Matt told me you had flown the coop." There was a pause. "Kate, I haven't talked to you in weeks. You haven't returned my calls. What gives?"

"Actually, my good French friend, Sophie, lost her mother a couple of weeks ago, and I'm helping her pull together some of the threads of her mother's life."

"That sounds like you," Melody said. "But there's something more going on. You keep avoiding me." Melody paused. "Is this about Lisa?"

Kate caught her breath. She had been trying hard to contain her feelings, and she felt she didn't dare uncork them now. She lay back on the bed and stared at the poster of some teenage idol on the ceiling.

"Probably," she whispered. "I'm sorry."

"Oh, Katie. You don't need to be sorry. I know Lisa coming back into your life must have sent you into a tailspin—how could it not? I can almost mark that date on my calendar as to when you stopped calling." Melody took a deep breath. "Is this a bad time to talk? I'd like to know what you are feeling."

"This is probably as good a time as any." Kate thought of Sophie and Julien downstairs sorting through their own family dilemmas. "How am I feeling? Melody, I've been holding my feelings in for so many years, I sometimes feel like I will explode," she confessed.

"So, stop tap-dancing in the dust and tell me what's going on. Tell me what you've recently heard from Lisa."

Kate paused. "Nothing recently. And that's what's bothering me. I've been leaving phone messages for her but . . . I know she's really busy in graduate school."

"But it hurts all the same."

"It's just . . . you know . . . reuniting with Lisa was the moment I've been waiting for for thirty-some years. Remember we used to talk about what would happen if or when my baby daughter returned? And yet, I was totally unprepared for her first visit. It was wonderful! It was delightful! And it was so desperately difficult!" Kate closed her eyes, remembering. "Gawd! What a mix of emotions! But don't get me wrong; it has been a joy to have her in our lives and as part of our family."

Kate thought back to the first phone call she had received from Lisa more than five months ago. It was a bolt out of the blue! Kate remembered how her legs had begun to tremble and she had slumped inelegantly onto a stool when she first heard her daughter's voice. She was shocked, but she immediately had determined to keep her on the phone for as long as possible. Days later, Kate received a lengthy letter from her daughter, and their relationship began to unfold. Phone calls, pictures, and more letters followed, and finally, they arranged for Lisa to fly to California for their first face-to-face visit. It was a dream come true for Kate, yet she was fraught with anxiety. And it wasn't easy for Lisa, either.

Breaking into Kate's thoughts, Melody said, "I'm looking forward to meeting her, Kate. In the photos you sent, she looks lovely . . . reserved, but lovely."

"Oh, she was frightened to death!" Kate let out a guffaw. "But, Melody, she *is* beautiful! Really, I mean it. She has rich curly dark hair—the same as Mom used to have—with alabaster skin and soft, slightly skeptical, hazel eyes. Actually, Melody, when she tilts her head to the side, she reminds me of you."

"Except that I don't have curly dark hair or hazel eyes," Melody laughed. "But I understand. Go on. Tell me more about her visit. You were so tight-lipped about it at the time, and I didn't want to pry."

"Actually, I was optimistic during her visit—I still am—but I was also trying to sort out my role—and I'm still doing that too. She had always known she was adopted and said she was comfortable with that, but she was also clear that she adored her adoptive mother and didn't need another mother. So the question I have is, who am I to a thirty-four-year-old daughter who doesn't need another mother? Exactly what role does that leave me? I don't mean to be whining, but I'm stymied."

"Oh, Kate, I can't imagine how difficult that situation must have been." The compassion in Melody's voice finally melted Kate's reserve, and a small sob slipped out before she could stop it.

"Yes," Kate said as she searched for a Kleenex. No light brooked the Goth curtains, and she stumbled over her shoes. "I haven't wanted to admit it, but this has been more painful than I allowed myself to . . . to realize." She located the tissue, blew her nose, and then resumed the conversation. After all these years of being without Lisa, all I wanted to do was hold her in my arms. But we were strangers; are strangers." Another little sob squeaked out.

"Oh, Katie, she will. I tell you, she will. It just takes time . . ." Melody paused. Silence filled the line. Kate heard Melody take a deep breath, then start anew. "So," Melody asked, "how was your first meeting?"

"Well," Kate paused, "it was strained. I could see disappointment in her eyes; I was not who she expected. I'm certain it was my weight . . ."

"Kate," Melody stopped her. "You've always been so hard on yourself. I'm sure that wasn't the case."

"I couldn't tell if she was relieved that we didn't look alike, but I can imagine she was." Kate's voice cracked. She cleared her throat.

"Katie, I wish you had told me this before."

"It is still too fresh, too raw. But . . ." Kate hesitated, "I can finally tell you some of it now." She snuffled. "Lisa was shy, reserved, and certainly wary. I knew she was scared stiff, but I didn't know how heavily guarded her defenses were. So, anyway, I found myself chattering on and on to fill in her silences . . ."

Kate paused and dabbed the tissue against her forehead as she relived those hours—those precious hours—with her daughter. There had been so much weight hanging on every syllable she uttered, and now in this far away bedroom in France, she could only recall herself babbling like a noisy brook that, after thirty-some years, had been disgorged. She slumped back onto the bed and wriggled under the covers.

"Before she arrived, I sat down with the family and told them the main reason Lisa was coming. She wanted to know who she was and who I was exactly, so she would be bringing plenty of questions."

"Like what?"

Kate turned on a lamp in the bedroom. The light cast a yellowish half-circle up the wall and onto the black-draped ceiling. She looked around again. Surrounded by the memorabilia of a teenage girl she had never met, she reimagined the day she was answering questions from Lisa, whom she had just begun to know. Kate was there to help her create memories and fill in blanks— which, frankly, felt futile to suffice after abandoning this sweet baby girl of hers.

"She wanted to know everything," Kate said. "All of my stories, why her knees bowed back, and why her fingers were formed the way they are. She wanted to know if our faces were similar, and because she resembled her father more than me, I was at a complete loss to explain. She wanted to know if I had any pictures of her father. No. Not anymore." Kate shivered and slid deeper under the covers.

"Lisa then turned to find a reflection of herself in her new sister and brother, and, of course, she resembled neither of them. But though they have different fathers, they're equally as beautiful. We all just stood in a circle of anxiety and resignation. None of us resembled the other—except Addy and Ian, of course—in spite of the fact that we were all related by blood—my blood."

"That's quite an observation. Go on," Melody encouraged.

"I don't really know what I expected from this first encounter, but it felt as if we all had been cast into a play and the director had failed to pass out scripts," Kate continued. "We all knew the importance of the moment, but none of us knew our lines." Kate shifted on to her side and kicked her foot out to catch the cool. "Melody, I can tell you, it was a beautiful yet exhausting experience. Thank goodness for Matt! He carried the day. He made each one of us feel comfortable with his sense of humor always at the ready," Kate said. "I'm sure it wasn't easy on him, either, as here was another child coming into our home who was not his own. Frankly, I don't give him the credit he is due."

"He's a gem, all right. Always has been. We both have been lucky like that!" Melody paused. "When I've tried to imagine what this scene must have been like . . . well, Kate, I don't know how you did it. Each one of you had to be completely vulnerable, and that must have scared the bejeebers out of you."

Kate chuckled. "You got that right. But I felt I had only one shot at it, and thank goodness everyone in the family understood the importance. So, in that light, I guess we did receive partial scripts to the play we were in. There were joyful moments all along, but it was also hard work."

"What did you tell Lisa about the circumstances prompting you to put her up for adoption?" Melody asked. "That had to be the most difficult."

"I told her the truth; it was during the Vietnam War. I fell in love with a soldier, a man named Dave, who stumbled under the weight and prospects of fatherhood, much less his M-16, and . . . But, now as I tell you, Melody, that explanation rings hollow and empty . . ."

Kate closed her eyes. How could she explain what it had been like? "Actually," she started again, "I told her it was 1967 and the Vietnam War was in full force . . ."

⚜

Kate, having worked summers in Colorado resorts between her years of college, had come to know of the war through those who were avoiding it. These were the times of the pot-smoking, tie-dyed joking, war-revolting young hippy men and women preaching their stances on war. What did they really know? What did any of them know? But this was also when President Johnson had put out an edict that gave young men a way out of the war. They could stay in college, have an influential friend pull strings, or get married. And the last option was the part that jaded Kate. During the summer of '66, she had received eight—how is that possible?—eight marriage proposals from men she barely knew. How serious could any of them have been? Was she really supposed to fall in love and get married? But once she became pregnant . . .

Now, sitting in this teenager's room, who was probably not much younger than she had been back then, Kate remembered the night she called Dave's house. She had received the results of her pregnancy test. She had become pregnant a couple of months before, when they spent New Year's together. He was at a party, and she could call him there.

Oh my, this feels like forever ago, Kate said to herself as she drew in a ragged breath. The sharp edges of these memories were not coming easily.

Dave had taken the phone call and cloistered himself into a small closet, the raucous laughter and music braying in the background outside the door. The music was too loud; he was trying to hear her, he had said. Funny, she could even picture him sitting there in the closet, listening to her words. But he said nothing. Nothing! Most of all she remembered the thick silence that rose up between them once she had poured out her news. They were hundreds of miles apart at the time, but it could have been thousands. She imagined a thick blanket of cotton had surrounded her, maybe protected her, but even today she couldn't remember if he ever responded. She had known many of the people at the party—the same drunken, over-privileged college kids she had worked with in Colorado the summer before.

Kate reached up and twisted a lock of hair around her finger before she continued her thoughts. *I suppose I knew at that moment our relationship was over,* she thought to herself. *No thoughts of marriage . . .* Of course, he said he would call her later, but the pathetic truth was that she never heard from him again. Dave's lack of response had told her all she needed to know. He was an empty suit—in this case, an empty set of fatigues—and when the spring term ended, Kate arranged to get a lift to San Francisco, left her unknowing family, and headed out on her own.

In that moment, Kate's mind flashed to a phrase she'd seen in one of Marcelle's journal entries. During the heat of World War II, Marcelle had taken her baby, Gérard, and left her dear love in Paris. Why? She needed to provide a safe haven for not only her baby, but also her son Thierry. But what were those words she had written? Suddenly, Kate recalled that special phrase. Marcelle had said her lover had "failed to have the courage of his love." That was exactly what she had told Lisa about her own father. Kate moaned, and her cell phone beeped. Her battery was almost dead.

"Oh, Melody, my phone is dying, but thank you so much for prodding me to begin to sort these feelings. I'll give you a call soon, and we can continue. I love you and appreciate your interest in all of this."

"Well, remember I am here for you whenever you need me. Thanks for calling me back. I love you, Katie."

"I love you too." *Beep. Beep.* And Melody was gone.

After she hung up the phone, Kate lay on the bed and thought about her conversation with her sister. She knew she was just awakening to the pain and anguish she had long ago submerged. Downstairs, she heard the faint strains of Sophie and Julien's laughter and the clattering of pots. Kate pushed the covers away from her and stood to go downstairs. She had faced enough for one day, and the promise of learning a new recipe compelled her to race down the stairs to join her friends.

CHAPTER ELEVEN

*M*emories of *T*ime's *P*ast

(*Souvenirs du Temps Passé*)

$$\text{\Lambda}$$

*B*ONJOUR, *MON FRÈRE,*" Sophie said to Julien the following morning as she kissed him and gave him a good-morning hug. Julien had already dashed out for fresh croissants for their breakfast, and before Sophie could fully open her eyes or be seated, her *petit déjeuner* was set before her. Julien grasped her hand and gave it a squeeze as he led her to the table. It felt good to have bridged the gap of dissension from the previous day.

"Looks like you better join me, Julien," Sophie smiled as she surveyed the pastries. "You have to save me from myself. There are way too many croissants here, and Kate won't be down until later. Too much champagne, I'm afraid."

"So, I'm your savior already?" Julien smiled back. "And, you, without your first cup of coffee? How can that be?" He pretended to ponder that question while pouring two large mugs of *café* and sitting down across from her. Sophie bit into the buttery croissant as a shower of flakes crumbled onto her blouse and into her lap. Julien snickered. "After all these years of French training, you would think you could get the hang of eating these," Julien laughed, tucking a napkin into the top of his shirt. "So what are your plans today, Sophie?" Julien asked as he bit into his croissant and was left with a good deal of pastry hanging off his mustache.

"Looks like you need some training, too," Sophie giggled. "I got hold of Yvon earlier, and he said he and Annie would love for us to visit early this afternoon. I think we'll head over there for a few hours."

Julien made a face and brushed the crumbs from his mustache. "He's originally from Papa's hometown of Pont-à-Meuse?" he asked.

"Yes. He knew our father and of some of the shenanigans Papa got into. Perhaps I should leave this alone, but there's something that just doesn't add up."

"Only one something?" he scoffed, taking another bite of croissant.

Sophie spread some raspberry preserves into her croissant and laid her knife down. "Do you remember what happened at Papa's funeral?"

Julien's mouth was full, but he shook his head. Julien and Sophie had rarely broached the subject of their father's funeral, even though it had happened over ten years before. Julien had successfully pushed his memory of that day far back in his mind, but Sophie simply couldn't leave well enough alone.

"Really, you don't remember?" Sophie rolled her eyes and wiped her mouth from crumbs before continuing. "Remember the deep container ashtrays at the back of the church used only to kill the butt of a cigarette?"

A quizzical look passed over Julien's face.

"Come on, Julien," Sophie wheedled. "Don't you remember what our cousin Jocelyne did before the funeral?" She began to giggle now.

Julien was now completely confused. "Papa's funeral, an

ashtray, and our cousin? Whatever are you talking about, Soph, and what's with the giggle?"

"Because this is so funny! Remember how the ashtray looked like a baptismal font?" Now Sophie could barely contain herself. "But, of course, it didn't hold holy water—only cigarette butts, remember?"

"That's . . . right!" Julien finally exclaimed, his memory creeping back to him. "I remember! I do remember now . . ."

"So when Jocelyne saw the ashtray in the back of the church, she took it, and began, with all the seriousness of a priest, to bless our father's body from the ashtray. She called it a 'smoker's blessing'!"

Julien jumped up to act out their cousin's antics. He moved through the officiating of ashes by marching around the kitchen and the invisible coffin, genuflecting to the cross, kissing the top of an imperceptible casket, and all while Sophie, his best audience, clapped her hands and laughed uncontrollably.

"Perfect! That was so perfect because there was never a moment that our father didn't have a lit cigarette in his mouth . . ." Sophie chortled.

"Whether he was dead or alive!" Julien laughed with her.

"Oh, Julien, it was terribly sacrilegious, but it was so funny and so fitting."

Fortunately, the small Gothic church, built entirely of dark grey river rock, had been almost empty when Jocelyne began her antics. She, along with a few other relatives, had joined the three siblings in setting up before the service. The funeral was not to be a full mass, as Jules had rarely, if ever, graced the insides of any chapel, much less a church, in all of his life. In his death, however, even the Catholic Church would give him grace and had opened their doors (and coffers) to allow his service. But grace was not on the minds of this little thespian group.

As Jocelyne was performing, a small door leading from the

sacristy opened, and a frail octogenarian made her way into the nave. Wearing a lace kerchief to hide the grey-white coils on her head and a yellowed cassock to cover her best and only long black dress, the organist clumped her way before the altar, turned, and faced the petulant sorts at the back of the church. The unholy look of contempt that unfolded from her wrinkled visage was enough to send the group skittering. Like capricious children, the three siblings abandoned Jocelyne to face the music, so to speak, but she, too, disappeared out the front door to have a cigarette of her own.

Before their father's death, Sophie and Julien had made an effort to become closer to him, while Thierry had made his own tentative peace. Gérard had tragically passed away a few years earlier. Sophie had put on a somber air, but afterward, she still did not weep for her father—not when he became sick and not when he passed away. Too many years of unresolved anger remained locked inside of her.

It was only Julien, the one son Jules claimed, who seemed least affected by their father's behavior and most impacted by his death. Even as he remembered this scene of hilarity from their father's funeral, a momentary shadow of sadness passed across Julien's face. But because Sophie was doubled over in laughter and was the most lighthearted he had seen her in weeks, Julien couldn't help but smile.

"We were breaking up so badly," Sophie shrieked, "and sure enough it was smoking that killed him. It wasn't bad enough for him to work as a miner; he had to go and die of smoking."

Julien joined in. "So, she blessed him with ashes from an ashtray! Why, I remember we laughed until we could barely stand. *Mon Dieu,* if *Maman* had seen us."

"I was so afraid I was going to pee my pants," Sophie said as she convulsed into another fit of laughter. "Anyway, my point is," Sophie said, wiping her eyes dry with her croissant-encrusted napkin, "while we were standing in the sacristy, a very large spray of blood-red gladiolas arrived for the funeral. They were quite beautiful, truly memorable, and one of our father's favorite flowers. I had been in charge of arranging the flowers, and you and Thierry were to set them in the sanctuary for the service. And here was an enormous arrangement. *Enormous.* Remember that?" Julien slowly began to nod his head as he reached over and brushed a crumb from his sister's upper lip.

"I pulled the card from the flowers," Sophie said, "and read it out loud. I remember it said, 'In loving memory of you, Papa.' I turned to you, Julien, to say, 'These are really beautiful, and *Maman's* going to be so pleased,' but when I started to throw my arms around your neck, you pushed me back and said, 'Sophie, I didn't send them.' Do you remember that, Julien?"

"*Zut alors!* Unfortunately, I do," grumbled Julien. "And then we turned to Thierry and asked him. He shrugged his shoulders and said he hadn't."

"The three of us stood in that little kitchen staring at the arrangement," Sophie said pensively. "We were dumbfounded . . ."

Sophie still remembered holding the card that had come with the flowers. After no one had admitted sending them, she had looked from those blood-red flowers to the card and back again. Cold sweat had formed on her forehead as she had staggered against the counter. The fragrance from all the flowers was overpowering in the tiny vestibule, and she swooned. Choking out her words, she asked her brothers, "What could this mean? Who are they from?"

Thierry, who stayed away from the fringes of any volatile or emotional issue, shrugged again and took a step backward. He leaned against the wall. Sophie had moved in closer to Julien, willing him to come up with an answer, but Julien stood his ground and remained mute. Just as Sophie was about to get into his face, their mother entered the room.

"And then *Maman* came in and asked who the flowers were

from," Julien recalled. "The three of us stood stark still, too terrified to move or say thing," Julien said, as he threw his arms in the air. "Poof!" he sent up a Gallic puff.

"Finally, you saved the day by grabbing the arrangement and taking them directly into the church. You said to *Maman* in passing, 'They're from Sophie. Aren't they lovely?'"

Sophie continued the story, "Well, *Maman* looked at Thierry and me, took the card from my shaking hands, and read it. I remember my heart was pounding so loudly I was certain she could hear it. She started to cry and reached for me, but luckily we heard the organ music begin to play. Ha! That horrible little crone saved the day! The service was beginning. I quickly raced into the church with the rest of the flowers as Thierry led *Maman* around to the front door to find our seats."

"I haven't thought about that in a long time," Julien said after a moment.

"We never talked about it afterward," Sophie said.

"No, we didn't." Julien sipped his coffee.

Sophie tilted her head to one side and peered at her brother. "So what did you make of it, Julien?"

"I guess I thought it was a mistake." He shrugged. "Some other funeral must have been missing some lovely flowers."

"Really, Julien? You thought it was a mistake?" Sophie said, poking Julien in the side.

"You, who worked as a policeman for over thirty years, didn't think that was odd? And knowing what you knew about our father's infidelities?"

Julien squirmed in his seat and got up to refill his already full cup. He paced back and forth beside the table but didn't sit back down.

"Do you know what I think?" Sophie finally said. Inside she was screaming, but she didn't want Julien to shut down. "I think we have some half brothers or half sisters somewhere,

Julien. That's what I think. Back in Pont-à-Meuse."

Julien spun around to face her and said, "Well, I think . . ."

Just then the telephone rang, and he disappeared into the hallway to take the call. He was gone a few minutes and then stuck his head back into the kitchen to say, "I've got to help a friend with an emergency situation."

"But . . ." Sophie sputtered, rising from the table.

"Sorry, Soph." Julien's coat was already on. "We'll talk later." And he was out the door.

"We'll talk later! We'll talk later! That's the story of my life," Sophie muttered loudly to herself, plopping back down into her seat just as Kate entered the kitchen.

"Good morning," Kate chirped, and she made a beeline for the coffee. "What's the plan for the day?" she asked Sophie as she poured a cup.

"We're going to St. Denis to see whether my father had other children," she said with a flourish.

Kate's eyes bulged as Sophie's comment registered. She blinked and bit into her croissant. She knew the explanation would roll out sooner or later.

It was midafternoon when the two headed down the streets of St. Denis, searching for Sophie's friends' apartment building. Sophie had stopped at a bakery in Nancy to purchase some sweets for their little gabfest. She was looking forward to seeing them.

"I've known them both since I was a teenager in Ste. Barbe." Sophie fluffed. "Although I've known Yvon longer, Ann-Marie was my first boss when I worked in a doll factory. The factory was five kilometers away from home, so I rode my bike to work. And, oh, that's when I realized there were hills surrounding our village." Sophie giggled. "As for Yvon, he was raised in the same village as my father. Plus, they knew both my parents when we lived in Ste. Barbe. They may or may not give insight into my parent's lives, but at least I thought I might start here."

"Mmmm hmmm." Kate sat thinking.

Sophie and Kate climbed out of the car carrying a box of pastries plus a bottle of champagne. They entered the front hallway and rang the bell, and Ann-Marie buzzed them up to the eighth floor. Ann-Marie, who was in her eighties, opened the door and stared at Sophie. She seemed at a loss.

"It's me! Sophie! We've come to see you, Annie. Annie?" The three women stood in the hallway staring at each other.

Suffering from dementia? Kate wondered.

Once the fog lifted and Ann-Marie recognized Sophie, she threw her arms around her and held her tightly. Sophie introduced Kate. Again, the blank stare. Sophie knew Yvon had told Ann-Marie they both were coming, yet Annie was still confused. Despite her condition, she was nicely coiffed and stylishly dressed in a black silk blouse and floral skirt. She was definitely expecting someone. With her very fair skin, blonde hair, and broad facial features, Ann-Marie reminded Kate of the Swedish women in her own family.

"So where's that big hunk of a husband of yours, Annie?" Sophie asked.

"He'll be a bit later, as he's completing some work downtown. Come on in, and I'll put on the coffee." After Annie led Sophie back into the kitchen, Kate wandered into the living room and found a mix of contemporary furnishings. A neoclassic sofa table of chrome and glass swept past a modern lemon-colored Danish sofa.

Kate could hear Sophie chatting animatedly with Annie and then heard both of them giggling like schoolgirls. Kate breathed a sigh of relief. *Ah, the healing effects of gossip.*

Almost as if he had been announced, Yvon bounded through the door with a warm smile. A tall man with broad shoulders, he had dark but slightly graying hair. As if he had run up the stairs, both his face and burgundy shirt were of the same hue. He kissed his wife and grandly swept Sophie up into a bear hug. His energy filled the apartment.

"I apologize for my lateness; I got caught up in some business," he said, his voice booming through the living room.

"Yes, Sophie," Ann-Marie said as she slowly made her way into the living room. "Instead of teaching, he is now St. Denis's vice-mayor. Didn't I tell you?"

Sophie feigned a gasp, "Yvon, you've always been an important man. And now this, too?"

An amused look crossed Yvon face, and he hugged her again. "I can't tell you how happy I am that you've come. Both of you." He looked at Kate and smiled. "This is a blessing to both of us." His countenance darkened, but he immediately switched topics and bounced through the room.

Taking full command as host, he made certain his bride was settled, before he seated Kate and helped Sophie serve coffee. Finally, he sat down in a seat across from Annie and Sophie.

"Before we begin, Sophie, we want to say how sorry we were to hear about your mother's passing," Yvon said kindly.

"Yes, that was rather sudden, wasn't it?" Annie said.

"Yes, it was. Kate, *Maman*, and I were planning a trip together to travel all over France. *Maman* was looking forward to returning to Brittany one last time . . . Yes, it is sad." Sophie paused and sipped her coffee.

"Because of the loss of my mother I have come to reconnect with those of you who knew both my mother and father. You see," she smiled, "I ran across some old journals of *Maman's* in the attic, and it brought back so many . . . *souvenirs du temps passé. . .* memories of times past. So, here I am, wanting to ask some questions, if that would be all right."

Yvon grinned at Sophie and practically leaped across the coffee table. "It's always nice to remember dear old friends. Annie would enjoy talking about that too, wouldn't you, my dear?"

Kate took a sip of coffee. "Ann-Marie, did you also grow up in Ste. Barbe?"

"*Mais oui!*" Annie turned toward Kate. "My father was a teacher in the same village Sophie's grandparents lived, in Pont-à-Meuse. We lived there until my father took a job in Ste. Barbe-Bouligny. And Yvon was also from the village of Pont-à-Meuse and lived there until he went to college. So we both knew your father's family well, Sophie. Yvon knew them even better than I."

Well, that was easy, thought Sophie. *I wonder how far they will take me?*

"Yvon, what can you tell me about my grandfather?" Sophie asked him. "About the family? I remember some things, but I've been gone so long."

At that point, Yvon rushed out of the room only to return with a photo album. He opened the album to a page and handed it to Sophie. He began pointing at photos of Sophie's family—Sophie's mother, her father, uncles, brothers, cousins. Kate got up to take a look.

Leaning over Sophie as she looked through the album, Yvon pointed at one picture in particular. "Here's a picture of my grandfather who was killed in July shortly before the armistice of World War I . . . They never found his body."

"My mother's father may have been killed around that time, too," Sophie said. "Because *Maman* was born on the last day of World War I, she never met her father."

Annie looked at her husband and said, "This is a very sad book. There are many pictures about our families, but so much of this book is about war." She started to close the album, but then an image caught her eye.

"Ah," said Annie, "but here are some pictures showing the young people when they were first drafted into the Army. They were drafted for one to three years of mandatory service. Don't you remember this, Sophie?"

Sophie patted Annie's hand. "I wasn't born yet, Annie."

"Oh, of course you weren't!" Annie laughed. "So, Kate, there was a great tradition for these young men to be honored in a special way." A mischievous spark flitted through her eyes; she smiled broadly.

"The *conscrits,* or draftees, were received at age eighteen and ordered to present themselves at a nearby army depot. Right, Yvon?" He nodded and took his seat.

"They had to go through a medical checkup," she continued. "Privacy was of no concern, so all these young men were lined up and stripped of all their clothes . . . along with some of their pride." She looked up from the book and beamed.

An already blushing Yvon picked up the story. "If it was determined that you were fit to become a soldier, you could return home, and then began the custom for the new recruit to celebrate his *Bon pour l'Armée* (Good for the Army). First, the men were covered in all kinds of blue, white, and red rosettes, stickers, and ribbons."

"But, instead of the stickers saying, *Bon pour l'Armée,*" Annie popped in, "they said, *Bon pour les Filles,* or Good for the Girls." Kate and Sophie laughed.

"Sounds like fun," Kate said.

"Yes," Annie grinned, "the young draftees then went to all of the houses of the village, and since they were considered Good for the Army, they also were considered good for a drink. They drank as many drinks as there were houses in the entire village. When Yvon went through that, he was served a mixed drink that about killed him. It was Ricard Pastis, and instead of pouring water over it, the hosts used eau-de-vie, and he has no recollection of being taken back home in a wheelbarrow. That was how it was in those little villages!"

Yvon smiled sheepishly. "*Oui.* I don't know how I survived. That was over forty years ago . . . Oh la la, now look at my hair!"

He stroked his slightly balding scalp and laughed.

"Say, speaking of drinks, we brought some champagne just for this occasion," Sophie said, jumping up. "Would you care for some?" She was met with enthusiastic nods as the three quickly put down their coffee cups.

While the flutes were being filled, Sophie piped up. "By the way, we went to Ste. Barbe with Julien the other day and had a look around. In fact, we went by the old *lavoir*."

"It still exists?" Annie asked.

"*Oui*, it's still there," Sophie said, nodding. "Yvon, wasn't that the washing-place where your father broke a rib?" They all started laughing wildly.

Once Annie caught her breath again, she said to Kate, "He was at my grandmother's house next door, washing out a cask to make his eau-de-vie. Do you know what eau-de-vie is, Kate?" Kate nodded, but Annie continued on. "It's a special liqueur that our men used to make, and it was like firewater. I guess he decided he needed more water, so he went over to the fountain. He must have been gallivanting around because he fell in. When he got out, he was soaked and pretty embarrassed."

"Yes, too many witnesses," Yvon laughed. "People said for years that he must have been drinking his own eau-de-vie at the time, but he never admitted it. I remember he came home to change clothes, and it was only later in the day when he sneezed that he felt a terrible pain in his side. He had broken a rib and was in excruciating pain. Many joked that he should avoid going near water even for eau-de-vie, but he did suffer a great deal of pain from that accident. I doubt that he complained much, though."

"Are you ready for the cake?" Annie asked as she got up from the settee. As Sophie and Yvon nodded in the affirmative, Annie disappeared into the kitchen with Kate in her wake.

"How is Annie doing?" Sophie whispered to Yvon.

"She has had a rough year with her depression."

"Oh, Yvon, haven't we all." Sophie patted his hand. "I suffer from it too, so I understand. But it seems like there's something more going on with her . . ."

"Oui, oui, I'm afraid her memory is not what it used to be. Happens to us in our eighties, but she struggles with memories of the past even more so now." He paused and blew out a Gallic puff.

"Maybe it is not such a bad thing to leave off some of our memories," Sophie said kindly.

"Now, that's a positive outlook, Sophie. I have to say I was pleased you were nearby and could visit. I knew she would be pleased, too. As you can see, she is enjoying herself immensely. It's been weeks since I last saw her smile." Yvon ran a hand through his thin hair. "So thank you and your friend for coming."

"You needn't thank me," Sophie said. "It's always a pleasure. You both have always been dear to me."

"Et vous, Sophie? How are you handling the loss of your dear *Maman?* That must be very hard on you. She was—well, Sophie, I never knew a more warm and loving soul, your mother."

"Well, thank you . . ."

"Yes, Sophie," said Annie, as she and Kate returned to the living room bearing a *gâteau de Nancy,* a chocolate and Grand Marnier soufflé-type cake. "Your mother was a very good woman, a very resilient woman."

Sophie looked over at Annie and thought, *"Very resilient." That's an interesting choice of words.*

Yvon jumped up and helped Kate with the four cake plates, the forks, and a bowl of *crème anglaise* and placed them on the coffee table as Annie slid onto the settee. Her energy was spent.

"Would you do the honors, Sophie?" Yvon asked. "You have provided us with some luxurious treats."

"Yes, Sophie, we won't have to eat for a week."

"Certainly," Sophie stood and lifted the cake knife. "I didn't realize you both knew my mother—so well. I knew you, Yvon, grew up in the same village as my father, but my mother?"

"Oh, but of course we knew her. Maybe more so after you moved away from Ste. Barbe, but we lived in small communities."

"Actually, now that both my parents have gone, I've been trying to understand them," Sophie blurted out. "I can't believe I've waited until now." She leaned over the *gâteau* and made precise incisions into it and lifted four equal pieces onto the plates that Kate was holding. Kate ladled a spoonful of the *crème anglaise* sauce over each slice and handed the cake around.

"It's not so odd, Sophie," said Yvon, gently. "We usually don't think to ask questions of our parents or challenge them about their pasts. But that doesn't mean we ever stop wondering—wondering if who we are is part of who they were. *C'est normal.*"

"Did either of you ask your parents questions about their pasts?" Sophie asked.

Yvon took a bite of cake and his eyes smiled as he swallowed. "Mmm, this is marvelous! But, heavens, no! What my parents' lives were like before I was born? Well, I guess the only way I found out was from overheard gossip, like the story of my father's broken rib. Anything that might have brought him shame or embarrassment, we never discussed. It was only because he was near Annie's grandmother's home that I was told about it later. Never at home."

"The same for me, Sophie," said Annie. "Because my parents were teachers, they had to live their lives in a very strict fashion. Our lives as children were severely scrutinized by not only our parents but also the entire community. There was not much room for a misstep in a small village."

Sophie sat down and looked at the elderly couple, "Well, Yvon, Annie, can you tell me what you remember about my parents? Please. I know there were problems. Serious problems. And I know of my father's cousin in Pont-à-Meuse . . ."

Startled, Yvon looked at Annie, then back to Sophie. "What

do you know about this cousin, Sophie?" he asked.

Sophie fussed with her cake. "Not enough. I know my mother was terribly upset whenever my father disappeared for days at a time. And he wasn't a drinker. Well, that's what I'm trying to find out."

Alarm crossed Ann-Marie's face. She cast a harsh glance at Yvon and then smiled back at Sophie. Picking up her fork, she began to eat, "Mmm. This *gâteau de Nancy* is quite delicious. I haven't had this in years. Do you have this recipe?" she rattled.

Both Sophie and Kate looked at one another. Clearly the door on this conversation had just slammed shut.

"No, Annie, I don't have the recipe. I bought it at a *pâtisserie* down the road from you." Sophie took her first bite of the bittersweet chocolate cake and almost swooned. "Mmm. This *is* good! I haven't had this since I was a kid."

So close, but nothing significant. Sophie couldn't shake witnessing the terrified look on both Yvon's and Annie's faces when the subject of her father's lover was raised. *Oh, I'm too hard on them. I need to let them be.* As the sun started to lower in the sky, Sophie announced that they needed to get going.

"Let me help you to the car, Sophie," Yvon said gallantly. Gathering together her jacket, purse, and remnants of half the leftover cake they insisted she take, Sophie gave Annie a long hug and promised her she would be back in a few weeks. They headed into the hallway. Once on the elevator, Sophie apologized to Yvon for bringing up her parents and their past.

"No need to apologize, *ma chérie.* You have a right to know about your parents. It seems unfair that *tout le monde* seems to know the truth, yet we children are left in the dark. I guess that is why both Annie and I felt so sorry for your mother. She, too, was left in the dark. But we admired her strength and tenacity to hold your family together."

Sophie followed Kate and Yvon out of the elevator, but she

floated out as if in a daze. "I'm not completely clueless about this, Yvon, but almost. Exactly what are you referring to? I don't know what you know . . . I don't even know anymore what I know!"

Kate looked down at the ground, scurried ahead, and got into the car to allow the two privacy.

"Let me start over," said Yvon, as they stood next to the car. "You see, I remember your father from the years shortly after World War II ended. I was only a kid at the time—maybe nine years old—but I remember how he would swagger down the streets of Pont-à-Meuse, and we used to run and hide. At the time, we made a game of it, but it was because he was always so angry. He would take a swipe at us kids, if he had a mind to."

"Okay, then that means I was probably a toddler at that time and Julien may not have been born yet . . ."

"I suppose so," Yvon said, contemplating the past. "But I remember my folks talking about how the war had changed your father—made him even angrier than before. And that the cousin you mentioned . . ." Yvon turned to look up at the apartment window where he had left his wife. He opened the trunk of Sophie's car and slowly placed her things inside.

"What about this cousin? No one has ever told me, Yvon. We've had to guess at who she was, but . . ." Sophie let her words trail off, hoping Yvon would fill in the blanks.

Yvon cleared his throat, cast another glance toward his apartment, then began. His words came slowly at first but then began to tumble out and pick up speed.

"I have no way of knowing what you know, Sophie, but your father's companion . . ."

"His lover," Sophie inserted.

"*Oui. Probablement!*" He sighed. "Years ago his *partenaire* lived only a few streets away from my parents' in Pont-à-Meuse. I only witnessed seeing him on one or two occasions there, but, it was clear, he was staying with his cousin for days on end. I remember he didn't hide it from anyone . . ." Yvon blushed.

"Yes. As long as he was not in Ste. Barbe—I'll give him that," Sophie bitterly spit out. She wrapped her arms about herself to ward off the chill and to buffer herself from whatever else was coming her way.

"My folks, of course," Yvon continued, "were more aware and were quite concerned . . ."

"Concerned? Concerned about what?" Sophie interrupted. "Wasn't this a long-term affair? Weren't people used to it?" Sophie leaned against the car in order to steady herself. The wind had picked up, and her hair, which kept blowing into her mouth, was sticking to her lipstick. She spit out her hair. She was struggling to focus on what Yvon was saying, but his words wavered in and out of her hearing. Or, did she want to hear? Did she dare to? He was talking about the woman's other children, their misbehavior, how filthy they were, and that their mother, it seemed, had taken little interest in their welfare.

What can this accomplish? Sophie wondered as Yvon told of the gossip his parents had passed on. *Where could this possibly lead? Why have I even asked these questions?* Even though she had tried to deny it to herself, she had always known there was someone Papa had loved more than her mother.

A frenzy of memories flew through her mind: the raucous laughter of an unknown woman followed by the low, guttural laughter of . . . of her father in that wheat field fifty years before. And her parents' arguments. Those horrible battles of words, which invariably ended with her father brutalizing their mother with every form of the word *putain* he could muster. Sophie imagined hearing, once again, the dull slam of the back door of their house as her father took off—for an hour, a day, a week—and her mother's pitiable crying as he left. *Had Maman never known happiness?*

As a child, Sophie would lie upstairs on her bed, her finger tracing the pink quilted squares of her counterpane as she tried to avoid hearing Papa's endless tantrums. His threats to abandon them were one of his most vicious—not just for them, but for their mother. All her mother had ever known was abandonment. Time after time, as her father made his departure known to the entire block, she pondered life without him. She fantasized about a life without stress, without turmoil. But how would they survive? If he left, they would be forced to move out of the *coron*—the squalid shambles of miners' housing she had known as her only home. How would they eat? She knew the shame of not being able to pay for groceries when *Maman* was forced to ask for credit. Papa made it clear that even though his wages were meager, they could certainly do worse.

So this secret desire of having him leave for good always bumped against the real fear of starvation. Held in the panicky grip of past fears, Sophie gulped, then shifted her focus back to Yvon.

"Those children were a real trial for our town," Yvon was saying. "No one knew who their fathers were or where they belonged . . ."

At those words, Sophie clicked back to her early morning conversation with Julien. Where had those funeral flowers come from? Was this where she finally would learn the truth? Was one of them her half brother or half sister?

"What did you say was her last name?" she blurted out.

Yvon paused and noted that Sophie had become frenzied in the few minutes they had been standing by the car. She was breathing heavily, and sweat was evident on her brow.

"Sophie, are you all right? I think this conversation is too much for you right now . . ."

"No, Yvon. Please tell me. This is what I need to know. Please tell me what her last name was."

"Well," he paused in thought, "I believe she used her married name . . . Benoît, if I remember correctly. But no one ever met this so-called husband of hers. She covered her tracks, though, by saying he had died during the war, and then she found herself pregnant . . ."

"How many children did she have?" Sophie interrupted. Visions of visiting a horrid little house with her father when she was small flashed through her mind. And the smell! That horrible smell of too many cats, too many dogs, and too many children made her begin to gag. She stepped away from Yvon and moved toward the front of the car.

He grabbed her arm to steady her, but he was just finishing his sentence. "Beaulieu was one of the names she gave to some of her kids."

Sophie stood back as if he had slapped her. "Beaulieu? Are you certain?"

"*Mais oui*, Sophie. That was one of the many names she used. No one knew who the fathers really were . . . but, well . . ."

"Were any of them called Zabél? Did anyone think they were my father's, Yvon? Was that what Annie didn't want me to learn?"

Yvon didn't answer; he just drew her into a bear hug and held on to her. "I'm sorry, Sophie. We have no proof. We know nothing for certain. Only gossip."

When Sophie finally opened the car door and slipped into her seat, she was totally distraught, absolutely wrung out. Kate kept silent but patted Sophie's knee. Kate had not heard the conversation between them from inside the car, but from what she happened to see through the window, it was clear the sharp attack of truth had taken a bite.

Sophie started the ignition, sent a sweet smile over her shoulder to Yvon, and waved as she backed up and then drove out of the parking lot. Once having driven down the road a few blocks, she pulled over to the shoulder, shoved the car into park, and laid her head on the steering wheel.

"*Mon Dieu*," she wailed, "and sweet Ste. Anne d'Auray," she called out to her mother's favorite saint. The only response was the wind buffering her car, blowing dust in swirls around her vehicle and back across the road. She looked over at Kate, took a deep breath, and said, "I don't know whether to laugh or cry. I wanted to know, but at the same time—I didn't want to know."

Kate slid across the seat and wrapped her arms around her dear friend, "Do you want to talk about it, Sophie?" Kate asked softly.

Sophie took her time to respond, "Yvon finally told me the name of the cousin. I thought I knew who she was all of these years, but now I'm shocked. I remember once going with my father to visit this . . . this cousin of his. I was probably six or seven at the time, but I remember I didn't like going there. The house was filthy. The cloying smell of urine was everywhere, and I remember crying and begging him to take me home. He became so angry with me for asking to leave that he never took me back again. And, the kids!"

"The kids? What do you mean? What kids?"

"There were so many kids—I didn't even talk to them—I didn't know who they belonged to. Even at that age, I knew my father's cousin was not married. And when I was older, there was talk about her always being pregnant. This morning Julien and I were talking about my father's smoker's funeral."

The change in topics was making Kate's head spin. "What does this have to do with your father's cousin?"

"Well, a spray of flowers arrived . . ." Sophie went into the entire description of the floral arrangement and the strange note that was attached.

Kate's hand flew up to her mouth. "Whoa! Did Yvon know who sent these flowers?"

"Yes. No. Well, I didn't ask him. But after what he had to say, I didn't have to. I suddenly knew . . ." She turned the key in the ignition and the car roared to life. As Sophie headed back to

Julien's, silence punctuated the women's conversation. Both were deep in thought.

Finally Sophie said, "I realized that the night I was molested at my grandfather's, my father was down the street with that—that woman—and I didn't tell him because I didn't want to *upset* him. He had such an awful temper."

"Sounds like you feel betrayed on many levels, Sophie," Kate said, softly. "And, your depression is linked to this event at your grandfather's?"

Sophie let the question sink in before answering. "I'm thinking it might be linked to my nightmares and to the hospital bill. Plus, tonight I found out the name of the cousin I had visited as a child was the same one who . . . who must have had a child by my father. Thus, the arrival of the flowers at the funeral!

"This morning I tried to put the pieces together with Julien, but he insisted the flowers had arrived at our funeral by mistake. Can you imagine? I had no way of being certain—until tonight." Sophie let out a deep breath. "And now, I'm certain that one of those terrible little kids who was hanging around that filthy house . . . was . . . is one of my siblings." Pulling into Julien's driveway, she could see Julien standing in the doorway, then walking outside to greet them, a champagne bottle in hand.

"Well, dear friend," Kate said before opening the passenger door, "you have a lot to take in and internalize. If Julien is open to it, perhaps, you two could talk it over tonight. It's his story too."

"Well, Kate," Sophie said, slipping into a different voice as she faced her brother, "you wanted to know about French family life, didn't you?" Sophie quickly blotted her face with a handkerchief, then smiled.

"Sophie, I make no judgments. We all have skeletons in our closets." Kate thought of Lisa. "Unfortunately, those are the very things in life that keep us from moving forward. Tonight you've been given the opportunity to move forward."

"But I should have known . . ." Sophie said as she watched her brother approach the car.

"You couldn't have known," Kate murmured. "Small villages rarely share their dirt with those who raise it. Just like Yvon explained today."

Right then, Julien flung open the driver's door and helped Sophie out of the car. Together the siblings locked arms and moved toward the house. Kate scooped up the leftover cake from the backseat and followed them inside.

CHAPTER TWELVE

$\mathcal{S}$etting the $\mathcal{N}$ightmares $\mathcal{F}$ree

A

SLIGHT BREATH OF A BREEZE whispered past Sophie's face as she turned over in bed. She caught a scent from the air, and without rising up or opening her eyes, she expected the freshness of pine or juniper. Even though it was late fall, she had opened the window a crack before hopping into bed. Once she slid between the sheets, all she could hope for was a good night's sleep—without being haunted by her nightmares.

Instead of smelling juniper, a cloying metallic odor filled her nostrils, and her eyelids popped open with alarm. What was that smell? Almost in answer, the curtain unfurled beside the bed, and she was certain she caught the scent of jasmine—jasmine on a soft, sultry, warm breeze. Much too warm for late October, but perfectly fine for late summer, she surmised, as she slid back into slumber.

A door slammed, and she startled awake. She couldn't make out anything around her; it was pitch dark. *Where was she?* Nothing seemed familiar. She tried to kick herself free from the sheets, but her legs felt like lead. Were they tied down? How could this be? Pushing down with her hands against the sheets, she found them wet. Had she been sweating? It was *so* warm in the room. Panic shot through her as she raised herself up on her elbow. She felt around to turn on the bedside lamp, but none was near. She reached into the dark in search of something familiar—the bedside table, her book, her cellphone—but her hand instead knocked against a cold metal bar. She rolled onto her back and attempted to slide out the other side of the bed. Again, her hand hit upon a metal bar. She recoiled with the pain as it radiated up her arm.

Dazed, she lay there rubbing her hand just as a door eased open into her room—very slightly—almost imperceptibly. The slight opening cast a thin beam of light onto her bed, and she could make out her surroundings. She was lying in a hospital bed, definitely in a hospital room, and it was the same room in which she had been having nightmares for the past forty years. Pushing herself up again, she decided to finally break free of this dream and put it to rest. She shot one leg out from under the sheet, but just as she attempted to fling the top sheet from her body, she found the sheet dark, sticky, and covered—in blood. Blood was everywhere. Pools of blood were forming around her bed and seemed to course from where? What was this?

The gauze curtains at the window billowed inward as the door opened a bit more, revealing a man—a tall, gaunt, yet familiar-looking man. *Like Papa, when I was a girl.* But just as she called out to him, he turned and fled. But he returned with men and more men, all wearing white and all wildly reaching for her—grabbing at her, pulling at her. Pulling her apart. Just as Sophie slipped into unconsciousness, the men transformed into wild dogs—into wolves—and she succumbed to an all-encompassing pain.

Sophie woke sobbing, the sheets damp with sweat. As she lay in bed, trying to calm her racing pulse, the image of the hospital room remained etched in her mind. She closed her eyes and breathed in deeply. Her tears dried along her cheeks. Now, more than ever, she was determined to return to Ste. Barbe and see if she could find anything in the old hospital records. *What happened back there, and who was involved?*

Sophie turned toward the alarm clock. 7:00 AM. She swung her legs out of the bed and decided the time had come. The time was now! She hurriedly pulled on the same clothes she had worn the day before and curtly informed Kate they would be leaving right away.

"I'll explain more in the car," Sophie said, her lips pressed into a thin line, "but get everything ready, as we won't be back for a few days."

Almost before Kate had packed or had one sip of coffee, Sophie was headed out the door.

"We're off to the Alsace, Julien," Sophie announced. "Would you mind helping us with our bags?" Julien gazed at her with a look of disappointment. He said nothing as he lugged their suitcases to the car. Sophie climbed into the driver's seat as Kate settled into her place. As the car stood idling in the driveway, Sophie rolled the window down. "I'll be back through here in a few days. I just need to move down the road right now," she said to her brother, giving him a small smile as she waved good-bye. He stood back and wished them *bon voyage.*

Kate had no idea what had transpired, but she felt the electricity of the moment. Sophie drove out of her brother's village at a fast clip, and instead of heading east toward the Vosges Mountains and the Alsace, she continued north.

"We're going back to Ste. Barbe first—you'll get a chance to see first-hand the point of my downfall," Sophie said, her eyes trained on the road ahead.

"We're returning? I thought the other day was enough for you?" Kate turned to face her friend and noted the determined look on her face. "Sophie, what's going on?"

Sophie sighed. "Oh, Kate, I had another nightmare last night; the most vivid so far." Sophie pounded the steering wheel with her fist. "I'm determined to find out what happened at that hospital years ago." She began to describe her dream to Kate, and even while telling her, her body began to shake.

Kate softly touched her arm. "I'm here with you, Sophie. You won't be alone."

After an hour, Sophie pulled up to the Hôpital de San Gabriel, Ste. Barbe's Hospital. It had been years since she had been there, and she was surprised to see the building had the appearance of a thriving enterprise. Before them, two connected structures stood three-stories tall; one was obviously an older section built with wine-red brick, and the second section was gleaming, in stark contrast, in white brick. Sophie blinked. She didn't recognize the building. In fact, the image in her mind's eye was so different from what stood before her that she sat rooted to the spot, staring ahead. *Is this the same hospital?*

She opened her purse and pulled out the yellowed hospital record she had brought with her. Yes, there in the header of the document was the image of the older section of this hospital. It was a disquieting feeling. Was she relieved they were the same? For a split second, she had almost hoped she had come to the wrong place. She must have muttered something out loud as Kate, seeing her perplexed reaction, asked if this was the only hospital in town.

"Probably," Sophie grumbled.

"Well now, it looks rather cheery," Kate exclaimed. "Look at those flower boxes lining the windows—and even with bunches of brightly colored tulips.

"Obviously plastic," Sophie muttered again. "Tacky, but

typical, since it's almost winter for crying out loud." She got out of the car.

"Do you want me to come with you, or do you want me to stay in the car?" Kate asked. Sophie was beginning to get grumpy and they had barely started their trip. Kate looked up just as Sophie hesitated on the sidewalk; she appeared lost.

"Why don't I come with you," Kate said, stepping out of the car.

"Yes, come with me," was Sophie's reply. "Which is the front door?" she asked. Kate shrugged, her eyebrows rising in surprise. This was beginning to feel like a repeat of yesterday's trip to Annie and Yvon's. She said nothing. Just then, a man came prancing down the steps of the new section.

Sophie stopped him, "Can you tell me where the main hospital offices are? I haven't been here in ages."

A wave of the hand over his shoulder followed by a once-over and a wink to both of them was all the direction they received. Retracing the steps of the prancer, the two found themselves in the center hallway, where they easily found signs directing them to the records department. Sophie turned down the appropriate hallway, but her feet seemed to be steeped in cement. What was she fearful of? What would she find here? Walking along the wide corridor, she failed to hear the soft music, see the sunlight dancing ahead of her, smell the clean scent of fresh flowers, or notice the ethereal French Impressionists' prints that tastefully lined the pastel yellow walls—Renoir, Van Gogh, Cézanne, Monet.

Inside the office of records, the two found themselves in a large room separated by a dark green laminated counter. Order and efficiency permeated the waiting area. Books were perfectly set into side bookcases, magazines were placed alphabetically in racks beside a row of green padded chairs, and the counters were bare of papers, pens, or paraphernalia of any kind. Sophie cleared her throat and stepped forward to the counter.

"Can you tell me how I retrieve records from, say, the 1950s?" Sophie asked of the woman in charge. A heavily made-up woman with carrot-colored hair looked up. She was twice the weight of Sophie but was possibly the same age. Sophie tried to decide if this was someone she knew or should know. The woman wore no nametag, and nothing popped into Sophie's memory. Here the illusion of order disappeared, as papers were strewn wildly over the surface of the woman's desk and her look was equally frenzied.

"Don't you have an exact date?" she demanded of Sophie.

Sophie pulled out the document she had wadded into her purse. "Looks like September 24, 1959. Would you have records from back then?"

"Oh, madame," the clerk replied with a slight sniff, "that is too far back. We have no records for that time frame." Her overly made-up eyelids dropped as if the subject was closed.

"Are you certain?" Sophie asked again. "Is it possible that the records are in storage, or in some microfiche system?"

"No, madame, I have nothing."

"Absolutely nothing? How can that be?" Sophie asked again, her voice becoming shrill.

"Because, madame, like I said, we have no records for anything before 1980."

"I don't understand. This hospital is the same hospital I came to as a kid," Sophie exclaimed. The woman ignored her and would not deign her a response.

"Records, due to new technology, can easily be accessed from anywhere in the world," Sophie piped, clearly exasperated with the woman. She turned to Kate.

"Why not here?" she asked Kate in English. "Unless, of course, people are too lazy to input the information. I should have expected as much. There is nothing about this miserable little town . . ." Sophie wailed. Tears had begun to slide down her face, and her ability to hold them back seemed fruitless. "This is solid proof of their idiocy," she spit out, throwing her hands into the air. Her face was reddening in a most uncharacteristic manner, and she turned from the counter.

Kate moved closer to Sophie and put her hands on her shoulders, gently turning her around. She could see Sophie was getting nowhere fast with this woman.

"We really don't understand," Kate said more calmly to the clerk. "Why, exactly, can't we get records before 1980?"

The clerk's carrot-topped head rose slightly, and a look of smugness graced her face and layer of chins. With a tight-lipped smirk and a toss of her head, she responded. "You're most correct, *mesdames.* You do *not* understand. In 1979, we had a massive fire, which destroyed parts of the hospital. If you kept up with Ste. Barbe news, you would know this included all of the records you've requested." She glared at Sophie while wildly tapping her fountain pen. Then she added in a clipped voice, "I'm surprised you do not remember."

"All of the records? All? *Mon Dieu,* that's awful," said Sophie, her knees almost buckling. "I'm sorry, but I've not lived in France for some years now. I didn't realize."

"Obviously! I can see that," came the curt reply. Case closed.

Sophie's body sagged as she took in the loss, but suddenly she straightened up. She couldn't give up; this was too important. She had come all this way. She gripped the edge of the counter and asked, "Could I possibly go into the older section of the hospital? This was where my father passed away," she lied. She couldn't think of any other reason to give, so lie she did. Sophie held her breath.

"You'll need a pass, madame." The clerk reached into her drawer and rummaged around with her pudgy fingers. She pulled out a bright blue pad of paper and tore off a sheet. Sophie started to panic that she would have to reveal who she was, but the woman said primly that Sophie was to be certain to return this form when she completed her tour.

Sophie took the blue hall pass, and together, Kate and Sophie started to retreat from the office. Sophie turned and received a nod of the woman's head and nothing more other than a stern admonition not to bother the patients. Promising as much, she spun around, and the two headed down the hall. They walked quietly from the sunlit hallways filled with paintings and music, then turned the corner. The walls in the older section were gunmetal grey with cracked, drab red linoleum floors. Evidence of pictures marked the walls, but only the silhouettes of pictures remained. No soft music followed them to this section of the hospital; only the sound of their own hesitant footsteps echoed as they walked. Just beyond this juncture, Sophie stopped short. She took in a quick gulp of air, then had trouble releasing it. Simply moving from the new section to the old had taken her by surprise. She hadn't paid attention before, but the scents and odors to the older section were decidedly more pungent—sharp with alcohol and pine-scented cleaners. She almost gagged, for within the antiseptic mix, she could detect the cloyingly sweet smell of jasmine. Her nightmare roared back into her mind and hooked into her core. Swaying on her feet, Kate quickly grabbed her arm and steered her to a set of metal folding chairs. They sat down.

"What's going on, Sophie?" Kate asked. "I'm here. Tell me what you're feeling."

While holding Sophie's trembling hand and awaiting her answer, Kate, too, looked around the hallway. The cold, austere corridor felt familiar to her as well. Almost on a whisper of a memory, she recalled that she, too, had been in a Catholic hospital during her youth. Same grey walls; same red linoleum floors. She remembered pictures of Jesus dying on the cross and statues of Saint Mary. Sad—all so sad. Tears sprang unexpectedly from her eyes as the memory unfolded. She was holding her father's hand as he led her, with her older sister Melody, through a hallway similar to this. He had just told them that their mother was struggling to give birth to their fifth sibling. It wasn't going well. "She might not make it," he had said. Scuffling along the floor, she stared down at her Buster Brown shoes as she was led along the red squares of linoleum to their mother's hospital room. "She may not be able to come home," he told them again softly. He had brought them to say goodbye. Kate turned seven that day.

"Kate, are *you* all right?" she heard Sophie ask. Kate shook her head to bring herself into the present. It had turned out well in the end. Her mother had survived the stillborn birth. But Kate was marked from that moment on. The Catholic nuns and nurses at the hospital had insisted on saving a dead fetus instead of her mother. She would never forget or forgive them for jeopardizing her mother's life. Ever-wary of Catholic hospitals, she vowed never to be brought to one. Why, she had even broken off her long-term engagement because her fiancé was Catholic; she couldn't take the risk.

Kate looked around once again to establish her bearings. "Sorry, sorry! This place just brought back some surprising memories." Kate shook her head and squeezed Sophie's hand again. "How about you? It must have done exactly the same. Please, tell me."

"Oh, I just remember," Sophie stammered, "that these are the hallways of my childhood."

"Are you certain you want to continue?" Kate asked. She had obviously become a little spooked herself, and although she was supposed to be the strong one, she felt queasy.

Sophie felt her own forehead. It was damp. Yes, she felt a momentary desire to flee, but then she stopped herself. The memory of her horrific nightmare had receded, and other than the strange aroma of jasmine mixed with cleaning solvents, she felt compelled to go on. "I'm here, and I need some answers." she whispered. Easing up from the metal folding chairs, they moved more quietly down the hallway.

A door was propped open to one room, and Sophie peered in

to see if she could remember anything from her past. She swallowed hard. There, between herself and the bed, was a white gauze curtain —ethereal in composition—too sheer for privacy, but, oh, so familiar. Sophie's legs began to shake. She reached back to grab Kate but caught hold of the doorjamb by mistake. Her movement pitched the door open, slamming it to the wall with a bang.

The head of an elderly man poked around the corner closest to the door. His hair was grey and greasy from lack of care; his weathered face was wrinkled from not only age, but also poverty. Only one tooth was visible in his mouth, and he gummed the words he spat in the women's direction. "Whatcha two want, little missies?"

When his gnarled hand stretched out to wave his cane at them, Sophie noticed his arms were covered in thick dark hair. Visions of her nightmare once again rose up.

"Whatcha want?" he repeated. "We don't need any visitors. Can't you read?"

Startled, Sophie looked back at the door and saw no signs indicating whether visitors were welcome or not, but there in a slot on the door was the name of the patient: A. Zabélle. Her father's surname; her own maiden name. A look of panic swept her face.

"You want for me to call the nursing staff? You lost or something?" the old man snarled again. He started to hoist himself up on his cane to stand.

Without taking time to apologize or respond, Sophie fled, dragging Kate along with her. Not only was her nightmare propelling her forward, but flashbacks of that slimy green bastard of a great uncle forced her to flee from the room and down the hallway. Quickly, they hightailed it out of the hospital and back to Sophie's car. As Sophie frantically pawed through her purse to retrieve her keys, she saw the bright blue hall pass tucked into the side pocket. Pulling it out of her purse, she crumpled it and threw it on the ground as if it bore the mark of the devil. She jumped into the car with Kate scrambling in to follow suit. Without any hesitation, Sophie squealed out of the parking lot and headed down the street.

"Did you figure out your nightmare back there?" Kate asked.

"I did; it was the same place." Sophie was hyper-focused on the road ahead of her.

"Where to now?" Kate asked, quickly buckling her seatbelt and holding on to the armrest as they went screeching around another corner.

Sophie took a moment to catch her breath before she replied. "This may surprise you, Kate, as I can't wait to get out of town." Sophie gave a wry smile. "But, unfortunately, I have to make just one more stop: the hall of records. I've come for answers, and now that I know the place of my nightmare, I need to check on *Maman's*, Gérard's, and Papa's records."

"At least you're not coming away with diddly squat," Kate said, succinctly.

Sophie grinned. Then, she began to laugh. The nervous energy that had sent her racing out of the parking lot began to ease, and her shoulders, which had been knotted up, relaxed back into place.

"Wow, Sophie! That was freakier than I thought it would be," Kate shrilled before she joined Sophie in laughter. "Part present; part past—I didn't see that coming."

"Me either," Sophie confessed. Both women had been so internally focused on their own demons that they were finding it difficult to come up for air. Laughter was a great salve.

Making her way back through the side streets to the old *mairie*, Sophie pulled into a parking place in front of the hall of records. Again, Kate was asked to tag along, and the two headed down the corridor to a small room at the end of the hall. In years past, Sophie had made a number of trips down this hallway.

"This place hasn't changed one bit," Sophie gasped. The

eighteenth-century building still exuded the same sights and smells as it had throughout Sophie's life, as well as throughout her parents' and grandparents' lives. Kate looked around her. Dark stained and hand-smudged wooden wainscoting lined the walls, and the once-white walls and ceilings were yellowed with eons of tobacco smoke. Even the ceiling lights appeared fogged with dust and grime, and no windows gave light or fresh air to alleviate the stagnant smell of years of little cleaning. A rank stench reached their noses, forcing them both to cup their hands over their mouths until they grew used to it.

"The last time I came here was to get a marriage license to marry Pierre Fradin, Gérard's closest friend. Oh, that was a miserable mistake—for both of us," whispered Sophie as she stood in line to speak to a clerk, the keeper of all family records.

"All births, deaths, name changes, address changes, and any recordings of a resident's life are recorded in this one place, although, thankfully, not my current marriage. That took place in Reno, Nevada." She flashed a cheeky grin. Sophie and Kate moved to the front of the line.

"Can I help you with anything, madame?" This time the woman in charge was soft-spoken, nicely dressed, and coiffed with the same candy apple hair tint as Sophie's sister-in-law but was half Sophie and Kate's age. She smiled kindly at them. Unlike the clerk at the hospital, her desk was immaculate and a real contrast to the rest of the *mairie* from what Sophie and Kate had observed.

"Yes, you may. Thank you so much. I am here to see my family's records. My last name was Zabél. Let me spell that for you; it has only one *l*, not two."

The woman disappeared behind a large computer screen and then popped up to say, "Ah, I see it *is* different from the other Zabélle. How is that? Are you related?" she asked.

"A mistake—one that happened right in this office back in the nineteenth century," Sophie answered, leaning closer to the clerk.

"It's rather a funny story, but evidently when my grandparents came in to get a marriage certificate, the clerk recorded the name in such a way that no one could determine the correct spelling. Odd, isn't it? I doubt that anyone, after a time, thought too much about it," Sophie rattled on, "but it did make for a good family joke." Sophie laughed, a trifle loud. "You see, there are no bad feelings."

The clerk smiled kindly. "At least we can rely on computers these days." Sophie turned to Kate, and they exchanged amused smiles.

"So, you want to see your own records?" the clerk inquired. "Or your father's entire records, which include your immediate family?"

"The latter. My parents have both passed away, but I also want to check on a few other details."

Sophie and Kate waited for some time before the young woman returned. When she did, she escorted the two back into a private room, where Sophie was able to take time to peruse the large hardbound, handwritten ledger.

"Hmm. Not exactly a computerized register after all," Kate noted, as she sat nearby on a small flower-printed chair.

"At least I'll be able to see the real handwriting of my ancestors," Sophie said, as she sank down at a miniscule desk. With trepidation, she opened the ledger and stared at the almost-indecipherable writing. Some ancient Loraine Franconian; some German; the rest French.

"So what is it exactly that you want to check out, Sophie?" Kate asked her.

"What can I possibly find here?" Sophie echoed the question. "My goal is to search first for any of *Maman's* records. But, if nothing comes up, I'm wondering if there is any extraneous family information that I might need."

"Like what? Do you think you can find out anything about your . . . your father's other child or children?"

"Ooh, la la! Now, that's a thought. But, I also want to check out Gérard's records. I want to see if our father actually adopted him like he promised. This was always a bone of contention in the family."

The comment took Kate by surprise. "Why? Do you suspect your father would lie? Do you think it matters to your family now?" Kate asked quietly, not lifting her head. Her thoughts drifted to her own daughter's recent search for identity.

"Why now? I am having my nephew, Christian, track down Gérard's real father, so it would help if I had his legal name. And it would be important to Gérard's children and their children." Sitting in that small room, her family's history in her hands, Sophie's thoughts slipped back in time.

<hr>

"You have an official letter here," *Maman* called out to Gérard in the backyard. "It's from the Navy!"

Sophie had watched through the back window as her brother rushed to the house, clattered up the steps, then bounded into the kitchen. He grabbed up their mother in a big hug and kissed her neck while tickling her until she let loose of the letter. It floated gently down toward the floor. Sophie leaned down to pick it up, but Gérard scooped it out of the air and danced around the kitchen table, laughing and singing.

"It's here! It's here! I'm finally free!" he hooted into the air.

"Shhhhh! Your father is sleeping," *Maman* whispered with caution. "Please, don't wake him. He needs his sleep." But it was too late. They stood stark still as they heard their father bellow from the floor above them.

"What the hell's all the commotion about? Don't you idiots know I'm sleeping up here?" The upstairs steps creaked with the weight of his downward movement. He was coming down to the kitchen. Sophie looked at her mother in panic and turned to run into the living room. Suddenly, her father appeared. Like a gangly vulture, he stood in the doorway, his ragtag robe hanging loosely across his scarecrow-like shoulders. Always the one to rain on the family's joy, he waited for their reply. When they were too frightened to respond, he grunted, "Open her up, boy. Let's see when you are finally leaving us. It won't be soon enough to my liking. It's your turn to face war."

The two had rarely spoken over the past few years. Following the day of their father's rage, there was nothing more to be said that hadn't already been worn as thin as a miner's glove. More time in each other's presence brought neither comfort. It was so sad. Sophie looked up at her older brother.

Gérard roughly tore open the envelope and began reading. A look of joy was replaced with one of horror; his body sagged as he grabbed the back of the kitchen chair. He dragged it from underneath the table as the dissonant sound of the chair scraped across the rough floorboards. Sophie covered her ears just before he slumped onto the seat.

"What is it, *mon chéri?*" *Maman* hovered over Gérard. She took the letter from his limp fingers and began to read. Her brown eyes grew wide as her eyebrows disappeared beneath her dark feathery bangs. A fury, of which they had no previous knowledge, lurked deep within her. Her rage burst forth as she turned toward Jules. Sophie cowered in the corner, for the shadow of her mother's ire moved into place between them.

"You lying, cheating hypocrite," she screamed at him. She lurched toward him with her fists raised. He caught both hands in midair, squeezed them tightly, spun her about, and sent her sprawling to the kitchen floor. His foot swung out and kicked her as he turned to close the back door.

"No sense in alerting the neighbors to your hysterics," he hissed. "So, what's this nonsense?" he said as he turned on the three of them.

Maman pulled her legs up to her chest and wrapped her arms around them. Her head fell to her knees and she sobbed uncontrollably, while Gérard's dazed expression gave Jules and Sophie no clue. Their father grabbed the letter and read aloud:

We hereby inform you that no official record in the name of Gérard Zabél is known to exist. Please submit a notarized copy of your official birth records to the Marine Nationale at your earliest convenience. Your enlistment application will be held until further action has been completed.

Papa's jaw dropped. In a split second, the expression on his hatchet face transformed from arrogance to panic, then back again. Sophie had never seen him look so surprised. He stared from Maman to Gérard and back to her again. Fear raced through his eyes. Like a rabbit ensnared in a trap, he searched for an easy exit.

"What's this about?" he stammered. "What do they mean there is no Gérard Zabél in existence? What? Are they crazy? That damn government can't get anything right! That's it! They've got this all wrong! See, they probably spelled the last name wrong. That's so like them."

Maman looked up at my father, who towered above her. She slowly pulled herself to her feet and in carefully enunciated words asked, "Did—you—follow—through—on—the—adoption? Did you actually file the paperwork when we first moved here? You promised me! You promised me that if I agreed to move to Ste. Barbe, you would adopt both my sons. Is this one more time you've made promises you failed to keep?"

"I did. I did," he stammered. "Don't blame me for the government's incompetence," he bellowed. "You can't put this on me. I won't hear of it. Who do you think you are, *putain*? They are your bastard sons. Who do you think you're talking to? When I brought you to Ste. Barbe, I went directly to the offices and filled out the adoption forms. Don't tell me that I didn't!" His voice seethed with venom, but she stood tall.

"Did you receive confirmation documents from them? I asked you many times over the past fifteen years. You promised that you had taken care of this issue. Do you have the papers? Where is your proof?"

"I won't stand for this," he said, raising his hand above her. He looked at Gérard, who rose from his seat and moved toward him. "This is not my fault," their father said as he stormed back up to his room, changed his clothes, and in minutes fled out the door and into his car. He remained absent for weeks.

❦

Sophie needed to know the truth. She breathed in deeply. "I wonder if there is a record that shows the legitimacy of his adoption," she said out loud. "Papa swore up and down—oh, how he swore—that it was the government's ineptness." She came to the pages that addressed the children born to Jules Zabél, and she found her name along with Julien's. But there were no other names listed: not Thierry's, not Gérard's, and no other births listed.

"Gérard must have enlisted in the Navy under *Maman*'s maiden name, Pourrette," Sophie said. "As far as I know, he never used the Zabél name after that. *Why did I assume my father had made these records right? That was his promise.* Sophie paused and turned the ledger sheet. Her head dropped closer to the page as she pored over the handwritten records. Kate watched her as Sophie's eyes scanned back and forth, line by line.

"Nope!" she said suddenly as she sat back up. "At no time do these records indicate that my father applied for or received papers for adoption—for anyone." Sophie shoved her chair back from the small desk. "Oh, how I remember crying and crying when Gérard left for the service. I remember thinking our family would never be the same again—ever!"

A knot formed in her throat, and suddenly Sophie began to cry. She sat back down and put her head on the pages and whimpered, "Papa was so intolerant—so evil—how did we survive him at all?" As her body silently shook, Kate desperately wanted to wrap her arms around her, but instead, she reached into her bag and pulled out a clean handkerchief and slipped it into her hand. She needed to allow Sophie her grief.

Kate, too, sat for a long while with her own thoughts. At one point, she reached out to console Sophie, but again she withdrew her hand. Her own thoughts turned again to Lisa. Had she lied to her daughter? Had she kept the truth from her once they came together? No, she felt she had been pretty honest, but honesty is a tricky thing. Sometimes too much is not always positive, and too little? Tricky as well. She wondered if this scene—the one of her distraught friend—had been played out by Lisa. Had her own daughter experienced anguish because of Kate's decisions?

Kate thought back over the past few months when she had finally forced herself to make contact with Dave, Lisa's biological father. It wasn't all that difficult. Just like Lisa searching for her, Kate had gone to the Internet, and within minutes she was carrying on a short conversation with Dave's father, who, thirty-four years before, had given her his son's phone number so she could tell Dave she was pregnant.

Kate was able to reach his home, where she spoke with his wife. No, Dave was out of town, but she would relay Kate's message. Leaving her maiden name and home phone number, Kate wondered if he would be brave enough to return her call.

A day later she found herself revealing to him that he was the father of their thirty-four-year-old daughter. Daughter! Those words rang in her ears even now. She had never called him after she had given birth. His earlier lack of interest had given her all the information she needed. She told him Lisa's birth date, told him that she had given her up for adoption and that recently their daughter had come back into her life. No, Lisa didn't want anything from either of them. She was a good and sweet girl. A beautiful girl—looked much like his side of the family. It was just that Lisa was curious about her roots and, perhaps, some medical information. Nothing more, she had said.

So Kate had been surprised at his gracious response—oh, he had finally grown up—and after they spoke, he made contact with Lisa by both phone and through letters. Kate gulped. Did he want Lisa in his life? But, Lisa had not pursued a relationship. Had Lisa denied him his rights? Had Kate denied him his rights? She slapped her lap. *Hell, no!* He knew all those years ago where he could reach Kate, but he had never tried. She couldn't mine that crater of impossible dreams. Kate sneezed, looked over at Sophie, but left her alone. She slipped back into the wallow of her own thoughts. Just then, the clerk popped her head into the small room and, seeing Sophie distraught, asked if she would like some water. Sophie sat up, smiled shyly, wiped her eyes, and nodded her head.

"How about you, Kate?" Sophie asked. "Do you want some water too?" Kate shook her head no but stayed quiet.

After the water had been delivered, Sophie did a cursory check of her mother's records and found only her mother's marriage record. "There's no indication of *Maman's* record of birth. That would be back in Vannes, so we can check that out when we meet up with Mimi in Brittany."

Sophie then pulled open her own record, where she found a copy of her birth certificate, a copy of a marriage certificate, and an annulment of marriage to Pierre. Then, in small print—barely discernible—she noticed a date listed: September 24, 1959.

"Kate," Sophie said, "there's a date here . . ." She pulled the paper back out of her purse once again—it was getting even more crinkled from use.

"What's the date?" Kate asked, getting up from the sofa and coming closer.

Sophie checked the date on the paper. Yes, it was exactly the same date. She felt a chill start at her fingertips and travel through her body.

"This record indicates that I had," Sophie stopped suddenly and blanched.

"Sophie, what is it?" Kate asked, seeing her friend's face. "What is it? What does this say?"

Sophie swallowed and in a ragged whisper said, "A stillborn birth. A stillborn birth? How could this be? How is it possible?" She looked from the record to Kate and back to the page before her. Kate bent down to look over the documents, but she couldn't decipher the French.

"Damn, Sophie. I'm of no help!" Kate swore. "I can't tell you if that's right or wrong."

Sophie's head was swimming; she could barely think.

"How could this be?" she repeated, louder this time. "I was told I could never have children!" Her voice shook. She wanted to scream. She slammed the ledger shut and staggered from her chair and back out to the clerk's desk. Kate followed. The clerk was nowhere to be seen. Without signing out, Sophie ran through the heavy doors of the *mairie* and back to her car with Kate once again racing to keep up. Sophie started to get into the driver's seat, but Kate opened the passenger door and suggested she ride. Without any hesitation, Sophie crawled in and crumpled on the front seat.

Kate climbed into the driver's seat, turned on the ignition, and rolled out of the parking lot. She began driving through Ste. Barbe as if she knew where she was going, but of course she didn't. Befuddled and with no discernible direction coming from Sophie, she finally pulled into the parking lot of a small highway café. She turned off the car and swiveled her body toward Sophie.

"Sophie," Kate leaned over and put a hand on her shoulder.

Sophie, who had been silent up to this point, sat stunned and appeared lifeless; she had no words. She grunted.

"Okay then," Kate began, switching into therapist mode, "let me see if I can help you. What memories immediately came up for you when you read that word, *stillborn?*"

Sophie pushed the button on the passenger seat and reclined the seat back. Holding her right arm over her eyes, the quiver of her lip and a steady stream of tears leaking down her cheeks were all the responses Kate received.

Finally, Sophie stammered, "How could I *not* know? How could I *not* remember something so important in my life?"

"Sophie, you do remember," Kate said. "Certainly your body remembers because that is where your truth lies."

"I don't understand. And, I keep mixing up my memories with my nightmares. I can't think . . ."

Kate reclined the driver's seat so she was in line with Sophie. "Maybe, Sophie, it's because they are one in the same," she said softly.

Sophie didn't move; she didn't breathe. Kate once again reached into her purse and pulled out a fresh packet of tissues. She set it on the console between them.

"How can this be?" Sophie murmured again from under the protection of her arm. "How could I have no memory of this happening?"

"Sophie, that's the mystery and beauty of the human body and mind. Women who have experienced sexual violence as children or even as young adults block the memories until their bodies are ready to handle their truth."

"Do you think that's what happened? Do you think this is related to my great-uncle?"

"That is something only you will know in time. No one at any age can fathom violence being perpetrated on themselves, whether as a child or young adult. Because the mind can't comprehend it, it closes that memory off until the person is ready, healthy, or mentally able to handle it. It requires time and a safe environment to allow memories to be unlocked. Then, slowly, as the individual becomes stronger, the memories began to eke out. That might explain your nightmares, Sophie! Each night, your body is urging you to push through the gauze of your memories to discover your truth. After what you told me about your dream last night and seeing your reaction this morning in the hospital, I would say it was inevitable that this memory would surface. You are almost there. And it culminates in your discovery about the stillborn birth." Kate paused but received no response.

"So," Kate continued, sliding closer to Sophie and alternately keeping one hand on her shoulder, her arm, or her hand, "let's backtrack a bit to the first thing you said when you discovered the word *stillborn*."

Sophie thought for a moment but did not uncover her eyes. "I guess I said, 'How can that be? I was told I couldn't have children.'"

"That's right. That's what I heard you say as you ran out of the *mairie*. And who told you that you could never have children?"

Again there was a long pause, as Sophie sorted back through time. "When I was married to Pierre. I remember the doctor told me . . ." she paused again, "that I could never have a baby. I didn't understand what he meant, but he said I had been 'internally damaged,' and I could never carry a baby to term. The news was shocking to me, as I had always wanted a baby. Not necessarily marriage, but a baby. Did I tell you *Maman* pressured me to marry Pierre because she was fearful I would become pregnant and have an out-of-wedlock baby? Ironic, isn't it," Sophie spit out. "I couldn't even *have* a baby. I remember the doctor being . . . impolite about it—rude, actually," she said. "His reaction was disdainful. Here I was hearing the most devastating news, and he seemed angry with me. 'Damaged,' he kept saying . . . 'Damaged.'"

"Do you think, Sophie—no, no, that's not possible," Kate said. "That's not possible."

"What?" Sophie sat up and turned toward Kate. "What isn't possible?"

"I'm just wondering if . . . if you experienced a botched abortion, but one that was officially listed as a stillborn on the records."

"Oh, *mon Dieu*, abortion was never an option. We're still a Catholic country and . . . no, no, that would not have been acceptable in a Catholic hospital now or back then."

"But," Kate said, gently, "that might explain the doctor's reaction to you. If he thought an abortion had been performed—and badly, I might add—then, perhaps, he was expressing his own moral feelings about it. Not professional ones, by the way . . ." Kate paused and watched as Sophie slid back down in her seat.

"Could this be a possibility, Sophie?" Kate prodded gently. "Could you be emotionally blocking an abortion?"

"I don't know how, Kate. How did I get pregnant in the first place?" The voice Kate was hearing was the voice of the frightened girl Sophie must have been at that time. "I had never had sex back then—why, it was several years later I finally allowed Pierre to have me—just before we were married! Pooh! I never liked it much, but he insisted."

"So, the date you have on that hospital record. How old were you in . . ."

Sophie pulled the yellowed document back out of her purse once again. "September 24, 1959." She counted on her fingers and calculated her age. "I was barely fifteen! I had just turned fifteen earlier that month. Why?"

"How old were you when you were molested by your great-uncle? What year did that take place?"

Again, Sophie put her head down and tried to think. "I know it was in early summer . . . I remember waiting outside on the front step for Papa until late that night. Even though I wasn't allowed to tell him what had happened, I remember sitting in my shorts and being upset that I had school, tenth grade, the next day. That would have been the same year. *Mon dieu!* Do you think that old bat actually impregnated me?" she shrilled.

"Is there anyone else who could have?" Kate asked.

Sophie slid down even further, pulling her coat up over her legs as, once again, a figure, unbidden, loomed large from her nightmares. The man, who looked so much like her father, paused at the open hospital room door to look in on her. Fears of incest had ruminated through Sophie's mind before, but she had always pushed them aside. She never figured she could have blocked a memory such as that. But now? When she hadn't remembered having a stillborn child, or an abortion? Again, she started to push the thoughts aside.

As if reading her mind, Kate leaned closer to Sophie, took her hand, which was tightly gripping a used tissue, and spoke softly. "You told me this morning about the man standing in the doorway of your nightmare. You described him as being . . ."

"Just like my father, when I was a teen," Sophie blurted out. "Yes, I've been fearful for years that Papa had molested me, but truly, I don't think . . . well, I just don't know anything now." Sophie's hands flew up to hide her face, her breathing became rapid, and she began to heave with sobs.

"Sophie, I apologize for bringing this up, but, truly, you are so close to finding out the truth. Let's go back to your dream," Kate said, pulling Sophie's hands away from her face. "Here's another tissue. Now, let's try to remember your exact feelings in the dream when you see this man in the doorway. Were you frightened of him? Or were you relieved to see him and so called out to him?"

Sophie once again blew her nose, wiped her eyes, and adjusted the seat back into an upright position. Several men walked past their car and peered in before entering the café. The looks they cast in their direction ranged from amused to concerned, but none stopped to give aid. Kate just nodded and smiled.

Finally, Sophie stammered, "Relieved. I remember calling out to him to help me, but then he disappeared and brought back . . . That's where it becomes frightening for me. All those hands reaching for me . . ."

"Good. That's a good clue, Sophie. I would imagine you are remembering a concerned father—your father—seeking help for you and bringing help in the form of doctors. Maybe overly aggressive doctors, but doctors all the same. If he had been your molester or rapist, you would not have called out to him. I don't know for certain, Sophie, but it sounds like he was there for you and, if he found you hemorrhaging, he must have been very, very concerned."

Sophie pulled a clean tissue from the packet and threw her used ones in the back seat. She dabbed her face as her breathing became regular again. "Do you think so, Kate? Do you think that's what happened?"

Kate adjusted herself back behind the wheel of the car and said, "It's a theory right now, Sophie, but it's also plausible. If you were raped in early summer by your great-uncle, then in September, time-wise, that might have been when you either began to notice not feeling well or possibly began hemorrhaging—thus, your trip to the hospital." Kate paused. "But what puzzles me is, if your father was never told about your great-uncle's rape, who do you imagine your father thought was the father of your child? Did you have a boyfriend back then?"

Sophie slapped her forehead and turned to face Kate. "Christophe! Papa hated Christophe! I remember him raging at me to never see him again. He must have thought he was the culprit—but, no, no," she laughed tenderly, "he was just a sweet boy. *Oui,* such a sweet boy." Sophie wiped her eyes with the back of her hand and climbed out of the car. She walked to the driver's side of the car and opened the door for Kate to step out.

"My turn," she said simply as she slid into the driver's seat.

$\mathcal{T}$he $\mathcal{S}$ilent $\mathcal{W}$ar

$\stackrel{\cdot}{\mathbb{A}}$

ITHIN MOMENTS, the two women were heading down the highway. Sophie, surprisingly, seemed to be in good stead. Kate kept an eye on her, though, as Sophie's recovery seemed too easily resolved. Nevertheless, Sophie's spirits were up and she had regained a heightened level of energy.

"So, I notice the signs we are passing say that Paris is two hundred kilometers away. Aren't we headed in the wrong direction for the Alsace?" Kate asked.

"Are we?" Sophie joked, tossing her hands in the air. She gave Kate an apologetic look. "Sorry, I've changed our plans. I hope you don't mind. I realized when I was searching through Maman's records that I've been avoiding the very search we vowed to take on: to find *Maman's* father. We're headed to Paris."

Kate thought over Sophie's response. "Are you feeling strong enough to do that right now?"

"Not to worry, Kate. I have my own prescription, which is to give myself time. Take more antidepressants, *mais oui,* but also give myself time. Traveling to the Alsace would be wonderful, but I would be avoiding the inevitable. Please, don't be concerned. I'm going to focus on *Maman* and our trip," she murmured. She thought back to her mother's dying words—Search for me. Search for Pourrette—and resolutely gripped the steering wheel.

"This was something *Maman* believed in and wanted to be a part of. I got a little sidetracked the last few days, but refocusing on my mother will help me stay away from my . . . my grief."

"Sounds like a good plan, Sophie," Kate soothed.

Storm clouds loomed ahead, but the sun kept pace by breaking through and promising respite from rain. *Maybe the weather will hold*, Sophie was thinking. A pain hit her stomach, and she casually moved her hand from the wheel to massage it away. *The truth is, I'm not certain whether I want to go forward or to stand still. While searching for answers surrounding my father, I was brought up short. So what might I find with Maman's life? Her life was such a paradox—filled with so much mystery. I thought I knew who she was.* A whimper slipped from her lips. *And now I'm slowly losing that part of her that I knew.*

Sophie realized Kate was talking to her, although she had missed the connective thread to the conversation. She changed the subject. "Say, my cousin Madeleine asked that we stop at her apartment when we come through Paris. She wants us to pick up some old letters and a journal, which had been left for *Maman* years ago."

"Journals? She has journals, too?" Kate asked, as she shifted higher in her seat. "Sounds interesting." She rubbed her hands together enthusiastically. "By the way, any chance of a restroom in the near future?"

"We're just pulling into Verdun. You're in luck," Sophie said as she wheeled into the city parking lot. Sophie got out in search of a restroom but realized most attendants were at lunch. After a madcap dash through several blocks, they located a restroom behind the very parking garage in which they had parked.

"I can't believe they've made this so difficult," Sophie wheezed with indignation.

"I'm just glad we found one in time," Kate laughed. "Keep your fingers crossed that I don't need instruction." Instructions were often needed at every stop, or necessary coinage was required, but this one presented Kate with a dingy hole-in-the-floor accommodation. Grateful for anything at all, she shrugged and made the most of it.

As she made her way out of the chilly restroom, Kate said, "I've heard of Verdun somewhere before, in relationship to World War I, I think."

Sophie took Kate's arm, and the two women began to stroll leisurely along the cobblestone streets. They turned to walk along the river's edge in search of lunch as Sophie regaled Kate with a short history of Verdun. As she pointed out significant points, places, and statues, Sophie's shoulders began to relax. The sound of the river was soothing to her soul, and the remembrance of her childhood school trips afforded her a comfortable digression from the morning's turmoil.

"Verdun is situated on the Meuse River and has always been a center of commerce—since before Roman times. Do you see the canals that stretch along this river?" She pointed toward the north. "The canals connect to the sea through Belgium and Holland—or the old County of Flanders."

"That's surprising," said Kate. "This area seems so landlocked, like Nebraska was, where I grew up."

"The Treaty of Verdun, where Charlemagne divided his empire, took place right here. Remnants of the medieval city are up on that hillside there." Her hand swept a wide arc to her left, and both women turned to the steep hills above them. "You see, I was paying attention on those school field trips." She laughed out loud.

"Our field trips in Nebraska were just that—in fields—fields of corn, sorghum, milo, wheat . . . Although, I was raised in Buffalo County, where in years past there had been some gruesome battles between Indians and the soldiers at nearby Fort Kearney. As kids, we used to play there, always hoping to find arrowheads. But there are not as many years of written history," Kate laughed. It felt good to be standing outside in the chill air and let loose for a change.

"Yes, I believe our history has less Indians," Sophie joked. The women continued walking. "Now, this is interesting. The Battle of Verdun was the longest battle ever fought during World War I. In fact, as school kids, we were taught it was the longest battle in world history. Over 700,000 casualties, including 250,000 deaths."

"700,000?" Stunned, Kate looked around her. "With all our talk of your mother's life, I'm starting to get a sense of war in a completely different light. Do you remember your mother telling us of her grandmother's stories of WWI? She said the only sound they heard for months was the *chink-chink-chink* of the chisel carving out yet one more name on the war memorial. How sad this all is." She looked across the river. "I'm sorry, Sophie. Are you all right talking about these things? About war? Yesterday, Annie had a rough time going back over her past, especially when it included wars . . ." Kate asked.

"Actually, I think digging into the wars will help us find out what happened to my grandfather. And, eventually, I may have a better understanding of my own father. Perhaps I've given him short shrift . . ."

Kate nodded her head. They crossed the bridge and then stopped to peer into the deep brown and gold waters of the Meuse. The earlier rains had churned up the river and turned the water into a murky residue that flowed beneath them.

"The German border isn't far away from here. My grandfather told me that one of the battles lasted for eighteen months because the Germans wanted to bleed the French white. He showed me pictures taken after the war here, and see . . ." Sophie pointed up the hill again to the modern city of Verdun. "The photos showed all of those buildings having been completely bombed and left to fall into the river below. The whole city looked like a ghost town."

Hints of sunlight sparkled off the wet stones, while along the water cries arose from a sculling team as it glided beneath them. On the opposite shore, a large grey tour boat awaited business from tourists who, like Kate, were caught up in the history of Verdun.

"*Déjeuner, s'il vous plaît?*" asked Sophie.

"*Mais oui, madame. Merci beaucoup!*"

Linking arms, the two walked away from the river, where they spotted a small café. Hidden behind white lace curtains was a small dark but cozy room that exuded the warmth they needed. They found a booth and slid in.

"Do you think we should try the quiche Lorraine? We are still in the Lorraine, aren't we?" Kate asked.

"We are, and we should. Good idea! Quiche Lorraine *pour deux!*"

Their eyes surveyed the contents of the serving case, where rather limp-looking salads stared back at them. And the quiche?

"Once those are microwaved, they will probably be rubbery, at best. What do you think?" The two women stared at the case and then burst out laughing. This was not exactly what they had in mind, but for the time being, it would do. They opted for wine instead of coffee and settled into their seats.

Sophie leaned forward and rested her elbows on the table.

"Kate, I've been telling you about the wars that took place here. Because it was fought on our soil, there was no escape, but what about your folks? How did they manage during wartime?"

Kate thought over the old stories she had been told and answered, "I can only respond about World War II, but I don't think anyone was anxious to go to war. We, like you folks in

France, had suffered a great many losses during World War I—in fact, many casualties right here in Verdun—and that was followed by the devastating Depression of the '30s. I have the impression my parents rushed into marriage, although my older sister wasn't born until a year later. But I believe they feared my father would be sent overseas and they would never be together.

Sophie nodded her head sadly, "Yes, we, too, didn't want to enter war. It never resolves anything, but we were forced into it once again by the Germans. They had not taken their loss well in 1918, so they were bound and determined to lay waste to us—so I was told."

"Bleeding the French white, like you said?" Kate asked.

"Exactly!" Sophie replied.

"Sophie, I know very few in the States suffered like your mother and all of France did while being occupied, but I still can't imagine how she was able to push forward and persevere."

"I doubt that war gave her many alternatives," Sophie said softly. "And I would imagine that is why my mother chose to marry my father—during the war."

Kate pondered her observation. "When I think about your parents, I try to understand the world they lived in. Certainly, the formidable power of war on your own turf has the ability to force change on everyone. People get married to total strangers and have babies with or without marriage, all because of the threat of being abandoned or left alone."

The sounds of a deluge reverberated through a nearby window. Sophie pulled her coat over her shoulders as stiffness ran through her back. The cold damp air edged into her bones. She snugged the coat more closely about her.

"Wait, have we ordered, yet?" Kate asked. The two giggled at their realization.

Sophie got up and ordered their food and returned with two glasses of wine. "I'm starting to realize how little I know about your life, Kate."

Kate laughed at that. "Here I've been thinking that you have been keeping your feelings rather close to the vest, and I imagine I have been doing the same." She shrugged, "Probably I've been hiding behind the protective mantle of my old job." Kate paused. "Do we have time to order a carafe of wine?"

"*Oui*! Great idea!" Sophie said as she signaled the attention of the waitress. She quickly placed the order and in moments the carafe appeared with two wilted salads and two steaming-hot wedges of rubbery quiche.

Kate took a slow sip of wine. "Mmm. *Délicieuse!* She raised her glass to Sophie, and Sophie, in turn, raised hers. "Love and war; war and love. They can make you do strange and crazy things," Kate said, remembering some words her mother used to say. "And I certainly found that out on my own."

Sophie looked at Kate inquisitively. "What do you mean? What happened?"

Kate took a bite of quiche and swallowed it down almost whole. She hesitated and then changed the subject. "Did I ever tell you about the silent war?"

Sophie shook her head.

"My mother told me the silent war was the period of time that followed World War II. This was when war brides got to know their husbands, sometimes for the first time. And this was before divorce became acceptable. Many were stuck in loveless marriages!" A faraway look drifted over her face and was gone.

Sophie nodded. "I understand. Marie mentioned something like that—that my mother went through a silent war, too, once she moved to Ste. Barbe. Most of my father's family never accepted her, and they treated her very badly." Sophie picked up her fork and began poking the limp salad around her plate, but her fork never touched her lips.

"I think much of what my mother was feeling—her feelings of not being wanted, not being accepted—I took on myself. I remember when I was in high school, I was in love with this boy named Christophe—I mentioned him earlier today, remember?"

Kate adjusted herself more squarely in her chair. "I've been waiting to hear about your Christophe."

"I mentioned that my father had refused to let me see him. He was adamant about it, to the point of becoming violent. I remember wanting to die," Sophie stopped.

"Didn't you suggest that maybe your parents suspected Christophe might have been the father of your baby?" Kate probed.

"If that's what happened, then yes. But both my parents were against him. It was so strange, as my relationship with Christophe was more in my head than in reality. If my brother Julien hadn't teased me in front of my parents, they would never have known. Oh, and then Julien made jokes about Christophe's limp. *Mon pauvre!* I believe he had had polio when he was much younger. My folks thought—can you believe this? They believed that it could be catching. It was so sad!"

Kate shook her head. Sophie refilled her wine glass as Kate began to unravel her own tale of love lost and of a baby born out of wedlock. She told her of her former fiancé's love-losing rigor after she told him she was pregnant and of her painful decision to go far away from her family to have her baby on her own.

"Much like your mother, Sophie—I had little choice in the matter," Kate said. "I didn't want to hurt my parents, and I wanted to do what was best for my baby. I was thinking about your mother's comment about Gérard's father lacking the courage of his love. That comment so resonated with me because I, too, had to go it alone. Because I never heard from Dave again—that was his name—that told me all I needed to know: he was not a man who had the courage of his love. I needed to move on. I think your mother, bless her heart, must have felt the same."

"For me, life in Ste. Barbe became too difficult to handle, and I tried to find a way out. Later, like I mentioned at the *mairie* this morning, I ended up marrying a soldier friend of Gérard's." Sophie ran one finger around the edge of her fork.

"Soldier? Was he in a war, too?" Kate asked.

An amused look brushed Sophie's face. "Have you heard of the Algerian War? Both my brothers were shipped out to Algeria. And that was how Gérard met my . . . well, the man I married. In the Algerian conflict."

"Did you love him?" asked Kate.

"Not really," she said, lifting her glass to her lips and drinking. "Like I told you before, my mother begged me to get married. I guess I consented just to be away from my father and all his strife. I was young—just nineteen at the time—and I thought marriage might make the difference. But it didn't."

"How long were you married? You've barely mentioned this before."

"Oh, pooh! It's such a sad story, but I was married ten years. I tried to love him, but frankly, I just didn't feel it. I felt . . . pretty dead inside. I attempted suicide a couple of times. He tried really hard to make me happy, but . . . I just couldn't . . . I just couldn't."

"Too bad you didn't realize until today what you had gone through," Kate said sadly.

Sophie looked into her empty wine glass, refilled it, and said, "The difference I was looking for was a change in me. And then, years later, I found my Jerome. He scooped me up and took me away from it all," she quipped. "Enough said about me!" The curtain dropped; she was done.

With lightly filled stomachs and probably too much wine, Kate and Sophie wobbled out the door, leaning on each other for support. Sophie got back at the wheel, they plugged new coordinates into the onboard computer, and they headed for Paris.

Once the landscape changed and the undulating hills began to flatten, Sophie eased onto Highway A4 heading to her Cousin

Madeleine's place. Other than comments about the weather and the landscape, nothing of significance passed between the two women. It had been a long day, they had consumed a bit of wine, and both were burrowed deep in their own thoughts.

"Have you visited your cousin before?" Kate asked as the buildings of Paris came into view. She gazed out the window awaiting her answer.

"Yes, I did, but it was some time ago," Sophie said. "My family came to stay with Tante Suzanne, Madeleine's mother. It was my first trip to Paris. I was so excited! I must have been eight or ten. It was one of those infrequent times when we got to ride in a car. Not our car, of course, but the Geoffreys, who were close friends of my parents. Oh, it was such fun! Julien, Gérard, my parents, the friends, and I were all crammed into their little *Deux Chevaux*, a car built for two. Or, perhaps, four, but it was tight." Sophie threw her head back and laughed.

Kate smiled. It was good to hear Sophie laugh again.

"So, once we arrived in Paris, we slept on Aunt Suzanne's living room floor. We didn't care—we were visiting Paris!"

Sophie glided off the A4 past the Périphérique and crossed the Seine River, then made her way across the city, while they caught glimpses of the Eiffel Tower as it came into and disappeared from view. Kate strained in her seat trying to take it all in. She had been to Paris a number of times, but she never tired of seeing Paris from absolutely every angle.

Sophie murmured, "My most vivid memory from that trip was when all of us were walking down Boulevard St. Germaine. We entered a neighborhood tavern and there was a man in the bar *Maman* seemed to know. Once she saw him, she ushered us out."

Sophie remembered holding her mother's hand as they had walked out of the sunshine and into the darkened barroom that day, but she suddenly experienced a visceral flashback. She could smell the stench of stale tobacco smoke and the reek of alcohol that had permeated the air. The floors, which were sticky, exuded the same odor. Forties music swirled through the air from an unseen jukebox. Everyone was laughing, as they were all having such a good time. Suddenly, Sophie's mother stood stark still. Her hand clenched hers, then went limp, and then flew up to cover her mouth. Sophie had turned to look at her mother and was struck by her startled expression.

"*Maman* had such a dramatic reaction when she saw this man," Sophie continued. "I remember standing on my tiptoes to see who she saw. My eyes hadn't adjusted, at first, to the dim light, but, eventually, I was able to see a man leaning against the bar staring straight back at my mother. '*Maman*, who is he?' I had whispered. She didn't answer. Even now, I can remember the light over the bar that framed the stranger in a rainbow of color. His hair was dark blonde, his facial features were slightly chiseled, and even though we stood there for only a moment, I swear it seemed like time had stopped. I remember peering up at my mother and realizing she knew this man; her face had softened, beautifully. But then suddenly, she swiveled around to catch sight of Papa. Terror filled her eyes, and that softness disappeared. Kate, I could have sworn I could feel *Maman's* heart beating. Without a word to anyone, she grabbed my hand, spun me around, and marched us all back out of the bar."

"What do you think that was about?" Kate asked her, enthralled.

"As I recall, my father, Julien, Gérard, and the Geoffreys were surprised we hadn't stayed, but then they hadn't noticed the stranger. But we all knew from the expression on my mother's face that there would be no discussion. Our group proceeded down the Boulevard and entered another establishment and had a great time."

Poof! Sophie breathed out as if she were holding her breath. Kate turned to look at her. Sophie's face exuded a tension, released.

Changing the subject abruptly, Sophie said, "I need to turn onto Boulevard St. Michel. I remember my aunt and cousins lived in a neighborhood near here, just off Boulevard St. Germaine . . ." she muttered to herself.

The sun was setting; the plane trees that lined the boulevards had lost most of their leaves, and their silhouettes were cast in a golden light. The broad sidewalks and gutters glittered with autumnal detritus, as the street lamps began to light.

"Who do you think that man was?" Kate finally asked.

Sophie paused. She was negotiating her way into a parking spot, but she failed and continued on down the block. "There was something so electrifying in that moment, Kate; maybe I felt it through my mother's hand, maybe it was my mother's movements, but I was certain the man across the room was someone important to her. I never forgot his face and . . ."

Once again, Sophie was transported back in time. The smells, sights, and sounds of her past grew stronger. She could hear the lusty laugh of a woman sitting near the bar. She could make out the tune, which had been playing that day, and suddenly the words came into focus. She hadn't understood the words before, but now, if her memory served her, she had heard Peggy Lee's rendition of "We'll Meet Again." Even now, she found herself humming the tune and catching the meaning to those poignant words, which her mother, too, must have heard. "We'll meet again; don't know where; don't know when; but I know we'll meet again some sunny day." *That sunny day?*

Sophie moaned out loud.

"What were you singing?" Kate asked her. "Sounded like one of the old World War II songs."

Sophie stammered. "I was?" She looked lost. Then she said, "It's funny, but I think that was the song I heard when we walked into that bar." She looked at Kate. "That was the song my mother heard as she looked across the room to see—for the first time in ten or twelve years—her old lover. Gérard's father."

"Really? It *was* his father? Are you sure?"

"*Oui*, I believe so. Of course, this event happened long before we knew Gérard had another father, so it didn't register as anything but *bizarre, curieux* even. But I'll never forget the startled look on the man's face, which mirrored *Maman's* reaction. And the experience was truly visceral! Even though I was young, I knew that moment held far more meaning than any of us could imagine. And now that I think of those words . . ."

"So perfect, so poignant, and so poorly timed," Kate said sadly. "How devastating that must have been for your mother! Did you ever ask her about it? I mean, years later?"

"At first, no. Like the dutiful daughter, I never asked. But after Gérard and my father died, she brought the subject up. She told me that the moment we walked into that bar, she recognized her true love across the room."

"What else did she say?" Kate asked, as memories of her catching sight of Dave twenty years ago at a highway stop came to mind. She had never approached him; in fact, she had hidden away, as she, too, had cowered at the thought of introducing her first husband to him.

"I think it was bittersweet for her," Sophie replied. "She said she was relieved that he was alive—she hadn't known all those years—but she said that she spent all the rest of her years yearning for him. She loved him so. And then I could understand why she so adored Gérard, her love child, so much."

"When did you start referring to Gérard in that way?"

Sophie scratched her head, and then said, "Obviously, after Papa had died." She paused again. "Probably after *Maman* and I had had this conversation. It made sense to me, Kate. And, I think it was my way of letting her know I recognized a love she had known."

"And she never told you her true love's last name." Kate

reached into the back seat to get her purse. "I can't locate my . . . whew, I just found it. My phone. I was thinking we'd have to return to Verdun." Kate looked down at her cell phone and noted a message from Lisa. Stifling her desire to check the message, she shoved her phone into her purse for later.

"I suppose this man hadn't wanted to break up my mother's marriage, especially if he thought she had found happiness." Sophie sighed. "Like I told you, what he never knew was that my mother had never stopped loving him. But she told me, as unhappy as she was during her marriage to Papa, her first priority was to hold our family together—always, the family came first."

"Yes, always the family came first," Kate nodded her head. Her head dropped toward her lap as pangs of guilt ate away at her about Lisa. She thought back on those lonely days she was at a women's college, where she quietly went to school, went to work, came back home to her parents' house, and studied, all while waiting for Dave's call. Day after day, week after week, she wanted to reach out to him. But was he her true love? Did she really believe he was the one for her? Memories of those carefree times with Dave and his friends had been great, but as a permanent partner? As she swiped her cheek dry of a wayward tear, Kate stammered out loud, "So, once again, decisions made during the heat of war continue to be honored. And once again, she walked away from her only love."

They sat for a few moments pondering the story Sophie had laid out. Then Kate sat up and asked, "Do you think your mother contacted him later?" She took stock of her surroundings. "Maybe your mother's family will know something?"

"My great aunt moved here long after the war, but we can ask, *oui?*" Sophie wheeled around the block one more time before finding a spot in front of Madeleine's apartment building.

$\mathscr{S}$earching $\mathscr{T}$hrough the $\mathscr{A}$nnals of $\mathscr{T}$ime

$\stackrel{.}{\mathbf{A}}$

*T*HE NEIGHBORHOOD SURROUNDING Madeleine's *pensione* had once been one of wealth, but the building appeared rundown from years of disrepair and neglect. Thin strips of paint from the front door and windows had fallen off like dead leaves, the trim had come loose, and Sophie noticed the building appeared to be listing to one side. Or, was she the one who was out of balance?

"Is this the same place you came as a child, Sophie?" Kate asked, taking in the forlorn-looking building.

"It's been years since I was last here. I won't know until I get in the apartment." She was feeling disoriented from the wave of memories that had washed over her all day and didn't feel certain about anything.

The women headed to the front door and entered an inner hallway. The room was cold; dingy slabs of grey marble lined the walls. Dim light beamed down from three naked bulbs high above them, and no shades were in place to cut the glare. A line of brass postal boxes, grimy with time and use, were inset into the wall along with a bell system for the upstairs apartments. No other ornamentation was visible. Sophie pushed the buzzer for her cousin's apartment and was automatically allowed in.

"Voilà! Nothing to it!" she said as the two women made their way through the door before it slammed shut.

"Are we planning to spend the night here, Sophie?" Kate asked. Trepidation seeped into her voice as they stood in the dark vestibule.

Sophie put a reassuring hand on Kate's shoulder and said, "No, when you were using the bathroom in Verdun, after I called Madeleine, I made reservations for us at a small hotel nearby."

"Goodness! Was I in there that long?" Kate gasped. She smoothed down her scarf and patted it into place.

After her eyes adjusted to the lack of light, Sophie searched for an elevator. The only beacon to penetrate the darkness came from a landing high above them. She inched over to where she could make out a sign indicating the *ascenseur* was broken.

Letting out a Gallic puff, she moved to the stairway, where a rickety set of stairs covered with tattered carpeting led them up the necessary three flights. They headed down the hallway and stopped in front of apartment number 210. Immediately, the door flew open, and a small, sprite woman of indeterminate age stood before them. Her hair, a white cottony mass, stuck out in every direction. Kate's eyes widened. The woman's features were that of a dehydrated apple doll—squinched-up eyes, sucked-in mouth, and heavily-lined, rouge colored cheeks. Her flashing black eyes stared out at them from two dark recesses. Kate stepped backward. But Sophie stepped forward and hugged her cousin as they became reacquainted.

"Madeleine, this is my friend, Kate. Kate, Madeleine." Kate reached forward to shake her hand but was scooped into a firm embrace. Madeleine began bubbling excitedly as she led them

into a small living area, where both the TV and heat were
blasting away. It was difficult to breathe, as the air smelled of
scorched kitty litter. As Kate looked around the apartment, she
realized there were cats—many cats. She felt light-headed and
quickly covered her mouth to avoid sneezing, but an allergy
attack hit anyway.

After seven sneezes, she mumbled, "I'm sorry. I have allergies,
but maybe the worst is over." She daubed her eyes with a tissue
and found a place to sit on a padded rocker near the only open
window. Madeleine and Sophie nodded in her direction but
quickly picked up their conversation. Madeleine, who had been
awaiting their arrival, poured cups of hot tea and served a plate of
biscuits for the occasion. Like a small bird, she flitted about the
room, then finally shut off the TV and sat down on the well-worn
sofa beside Sophie.

Kate looked around. The five cats must have taken offense to
her sneezes, for they had disappeared. The walls above Madeleine
and Sophie were covered in photographs. Kate looked for
someone she might recognize but saw no one. She sat quietly,
tuning into an occasional French phrase, but almost dozed off.

"I'm so very glad you came to visit, Sophie," Madeleine began.
"It has been years since you were last here, but my mother always
spoke well of your mother and all of you. I believe they were close
at one time . . . But I wouldn't know when that would have been."
Her thin forefinger touched and retouched her bony chin.

"We're glad to visit, also. Thank you for allowing us to come
on such short notice. Everyone connected to my mother is a
special delight. I miss her very much."

"I'm sure you do, *ma chérie*," said Madeleine. "I feel that way
about my mother, and it's been years. I didn't know your mother
well, as she was older than I was when we were growing up in
Vannes. But I do remember my mother's concern for her welfare."

Sophie hesitated and then dove in. "That's one of the reasons for my visit. Now that she is gone, I realize how little I know about her side of the family.

Madeleine nodded. "I was maybe five or six when our Grandmother Tetiau passed away, but I remember visiting her home when your mother was still living there. I remember homemade jams slathered on hot-from-the-griddle crêpes along with her laughter and plenty of hugs." A wistful expression swept across her face but lasted only a moment. She blinked her eyes.

Sophie turned to Kate, smiling broadly. "She's telling me of visiting my great-grandmother's house and how she loved the crêpes. As you've said before, dear Kate, memories are always wrapped around food."

Kate sat up and tuned into their conversation. She took a sip of tea, which she found soothing to her scratchy throat, and reached for a biscuit. Suddenly, Madeleine jumped up from the sofa and disappeared into her bedroom.

While she was gone, Sophie began looking at the photos and pictures on the wall. Her eyes swept the room.

"Do you remember being here, Sophie?" Kate asked her.

Memories of Sophie's one and only stay in this apartment came tumbling back—the same grey and pink striped wallpaper, the same crocheted doilies littering the headrests of the overstuffed chair and sofa. Even the rose-printed chintz covering the rocker, in which Kate sat, seemed familiar.

"Yes," she said, "I do." Sophie slid back onto the sofa just as Madeleine returned.

She held a packet of yellowed envelopes and an old diary, which she laid in Sophie's lap. Before sitting down, Madeleine placed a child's-size pair of bifocals onto her beak of a nose, then lighted back onto the sofa, almost on top of Sophie. She let out a squeak, which was followed by both women lapsing into a fit of laughter. Madeleine scooted farther down the sofa.

Madeleine began, "These are some letters and a diary I ran

across after my mother passed away. She died over thirty years ago, but I didn't think to read them, until . . . until I heard of your mother's passing." Madeleine's hands suddenly fluttered around her mouth and then dropped back into her lap. A look of guilt flashed across her face as her cheeks reddened.

Placing one hand on her cousin's, Sophie said, "This is wonderful, Madeleine. I can't tell you how precious this is to me." She turned the envelopes and diary over in her lap.

Spurred by Sophie's positive response, Madeleine said, "In fact, there is one letter that was addressed to your mother but was never sent. I'm not sure why." She paused to think. She blew out the slightest of Gallic puffs. "And the diary appears to have been written by your Grandmother Honorine, my mother's little sister. Did you ever meet her?" Madeleine turned toward Sophie and peered up at her. Her beady black eyes suddenly enlarged three sizes. "Oh, probably not. She died fairly young. But it appears Honorine often corresponded with my mother, once she came to live in Paris. My mother never threw a letter away, so I have sorted through the ones that might be of interest to you. In the diary, there is mention of a gentleman named Raymond Pourrette. Do you know who that might be?"

Sophie's eyes popped open, but she nodded and tried to calmly listen to Madeleine's words. She felt like leaping off the sofa. She couldn't believe her good fortune. Maybe the mystery to her mother's identity could finally be solved. Trying to remain composed, her fingers ran lightly over the precious packet in her lap, but inside she could barely contain herself. *Raymond Pourrette! Raymond Pourrette!* She had only been in the apartment—what? Twenty minutes? Thirty minutes? Kate apparently had missed this tidbit. She wanted to scream to Kate and run into the hallway to open the letters—now. Instead, she feigned composure and not once looked at the treasure in her hands.

A very long hour passed as Sophie sipped her tea and tried

to focus on her conversation with her second cousin.

"Kate," Sophie asked, startling her, "do you remember me telling you of my first visit to Paris? It *was* in this apartment that we all stayed. I was about ten. Madeleine says she was grown up by then but remembers our visit. After her mother died, she moved in here and has been here ever since." She stood up and motioned to Kate that it was time to go. She carefully placed the worn packet of letters and diary into her purse and hugged Madeleine as she said her *adieux*. Kate followed suit, and the two backed out the door.

After they had walked down the darkened hall, Sophie began giggling and jumping up and down. Her restrained response was at an end.

"What is it, Sophie," Kate asked. "What did I miss in there?"

"It's not in there that you missed." Sophie danced up and down. "It's in here!" she said, pulling the diary out of her purse. "This is a journal written by my Grandmother Honorine. She tells all about Raymond! Get it? Raymond Pourrette!" Sophie grabbed Kate and spun her around, and the two raced down the stairs and out into the night. Sophie let out a whoop, and they grabbed each other and danced in a circle like foolish schoolgirls.

"Miracle of miracles," Sophie kept shouting. "I can't believe it! I can't believe our good fortune!"

With an attempt to tamp down their excitement, they checked into their hotel and then dashed out for some dinner. It was well past 8:00 PM, and both were starving. The afternoon's repast of rubbery quiche hadn't sufficed. After ordering their first course along with wine, Kate dragged her chair closer to Sophie's. She leaned in as Sophie pulled the first of the letters from her purse.

"Would you look at this?" Sophie exclaimed. Kate peered at the yellowed pages on the white tablecloth but couldn't make out a single word.

"That's not French, right?"

"*Oui*, it is Breton." Sophie carefully opened the envelope and pulled out a sheaf of pages.

"This letter," she announced, "was written to my mother and is from Great-aunt Suzanne. I think I can make out most of this," she said, haltingly, "but, like Madeleine said, it's curious that the envelope was never mailed."

As the wine was poured and Sophie pulled her glasses from her purse, Kate said, "Seems to be a family trait—either to send letters that are never opened or to never send letters once they've been written."

Sophie nodded her head but was deciphering the first pages. She read the date. "Oh, it was written in 1971, over thirty years ago. Must have been just before Aunt Suzanne died." She thumbed through the letter. "She must not have finished before she got sick."

Sophie read silently down through the first page, starting, stopping, and then finally laying the letter down on the table.

"What does it say, Sophie," Kate whispered. Sophie picked up her wine glass but put it down again, unable to hold the glass steady.

"Are you all right, Sophie? What is it?"

Sophie sat quietly for a few moments. On the one hand, she was savoring each and every word she was able to read, but on the other hand, the enormity of what she was discovering about her family was overwhelming. Here, before her, were the very answers her mother had been desperate to learn.

Kate, by now, was beside herself fidgeting with her fork—racing her fingers up and down the tines—and folding and unfolding her napkin. *Should I leave Sophie alone?* she thought. Instead, she took a gulp of wine and began coughing and sputtering.

"I'm sorry, Sophie," Kate rasped. "Maybe this subject should be left alone."

"Nope, my dear friend," Sophie laughed. "I'm sorry; it's taking me a while to digest. I'm trying to sort out the context of this information. Get out your pad of paper so we can chart this."

Relieved to be of help, Kate pulled her leather satchel out. Along with a pad, she quickly produced a couple of pens and started to place them on the table when the waiter arrived. He placed two hot plates of bubbling escargots before them. The women looked at each other, grinned, pushed the papers aside, and dived into the succulent garlic-butter-infused snails. After daubing slices of baguette through the remaining pools of butter, licking their fingers dry and swilling down more wine, Sophie returned to her Aunt Suzanne's letter.

"Okay Kate, my Aunt Suzanne is writing to my mother to tell her about her father, Raymond Pourrette. Raymond Pourrette," she repeated. "I am having a hard time taking this in, as *Maman* never knew her father's first name. No one talked about him. She always assumed she was born out of wedlock. But Aunt Suzanne writes that she knew him—knew Raymond Pourrette—and she liked him very much.

"It appears my mother requested the information from her, but, well . . ." She turned the pages over and scanned quickly through them. "You're right, Kate. This does seem to be the story of my mother's life. Letters carefully written, but never sent, never opened."

"Oh, God," Kate said touching her chest, "the heartache she endured!"

"*C'est vrai! C'est vrai,*" Sophie said more calmly than she felt, "but maybe this will help my family and me understand who our grandfather was."

Sophie reached over and helped herself to more wine. She topped off Kate's glass while she was at it.

"Well, here's to finally finding answers for your mother, Sophie," Kate said, raising her glass in a toast. Kate clinked her glass with Sophie's and slowly sipped her wine as she waited for Sophie to continue. Finally, she asked, "So what does the rest of the letter say?"

Again, the waiter appeared and placed two separate plates of chicken before them. Kate tucked into her plate of chicken fricassée as Sophie began to play with her *chapon sauté à l'estragon.*

"Aren't you hungry, Sophie?" Kate asked as she stuffed a bite of fricassée into her mouth.

"I guess I'm more hungry for the truth," Sophie said, as she slid her plate aside.

"Now, to find out about my Grandfather Raymond. How nice to know his name." She took a sip of a wine and began translating the letter that had been conspicuously lying near her plate.

"My Aunt Suzanne is telling my mother how my Grandmother Honorine first met Raymond. She says, 'First, turn to the diary and begin by reading the pages for February 2, 1916.' She says, 'I know about this story because I was a part of it, but I think you will be able to understand your mother Honorine, with this reading.'" Sophie put down the letter and began thumbing through the brittle pages of the diary. "Okay, I've found the entry. My grandmother writes . . . I can't believe I'm actually seeing her diary, too!" Sophie looked up at Kate, her face glowing in the candlelight. The expression on Kate's face must have expressed impatience because Sophie burst into laughter and said, "Okay. Okay. I'll get on with it."

It was February 2, 1916, the night of Candlemas. A cold, biting wind blew off the Breton sea and down the narrow streets of Vannes, as Honorine and her mother made their way from the St. Patern District down the steep hill to Cathedral St. Pierre. The long-awaited annual *fête* would take place this evening, and for Honorine, this was a night of great longing. At seventeen, she no longer saw herself as a girl, but a woman, so she found it galling she needed permission from her mother to attend the ball. Yes, she could go as long as her older sister, Suzanne, accompanied her.

The evening service of Candlemas was unusually long, as the lighting of candles for Mary and the Christ Child also included special prayers for those away at War. At War! What did Honorine know about such things? Other than the older boys marching off over two years ago, she knew nothing. She could barely sit still, and she kept wiggling her feet back and forth in order to catch a glimpse of her new black shoes, the gold clasp capturing an occasional glint from the ever-brightening candlelight. She was relieved her father, an accomplished shoemaker, had finished them in time.

As the last *amen* was uttered, a collective sigh went up, and kneeling benches were slammed into place. After hugging her mother, Honorine flew down the side aisle and out of the Cathedral into the icy, cold night. Honorine became impatient, as her older sister was not waiting outside for her. Where was she? Suzanne hadn't attended the service. Disquietude began to unhinge Honorine, but she forced her feelings down and raced along the cobblestone streets to the *mairie*, where the ball was slated to begin.

⚜

Earlier that evening as Honorine had been readying for church, voices could be heard in another part of town.

"What makes you think I *need* to go to this ball?" Raymond said as he slipped a bookmark into his novel. He sat up on the sofa and stared straight into his cousin's eyes. It was almost like staring into a mirror—except for his cousin's unruly hair.

"I'm not like you. I've never been a lady's man," he said, ribbing his cousin, Pierre. "I've barely spent time with a woman."

Twenty-four-year-old Raymond Pourrette had come to

Vannes to visit his cousin while on leave from the Front. He wasn't allowed many leaves, so his time was precious. But during their youth, he and his cousin had become very close, even though they had grown up in different provinces. Having spent a few days with his parents in Paris, Raymond had come to Brittany to convince Pierre to join the war effort. He hoped he had succeeded.

"I suppose the reason you are not a lady's man has to do with your mother, dear cousin," Pierre said in jest. Pierre knew his aunt held a firm grip on Raymond, her only child, so Pierre never missed an opportunity to tease him.

"I don't know how it is that we, as cousins, could look so much alike but be so different," he laughed. He was right, though. They were very different—in temperament, demeanor, and in the way they were raised. But to see the two together, you would have thought they were twins.

Raymond sported a carefully groomed, jet-black mustache, unlike his cousin's scraggly one. His diminutive features were finer than Pierre's, but those piercing black eyes were definitely a family trait. No doubt about it.

Raymond's dark brown hair was the same color as Pierre's, yet he wore his swept straight back off his forehead and cropped short. Pierre, a fisherman and the son of a fisherman, wore his hair long and unruly. *The long hair will have to go once he enlists,* thought Raymond, but he said nothing.

In spite of being close, their lives had followed different paths. Raymond had been raised in Paris where his father, a former Vannetais, was a Parisian merchant. His Parisian mother made certain he knew that his life was one of luxury.

Pierre's mother, a sister to Raymond's father, carried on the traditions of all families connected to the sea, and she raised seven strapping fishermen as sons. For Pierre and his brothers, his cousin's life in Paris was an illusion too far removed and never to be envied.

"Okay, okay, so you insist I go to the ball," Raymond said again. "You know that I dance better than you, don't you? I've had more training, plus I have *savoir faire*. Are you prepared for that?"

"At least the dancing I've done was with girls—not with other boys in a prep school." He lunged at Raymond and pulled him to his feet as they enacted some quick ballroom steps. Their laughter brought all the family tumbling into the parlor to see the two young men waltzing about in a farcical dance.

✾

Papier-mâché flowers in deep purples and rich pinks were strung throughout the ballroom, while candles, which were scattered about the room, gave off a golden glow and an air of mystique. Celebrations during the war years were few and far between, so everyone came together to make this festival an exceptional affair. As the Vannetais began to fill the room, a look of joy lit their faces. That was replaced with the awareness that few young men would be in attendance, but those who were there became the envy of every available young woman. A tremor of excitement flowed through the mademoiselles lined up against one wall.

Honorine hesitated at the ballroom door. She was a petite young lass who looked much younger than her seventeen years. But her goal that night was to appear older, taller, and much more worldly. She shifted onto her tiptoes. Unfortunately, her dark curly hair, which had been hurriedly pinned beneath her *coiffe*, had sprung loose as she ran through the streets and had cascaded onto the white lace collar of the borrowed emerald-green dress. Feigning a look of confidence, she searched the faces of the crowd for her sister. Once she spotted her, she glided onto the dance floor and over to the other side.

"Suzanne? Suzanne!" she hoarsely whispered. "Why didn't you wait for me at the cathedral? Didn't you think I would come?"

Honorine was sounding hysterical. Her composure had slipped and was now dangling around her ankles.

"Yes," Suzanne said, tucking Honorine's hair back into her coiffe. "I knew you would come, but I was helping with the food. Were you able to convince mother that you could go unattended?"

"Of course not, Suzanne," Honorine said, stamping her foot. "Don't be silly. I told her you were waiting outside the cathedral to accompany me. I thought . . ." She let out her breath, then took in a new one. "Just because you're older, you . . ." she stammered. She didn't finish her sentence, as the music interrupted her in deafening decibels. The high-pitched whine from the oboe-like *bombarde* was joined in accompaniment by the traditional bagpipes of Brittany, the *veuze* and the *biniou kozh*. All conversation came to an abrupt end, as those attending the ball created room on the dance floor: men on one side, women on the other.

Once the music began, Raymond panicked. He realized he was out of his element. All of the ballroom dancing classes he had endured in school flew directly out the window. The Breton-style of dance was unlike anything he had known, as was the music. Pierre broke into laughter when he saw the look of terror cross his cousin's face.

"*Savoir faire?*" he smirked. Where is your *savoir faire* now, my cousin?"

Blushing slightly, Raymond looked away from Pierre as his eyes fell upon Honorine. "Who is that lovely young lady?" he asked. He straightened up and adjusted his tie.

"Oh, she's nobody," was his reply. "She's much too young for you."

"How young could she be? She's here without a chaperone."

"She's well-chaperoned," Pierre said. "Her older sister, Suzanne, is standing behind her. But she's not your type. The dance hasn't begun, and her hair is already a mess. Your mother will charge me with setting you up with a fallen woman." Pierre grinned and tossed his own hair back. He started off in another direction, leaving Raymond to fend for himself.

"*Un moment*, Pierre; you wanted me to come to this ball. So the least you can do is introduce me."

"All right, all right. I guess I owe you this one." The two cousins crossed the dance floor, where Pierre introduced Raymond to Honorine.

Honorine turned her head coyly, and when she looked up into Raymond's dark brown eyes, she could make out her reflection. Through her nervousness, she sensed his, although, in her limited experience, she estimated that he was possibly the most dashing of all the young men in the room. Her breath caught in her throat and she felt her hands perspire as he took her hand in his. She looked back at her sister, Suzanne, who stood there grinning in a most unbecoming manner. Raymond led her onto the dance floor, where she realized he was not from Brittany and that a dance lesson was in order.

⚬⊙⚬

After a few short months, on May 9, 1916, they were married. A couple of days later, Raymond prepared to return to the Front.

"Are you all right, *mon mari?*" Honorine asked her husband. Standing before the mirror brushing her hair, she could see him sitting on their bed—his expression had turned to one of distress.

"*Mon mari*, my husband," she let the words roll off her tongue. She rushed to the bed once again, for here was her world. Her love. He was preparing to leave for the war, and he looked quite worried.

He cradled her face with his hands and kissed her mouth, her ears, and her neck and wrapped her into his arms.

"To think of leaving you after such a short time is too painful. To think of leaving you at all is heart-wrenching." The ease they found with each other surprised them both. Neither had known intimacy before, but their early clumsiness seemed all the more endearing. And the more they made love, the more they hungered for it. It was an unquenchable thirst, one that scared them both, as they knew they would shortly part.

"How can I possibly leave you?" Raymond whispered as he inhaled the fragrance in her hair. "I can't bear to think of us apart, but, my Honorine, I must. I've received word from my parents and I must return to Paris to bid them *adieu* before heading back to the line. I'm sorry my mother took the news of our marriage badly. If she only knew you . . . If she only knew I found the love of my life." His mouth once again found hers.

"Don't worry, *mon amour*. I will go to her and tell her how much we are in love. Surely she will understand, for we both love the same man. Our Breton proverb says: *Dounoc'h eo kaloun ar merc'hed 'vit ar mor douna euz ar bed.* The heart of a woman is deeper than the deepest sea. My love for you will never end. Your mother will understand, for she loves you too."

"Please wait, Honorine. She is terribly displeased with me. You see, her dream was for me to marry a *Parisienne*—a woman of her choosing. I would hate for you to suffer her wrath. You see, *mon lapin*, you have taken her only son. Let's give her some time."

❦

"That's it," Sophie said, turning the page, her disappointment palpable. "There's no more . . . wait, wait, I was too quick. What's this?"

Kate sat quietly but began to tap her pencil. She looked pensively at Sophie to commence. Finally, Sophie shot her a look over the top of the diary and began again.

May 9, 1918

Today is our second wedding anniversary, but this long war continues to rage on. When will you, mon amour, return once again to my side? It has been three months. In spite of keeping busy

while working in the fields, you are always with me—in my head,
in my heart. I miss you so, and love you so. Bon anniversaire! I
have news, but I want to tell you in person. Come home soon!

On Raymond's last visit—February 9, to be exact—he became
concerned for my welfare. My impatience for this war to end must
have tugged hard on him, as he requested Michel, Pierre's younger
brother, to watch over me. He meant well, although I've given
Michel little to watch. With all of the men off to war, only we
women are left to handle the many jobs—bringing in a catch,
gleaning the fields . . . I tire so easily and have little reserve—and
now this!

I must tell Raymond, but I don't know what to say. When
Michel came to visit last night, he was drunk. It was his eighteenth
birthday; he had enlisted in the army and soon would be going to
the Front. Finding me alone, he grabbed me, told me he loved me,
overpowered me, and raped me in my bed. He said he had been
lusting for me for months now . . . I don't know what got into
him. *Viol!* I cried out, but no one heard. *Viol!* I cry even now. *Mon
Dieu!* Whatever am I going to do? I am sick with grief! I am so
sick. And this is my second anniversary!

June 15, 1918

Before Michel left for the Front, he returned to beg my
forgiveness. Why did I talk to him? I am still so angry! Maybe I
wanted to hurt *him.* I blurted out that I am pregnant, and he
immediately assumed the baby was his—Raymond's and my baby!
(I have yet to tell Raymond.) I told him I despised him, that I never
wanted to see him again. When he left, he was stunned, angry, and
heartbroken. He swore he would tell Raymond the baby was his!
Zut alors! Whatever can I do? What will Raymond think? It has been
so long since I last heard from my dear love, and I miss him so.

I have yet to hear from Raymond. I don't know what to think. I talked to Pierre, today, as he was back for Michel's funeral. Poor young Michel. As angry as I am at him, I didn't expect this! I spoke to Pierre only once after the funeral, and he explained that one day while he and Raymond were burrowed in a foxhole, they heard a familiar whistle—one they had known since childhood. As they turned to the sound, Michel slid down into the mud beside them. It had been months since the three of them had been together. Pierre laughed as he told me the story; he was desperately holding onto the memory of his little brother.

Pierre asked him what he was doing on the Front, but Michel looked confused—staring at Pierre then Raymond and back again. "In the mud, we cousins looked alike. Michel didn't recognize me."

"I asked for this assignment," Michel responded. "Aren't you happy to see me, *mon frère?*"

"Of course," Pierre said as he embraced his brother. "Only surprised."

Pierre told me the first thing Raymond asked Michel was, "How is Honorine?" (He told me Raymond talked non-stop about me. That made me smile.)

Pierre said to me, "At that point it had been weeks since he had seen you, Honorine, and I'm sure the images of you were beginning to dim, even though he keeps a photo of you close to his heart."

"So, what did Michel say?" I asked Pierre.

"Raymond slapped Michel on the back and gave him a bear hug, but Michel's answer was . . ."

I held my breath. What did Michel say?

"I don't know," Michel had quipped. "What does it matter?"

"I detected a defensive note in my brother's tone," Pierre continued, "but just then, we had to dive for cover. I figured there would be plenty of time for talk later on. But that talk never took place."

Oh, where does the truth lie? Did Michel tell Raymond of my pregnancy? I had so wanted to tell him in person, but now?

"What happened to Michel?" I asked, terrified of the answer.

"An unexpected tragedy occurred only a few days after Michel arrived."

He mentioned something about "friendly fire." I wanted to ask him more, but he was suddenly surrounded by his family and had to leave. The look of despair on his face left me shaking, and before I had time to send my love to Raymond, I was told Pierre returned to the Front.

August 25, 1918

It has been months since I last received a letter from Raymond. After Michel's body was returned, no word has arrived—no letters from *mon ami.* I don't know if he is dead or alive. The latest reports mentioned the Second Battle of the Somme. They are fighting valiantly, but oh, I am so frantic, so desperate. Every morning, I go to St. Patern's to pray for my dear husband's safe return.

November 15, 1918

Our beautiful daughter, Marcelle, has been born. She was born during the celebration of the end of the war. November 11, 1918! She is so lovely and looks so much like her father. I can only pray that Raymond can now come back home. The war is over.

January 6, 1919

It has been months since the war ended. I received word today that Raymond's body had been found in Somme near the village of Albert. He was killed in action. I can't believe I'm writing these words. Perhaps I knew it all along. How can I tell my lovely daughter that her father will never hold her, never kiss her sweet cheeks. She is all I have left of my sweet love.

January 28, 1919

The body was returned, as promised. I don't know how to feel. I've cried so much this past year that I have no more tears left. The body was not Raymond's. It was his cousin, Pierre's. Yes, they looked alike, but how is it that Raymond's identity tags were found on Pierre's body? If Raymond is still alive, why has he not returned to me? Does he think our baby is not his? Oh, I am so devastated, and I feel so alone. Standing over dear Pierre's body, I can only surmise that the truth I seek lies here—with the dead. If I hear from him no more, I have no choice; I must move on.

Sophie sat quietly playing with her fork, unaware of the dessert before her. The profiteroles filled with ice cream and drizzled with chocolate lay soggy in a puddle on her plate. She slumped in her chair, her wall of reserve washed away after reading her grandmother's diary. How could she possibly make sense of this?

Grand-mère Honorine got married, she thought, *and was under the protection of her own family when she was raped and became pregnant. Or was she pregnant before the rape? Who was my mother's father?* Sophie's head dropped to the back of the chair with a thud. Did Sophie's grandmother abandon Marcelle to flee to Paris? Was she running away from the humiliation of having a child out of wedlock? But, she was married!

Marcelle, too, had suffered the indignity of rape and gave birth at the age of seventeen to Thierry. Sophie tried to breathe. Finally, she gasped aloud. *Was there no end to this familial story of rape?* When her mother gave birth to Gérard, she suffered even more humiliation as an unmarried mother. The words *saleté réfugiate,* or *filthy refugee,* coursed through Sophie's mind as she recalled her mother telling her of traveling to the Free Zone to save her sons. There, too, she had been scorned, demeaned, taunted, and jeered once she got off the train in Evaux-les-Bain . . .

The same village she had just been buried in. *Oh, the irony!* And, of course, once she married Papa, she suffered more disparagement from his family. For her mother, the humiliation had never ended. From start to finish, her mother had believed herself to be a *batârd*, a bastard, and yet, was she?

Sophie could still hear her mother's words: "Never allow yourself to become pregnant without the benefit of marriage. You must promise me!" Was this solely because of her own experience? Or was this in response to Sophie's stillborn baby? Her mother must have known. Had this been her mother's way of protecting her? The more Sophie delved into both her mother's life and her own, the less she understood. *Oh, the indignity of it all!* Three generations of women raped and made to pay for the irresponsible follies of men. Sophie collapsed onto the table and wept.

Reaching across the table, Kate stroked Sophie's hand, but she, too, sat in silence. Her own thoughts were reverberating wildly through her head: *If I hear from him no more, I have no choice; I must move on.* Honorine's words hit her like a punch to the stomach. How had she been able to move forward? What obstacles was she forced to overcome? Kate knew of Marcelle's history, so from what wells of inner strength had these two women drawn? They both grew up under the tenets of the Catholic Church, but was the Church there for them in the long run?

How had she, Kate, found the inner strength to move forward during her pregnancy with Lisa? Had it been faith, fear, or pure unadulterated ignorance? *All three of us were young,* Kate thought, *so maybe we didn't know we could fail. And how had that worked for them? All three of us lived our lives based on the tragic circumstances of the past—a past we could never change or take back. So where did that lead Marcelle and Honorine?* Their children and grandchildren never knew their secrets and questioned their own identity. *What does that teach me?* Kate asked herself. She still had a lot of soul-searching to do before she could even answer.

Kate paid the bill and urged Sophie to her feet. The day had been one long over exposure to mental anguish, and both were exhausted. Shambling along the sidewalk, they made their way back to the hotel and collapsed into bed without another word.

CHAPTER FIFTEEN

A Close Encounter

A

*T*HE FOLLOWING MORNING, after showers, a quick croissant, and a *café*, Kate and Sophie prepared to head up the highway. Again, Kate watched Sophie for signs of depression, but as Sophie explained quite succinctly, "I can't get depressed; I'm already on meds."

"If you say so! By the way, were you able to get any sleep last night?" Kate asked as she walked over to the window to check the weather. "I kept dreaming of World War I, and then I woke up to noises coming from the streets." She noted a heavy fog lay over the city, so she pulled her blue knit sweater over her head, adjusted her hair, then closed her suitcase.

"*Mais oui*," Sophie said with a chuckle. "You are in the heart of Paris—a city that never sleeps. But I can officially tell you, there were no wars last night." She grabbed one of her colorful scarves, wrapped it around her neck, and tied it deftly. "So, should we be off?"

The cold grey mist lifted slightly off the Seine as they passed over the Quai d'Orsay near the Tuileries. Sophie looped around and then headed up the Champs Élysées, past the Arc de Triomphe, and back to the Périphérique. Eventually, she swept north out of the city. They were heading to Normandy to spend the night, but they could take their time. Sophie slid back into a comfortable position and clicked on the cruise control. She did enjoy driving.

The morning fog lifted, and the sun turned the day into a wonderland of frost-coated etchings on all edges of nature. The pearlescent sky transformed from grey into a bright blue dome, with the sun almost blinding them as the car continued north on their journey.

"I wonder," Kate asked after some time, "if your Grandmother Honorine went in search of Raymond in Paris? That was where he was from, wasn't it?"

"That was where she went in search of work," Sophie said, sitting up a bit. "If she didn't know if he was alive or dead, maybe she checked the Parisian records for a death certificate. Hmm. Something to contemplate." Her fingers thrummed the steering wheel.

"Or if she got a divorce from Raymond to marry again. I doubt that would happen, but she did marry again. Right? Your mother had a stepfather."

"No divorces back then," Sophie said matter-of-factly. "I'm going to ask Christian to check the records for Raymond. He's quite tech savvy, as he began searching the records for *his* grandfather. You know, Thierry's real father? I told you *Maman* had been quite forthcoming with him before she died."

"Yes, you did. You know, this is beginning to feel like a mystery that is solving itself, doesn't it, Sophie?"

Sophie hesitated and then nodded in agreement. As they drove through the open countryside, they followed the A16. The morning sunlight danced across kilometers of rust-colored fields and filtered down on them as they passed through dense forests, followed along rivers, and crossed over streams.

Kate was peering out the window when she asked, "Where are we, Sophie?" They had been driving for well over an hour, and the cityscape had long since disappeared.

"About one hundred kilometers or so north of Paris, not far from the city of Amiens. We're near where one of the bloodiest battles of World War I took place. Whole regiments were mowed down by the Germans during the summer of 1916." She clicked on the turn indicator to exit the highway and drove down a side road.

"I need to stretch my legs," she said, as she pulled over to a small parking lot. A granite obelisk rose out of the bushes high above the Somme River. The two climbed out of the car and walked over to the war memorial, where Sophie swept tall weeds and debris aside with her hand.

"Ah, ha, Kate, this is what I was hoping for. This monument marks the site of not one, but two World War I battles that were fought here. The First Battle of the Somme, this says, was in July 1916. It was one of the bloodiest battles of the War . . ." Sophie continued reading to herself and then said, "Then, the Second Battle of the Somme was in 1918."

"1918? Are we anywhere near Albert?" Kate asked.

Sophie turned and stared up and down the road, as if road signs would magically appear. "You know, it might just be up this road twenty or more kilometers. Why do you ask?" A mysterious gleam caught in Sophie's eye, but she said no more.

"Albert! Albert!" Kate said, almost jumping up and down. "Don't you remember Raymond Pourrette may have been injured at the Second Battle of Somme near Albert? Wasn't that the last place Raymond Pourrette was known to have been alive? That wasn't long before your mother was born, Sophie. Albert, huh?"

"Okay, I've got it now. But what are you thinking, Kate? Are you thinking, after all these years, we could find Raymond Pourrette in Albert?"

"Probably not," Kate said, her exuberance dwindling.

"Actually," Sophie said with a smug look, "I was thinking we should stop by to see what Albert looks like, get the lay of the land, see if there are any cemeteries . . ."

"Oh, you little minx!" Kate laughed. "You were intending to head there all the time," she said as she chucked Sophie's chin. "So, are you saying we're close by?"

Sophie nodded and strode back to the car, beaming at Kate over her shoulder.

"Ah then, while we're there, maybe we could find a little café?" Kate said, as she scrambled after Sophie.

Sophie eased her car back onto the roadway, and, with a bit of assistance from Justine the GPS, they found the D938. Just beyond a broad sweep of low-lying hills lay the village of Albert. As they reached the outskirts of town, they spotted the Albert French National Cemetery. Twenty-five-foot-tall white stone pillars supporting iron gates marked the opening of the graveyard. Beyond the gates, white stone crosses stretched across a wide expanse. Sophie stopped the car, and both women climbed out and made their way up the steps to the iron gates. Sophie pushed on the gate, but it didn't budge.

"Hmm! Looks like we need a key to enter," Sophie said, looking around.

Kate peeked inside to see if there was a directory but couldn't get her head through the bars.

"Don't get stuck," Sophie chortled. "I'd hate to leave you behind!"

Kate grinned. "It was worth a try! We might have found our peripatetic Raymond Pourrette!" She shaded her eyes and scanned the field. "How many soldiers do you think are here?"

Sophie counted the number of rows and estimated a number. "I would guess over several thousand, but maybe we can find more detail in town." They spun around and returned to the car.

The road curved gently into town, where three church towers

loomed above the village. One in particular caught their attention. Sophie drove straight for it and pulled into a parking lot in the *centre ville.* They clamored out of the car again and made their way to the base of the Basilica. Peering up from the base, the two noticed the building had been recently restored. The six-story red brick edifice, the Basilica of Notre Dame Brebieres, was stunning in the sunlight with white Romanesque arches gracing every window, doorway, and opening on the bell tower. Crowning the steeple was a shiny gold leaf dome topped with a Madonna hoisting her infant, the Christ Child, above her head.

"Most impressive," Kate said, as she tilted her head back. Sophie was busy reading a sign at the church when she heard Kate shout, "Hey, I think it says here that the World War I Museum is just to the *nord* side of this church. Let's go see if it's open. What time is it?"

"It's lunchtime, so I would imagine it's closed, but we can try," Sophie said. The two skittered around the side of the Basilica to find the museum closed.

"Drats," Kate said. "Okay, then, it's lunchtime for us." They walked half a block to the main street, which was thronged with parked cars but was almost empty of people. The entire village appeared to have locked every door and shuttered every window. The silence was deafening.

"This reminds me of the small town I was raised in," Sophie giggled.

"Me, too! We used to joke about the streets being rolled up at night, but during the day? Not so much!" Kate said.

"I bet I know where to find them," Sophie said as she strode across the street and into a small hotel, La Victoire, which advertised a tavern.

Walking through the beveled-glass doors, they found themselves in a small but well-appointed lobby. The front desk was tucked into a side alcove decorated with Victorian-print wallpaper and brass lamps that lent warmth to a small table. A handful of brochures advertising local businesses was fanned out, including several brochures listing tours of WWI battlegrounds. Sophie scooped up several tour guides and caught up with Kate, who had disappeared around a corner.

Tantalized by the spicy aroma of grilled sausages and onions along with the bitter smell of hops and beer, Kate had followed to where she heard friendly voices and a buzz of activity. Entering the dining area, they found it to be a warm, comfortable-looking brewpub. Beer mugs lined the shelves above the bar, and two bar maids feverishly drew frothy steins of beer and slid them along the counter. The two women were shown to their seats, where they slipped into a cushioned banquette.

The menu was one of charcuterie: andouillettes sausages, coq à la bière, and potjevleesch. Sophie gave Kate a quick tutorial on two of the Flemish-style foods. "Coq à la bière is a rooster who has seen better days but has given his life to be boiled in ale. And, potjevleesh is made up of the lives of chicken, rabbit, and veal mixed together and suspended in death in a fatty jelly made with onions and herbs."

"On that note," Kate said, "I'll follow your lead and order andouillettes sausages, *s'il vous plaît.*"

Once the daily specials had been ordered, Sophie requested the pièce de résistance: the house-made beer. She sank further into the banquette and said, "Ah, more than wine, I love my beer!"

She scanned the brochure once again and said, "After lunch, let's go see what we can find out about the museum. They may be open later. And then we can check out the cemeteries."

An elderly gentleman at the table near them overheard their conversation and caught Sophie's eye. "If you want to know anything about Albert, I could certainly fill you in. I've lived in Albert all my life," he told them. From the looks of him, that had been a lengthy period.

"All right, monsieur," Sophie said, waving him to join them. The man was all angles and sharp points—nose, knees, elbows, shoulders. His loose-fitting jacket and pants hung from his body as if by magic, but the twinkle in his bright blue eyes was clear and spoke of years of mischief. He bowed, doffed his dusty beret, and then, not knowing where to place it, slapped it back on his head.

"My name is Monsieur LeBlanc, mesdames," he said as he slid onto the banquette. He and Sophie conversed through a couple of beers apiece before the meal arrived. Monsieur LeBlanc squeezed himself up close to Sophie and was speaking animatedly about his hometown. Kate was satisfied to catch partial snippets of his dialect but was looking forward to hearing Monsieur LeBlanc's story. At one point, he dragged them from the comfort of their seats, his napkin still tucked under his collar, to lead them out the front door of the hotel to point wildly up at the golden tower of the Basilica.

"I can't stand it anymore," Kate said to Sophie. "What on earth is he saying?"

"He's telling us the story of the 'Leaning Virgin'. He says the tower on the Basilica was considered a landmark during World War I. It was hit by German bombers early on in the campaign, leaving the statue of the Madonna leaning precariously at a ninety-degree angle. During the next three years as the war continued, superstition had it that when she—the Leaning Virgin—fell, the war would end. The myth inspired frequent pot shots by disgruntled troops of the French, Australian, and British sides, for they were all hoping to bring the war to an end." Sophie finished her translation with an appreciative laugh.

"*Avec plaisir*," Monsieur LeBlanc beamed. "Of course, it was only a myth, but it made for a great story back then." His blue eyes sparkled.

"It's still a great story," Sophie said as she put her hand on his elbow and the three made their way back into the brewpub. Now there was no turning back. The old man continued non-stop chatter with the two, waving his hands with great exhilaration, and once, between swigs of beer, he stood up to pantomime the digging of holes. Sophie threw her head back and laughed long and hard, then gave Kate a quick explanation of his antics.

"He told me that the underground shelters, which were built during World War I, are where the museum is now. The museum has some impressive photos of life in the trenches during the battles of the Somme in 1916 and 1918—" She stopped short, as Monsieur LeBlanc interrupted her translation.

"I remember when the shelters served as bunkers for Albert's residents during the bombings in World War II. We spent many hours and evenings huddled in there and were grateful they were available to us." He wiped his brow, as if it had been last night.

Sophie asked him how old he was during WWII. He replied, "I was sixteen at the time, but I remember it well. *Mais oui,* there were many times when we crawled out of those bunkers that *Maman* would send me ahead to see if our house was left standing. For many, that wasn't the case," he said, shaking his head sadly.

"He really has a great memory," Kate remarked, smiling at Monsieur LeBlanc. "Say, I wonder if there are any pictures of your grandfather in the museum. Did you ask him if there is a list of those who died or went missing during World War I?"

"*Oui!* He said there may be records at the museum. But he says he doubts we could find anyone in particular. There were thousands and thousands of men who died here. It would be a monumental job."

Monsieur LeBlanc nodded his head, "*Pas impossible,*" he said, lifting his hand and waving one arthritic finger back and forth.

"But pretty iffy, huh," Kate said.

"Yes, and we have to hit the road soon if we want to make it to Mont St. Michel before it's too late."

Sophie signaled for the check, and the two women were

rummaging through their purses when Kate asked Sophie, "Did you ask this gentleman if he is familiar with the name Pourrette? Raymond Pourrette?"

Monsieur LeBlanc's eyes popped open with surprise. "Pourrette? *Mais oui?* Why, he lived here after he was wounded during World War I. He eventually moved back to Paris, but that was many years ago. Why do you ask?"

"I think," Sophie stammered, "he may have been my grandfather. I'm just trying to find out."

"Your grandfather?" Monsieur LeBlanc sat still for a moment looking her over and then squinted into her eyes. "Well, that's possible, but my first reaction would be one of surprise. If we're talking about the same Raymond Pourrette . . ."

"Oh, I can't be certain, but what I've just learned is that my mother's father, one Raymond Pourrette, may have been wounded near here. My mother never actually knew him, as she was born on the last day of The Great War and he never came home. No one knows what happened. So she carried his name all her life but never knew anything about him. She passed away . . ." Sophie choked on her words. "I'm sorry. *Maman* passed away only a few weeks ago, but her last wish was for me to find her father." Sophie picked up her napkin and dabbed at her tears as they began a downward slide. Monsieur LeBlanc took Sophie's hand into his.

"Well, Madame, let me tell you what I know," he said, after clearing his throat of a lifetime of smoking. "The man I knew named Raymond Pourrette became a close friend to my father and hung around here after the war ended. He was wounded near here in Albert. In fact, it was my father who found him, pulled him out of the mud, and brought him home. My grandparents helped him convalesce. He and my father became very close, like brothers. He told us he had no brothers and that all the others in his family had been killed. Now, I wasn't born until '25, but I remember his visits. He walked with a limp. 'Vestiges of war,' he said. And he would often show up for holidays and was good to us kids, because . . . because he said he didn't have a family of his own."

"Other than his leg being injured, or walking with a limp, did he have any head injuries?" Sophie asked somberly.

"Are you asking me if he had a brain injury? Oh, Madame, I wouldn't know about that," he said, scratching the stubble on his chin. "I was much too young." He paused. "He was just a nice man who seemed sad and lonely—except when he had us kids tumbling into his lap. But now, let me think about this. Yes, I believe he said he was originally from Paris, and he eventually moved back there and got married. I remember we were really happy for him." He paused again, lifting a tobacco-stained finger to thrum on the side of his head. "You know, come to think of it, he *did* have children. I'm sorry, but this part is hazy for me. It must have been right before World War II began . . ."

Sophie immediately thought of her mother making her way back to Paris, pregnant with her brother, Thierry. That was shortly before the war began. *Had her mother's own father been close by all that time?*

Kate's reaction was quizzical. "Why does he remember him so vividly?"

"That's easy, mesdames," Monsieur Le Blanc said. "He was my godfather. You see, my name is Raymond LeBlanc. I was named after him." A smile broke across his wrinkled face.

Sophie began to ask another question, but when she saw tears appearing in his eyes, she brought their conversation to an end.

"Thank you, sir, for your time," she said, clasping the old man's hands. "I'm certain you are talking about another Raymond Pourrette, but it was a great pleasure meeting you and hearing your stories."

"Well, if you have any more questions, please come back to Albert. I'll be here until the day I die," he said as he removed his napkin from his collar and wiped both eyes dry.

"I'll do it, Monsieur LeBlanc. I'll do it." Sophie kissed the man and paid for his lunch and beer, and the women headed out the door.

"What do you make of him, Sophie?" Kate asked when they were outside.

"I'm not certain; it may be a fit. It may not, but I didn't want to upset him, just in case we were talking about two different people. Like I said before, I'm going to have Christian check on the name in the Paris archives. I don't know what else we can do, as I doubt my grandfather is still alive." Sophie was clearly shaken by her encounter with Monsieur LeBlanc.

"That was rather uncanny that we should actually speak to someone who may have known your grandfather, though. What are the chances? And do you remember when your mother mentioned a stranger in the park who limped? That was when your mother lived in Paris as a child." Kate looked over at Sophie for her reaction. "Are you all right? Do you want me to drive, Sophie?" Kate asked as she slipped her hand through the crook of Sophie's arm.

"I'm fine. I'm just trying to digest the fact that a real person is actually behind the name Pourrette. All of these years of wondering about our family puzzles, and now the answers seem to be magically falling from the sky. Well, that's it! I was meant to know this information! That's all there is to it! *Maman* must be directing this from above." She threw a kiss toward the heavens. "So off we go," she said, with a snap to her step.

As they drove along the banks of the Baie du Mont Saint-Michel, evening mist began to rise from the deep grasses, and the setting sun sent radiant shafts of golden light across the windows of a grey stone manor, which loomed before them. Following along an entryway lined with lime trees, they pulled up to a four-story manor house that was covered in a thick beard of ivy. An elegant staircase, which swept down from the center of the house, held a bevy of young men, who rushed down the steps to assist them. The women were hustled into the manor's main hallway, where they were met by their hosts before being escorted four flights up to their room. Having driven across a large swath of France that day, this was a welcome greeting.

Once they had settled in, Kate and Sophie made their way back down to the main dining room, where a large open-pit grill was set into the main house wall. The heady aroma of the house specialty, *pré-salé d'agneau*, tantalized both Sophie and Kate.

"What is *pré-salé d'agneau*, anyway?" asked Kate. They had ordered a bottle of local apple cider while awaiting their dining table.

"It's quite well-known around here," Sophie replied. "The lovely lambs that graze by the bay consume salt-encrusted marsh grasses. The salt serves to season and flavor their meat, a very rare delicacy from this area."

By the time Kate and Sophie were led to their table in a glass-enclosed dining area, the sun had been down for some time and only the lights high on top of Mont Saint-Michel, the infamous island, shown across the kilometer of the bay that separated them. A light fog that had been rising off the water eventually consumed the island, and Mont Saint-Michel disappeared from sight.

On the following morning, Kate awakened to see Mont Saint-Michel rising above the tidal plain like a golden crown in the morning light.

"Why are we here, Sophie?" Kate asked, turning from the window.

"Hopefully we can meet up with Christian. He lives not far south of here, and if his schedule works out, we may be able to see him tomorrow. But, for today, you can do some sightseeing by yourself while I make some phone calls."

After breakfast, Sophie drove Kate to the base of Mont Saint-Michel and bid her *adieu.* By the time Kate located Sophie in the parking lot hours later, it was after 3:00 PM. Kate was worn out, but happy. She had joined an English-speaking tour and had hiked all the way to the top of the Mont. Kate reveled in these moments of gathering history and was ready to babble on and on, but Sophie seemed preoccupied. As they sat on the wall below the massive Mont, Sophie blurted out, "I've heard back from my nephew, Christian."

"Yes?" Kate caught the grim expression on Sophie's face. "Is there something wrong? "

"I'm just trying to sort out what he told me."

"What did he say?"

"He researched the name Raymond Pourrette by going online to the French registry. He told me that Raymond Pourrette died in Paris in 1970! 1970! Can you imagine that?" Sophie's face was strained, her eyes red.

"Which might fit with what that little man in Albert told us, right?" Kate was busy thumping her chin with her fingers when she looked up to see Sophie's face fall. "What is it, Sophie? What did I miss?"

"I'm thinking that all of those years my mother lived in Paris, it seems her own father was living possibly within blocks of her. All those years she considered herself a bastard."

Sophie tried to pull herself together but instead she felt weaker. Over and over again, like a reel in a movie, she kept imagining what may have happened between her grandparents: why they had refused to reunite in spite of being in love, why they had never sought each other out. Or had they? Sophie appeared to wilt; her arms hung limp at her sides. Kate put her arms around her friend and drew her close. She felt so small, so frail, that to Kate, it was like holding a rag doll. Receiving directions to the car, Kate led Sophie to the passenger side and let her in. She sat mute, staring out at the mainland in the distance. The tide was coming in, and the water was rising quickly. Kate climbed into the driver's side and started the car but sat with the engine idling to warm Sophie.

"And there is another thing," Sophie said, not breaking her gaze from the horizon. "The records indicate that Raymond Pourrette remarried, in 1939—within months after my Grandmother Honorine passed away. So he must have known where she was because he had to wait until her death before he could remarry. There was no divorce recorded."

Kate braced herself against the driver's seat.

"Just like Monsieur Le Blanc told us, Raymond had three other children. Sorry, but I can't contain this any longer." Again, her body heaved forward, and she sobbed. Minutes elapsed before she sat up and wiped her face dry with Kate's handkerchief. Her small body straightened. "I didn't want to believe Monsieur LeBlanc, but it's true. My mother had siblings!"

"Really! That's a . . . low blow, isn't it," Kate said, somberly. Her brow furrowed.

Sophie smiled weakly. "I don't know, Kate. This is all new to me. I'm not certain what anything means anymore. That's why I brought you along. Remember? You get to sort out all these answers."

"Nothing like pulling a rabbit out of a hat!" Kate smiled. Then she turned serious. "If you were able to find the names of the other siblings, would you want to find them? They may or may not know of their father's previous marriage." She took a deep breath and turned off the engine and opened the window a crack. It had suddenly gotten hot in the car.

Sophie took a moment to think, then said, "From the bits of information I read in my grandmother's diary, we don't know for certain that Raymond *was* my mother's biological father. Raymond was away during World War I. What if, after all of this, he wasn't *Maman*'s father?"

Sophie tipped her head back on the headrest and closed her eyes. The wind whipped up, blowing through the windows Kate had just opened and sending Sophie's dark brown hair into spiky points. Kate smiled at her and reached over to smooth down Sophie's newly formed horns.

"I guess I would choose to believe your grandmother knew she was pregnant with Raymond's baby. She mentioned several times in her diary not feeling well. It may have been Raymond who was misled."

Sophie sat quietly contemplating the dilemma. "You're right," she said. She swabbed her face with a tissue. "Barging into Raymond Pourrette's family might bring more pain and shame on everyone. Plus, I'll have no more answers than before."

"Believe it or not, Sophie, sometimes the truth doesn't always set us free."

Sophie nodded her head and then waved for Kate to follow. She got out of the car and led Kate back to the edge of the car park, where they watched the rising water. Small grey-green waves were turning larger as the wind whipped up white caps. Trees on the opposite banks were bending their heads as the last of their leaves were dispersed into the water around them. Clutching her coat about her, Sophie said, "Over there, Normandy ends and Brittany begins, where the River Couesnon runs into the sea." Their eyes scanned the shoreline across from them, searching for the elusive river.

"In days past," Sophie continued, "the river could be found either to the left or the right side of Mont Saint-Michel. This meant that the border between Normandy and Brittany could move with the rains, the tides, or the flooding of the river. They used to say, '*Le Couesnon, dans sa folie, à mis le Mont en Normandie,* which means, The Couesnon, in its madness, has put the Mont in Normandy. But, of course, nobody knows when the next change will take place—perhaps in Brittany." she said with a shrug.

"Sounds like another crisis of identity rises to the fore," Kate said.

Sophie giggled as she slipped back into the driver's seat and they returned to the manor for a final night.

CHAPTER SIXTEEN

The Heart of A Woman

HE FOLLOWING MORNING, as they were heading west to Brittany, both Sophie and Kate felt Marcelle's omni-presence. One of her final wishes was to travel with the two of them to her birthplace, and it felt as if she were along for the ride.

"Say," Kate said, "Your mother mentioned that crossing over into Brittany is a point of departure from France. What did she mean?"

"A perfect time to ask," Sophie said, as she made a right turn onto the autoroute. She pointed to a sign before they passed by.

Kate caught only a peek but realized the sign was no longer written in French. "What did it say?" she asked.

"Well, I know a little Breton, but this looks to be Gallo, which is the language of eastern Brittany. I would imagine it says, 'Welcome to Brittany.' Or possibly it says, 'You are now leaving France. Good riddance!'" She laughed heartily at her own joke and then began to cough. She cleared her throat.

"To say that Brittany's past belongs to its present is not a paradox here, Kate. The Bretons remain faithful to preserving their origins. As my mother taught me, Brittany holds within its soul its own language, history, customs, and legends. And these legends, whether natural or supernatural, form an integral part of each Breton." She cast a glance in Kate's direction.

"*Maman* gloried in the knowledge that at any moment, an elf or a *korrigan* could spring into view amidst the moors of flowering gorse and broom. Keep your eyes open—just in case!" She laughed again. A renewed lilt filtered into her voice, and when she threw her head back to laugh, a fresh sparkle took up residence in her eyes. The look of anxiety from yesterday was gone.

"Do you know much about the mythology of Brittany?" Kate asked Sophie as they wended their way along the coastal roads. Just then, Sophie's GPS, Justine, began to make some odd comments. She seemed quite disturbed.

"What's the matter?" Kate asked. "Is she having trouble reading the signs in Celtic? Or is it Gallo?" She chuckled to herself.

"She does seem to be lost and is pretty upset. Maybe Justine has seen a *korrigan*. That's what it is, I'm certain of it." She giggled. "How about you?"

"Have I seen a *korrigan*? First, I would have to know what one is." Kate laughed.

"*Korrigans* are traditional Breton gnomes. They're neither good nor evil, but they come out at night and entice people into dancing. It is only at daybreak that they release their captives and then disappear from sight once again. I think *Maman* had a bit of *korrigan* in her too, don't you?" Sophie tittered.

Kate nodded, "That reminds me of the old Irish myths my mother used to tell us kids. Marcelle reminded me often of my mother." A smile slipped across Kate's lips, and a faraway look came into her blue eyes. An image of sitting on her mother's lap while listening to the stories of mermaids flitted into mind. Her mother's warm, soothing voice rolled over her from the past. Kate shook her head, bringing herself back into the present.

"Oh, *Maman* loved her myths," Sophie said. She shoved the sleeves of her sweater up her arms.

"I especially remember your mother telling us the legend of the City of Ys. That was the story of the king and his mermaid daughter, right?"

"The City of Ys . . . yes, that was the one about good King Gradlon who built a city off the coast of Dourarnenez, out in the sea, for his beautiful daughter, Dahut. But, as the legend goes, when she began practicing the ancient Celtic rites, or 'witchcraft,' to lure handsome men to her, the God of the Catholic faith intervened. He destroyed the City of Ys turned the then-pregnant Dahut into a mermaid, and left King Gradlon on the shore to mourn his loss."

"That's it!" Kate exclaimed. She pivoted in her seat to face Sophie and recited, "Even now, the ringing of bells at night will bring Bretons to their windows to peek out in anticipation of this ancient city rising up from the sea." She beamed. "Can't you just imagine your mother as a little girl thrusting her head out of the window listening, listening for the bells in the sea?" Kate leaned back in her seat. "You know, Sophie, when I first heard the tale of the City of Ys, I remembered a similar Celtic version my mother told us when I was young."

"Kate, do you think," Sophie interrupted, "the myths are part of your draw to my mother? Or maybe there's a connection to your own mother—through these myths or legends?"

Kate paused to think, then shrugged. "Good question . . . I'm not certain. The legend is about a town swallowed up by water, a lake in Northern Ireland known as Loch Nog or Loch Neagh. And it's also about a beautiful maiden, whose name was Annie. Anyway," Kate continued, "in the land of Nog, or Neagh, there was once a wellspring, which was known far and wide to contain purifying water. If one was to drink from it, you could receive enlightenment and wisdom, so it was considered sacred. But it was also common knowledge that if ever the wellspring was left uncovered, the waters inside would immediately seek to be free.

"One fine day, Annie was sent to the well to bring back a pail of water for her mother. Now, Annie's mother was known to dabble in Celtic rites, also known as witchcraft. Because of her mother, there were some who failed to see Annie's good qualities and therefore sought to destroy her. Waiting near the well was an evil spirit disguised as a frail old man. Prevailing upon the young maiden, he asked her to remove the lid and fill his pail. Eager to help, she lifted the heavy lid and leaned over to lower his bucket into the purifying waters. When she was most vulnerable, the old man leaped upon her and attempted to push her into the well. Terrified, yet strong, she broke free and bolted from the well as fast as she could go. The old man disappeared just as quickly, forgetting to replace the lid. The uncovered well sought to find its own life-giving freedom and immediately overflowed. Within hours, the water filled the entire valley, drowning and destroying the nearby town and the population therein. All living creatures, crops, and dreams, whether Christian or pagan, were swallowed up by the water, creating the lake known as Loch Nog (Neagh).

"Now, when the weather is calm, fishermen have reported seeing an underwater city, with church towers rising to the top of the lake, and according to legend, mermaids can be seen dancing among the beautiful columns of the palaces inhabited long ago. Like in the myth of Dahut!"

"Oooh, I love that, Kate," Sophie said, loudly clapping. Sophie settled back, thinking of the myth Kate had just recounted. "You know, Kate, it is said that legends are not necessarily history, yet legends are part of history. And you'll find while we're in Brittany, legends and mythology are a part of everyone's history. Certainly *Maman's*!"

"Remember when your mother told us how she used to play the role of King Gradlon? I loved that. I can just imagine her as a spunky and spirited little kid," Kate said. "Do these legends continue to impact people today?"

"That's what I was just saying. I'm not sure you can separate the myth from the man, but we can ask Mimi when we see her tomorrow night. Until then, keep your eyes open. That spirit—or spunk, as you call it—came from right here." She pointed to the thick forests and vales around them.

"Ah, she would have loved this trip, right Sophie?" Kate said while enjoying the dense forests they were passing through.

"I believe she is, Kate," Sophie said quietly.

"You feel her presence, too, don't you?" Kate said, casting a grin in Sophie's direction.

"I do. And, even more so today! Maybe it's because we are coming home," Sophie said.

The road before them curved and undulated up and down the hills and through the tiny villages along their route. Every now and again, they would round a bend and the sea would leap into view.

"This was where it all began, Kate," Sophie said. She paused and turned to face her friend. "This is where the character of my mother developed and where she rose up to become the strong woman she was. This is where she learned that the heart of a woman is deeper than the deepest sea—which governed her entire life." Kate nodded but sat back to soak it in.

As the women ventured farther into Brittany, rain fell gently upon them, off and on, light and misty at times, changing slightly with the wind. The early-November air felt cool but surprisingly not cold, so as they traveled around the fringes of Brittany's coastline, they popped in and out of the car to enjoy the seascapes. It was early afternoon when they veered off the main road to stop for lunch in the walled city of St. Malo. The tide was extremely low. Old tugs and sailboats listed heavily to one side with their keels resting lazily in the mud. The two followed a path where locals walked along the sea wall with their dogs, stopped to chat with old friends, or entered the city gates. Seagulls and pelicans skulked about the edges of the water in search of lunch, as the smell of salt, sea, and seaweed wafted up to the two as they sought out a *crêperie.*

Later, as they headed up the Cote d'Emeraude, the sun began to pour through the clouds, and Sophie said, "On stormy winter days like this, when the rain is pelting the moors, the Cote d'Emeraude honors its name. The sea is never slate gray but always this emerald green in color." This day was no different, and with the sunlight dancing across the water and the surf crashing along the rocky shoals below them, they were forced to shield their eyes from the flashes of sunlight as they drove from Dinard toward St. Brieuc.

"Sophie, didn't you tell me that Thierry's father came from St. Brieuc?"

"Yes, that's what Christian told me yesterday."

"Are you planning a stop there?" Kate asked.

She shrugged. "That's a dilemma I seem to find myself in. Once I receive these little tidbits of family history, I don't know how far to push them. How much do I *really* want to know?"

Sophie navigated in and around fishing villages cradled in protective coves, then up and around bracken-covered cliffs with heather stretching into purple fingers over the hillsides.

"So there's nothing you want to check out in St. Brieuc? You won't be back here for a while." Kate looked at Sophie to see how she was managing.

"It will keep," Sophie said, after a moment's time. "Christian needs to sort this out on his own. I have my own stories to sort."

Stories to sort, Kate thought, *stories to sort.* "Speaking of stories to sort, I'm curious to know more about your mysterious Christophe," Kate prompted.

"Ah, it's no mystery," Sophie said as her face softened. Her shoulders relaxed and she breathed in deeply. "He was my first flirt. For sure, he was the first to capture my heart." Her hand lightly danced across her breast.

"How old were you when you first met him?"

"I was a young teen—maybe thirteen or fourteen years old. Hmmh. Let me think about this. He was from my father's village of Pont-à-Meuse, but he attended high school in Ste. Barbe. Yes, he was bussed to school in Ste. Barbe each day." She patted the steering wheel, as if touching base with her past.

"How did you meet?"

"Oh . . . Poof! One day when I was crossing the schoolyard before school, I saw the bus pull to a stop and happened to look up as he started to get off the bus. Just then, some bully shoved him out of the door and onto the ground. I went over to help him up. He was rather small in size, as was I, so we had that in common. I remember the smile on his face when I helped him up was the most beautiful smile I had ever seen. Again, I was so young." Sophie turned and grinned at Kate.

"He seemed so grateful to me. I told you that he had had polio as a small child and walked with a limp. Unfortunately, kids made fun of him, but I rather liked him. He was such a sweet boy, always so kind to me."

"Sounds like it was mutual," Kate said. "So, tell me about your torrid love affair."

Sophie threw her head back and laughed raucously. "Oh, la la. Well, actually, I'm going to surprise you, as there's not much to tell. We saw each other only in school. We didn't have the same classes, so we mostly passed notes when we would go from one class to another. Sometimes our fingers would touch, and I remember it felt like fire flowing through me. But, alas, we were never able to meet socially, and we were never alone."

Kate contemplated this. "Did your folks meet him?"

"Heavens, no!" She paused. "Well, I don't know now." She took a moment to think. "I just remember my father insisting that I stop seeing him. Oh, the heated discussions we had around our supper table until . . ." She paused. Her eyes drifted up and off the road before her. The car listed to the right.

"Until? Until what?" Kate grabbed the wheel but prodded Sophie to continue. "Don't leave me hanging here."

"Ah, dear Christophe. He was my first love, and like my mother taught me, the heart of a woman . . . This sounds rather melodramatic now, doesn't it?"

Kate glanced out the window just as the bright green waters of the Breton sea came into view. "Yes, that was exactly what your mother quoted. The heart of a woman is deeper than the deepest sea. And here we are near to that very sea."

A beatific smile spread across Sophie's face. "It was also something my Grandmother Honorine mentioned in her diary, remember? Anyway, I was only fourteen or fifteen, but I opened myself up to him, although not sexually. I was much too frightened for that! Even though I may have wanted to, I couldn't consent to . . . So when he turned away from me, I thought I couldn't face life without him. Probably, I was overreacting, but what teenager is not?" She shook her head with the memory.

"I remember the night," she said, drifting back and forth on the road, "that I rode my bike out of Ste. Barbe and along the back routes to Pont-à-Meuse. I hadn't been to Pont-à-Meuse since that horrible night with my uncle, but it was a warm fall night. Haven't I told you all this before? I, for the first time, searched for Christophe's house. Why I went, I don't remember. Maybe to tell him I loved him. Maybe to give myself to him . . ." She blushed. "But I never got the chance. As I started down the dirt road to his house, I recognized my father's car sitting in what I assumed was Christophe's driveway.

"I thought my father had gone to put a stop to our love. And it worked. Even though my tears were blinding my way, I fled back into the night, terrified my father would find out I had disobeyed him. I must have flown home. But it was that night that I first committed . . . no, attempted suicide. I just wanted to die. Like a young Juliet without her Romeo, I wanted Christophe to come to me. But it never happened. He never came to the hospital. And I never got over him."

"You say you attempted suicide *that* night?" Kate didn't wait for her answer. "What time of year was this again? Could this have been in September, by any chance?"

Sophie looked over at Kate, her eyebrows furrowed. "Yes. Why?"

"I'm wondering if your attempted suicide coincides with you ending up in the hospital due to your . . . Well, your pregnancy." Kate said haltingly. She was wading in too deep, but she couldn't turn back now.

"You mean my stillborn?" Sophie shrilled. Her hands flew off the steering wheel as she clutched the sides of her head. Kate once again turned the steering wheel as they swerved out of the way of an oncoming car.

"Whew, boy! That was close," Kate gasped, as Sophie took back the wheel. Shock was all that registered on Sophie's face.

"I'm so sorry, Sophie; I didn't mean to bring this up in this way," Kate pleaded. She, too, was feeling undone.

Sophie pulled onto a side road overlooking the sea. All was quiet except for the crashing of waves far below. She turned off the ignition and sat back. "I need to get a grip," she breathed heavily. "I almost killed us back there! I can't believe it!" She was shaking from head to toe. Rolling the window down, she began fanning herself. The salty odor of the sea blew into the car. Low tide. It was not unpleasant, just familiar, and both breathed in deeply.

"Let me think a moment; let me think!" Sophie whispered, as

her hands continued to flail at the air. Once her composure returned, she shouted, *"Zut alors!* It *was* in the fall!"

Sophie remembered it had been early dusk, and the sunlight was beginning to fold in on itself as she rode her bicycle down the back road to Pont-à-Meuse. She dipped down into the woods, where the dappled light rapidly changed from golden to dark to light once again. Following the creek, Sophie had recognized this as a place from her childhood and felt it beckoning her return. Instead, she stood and pumped her way up the steep incline, making her way out of the vale. The path was awash with golden and burnt orange oak leaves that crunched noisily under her tires. The pungent scents of fall—earthy, musty odors of moss, chanterelles, and a past season's detritus filled her nostrils. Somewhere, a fire had been burning dead leaves, which cast a light blue haze across the valley before her. Even though her heart was in her throat, she was looking forward to seeing her love and saw beauty everywhere—until she spotted her father's car in Christophe's driveway.

"Yes, it was fall!" Sophie said out loud again. "On my return trip home, I remember my legs were pumping so fast because I was afraid of and angry with my father. I raced into the kitchen, grabbed the bottle of *aspirine*, and disappeared into my bedroom, where I choked down a handful of pills and waited to die. Unfortunately, I got terribly sick to my stomach, and once Papa got home, he and *Maman* rushed me to the *salle des urgences.*"

Suddenly, Sophie sat straight up in the driver's seat. *"Mon dieu!* Do you think I caused my baby to die?" As if a flood had been unleashed, tears poured down her cheeks and she began to rock back and forth, keening uncontrollably.

"No," Kate soothed, as she slid over to Sophie. "A few aspirins would not have made you lose your baby." She held her tight and stroked Sophie's hair. Speaking softly in her ear, she asked, "Have you had any more nightmares . . . about the hospital . . . or your father?"

Sophie sat up; she blinked back her tears. "No," she said with surprise, "I haven't! Isn't that interesting? Not a single one. What does that mean?"

"It means that whatever you feared in your dreams no longer holds power over you—and that includes your father."

She sat for a few moments, allowing those thoughts to percolate, and then climbed out of the car to gaze out to sea. Kate joined her.

With the wind whipping their faces with sea spray and the bitterns and seagulls swooping nearby, they both thought about their previous conversation but remained quiet.

When the wind turned icy and began to seep through their coats, Sophie said, "The Bretons were used to this cold and living by and with the sea. Of course, they knew no different, but as Bretons used to say, *Me zo gañet é kreiz er mor*, which means, *I was born in the middle of the sea*. I think one of the things my mother loved best about her native land was it was surrounded on three sides by the sea. Even though Brittany feels so removed, so remote, I believe that was part of the identity—her inner identity—a kinship with the light and the melancholy." Despite the cold, the two women stood, facing the wind, until the sun dipped below the horizon.

CHAPTER SEVENTEEN

Confronting the Past

A̲

$\mathscr{A}$FTER SPENDING THE NIGHT in Quimper, Sophie and Kate headed to Damgan, where they would stay several nights with Sophie's friend Mimi. An easy silence had settled between the two friends as they drove along, lulled by the passing scenery.

"Kate, I've been wondering," Sophie asked, "how were you able to handle being alone when you gave birth to Lisa? Your experience must have been similar to my mother's, except . . ."

Kate squirmed and twirled an errant curl, which had drooped onto her cheek. She contemplated how to answer. "Except that I gave her up for adoption," she said. "Yes, it was a lonely and frightening time, but I felt there were no other good options. I wanted to give my baby a fresh start in life—one with legitimacy." She shifted in her seat to face Sophie. "To be a single mother at that time was very shameful—as it would have been for your mother." Kate breathed out heavily. "Those were different times back then."

"I'm sure. I know my mother felt the shame of not only being a bastard, but also in having two illegitimate sons, so it's no wonder she rarely talked about her experience."

"When I first learned what Marcelle had gone through, it hit me like a punch to the stomach," Kate said. "I don't know about your mother's experience in living in the convent, but where I gave birth to Lisa was probably similar. It was run by the Salvation Army and was known as the Home for Unwed Mothers." Kate stared out of the window, blindly watching the traffic file past them. She saw nothing; she could hear nothing. Sophie waited quietly. At last, Kate continued.

"There was no real choice in the matter. I had to place my baby up for adoption. Abortion wasn't legal back then. And because I feared I could ruin my father's reputation—he was a minister at that time—I knew I would have to return home alone. None of this was spoken about amongst my family. It was just the way things were done back then. So I headed out to California and lived and worked with a family until I gave birth."

"What was that like?" Sophie asked. "Were they kind to you?"

"They were a blessing to me, and with their help, I was never alone. I helped with their three young children, cleaned the house, and did some of the cooking. In return, I had free room and board, and we traveled up and down the entire Pacific Coast that summer. Ironically, it was the Summer of Love in San Francisco—the summer of '67."

"When did you go the Salvation Army home?" Sophie asked.

"When I was in my ninth month, I moved into that facility."

"What was that like?" She glanced over at Kate. "Do you mind talking about this?"

Kate laughed. "I've never, ever talked about it. It feels rather—cleansing." She reached back into the forgotten corners of her memory. "The home itself had once been a regal turn-of-the-century mansion. A porte cochere covered in purple morning glories led to a wide veranda, which wrapped around the front of the house. Rocking chairs lined the veranda, and during that summer, they were filled with young women such as myself. Because the house was situated on twenty-five acres of woodlands, it was very secluded. Very beautiful and serene."

"Sounds like a resort, not a convent," Sophie said.

Kate chuckled. "Right! Maybe on the outside it looked good, but on the inside of the house it was quite plain, clean, and simple. Conventish! I shared a room with many girls, and the staff lived down the hall. I suppose there were about thirty girls at the time. One wing had been converted into a hospital of sorts, so that was where Lisa was born. I would have to say we were treated fairly but were expected to help with the cooking and cleaning and attend twice-daily Salvation Army prayer services and morality lectures."

"Oooh, like you Americans like to say, 'that's the rub'!" Sophie giggled.

"Exactly!" Kate smiled. "But I took it as penance needing to be paid. I'll never forget when the counselors told us that one out of four of us would return to give birth to another baby. That was a shock! I silently promised myself I would not be one to return. I did make some good friends. Perhaps like your mother, I never felt alone." Both sadness and relief welled up in her and flooded over. She grabbed a tissue and blew her nose.

"Well, anyway, the most difficult part was to hand over my beautiful baby for adoption. My lifetime goal of being a good mother was not to be," Kate snuffled, "for as soon as Lisa was blessed and baptized, I had to relinquish her. But if I couldn't be there for her, I could make certain the family that adopted her would be there for her in a way I couldn't as a single mother."

"And now you regret it?" Sophie asked.

"Every day. Even though I felt I was making the best choice possible for her, I will never be wholly satisfied with the decision I made."

Sophie nodded. "Yes, I believe my mother wrestled with having to leave Thierry behind during the exodus and then again when she left him at the farm after the war. She never felt like she had made the right decision—especially since she trusted my father would bring Thierry to live with us in Ste. Barbe . . . like she trusted that Papa would adopt Gérard." Sophie sighed deeply. "I guess you hope and pray for the best . . . and then you move on!"

They continued driving down the E60 along the Morbihan Bay, where Sophie and Kate eventually arrived in the coastal village of Damgan.

"My friend Mimi was born here in 1945," Sophie explained.

"So she's our age, then," Kate noted.

"*C'est vrai!* She spent her summers in Damgan with her Breton paternal grandparents and her winters in Ste. Barbe with her Polish maternal grandmother. Once World War II was over, her parents moved to Paris to find jobs, and like my mother, Mimi spent her first eight years with her maternal grandmother in Ste. Barbe, far from her parents. That's how we met and became close friends. But it was during those warm summer months of her childhood that she got to know her paternal grandparents and her parents and, of course, grew to love Damgan and all of Brittany."

"Similar to how your mother got to know her own mother, right?" Kate asked.

"*Oui.* We shared many memories of our early childhood together," Sophie said as she turned off the highway onto a connector route into Damgan, "and, it was in Ste. Barbe that she sought the comfort of our home and my mother's kitchen."

"I can't wait to meet her," Kate said. "What brought her back to Damgan?"

"A long story I'll cut short. Once she was widowed, she and her sons moved from Paris to her Breton roots to help her ailing father in Damgan. After he died, she remained in his childhood home near the sea—where we will be staying. She wanted to remain near her sons and the same friends she had known during the summers of her youth. A friend in Mimi is a friend forever!"

As they pulled through the blue wooden gates of Mimi's driveway, they entered a yard filled with bare plum trees and flowerless flowerbeds. Up the sandstone walls of her house grew deep green fingers of ivy, which spread up and around the doorway, around the windows, and about the house in a gentle embrace. A matching blue front door was tucked back into a portal with a niche high above holding a small stone statue.

"What is the statue above the door?" Kate asked.

"Ah, that's Sainte Anne—the patron saint of Brittany and the protector of all houses with blue doors," Sophie quipped. She recited the lines:

C'est notre mère à tous; mort our vivant, dit-on,
Sainte-Anne, une fois, doit aller tout Breton.
[She is the mother to all; whether dead or alive, we say,
To Sainte Anne, one time, as Bretons, we all must go to her.]

Charming," Kate commented as they walked up to the door. Sophie knocked, then waltzed into the foyer and called out Mimi's name. Kate tiptoed sheepishly behind. Immediately, they were met by a very happy-to-see-them small bulldog named Lulu who jumped up and down excitedly. Mimi popped her head in from the kitchen. A woman of strong northern-European good looks— blonde hair, deep blue eyes, and a fair complexion—greeted them warmly. It had been a couple of years since Sophie and Mimi had seen each other, and they embraced like sisters. The French banter raised the roof with shrieks of delight. Mimi apologized to Kate in broken English, "I'm sorry. We *do* get carried away. Let me show you around."

Not long into their arrival, Kate's stomach began to act up, and she was put immediately to bed. Mimi and Sophie were given the evening to eat a leisurely dinner and catch up on old gossip.

Later in the evening, the two took a bottle of wine into the living room and curled up to chat on the couch.

"I did get to the Hall of Records to look up your mother's birth certificate just like you and your mother requested of me," Mimi explained. "But I found nothing."

"Nothing?" Sophie echoed.

"Nothing! I was just as shocked as you," Mimi replied.

"How can that be? There were no records of her birth, her marriage, or anything in Ste. Barbe, and she spent over forty years there. And now you're saying that even in Vannes, she doesn't exist?" Sophie stood up, holding her empty wine glass and thinking out loud. "I can't fathom this. I don't know where else to look."

"Sophie, your mother was born on Armistice Day—the end of World War I . . ."

Sophie nodded her head, "Yes, I know that. The date I gave you to check was November 11, 1918, right?"

"Right, but let me finish. There was so much celebration on that day that they failed to record her birth. In fact, no births were recorded for several days thereafter. I'm sorry. It seems like an idiotic blunder, but a blunder all the same. I even searched through the records for several days and weeks before and after that date, but I came up with nothing for Marcelle Pourrette. I really tried to find this for you because she was such a special woman and like a mother to me, but I found nothing. I'm so sorry." She hung her head in despair.

As Sophie sat back down, she began to wonder if the Pourrette name was even the name they should be after. Could her mother have been named after that rascal cousin of Raymond's after all? Something wasn't right, but she was determined to continue her search. She had come this far. Sophie poured herself and Mimi more wine, settled back on the sofa and said, "It's all right, Mimi. Something will turn up."

The next morning, Kate was greeted with bright sunshine breaking through the lace curtains and the indistinguishable wet nose of Lulu burrowing under the covers. *Am I in her bed?* Kate was still a little shaky but was feeling much better than the day before, and she was looking forward to visiting Vannes.

"How are you feeling, Kate?" Sophie asked, poking her head into the bedroom.

"Much better. I'm so sorry for last night. I don't know what hit me, but I'm grateful to you and Mimi for putting up with me. Did you two get caught up on all the gossip?"

"Yes, we were up late making toasts to our pasts!" She laughed. "Are you ready to head to Vannes?"

"I wouldn't miss it. This is like putting the final pieces of your mother's puzzle into place," she said excitedly, hopping out of bed. "I'm looking forward to it—seeing the market, the ramparts of the ancient town, the old *lavoir*, and . . ."

"Then I guess we better get going," Sophie laughed.

After a quick Breton breakfast of bread, salted butter, jam, and a mug of café au lait, the three scurried out the door. The morning air was crisp and sparkling as they drove along the beach observing a rough and rambunctious sea. In no time at all they arrived at the walled city of Vannes.

"The market in Vannes," Mimi said, "attracts several thousand visitors every Wednesday and Saturday—like today—because of its seasonal vegetables and meats, and because Vannes lies on the Gulf of Morbihan, they can offer the freshest of fish. We'll start at the traditional market, which is held in the Old Town near the ramparts." Kate's eyes lit up.

After parking the car, the three scooted across a connecting bridge, which linked the outside world to the inner city through Porte Poterne. Before clipping down the steps into the market, they stopped to catch the view. From this vantage point near the top of the ramparts, Mimi was able to point out the most sought-after landmark, the Cathedral Saint-Pierre in the center of Vannes, and below them, the lovely flower-filled moat.

"There they are, Kate," Sophie said, pointing to a row of old buildings below. "The *lavoirs* my mother told you about!"

"Is this something exciting?" Mimi asked.

"Oh, *mais oui!*" Sophie exclaimed, "Maman wove many of her early memories around this place. Right, Kate?" Kate was busy taking photos but nodded her head vigorously.

Through the promises Sophie had made her mother, she had returned to Vannes, her mother's hometown. She peered below, where her mother's beloved *lavoirs* still sat! To Sophie, those ancient washhouses with their thatched roofs bent low over the Marle River looked much like a group of old women bent over and enacting their timeless job of clothes-washing. She tried to imagine her mother playing atop the ramparts, then rushing to help her grandmother with the laundry at the *lavoir*.

⁂

The seaport of Vannes had been Marcelle's jewel. Many an afternoon, she stood high atop the city ramparts with the air of a monarch surveying her bounty. She had learned from her grandfather that playing the part of legendary King Gradlon was a far headier role than that of his wayward daughter, Dahut.

Marcelle raised a hand to cover her eyes from the glint of the sun. She gazed out to the waters beyond. Perhaps. Perhaps she could catch a glimpse of Dahut, the former princess. She struck a stalwart pose. She imagined the King standing on this very spot, awaiting the hour when the bells would ring. Cocking her head to the side, she, too, listened for the ringing of the bells. This was the sure sign of the City of Ys rising from the sea once more.

Marcelle's only school dress flapped about her legs. A cool wind picked up, and her homemade crown wobbled on her head. Below, along the fisherman's wharf, red and gold flecks of light danced along the waterway. The bright red sails of the fleet of tiny oyster boats, the *sinagots,* pulled up to the dock with the day's catch from the Gulf of Morbihan. "Morbihan," she rolled the word off her tongue. It meant "small sea" in Breton, but to Marcelle this was her whole world.

Suddenly, Marcelle pinched her nose. The putrid smell of the nearby tanneries mixed with the smell of lye soap drifted up to where she stood. She remembered her grandmother awaiting her help at the *lavoir.* Dashing down the ramparts, jumping off the wall onto the steps, she raced down to find her. Marcelle could hear the sound of the paddles beating, beating, beating the sopping-wet hemp clothes of a week's or a month's worth of wear. She dashed off so that she'd be there for her dear *grand-mère* when she needed help.

꿈◈

Sophie slowly opened her eyes again. This was why she had come! This was the connection she was seeking. This was where her mother's story had begun, and maybe this would be where her mother's story could find a peaceful end. Sophie was suddenly aware of Kate and Mimi talking.

"Vannes may have been the only place your mother knew contentment," Kate said calmly. Mimi's eyes opened wide, and she turned to look at Sophie for an explanation.

Sophie said, "*C'est vrai,* Kate." She turned to Mimi to explain, "*Maman* shared many of her Vannetais stories with Kate. She certainly could weave a wonderful tale, right Kate?" She sighed. She looked below once again; her mother's history lay at her feet even though now above the washhouses were expensive half-timbered residences with wooden window boxes filled with bright red poinsettias. Times had changed. "Yes, this was probably my mother's favorite place."

"I wonder if Marcelle would have been surprised to know this has become a place of honor in her town." Mimi asked. "They say it's the most photographed building in the city."

"A thing of beauty is a joy forever . . ." quoted Kate.

"Oh, but I do not think the *lavoirs* were originally considered a thing of beauty," tittered Sophie.

"No," Mimi joined in, "the washer women thought of this place as a place for hard work and, maybe, a sprinkling of gossip."

Just then, a fresh mixture of aromas from both land and sea commingled in the air, and the three breathed in deeply, crossed the bridge, and shambled down the stairs into the square below. People were everywhere, and a cacophony of noise belched forth. Old friends greeted one another with excited calls, hands reached out and were shaken, cheeks were brushed with *bisous*, and the chatter swelled. Gestures became more dramatic, as hearing was almost impossible and progress slowed. Children chased each other through the streets and then, disoriented among the legs of everyone, called out in alarm to find their parents.

The three turned at the Place des Lices and walked through the neo-Moorish archway, decorated with brightly colored enameled bricks, and entered an immense indoor marketplace with aisles filled with vendors—the butcher, the baker, the vintner, and the dairy farmer.

"Typical Breton products are displayed here, such as goat cheeses, or, more unusually, *pienoire* cheeses made from the milk of the Breton cow," Sophie said.

"Yes, Kate, look over there," Mimi said, pointing to a number of women seated quietly on a bench near the door. "They are known as the *p'tites dames au beurre*, or the eggs and butter ladies. They come each market day from surrounding villages with their wicker baskets filled with freshly churned butter and large farm eggs. Nothing better," she smacked her lips.

On tables and in cases, *galette-saucisses* competed alongside Breton onion tarts, *far Breton aux pruneaux*, and *kouign amann*.

Long lines of jabbering women waited for their share of the freshly made *blé noir*, or buckwheat crepes.

"Are homemade *crêpes* becoming a thing of the past?" Kate asked. "Has convenience taken a bite out of tradition?"

"Ah, they are not so different from us, are they, dear Kate?" Sophie answered with a smile. Kate nodded and grinned. *"C'est vrai! C'est vrai!"*

Following quickly behind Mimi, Sophie and Kate entered into the fray as they gathered up fresh bread, sweet buns, and local cheeses. They sampled wines and hard cider and were charmed by sales clerks wearing traditional Breton costumes. Sophie and Mimi took turns purchasing specialty charcuterie, including *morlaix* ham and *andouilles de bretagne* before darting out the door to the fresh vegetable and flower markets. Time was of the essence, and the winter vegetables were being plucked up quickly.

With too much in hand, the women finally reached the fish market, a restored nineteenth-century hall, where they threaded their way through the aisles. Tables stretched the full length of the hall and were piled high with fresh fish just pulled from the waters off Quiberon, along with mountains of bulots, clams, cockles, scallops, winkles, spiny lobsters, crabs, shrimp, and langoustine. They picked up a dozen oysters and three filets of sole, all for the day's *déjeuner*.

They sped back to the car, dropped off their purchases, packed the fish into a cooler, and returned to the main portal and the harbor, Port de Plaisance. Here they ducked into a dark tavern to soak up their surroundings with a cup of hot tea and a sweet biscuit. As they sat overlooking the square, Place Gambetta, they watched the sailboats bob in the breeze along the quay.

The name of that quay over there is Quai de la Rabine—" Before Mimi could finish her sentence, Sophie began to hoot with laughter.

"Quai de la Rabine?" she chortled. "Reminds me of a story about an old Vannetais uncle of mine who used to take us fishing.

Well, almost fishing. He preferred talking about it more than actually doing it, but it was right there," she said, pointing across the street, "that he found solace in one of those little taverns." She looked around her. "Or, maybe this one," she laughed raucously. "I remember the name, Quai de la Rabine, reverberated through our entire house, as my aunt was always worried he would drink too much and not make it home at night. But he always arrived home, sometimes a little worse for wear, but always riding his wobbly old bicycle up the cobblestone streets." She laughed again. She looked at the surprised look on Kate's face and said, "Oh, there are plenty more of those stories to be told." She smiled as she fluffed her hand into the air.

"Was that your mother's Aunt Suzanne, Sophie?" Kate asked her. A serious tone had crept into her voice. "I didn't realize you had visited here."

"Only on a couple of occasions when I was a kid. But, *non, non,* it was my mother's Aunt Margot. My great uncle was named Marcel. He was a real character, that one. Funny, I haven't thought of any of them for a very long time . . ."

"But, Sophie, are any of them still alive?"

Sophie let out a Gallic puff. "Nope. I'm thinking they're all gone. My cousin Madeleine told us in Paris that we are all that's left." She waved her hand through the air, hoping to abandon the subject.

"But, Sophie, what if there were still family members here? Like Marcel and Margot's family? And what about looking up marriage records for Raymond Pourrette? We could give it a try—since we're here." Kate wheedled Sophie with a smile.

Mimi shifted in her seat. "Who is this Raymond Pourrette?"

"If I hadn't been so tired last night, I would have told you about my grandmother's diary. When we stopped at my cousin Madeleine's in Paris, she gave me letters and a diary. It seems my grandmother was married to one Raymond Pourrette."

Mimi's eyes snapped open. "What? Your grandmother was married? Was this before or after she gave birth to your mother?"

"Before, by one and a half years. Isn't that something? It turns out my mother was not an illegitimate child. All her life she never knew the truth, but the tragedy is that we easily found out after she passed away!"

"So that's where the name came from. I know she always wondered," Mimi said softly. She lifted her teacup, then set it back down.

"On my mother's death bed she asked me to find out the truth and . . . well, we've come up with some of the truth, anyway."

Kate nodded her head and sipped her tea. She may have spoken out of turn when she suggested pursuing records for Raymond.

"If you need more help on this, Sophie," Mimi said, "I'd be happy too, especially since I came up empty handed with your mother's records."

"Well, let's think about it. We know that Raymond was born in Paris, so I doubt if there are any records here—other than possible marriage records."

A clock in the tavern chimed, and all three heads turned in that direction. It was nearing 1:00 PM, so they paid their bill and strolled into the square. As they arrived at the Gates of Sainte Vincent, people began disappearing off the streets. The market and shops had closed for the day and everyone, except them, was heading home for *déjeuner*.

"Ah hah," exclaimed Sophie, "we have the town all to ourselves! The streets are empty, Kate, and it's a perfect time to show you the city of my mother's youth!"

The three began their hike up the streets to find Marcelle's childhood home. "Let's take this street," Mimi said, veering off to the left. "Rue Noé climbs up the hill toward St. Patern, where Marcelle's home was located. I never walked this way with her, but she talked about it often."

The steep hills became more and more difficult for Kate to walk. Midway up, Kate stopped to get her breath. "What does Rue Noé mean, anyway? Steepest hill in the city?"

"Almost. It means Noah's Street, like Noah's Ark. I guess that's another reference to prompt people to get up and away from the rising tide," Sophie said. "When we were kids, *Maman* used to describe the Vannetais homes as old buildings that sagged so closely together that their upper stories touched one another across the lanes. It was as if old friends had come to confide in one another, she would say. And, the streets? Why, she described them as being built wide enough for a small horse-drawn cart, but now, motor scooters race back and forth, forcing pedestrians to scream and press themselves up against the stone walls." Sophie let out a gale of laughter. "And look at what we've found! At least the motor scooters are home for lunch."

The half-timbered buildings, which rose three, four, or five stories from the cobblestone streets, were of thirteenth-century vintage—the narrow stone bases of each shouldered additional upper stories, which seemed to telescope upward into expanded space. Like Marcelle had described, the upper stories leaned so closely to the other buildings that it was clear they relied on each other for support. The timbers themselves were woven into crosshatched designs across the face of each structure, which may have been for support at one time, but now? Some were straight, but most had heaved with the weight of time. Windows, which had been placed high above the streets, now listed in their frames to the right or the left, depending on the whim of the burden above.

"Do you know why these buildings are built in this way, Kate?" Sophie asked her.

"Don't have any idea."

"Taxes! Plain and simple! You see, the square meters of the bottom level—the one that rests on the ground floor—is the one that determines the tax rate. The smaller the base, the smaller the tax. But once the next story is built, and the one after that, the tax remains the same as what was first determined. Voilà! Cheaper taxes!"

Above their heads, specialty signs squeaked as they swung in a light breeze. The weather was shifting and changing. "See these signs?" Mimi asked Kate. Kate nodded. "In the early years, most people couldn't read, so many stores greeted their customers with symbols instead of words representing their products: over there is a sign of a horse head for the *boucherie chevaline*, the butcher of horse meat; across the street is a spoon and a fork for a café; the charcuterie, here, is represented by those large hams and sausages dangling above our heads; and, over there, is a boot or a shoe, which represents a *cordonnier*, a shoe shop."

"Ah-ha! I wonder if that was where *Maman's* family built their livelihood." Sophie asked out loud. She began to walk across the street.

"The family used to live above the store, didn't they?" Mimi asked.

"Yes," Sophie said, "but that was before my mother was born. It seems they lost the business and were forced to move farther up the hill. *Maman's* grandfather still worked as a shoemaker, but he no longer held the privilege of living above the family store. Oh, but *Maman* said they were all happy," she added.

The three plodded up the street and crossed over to Cathedral Saint-Pierre.

"Now, this was the place of my mother's baptism and her first communion," Sophie whispered as they entered the massive doors of the Gothic-style cathedral. Quietly, they wandered through the austere church peering through the dim light at the altar and up through the stained glass windows. The massive rooms held tightly to the damp and chill, and even though they thought to remain longer, after only twenty minutes, the three rushed outside to catch some of the sun's warmth radiating off the outer stone walls.

"I was going to ask if they have church records here, like for weddings, baptisms, that kind of thing. But it is so cold in there, my lips are turning blue. Are my lips blue?" Kate asked, turning to face Sophie.

"Definitely blue! Can you imagine how frigid that place must have been during the cold, cold winters here for my mother?" asked Sophie.

Mimi laughed. "Your mother used to tell me about how bone-rattling cold she used to get sitting in this church. Also in the church nearest her home, at St. Patern's."

"No wonder she wandered off from her ritual attendance," Sophie said with a shudder. Mimi flashed a look in her direction but continued walking slowly ahead of Sophie and Kate.

"I'm sorry, Mimi," Sophie said. "I know the Church has been a real comfort, especially after the loss of your husband and father. It simply had a different impact on *Maman*—even though she wove a great deal of spirituality into her everyday life. And, say, didn't we used to go to church together in Ste. Barbe? But I, too, walked away from the Church once I got a divorce. Not that I had any choice at that point . . ."

"Oh, Sophie. I'm not judging you or your mother. In the world of turmoil I grew up in, and having lived with an alcoholic husband throughout most of my adult life, the Church was my only constant. My rock."

"In my case," Kate said, "I, too, had an alcoholic husband, but once I divorced, the Episcopal Church wasn't very accepting of me either. I think they had a difficult time with a single woman floating around untethered."

The three continued up the cobbled streets, passed through the Porte Prison gate without comment, and then, Kate stopped short.

"Wait a minute! Isn't this the ancient gate left over from the third century A.D.?" She spun around to look behind her. "Isn't this the gate of the St. Patern district near Marcelle's home?"

"Yes, on both counts," Sophie replied, a smile appearing on her face. "Do you remember when *Maman* talked about helping push the laundry cart up from the *lavoir?* She said they would go through the cart gate, which is unique, I understand. There it is." She pointed behind them.

"*Oui!* This district is the original site of the old Gallo-Roman city," Mimi said. This plaque says that it is 'a remarkable example of a fortified gate, controlled by a double drawbridge system, one for the cart gate and the other for pedestrians.' We're getting close to Marcelle's home."

Hurrying down the street, as their goal was before them, the three stopped at the first church they saw. Once again, Mimi stopped in front of a plaque and began to read. "It says here, 'Saint Patern's Church has not ceased to confront its past, for the traces of memories still remain.'"

Kate nudged alongside Mimi and stared at the French inscription. *Why, this was exactly what Sophie and I are seeking: a confrontation of the past and a trace of some remaining memory.* Before them was the home church of Marcelle's youth, St. Patern's. Kate stared up at the building before her. The exterior of grey granite seemed even more austere and was much more rough-hewn than St. Pierre Cathedral.

Mimi continued reading, "'During the fifth century, St. Patern, one of the original seven saints who fled to Brittany from England, established this as a place of worship. This current church was rebuilt in the eighth century, and it still preserves the patronymic memory of this saint.'"

"No wonder the church looks old," Sophie said.

Mimi turned to face Sophie and Kate. "You see, Patern was the very first bishop of this city, and he was later made a saint. People still call upon him when there is a drought."

"A drought? I thought they were fearful of high water! So, what is the story around St. Patern becoming a saint?" Kate asked.

"Well," said Mimi, "the story goes that when St. Patern left the city for a few years, the rains in Vannes stopped. But after his death, when his body was returned and he was interred here, the rains immediately began to fall. Thus, whenever there is a drought, you will hear great outcries to St. Patern."

"I'm certain my mother called upon him many times, but probably not for rain. Although, I think she mostly called upon Sainte Anne d'Auray throughout her life. But I know that this saint—this church—was a true touchstone for her."

"Touchstone, yes! I remember Marcelle telling us," Kate said, "she lived so close to St. Patern that she could almost reach out of her upper-story window and touch the stones of the church across the street. That certainly would make it a touchstone, so to speak."

The women moved around to the side of the church. The bell tower, which overhung the narrow streets, was bordered by half-timbered buildings. One in particular, at the corner of Street Saint-Patern and Place du Général de Gaulle, displayed the decorative richness of the architecture of the fifteenth century. Just then, the church bells began to chime.

Kate practically leaped out of her skin. "Whoa. That scared me," she exclaimed. They began tittering and then collapsed into laughter, as the bells had surprised them all. Finally, they had arrived at the destination of Marcelle's home and her home church, and the three were acting like foolish schoolgirls.

"My mother used to tell me the church bells would awaken her every morning."

"I would have thought the bells would have kept her up all night long," Kate laughed.

"They probably did, but they were a real comfort to her too. Oh, how she longed to come back here before she died—right here —to hear these very bells just one more time."

"You're right, Sophie. This must have been one of the constants in her young life." Kate turned away from the church, then back to Sophie.

"So exactly where did she live?"

"Right up there," Sophie said, pointing at some windows in a half-timbered building. On the bottom floor was a business, which appeared to be closed for the day. No sign or symbol was hung to designate what business was conducted there. The women moved closer. The store windows were streaked with dust and grime, and, as they peered through the mottled glass, they could see the store was empty. The dark green paint on the outside timbers had chipped and peeled away, baring the original wood of the fifteenth century. A weathered green side door, which was slightly ajar, led up a set of dark, rickety-looking steps to the apartments above. Nothing could be seen above the fifth step. It was pitch black.

Sophie moved toward the door to peer up the steps. She pushed the door slightly, and a loud creak resounded through the empty hallway. She jumped back, then smiled sheepishly. "I guess no one's at home," she said, her voice quavering.

"Say, Sophie," Mimi asked, "did your mother ever tell you who *she* thought her father was?" The question came like a bolt out of the blue.

As if stung, Sophie jumped back. "No. She would never talk about it."

"I was just remembering a time," Mimi said, "when we were together at your house in California, and she and I got to talking about questioning paternity . . . I don't remember how we got onto that subject, but she said, 'When I was still living in Vannes, some of the kids in my class used to tease me about being sisters or cousins with another boy in class. Of course, I said that wasn't true. I even fought with one of the girls who made the claim. But the truth was, I didn't know.' She went on to say, 'He certainly looked a lot like me. I remember sneaking a peek at his father one day after school, as I wondered if . . . well, maybe he was my Papa, too, but their last name was not Pourrette. And I could never bring myself to ask *ma grand-mère*. So I never knew.'"

"Really," Sophie said, turning toward Kate, who joined them in their circle.

"Did Marcelle happen to mention the last name of this boy?" Kate asked.

"Seems like it was something like . . . Wow," Mimi said, scratching her head. "This is a stretch, but what I remember her saying was that it was like Bréhat. *Oui!* That was it because I remember one of my cousins had the same surname and my first thought when Marcelle mentioned it was that maybe we were related. Funny how things pass through your mind!" she said, throwing her hands into the air.

As they stood on the corner contemplating the information, the heavens suddenly opened and the skies, which had been threatening rain all day, gave way to the spirits of St. Patern. The women scurried down the streets, clattering over the same cobblestones that Marcelle had run across seventy-five years before. Laughing again like schoolgirls, they raced all the way to Mimi's car and jumped in.

Just as Mimi pulled out of the parking lot, Sophie looked back at the walled city of Vannes. A feeling of contentment swept over her. She relaxed back into her seat. The promise she had made to her mother to return had been kept, and in so doing, she had experienced a most remarkable closeness with her. To see Vannes again had been one of her mother's deepest desires, and today, Sophie had fulfilled her dream.

Back at Mimi's, and after a fine *déjeuner*, Mimi said, "I just put a pot of coffee on. I thought we needed to have some clear thinking." The three women settled into the living room.

"Marcelle and I shared so much in common," Mimi began. "We both were basically abandoned by our mothers to be raised by our grandmothers, and even though our married lives were different in the beginning, we both had hardships and broken hearts. Yes, I would say that we shared parallel lives—just one generation apart."

"You know," Sophie said softly, "my mother used to sing a song for us when we were children. She said it was one of the few she remembered her mother singing to her. And the chorus was something like . . .

Plaisir d'amour ne durent pas toujours
Chagrins d'amour durent toute la vie!
(Love's pleasure never lasts
But the pain of lost love will last forever!)

Mimi said mournfully, "Those words hold more than just great truth. This was the experience your mother and I shared in common, lost love."

"That was part of what we were wondering about," Kate said softly.

"Yes, is there anything more you can tell us about *Maman*?" Sophie scooted in her seat to face Mimi.

"I don't have to tell you what your mother put up with from your father. I don't presume to know more than you do, Sophie, but . . ."

"But Mimi, my mother's lost love was not my father. It was Gérard's father. That much was always clear to me. Did my mother ever talk to you about Gérard's father?"

Mimi kicked off her shoes and shifted her feet underneath her. "I suppose I'm not betraying your mother's trust now." Mimi shifted again, trying to find a comfortable sitting position. "Remember that I told you, Sophie, that she had written to me?"

Sophie nodded and tilted her head to one side. She realized she was holding her breath.

"She told me . . ." Mimi said, as she reached for her cup, "about a time when you all went to Paris with some friends, and . . ."

"To Paris?" Sophie asked. "Oh, *Mon Dieu*. I know when that was. I must have been ten or so."

Mimi shrugged her shoulders. "That sounds right."

"I knew it," Sophie slapped her knee. "I told you, Kate. Remember? When my mother and I walked into that dark bistro in Paris, she saw a man across the room. I felt there was something electric about the moment."

Kate nodded.

"It was André, wasn't it?" Sophie asked Mimi. Before she could respond, Sophie said, "I finally learned his name from my mother's friend, Sophie Marie Chirade, a few weeks ago. Go on."

Mimi was startled by the mention of not only André's name, but Marie's name, as well. Along with her letter from Marcelle, she had received a letter addressed to Sophie Marie, but she didn't realize the connection. It was all coming together.

"Wait here," Mimi said, jumping up to head to her office. She returned with a letter addressed to Sophie Marie.

"What is this?" Sophie asked, picking up the envelope and turning it over in her hand. She recognized her mother's handwriting immediately.

"When you mentioned Sophie Marie's name, I remembered that your mother had enclosed another letter with mine. She requested that I give it to you when you came to visit so that you, personally, could deliver it to Sophie Marie."

"It's hard to believe she planned all this out ahead of time," Sophie said, her voice almost a whisper. "I had no idea how ill she was until I was called to her bedside."

"She loved you deeply, Sophie," Mimi said, "and she trusted that you, of all people, would follow through for her. She knew you."

The three women sat in silence, sipping their coffee, and for a moment Marcelle's presence was so strong that each felt like she could reach out to touch her.

CHAPTER EIGHTEEN

Restless as a Devil
in Holy Water

A

As SOPHIE DROVE OFF the next morning, she shouted to Mimi who waved from her doorway, "*Ken avo; au revoir.*" Sophie turned to Kate and said, "That's Breton for *Good bye for now.* I'm certain we will be back again soon."

Kate nodded her head but was quietly reflecting on her past few days in Brittany. She couldn't help but feel a strange mystical pull. After a while, she said to Sophie, "Are you having a difficult time leaving Brittany, Sophie?"

"I've always experienced that feeling—like a large magnet pulling me back to a place I've never lived." Sophie smiled at Kate.

"Maybe it's because we don't have all the answers we came for," Kate said, "or maybe what we're searching for remained elusive."

"Like the *korrigans?*" Sophie giggled.

"Maybe," Kate grinned. "When we first drove into Brittany, my goal was to try to understand your mother's character. But now that we're leaving, I feel what I gained is already slipping away. It feels so palpable yet so evanescent at the same time.

"Yes," Sophie glanced at her, "I feel the same. Maybe we can sort it out."

"Okay," Kate paused. "I learned that the Breton strength of character comes from the influences of the Celts and the Catholics, two antithetical yet intertwined belief systems. This makes sense to the Bretons," Kate said, "but it doesn't make much sense to those who were not born or raised here."

"*C'est vrai*. My mother's belief in St. Anne and Dahut and her romantic belief that women who live and love deeply may eventually find happiness came from Brittany," Sophie added.

"But where did your mother's strength come from? Her courage and perseverance?"

Because of the passion in Kate's voice, Sophie gave her friend a searching look. "Are you looking to find *Maman*'s source of strength for yourself?"

Kate thought for a few moments. "Perhaps I am. I guess I've been searching for my own wellspring of courage: the courage to ask for and have a solid relationship with Lisa."

Sophie pursed her lips in contemplation. "Well, she was not successful in convincing Thierry that she had not wanted to abandon him, so . . ."

Kate stared out the window, avoiding the reflection of her own face in the glass. "Changing the subject, when do you think your mother decided to open up more—before or after your father died?"

"Definitely after, but there was a time after Gérard took his life that she began to open up as well."

"You've never talked about Gérard's suicide," Kate said in a level voice. She glanced at her friend; Sophie's jaw seemed locked in a strained position.

"Sometimes, Kate," Sophie said slowly, "when I seem reticent in answering, it's because this is all so foreign to me—to open up in this way—to even open up the line of thought much less search for answers. But," she paused, "you do need to hear his story. After all, he was my mother's love child. So where should I begin?" Sophie asked herself as she let out a sigh.

Sophie first negotiated a tricky turn onto N165 toward Nantes and then said, "Julien, Thierry, and I always felt a special love for Gérard, who suffered so much from my father's ire."

"I missed meeting a fine brother in your Gérard," Kate said.

"You did, Kate. Oh, you did," Sophie replied. Her eyes welled up; she looked away.

"Sophie, if this is too painful, we don't have to discuss it."

"Oh, pooh! It just seems like one more tragedy in a long line of tragedies. I hadn't thought of our lives in this manner before, but after this trip—well, sometimes the very thought takes my breath away . . ." She paused, let out a deep sigh, and began anew.

"It was a year or two before Gérard's death. I had been married to Jerome for only eleven or twelve years. Gérard and Thierry had become good friends—actually like brothers—and, even though Thierry never traveled down to Gérard's home in the south of France, Gérard made a special effort to spend time with him and *Maman*. They would talk and laugh, go fishing, have a few beers I suppose—and they became very close. My parents had moved from Ste. Barbe to Fontanière by then, by the way." Sophie paused to think, her fingers tapping on the steering wheel.

"Some of this surprises me even now, because Gérard often went to help my folks out. He did odd jobs for them, like rewiring the old house, and he worked on the ancient plumbing. Things like that. He was always quite good with his hands and was always anxious to help *Maman* in any way."

"So the relationship between Gérard and your father had mended?" Kate asked.

"I suppose so," Sophie paused. "You know, if you never bring up an uncomfortable subject, life can move along quite smoothly." She grinned. "Like we French say, *Quand les poules auront des dents.*"

"What? What do they say?"

"It means 'when hens have teeth.' Maybe you would say, 'when pigs fly,' but that's when things would be discussed in our family." She giggled. "Oh, never mind. We learned early not to discuss anything that might make our father upset or angry. And Gérard was always such a happy-go-lucky type. He was always singing, or whistling, even if it was off-key. I never minded," she said soulfully, "as it meant he was happy.

"When Gérard and his wife, Jacqueline, had saved enough money to build their own home, my parents drove down to Provençe to help them out. We all pitched in from time to time, as this project stretched out over several years. I understand that everything was going really well, until Gérard's accident. I wasn't there when it happened, but *Maman* told me pieces of the story."

⁓✺⁓

"Papa, could you hand me that wrench? Over there on the work bench behind you," Gérard called from underneath his car.

Lying on his back on the dirt floor of his new garage, Gérard's feet extended out from under the front bumper only a meter. From this angle, he could see his stepfather's legs cross and uncross while he sat on the wooden sawhorse smoking one cigarette after another. The wrench was handed to him, and Gérard continued the work on the undercarriage of his car.

"Looks like the last mechanic rigged some faulty wiring under here and did a bad solder job as well. It shouldn't take me any time at all, and then we can get back to work on the house. Could you hand me that soldering iron next to you? It's the silver grey one hanging on the hook above the workbench. Could you plug it in and get it warmed up?"

"Sure thing, Gérard. Do you want me to crawl under there and hold your hand too?" Jules joked.

"Why not. There's just enough room, Papa," Gérard laughed.

Once the soldering iron was heated, Jules placed it on the floor beside the car. Gérard moved the wires into place and picked up the soldering iron to begin. He was aware of his stepfather's feet move across the garage, and then he noted that a lighted cigarette was tossed near the car. It startled him at first, but he chose to say nothing. Whistling as he worked, he noticed Jules had sat down again on the sawhorse to watch the proceedings. He lit another cigarette.

Suddenly, a loud flash of light appeared, followed by an explosion that filled the garage with dust and black smoke. As Jules stood to run from the room, smoke filled his already badly damaged lungs. Too many years in the mine; too many cigarettes. He found himself standing in one place choking and coughing.

"*Zut alors! Zut alors!*" Jules swore as he gasped for breath. Tears poured from his eyes as he fought to find the doorway. Once he spotted it, he tossed his cigarette and ran.

"Help me," he heard Gérard cry. "Help me, Papa. I'm on fire!" Panic seized him as Gérard began to scream.

Jules's body locked up; he began to shake. He shook so violently that he was unable to move in any direction. He couldn't think, and a smell he couldn't identify wafted toward him. His stomach churned. Somewhere outside of himself he heard the screaming continue.

"Papa, please help me get out! Please, please!" The smoke continued to boil out from underneath the frame, and flames licked over the car.

Again, Jules heard his stepson's shrieks. He could not move— not forward, not backward, and certainly not toward the car. Fire was moving along the floor, and he expected the car to explode. As if observing a scene on television, he turned to look as Gérard crawled slowly from underneath the burning vehicle. His clothes were engulfed in flames, yet he dragged himself, gasping for air, across the dirt floor and out the door, where he rolled in the dirt beyond the garage.

Before Gérard reached the door, Jules was nowhere to be seen. He had disappeared into the house, shaking and crying hysterically. During Jules's feeble attempt to tell Marcelle about the accident, he was stuttering so badly she couldn't interpret what had happened. Precious moments were lost. Marcelle suddenly raced out the back door with a blanket and found her son lying facedown on the ground.

"*Mon Dieu, mon Gérard,*" she wailed. What has become of you? What has he done to you?" She reached out to touch him, but even her hand, a mother's hand, withdrew as horror sank in. She threw the blanket over him, smothering any remaining flames. She looked toward the garage, then grabbed a hose and bucket and raced forward. Without a single thought for her own safety, she put the fire out. Why the car hadn't exploded is anyone's guess.

When she returned to Gérard's side, Jacqueline, his wife, had come from the market and was holding Gérard's head in her lap. She was weeping uncontrollably.

"*Maman,*" Gérard wheezed from under the blanket, "please get Papa to take me to the hospital. I must go now! He has the only working car . . ."

Marcelle shrieked at Jules, who appeared at the back door. His white angular features were covered in black soot. He cowered inside the door, where he continued to shake uncontrollably. What was that expression on his face? Was that anguish?

"Please," Gérard pleaded, "Papa, please. I must go to the hospital. You are the only one who can drive." Jacqueline looked at Marcelle. Neither woman had learned to drive, nor had they realized, until that moment, that their decision could mean life or death for a loved one. Tears streamed down both their faces, and hysteria began to set in.

"Jules," Marcelle screamed, "take your son to the hospital!"

"I can't," he whimpered. "I'm shaking too badly; I can't move. I don't even know where to go!"

"Then I'll drive myself," Gérard said as he pulled himself off the ground. His tattered and burned clothing fell off in bits and pieces. The smell of burnt flesh nauseated them all. The urge to retch was overpowering.

"Where are the keys, Papa?" Gérard wailed. "I'll drive myself; just come with me. I need your car—now!"

❖

Gérard had lain in his hospital bed unconscious for the past two days, and upon waking, he whispered to Marcelle, "*Maman*, has he always hated me?" The question came as a shock. "Has my stepfather always hated me?"

It was a question Marcelle had asked herself many times since Gérard was a little boy. Standing beside his hospital bed, she ran the question through her mind. *Had Jules always hated Gérard?* Maybe the real question was: *Had Jules ever forgiven her for loving Gérard's father?* Even though she remained true to Jules all these years, he must have instinctively known where her heart lay. Even though the heart of a woman is deep, eventually her true feelings will surface.

Before the war had ended, Jules had convinced her to put aside her feelings for André, to marry him, and to move back to his hometown of Ste. Barbe. She had been blinded by his promises of loving and adopting her sons and, as he used to say, "legitimizing her life." He knew that her greatest desire was to have a stable family. Had he ever intended to follow through on those promises? Hadn't he abandoned her almost immediately on arriving in Ste. Barbe, when he returned to his lover? What she knew by heart was that this man of action acted only when it served his best interests.

She dropped her head into her hands as she sank into a chair beside Gérard's bed. Her beautiful son, who lay with over 60 percent of his body burned, had almost died in that car fire. And now that he had finally awakened, his first words were about his stepfather. Disgust roiled through her as she convulsed forward. She had lived her life in denial, a refuge she had adopted as a child, and now Gérard's words brought those walls of hers crumbling down around her.

His question was a legitimate one. He was possibly dying because of the inability of her husband, his stepfather, to respond in a timely way. Yes, she knew Jules had been shaken by the explosion, and he had seemed too weak and frightened to save Gérard. She, herself, had responded, but she couldn't shake Jules's expression as he peered from the kitchen. Was that fear? Or was it that menacingly hideous smirk she had seen all too often over the past forty years? The image haunted her. She remained silent, tears running down her cheeks.

She couldn't help but ask herself: Hadn't he been trained to react quickly while under fire during the war? Hadn't he thrived on the adrenaline rush of both war and the harrowing aspects of his job as an iron miner? What was it he used to say? Ah, yes: "Danger is my middle name." She shook her head in despair. No, *s'agiter comme un diable dans un bénitier*; no, he had been as restless as a devil in holy water.

Instinctively, Marcelle reached out to take her son's hand, but she quickly withdrew it when she realized his hands were heavily bandaged. She looked past the gauze mask on his face to those unbelievably deep blue eyes and saw him watching her, waiting for her answer.

"Son, only he can answer that question for you, but it wasn't you he hated. It was me. He must have always sensed that because you were a product from my greatest love, he could never have my heart. And he has spent a lifetime punishing us both.

"What about my real father, *Maman*?" Gérard's voice barely scratched the air between them. Marcelle leaned closer to hear his words. "Has he always hated me too?"

Just then, the hospital door banged open, and a team of doctors and two nurses pushed into the already cramped room.

"Please wait for us outside, madame," the plastic surgeon barked at Marcelle. Quickly, she squeezed out of the room, casting a quick look at her son. "Later, Gérard. We'll talk later," she called to him.

The surgery and recovery that followed lasted several months, and while Marcelle remained nearby for those many weeks, she was never left alone with him, and her son's questions went unanswered. For years she had ruminated in telling him more about his real father, but she had always held out hope that Jules would come around. "Learned hopefulness," she had heard it called. The past few years had actually seemed good between them. But now she questioned if it was all a ruse. On Jules's part, anyway.

And she had her own questions, questions that had caused her sleepless nights. Was it possible that Jules had started the fire in the garage that day? Was he really jealous of his stepson's success? Or his new house?

"Sophie, do you believe your father tried to save Gérard?" Kate asked as the countryside outside the car began to change. Hard rocky scrabble gave way to soft rolling fields and wide river valleys.

"It was all too horrible to consider back then," Sophie said after a pause. "When I first received word from the family that Gérard had been in an accident, Jerome and I had been relocated to Spain where we were settling into our new apartment. We left the house immediately and drove all night and deep into the next day to arrive at the hospital to be with him. My father seemed so stricken with grief that it never occurred to me that he might have been responsible."

"Had your father ever shown such strong emotions for Gérard before?" Kate asked.

A lengthy pause followed Kate's question—long enough for her to start back pedaling. "Oh, what do I know anyway, Sophie? I was just wondering what he was feeling in his anguish. Sadness? Contrition? Guilt?"

"Guilt?" Sophie repeated. "Why would he feel guilt?"

"Oh, I don't know. Maybe for not responding more quickly to save Gérard," Kate said.

"Well, that's certainly possible, but . . ."

"Is there any possibility that he caused the fire in the first place? Your father had been smoking in the garage . . ."

"Well, I thought the car caught fire because of Gérard's soldering iron—that he had caused the accident on his own. I just think my father's nerves were shot and he simply didn't know how to respond."

"Did your parents have any problems with each other after the fire?"

"Like what?" Sophie asked.

"Like getting along with each other after they returned to Fontanières?"

Sophie paused to think. "Come to think of it, they began to fight more regularly. Certainly more so once Gérard died. I never knew what happened, but they couldn't stand to be in the same place at the same time. That lasted the whole year after my brother's death. Sometimes I would have my mother stay with me in Spain, and other times my father would come visit." Sophie's throat was constricting; she felt she could barely breathe. She wheeled over the River Mayenne into the city of Angers and pulled into a parking lot facing an immense castle. She breathed in deeply. Her hands were shaking. "When I visited, I felt like I was trying to hold their heads above water. Their marriage had become a condition of reality, not of choice. And I felt my visits took their minds off Gérard."

"So what caused Gérard's death?" Kate asked as they sat in the car at the base of the Chateau d'Angers. She didn't dare look at Sophie as her words hung in the abyss between them.

"His service revolver," Sophie said matter-of-factly. She laid her head against the steering wheel and sobbed openly. Kate reached into the backseat and grabbed some Kleenex.

"I remember getting the call," Sophie moaned, wiping her eyes with her hands and then taking the offered Kleenex. "We were still living in Almeira, Spain when my brother Julien phoned to tell me that Gérard had taken his life. I literally began to howl—howl, like a wounded animal. I remember hearing Julien's words and hearing the howls, but I was unaware those sounds were coming from me. My poor Gérard! My poor, dear Gérard! His life was so very tragic; his death, so senseless." Sophie blotted her reddened face and now-swollen eyes.

"Was he in a depression after the fire? Was that why he took his life?" Kate asked cautiously.

"I asked Jacqueline, his wife, why she thought he had committed suicide. She didn't think it was depression that took him because he seemed fine the night before. But they did find the letter from my mother in his pocket—along with a note from his father."

"My God, Sophie," Kate whispered.

The two remained in the car for what seemed like hours. The car engine continued its hum. Kate unhooked her seat belt and slid over to Sophie. She once again held Sophie in her arms and let her sob until she had no more tears.

CHAPTER NINETEEN

*F*ilthy *R*efugee

(*Saleté Réfugiate*)

A

*W*HEN THE WOMEN EMERGED from the car, they both were spent. It was only midmorning, so Sophie encouraged Kate to take a tour of the Chateau d'Angers. Kate numbly proceeded across the moat over the drawbridge to the entrance of the castle. She purchased her ticket and stood in the inner courtyard awaiting the beginning of the tour. The sunlight fell on her shoulders and warmed her as she reflected on the conversation about Gérard. Now that the darkest of Sophie's family secrets had been revealed, she expected Sophie to take a few steps backward; maybe withdraw. Kate, too, felt like withdrawing. Gérard choosing a drastic end to his life after reading his father's letter left Kate weak in the knees. A terrible thought flitted through her mind. *Could Lisa choose this course?*

Blindly, Kate headed into the queue. The tour took her into the feudal fortress, which was built in the 1230s by the mother of Louis IX. Built of limestone and schist, the foreboding building with its seventeen towers had remained austere until a succeeding monarch, King René I, had added charm to the castle with gardens, an aviary, and a menagerie. Kate realized she was in no mood to confront this past. She dropped off the tour to give more thought to Gérard's story.

Wandering back into the sunshine of the formal gardens, she found a stone bench where she could sit and think. Just as Marcelle's story as an out-of-wedlock mother had brought special pain and insight to her, this story of Gérard's death, and the letter he had carried with him, brought new questions and fears for her. *When does a mother reach out to tell her child the truth? What if the truth is more difficult to accept than the unknown? How does one know when or what to reveal?* She could imagine Marcelle mentally anguishing over whether or not to tell her son of his father's identity. But who was she protecting? Her son? Her husband? André? Or herself? And, why had she waited so long to tell him his real surname or any other specific details? Kate had wrestled with similar questions. Why had it been so many years before she had revealed Lisa's birth to her own family—much less search for Lisa? Yes, she had sent letters to the adoption agency encouraging contact with her daughter, but should she have done more? Instead, she had waited for Lisa to make the first move. Thirty-four years she waited.

So when had Marcelle told Gérard more about his father? And, was this why he chose to take his life? Kate just wanted to weep—for Marcelle, for Gérard, for Sophie—and for her own daughter, Lisa.

Kate closed her eyes. *God, please send me your answers,* she silently prayed. *Teach me what you want me to learn. May I remain open to your answers and your wisdom. Amen.*

Kate wandered back through the garden and back to the drawbridge. She peered over the edge down the twelve-meter walls to the grassy floor below. Like the garden spot she had just left, she could imagine summertime splendor to be resplendent here—just like the gardens surrounding the *lavoirs* in Vannes.

Geometrically formed gardens with ornamental borders filled the thirty-three-meter-wide swath of the former moat. Her eyes were drawn back to the castle; almost eight hundred years of history had played itself out here. Wars, battles, legitimate heirs, non-legitimate heirs. Right here.

Aware that the tour she had ditched had been dismissed, Kate moved farther back into the garden, where she sat once again. She checked her watch and calculated the time in Lisa's time zone. 7:00 AM. She had enjoyed her recent phone calls with Lisa but now was plagued with the daunting thoughts of how she had handled the subject of Lisa's biological father. Had she handled that well enough? Had she shared all she needed to share? Does anyone? And who had Kate been shielding all these years with her silence?

She pulled her cell phone from her purse and punched in Lisa's number. Kate hoped to catch her daughter before she left for grad school.

"Lisa? Lisa, this is Ka . . . This is OM," Kate stammered, using the term Lisa and Addy had coined for her, Our Mom, or OM. She gulped. That was the sticky issue Kate continued to work through: who was she if not Lisa's mother? No matter how often she called her daughter, she was always paralyzed with fear—fear of saying the wrong thing, fear of being rejected, fear of not being a part of her daughter's life. "Am I calling too early?"

Lisa's sleepy voice came over the phone but it immediately warmed with recognition. "Oh, hi OM! We're good. How are you? Are you still in France?" Kate could hear her daughter's covers rustle. She assumed she had awakened her.

"Yes, I am," Kate said, looking up at the mossy wall of the castle near her. "Did I catch you too early in the morning?"

"No, no, this is perfect. My alarm went off just moments before you called, and I have another hour before I leave. This is perfect. OM . . . I'm so glad you called because Neil and I have made a change in plans for our wedding."

"Is there anything I can do?" Kate stood and paced up and down the pebbled walkway past the parterre.

"Yes, that's why I'm glad you called. There *is* something you can do. You can come! We're hoping to move the date up to December 30, the day before New Year's—that is, if you can make it. And that's not so far away—just next month. Will you be back from France by then? Because we don't have to . . ."

"Next month? Really? Oh, of course, I'll be back from France by then. Oh, Lisa, we'll make this happen! I'm so excited for you." She caught herself spinning around in the empty garden, giddy at the prospects. Giddy at the idea of being included in not just the planning, but also the event.

"And of course, I want Addy, Ian, and Matthew here, too. I know that's a lot to ask, but I would love to have my whole family here. I know this is late notice . . ." her voice trailed off.

Kate latched onto those blessed words, *my whole family, my whole family*. It took her breath away. When she tuned back into what Lisa was saying, she heard, "And, OM, don't worry! I don't *have* to get married, honest." Lisa laughed again. It was a lilting laugh—one without the normal tension clinging to her voice. In the background, she could hear laughter. Neil's laughter. Lisa sounded more relaxed than Kate had ever heard her. She sank onto a wrought iron bench, then jumped up and let out a yelp.

"What? What did you say?" Lisa asked.

"Oh, nothing, honey. I just sat down on a freezing cold bench in this . . ." She looked up at the massive castle before her and swallowed down the trepidation she had felt only moments earlier when she had placed the call. "I'm in a garden at an eight-hundred-year-old castle in the Loire Valley. But, back to you," she said, as she sat back down. "What would you like for me to do? How can I be of help to you, Neil, and your mom?"

Their conversation flowed unabated for ten minutes more when Kate heard the honk of a horn. She popped her head up and could see Sophie waving from the car. She waved back, and after bidding her daughter a good day, she hung up and zipped across the drawbridge and into the street to join her. Sophie, too, was in good spirits.

"Christian is going to join us at Thierry's the day after tomorrow," Sophie told her. "Julien said he could make it too. It will be a whole family affair," she said, excitedly clapping her hands.

"Speaking of family affairs, I just spoke with Lisa, and she wants . . . now, get this . . . she said she wants 'her whole family' to come to her wedding. 'Whole family'! Looks like we've hit the jackpot, Sophie," Kate gushed.

Once in the car, Kate continued bubbling about Lisa's wedding. "Lisa tells me she has found a place for her wedding," she carried on.

"Place? Like a church?" Sophie asked, as she negotiated a difficult transition onto the highway.

"No, I don't think so. It seems she and Neil are . . . um, Buddhists. So, I don't know what to call the place. I swear my kids do keep me on my toes. One is a Rastafarian, one is a pagan, and now this one is a Buddhist. I'm sure when my Episcopalian priest father finds out *this* turn of events . . . Whoo boy! So, Sophie, I will definitely have to change my flight back home for sooner than later. Do you think that's possible?"

"*Mais certainement!* How soon do you have to go?"

"Well, since the wedding is December 30, I probably will need to go home by next week. Oh, good Lord! We're nearing mid-November! And to think she made her decision based on if my family and I could come! That pleases me so much!" she rattled on.

The two women slipped into their own separate thoughts as Sophie drove east. The flat plains of the Loire River Valley gave way to mountains, which rose up to great heights and cascaded down into steep knife-edged valleys. They were entering the

Massif Central and the land to which Marcelle had fled over sixty years before during the war.

Kate found herself daydreaming: about her daughter's upcoming wedding—the daughter who had so recently entered her life—and about if she, indeed, had followed Marcelle to France to find answers to resolve her turmoil regarding Lisa. Had she? She was feeling contentment as she gazed at the passing countryside. She tried to imagine what it had been like for Marcelle when she first passed through this same region on her long train ride from Paris. Marcelle was seeking safety when she came through here and was desperate to reconnect with her young son. Kate opened her eyes more fully as if to gain clarity into Marcelle's life. The extensive fields and vineyards, which had blanketed the Loire Valley, gave way to small plots of ground enclosed by meter-high rock walls. Within the enclosures, rust-colored and bloodred weeds waved gracefully as the wind lifted and rose through the landscape. All seemed to grow in abundance and to dance to the same tune the autumnal wind was playing—dipping and rising in unison.

"What time of year did your mother first go to the *Auvergne,* Sophie?" Kate asked, breaking the silence. "Was it in the springtime? Or, in the fall, like now?"

Sophie furrowed her brow. She looked around her, as if seeing outside the car for the first time that afternoon. She, too, had been lost in her thoughts. "I think it was in April or May." She rubbed her eyes a couple of times. "Other than a change of seasons, I would imagine what she first saw looked much like this."

Sophie had been muddling over in her mind how she was going to handle Thierry: her explanations of what her mother's letters meant for him, why she and Kate had been exploring their mother's past, plus what kind of buffer she could provide for Christian when he revealed who Thierry's father was. And Julien? She was surprised Julien had accepted her invitation to join them.

"By the way, has Thierry mentioned your mother's letters to you? Has he talked about them?"

Sophie quickly glanced in Kate's direction. *Has she been reading my mind?* "No. No, that's not his way. He never brings up topics which could be . . ." she fluffed her hands about her face, "considered uncomfortable—to himself or others. When I've called him from the road these past few weeks, I've never brought it up. But I plan to talk with him about it soon—maybe tomorrow."

They rounded a curve on the narrow road and caught a glimpse of a woman herding cows as she walked up and over a knoll. Only the red-checkered head scarf bobbed along the hillside until it disappeared from sight. High on a ridge above them they could see children riding their bicycles as a small herd of goats skittered down the hill out of the children's way. Sophie slowed and rolled down her window as the children's laughter cascaded down the hill toward them. She waved at the children and laughed as if she were joining in their fun.

"You're probably right, Sophie," said Kate. "These rutted old roads may have been worn with time, but I would like to believe we are seeing the land your mother first saw back in 1943." She watched with fascination as the children climbed higher and higher on the ridge until they, too, disappeared from sight.

Sophie rolled up her window and wound down the hill and through a small village holding a clutch of dilapidated stone houses. She pointed at an abandoned *lavoir* next to a scum-coated pond. She slowed but did not stop. One more time, images of women scrubbing their families' clothes flitted through Kate's head. Other than tradition, why this was such a passion for her, she did not know. Although the village seemed uninhabited, chickens and ducks made their way across the road and waddled into a roadside garden. Without hesitation, they busied themselves by rummaging through the withered leaves for an afternoon snack.

As a formal introduction to the area, Sophie announced, "We are finally in the region called the Auvergne. This is central France, the 'heart of France.' Once you've met my brother and the people of Auvergne, you will understand that this is true. They are all heart!"

"It's beautiful!" Kate exclaimed. "Very pastoral. Is it mostly farming country?"

"I suppose farming is how most people still survive, even though a farmer today can barely eke out a living. But the work is such a part of who the farmer is that he can't leave the farm behind. Perhaps my brother will tell you some of his story. But I must tell you, the people here are shy, not used to strangers, and you'll find reluctance in them to open up. Don't be hurt by that. They have good minds, but they do not wish to display intellect as a means of discourse."

"Yes, I remember the reluctance to strangers your mother experienced when she first arrived in Evaux-les-Bain. From your mother's journal, remember?"

"Yes, as I recall, that was the first time she was called *saleté réfugiate* . . ."

Gare d'Austerlitz, Paris
April 1943

The train was packed with people like Marcelle, hoping to find a new life and a place without fear. She had not wanted to leave Paris, but she could no longer wait for her love, her André.

She had no choice. She had to move on. Sadness had gripped her heart for days before she left, for somehow she knew deep down inside that André didn't have the courage of his love.

The train, itself, stunk to high heaven—of cigarette smoke, bodies too long without a bath, baskets of food that had seen better days, plus the reek of urine and coal smoke. German soldiers pushed their way onto the train, shoving into the best seats and elbowing the elderly and children into the aisles. When she first saw them, a wave of fear enveloped her. She was not used to having soldiers so close by. Immediately, she clutched her dear Gérard close to her breast. Eight months old and he was all she had left of her love. Her love.

There was nowhere to sit, so she crouched down in the aisle. As the train lurched forward, she caught a glimpse of André through the window, but barely a glimpse. She hoped this wouldn't be the last time she would see him.

She sat down on her few belongings and shoved her inadequate basket of food under a seat. She looked around for facilities. If there were toilets, they were far away, and of course, no food service was available, not that she had money for such things. Again, a wave of weariness swept over her. She steadied herself for the lengthy ride to the *l'interieur* of France, where she hoped her son Thierry would be waiting.

As she peeked down the aisle, a German soldier caught her eye and gestured for her to take his seat. Grateful, she swallowed the revulsion she felt for the Germans as she rushed forward with her baby. Quickly, she piled her things in the seat and stayed there for the duration of the trip.

Train travel had become quite dangerous, as the trains had become targets for allied strafing. She tried to block this from her mind, as there was no other means of travel.

She allowed her mind to drift back to Paris. The city had become so dismal, so bleak, so hopeless. The sky had seemed a ceaseless grey, with the black soot of progress drifting down upon her. But whose progress was it? She had not experienced it. She had scrambled to make enough money to pay the nurses who kept her sons, and if she had not been sharing her life with André, she was not certain how she would have survived.

The train had stopped and started at every village along the route. The German soldiers were continually getting on and off, checking their papers over and over again, and riffling through their meager belongings. But why had the train stopped so long in Orléans? What was happening? Was that the backfire from a car, or a gunshot? Suddenly, she heard someone selling café au lait from outside the train window. She propped Gérard on the seat, lowered the window, and ordered a cup of *café*. The hot, rich brew was like a salve on a cut. For a few moments, it helped stave off her fear, but, as she held the cup in her hands, she noticed she was shaking. Once again she was facing the unknown, alone. A blast from the train whistle brought her to the present. Just as the train lurched forward, she passed the cup out of the window.

After a time, the landscape shifted dramatically, as they arrived in the mountains of the Massif Central with its volcanic peaks and lunar landscape. She cleaned the window to peer out. A thrill of anticipation rippled through her, and she held Gérard up to the window so he, too, could see. The train crossed and recrossed rivers and gorges and entered onto a fertile river basin of the Limagne. She looked for cows, sheep, or goats to point out to Gérard, but she spotted very few. Yet the fields of wheat had ignored the happenstance of war and were turning chartreuse green and growing tall, almost as if in a spirit of rebellion.

When she saw the deep gorges filled with the spring runoff, she suddenly was anxious to wash herself clean of the dreary grey of the past and of the dinginess and terror of war.

As she tried to relax, fear once again became her companion. Outside the window, the glint of a plane swooped down over them. Because the allies were targeting railroad bridges, she prayed for safe passage as she stared down to the deep gorge below her. There was nothing she took for granted. She bit down hard on her lip to keep from crying and immediately prayed to Ste. Anne to keep the war far away from the free zone.

She arrived in Evaux les Bains and stepped off the train—with baby, luggage, and all. She, of course, had no idea which direction the village of Mainsat was. The local peasants reminded her of her beloved Bretons, who wore a similar regional dress. She felt like she was home.

Alas, it was not long before she realized, through the differences in regional dialect, that she understood no one. It took her a few minutes to ask for directions. During that interim, her presence was met with distain and antipathy. Finally directions were given, and she began to head out of town. She picked up one piece of luggage, readjusted Gérard on her hip, and began to kick her other bags down the road as she made her way out of town. She was ashamed to hear catcalls. Then, the words *saleté refugiate*, were hurled in her direction. By their tone she knew she had not been accepted. It was then she realized those words meant *filthy refugee*. She almost dropped to her knees. Where or when would she ever find acceptance?

Mainsat

May 1943

The thick wooden door, cracked and covered in peeling white paint, echoed with her knock. Standing back from the door, Marcelle waited for an answer. She could hear voices inside the house—loud whispers. She knocked once again and waited, shifting Gérard from one hip to the other. She took a look around. The door, which was set deep into the meter-thick farmhouse wall, was made of grey volcanic rock. The two-story house was worn out and was missing roofing tiles. Above her, two of the window shutters swung recklessly in the cool spring wind. Banging. Banging. The acrid odor of manure stung her nose yet commingled with the sweet smell of hay and grass. She was a city girl and knew little about farms. The dairy farm where she had been raped loomed in her mind. She wanted to run. Instead, she sneezed.

The door squeaked open a crack, and a gruff voice bellowed out at her. "What do you want, missy?" The Auvergnat dialect was the same as she had heard in the village of Evaux-les-Bain. It was a mixture of French and Occitan, but until that day, she had never heard it before. She leaned toward the door, as she wasn't altogether certain what had been asked of her.

"Monsieur Ambert, I'm Mademoiselle Pourrette, the mother to Thierry Pourrette. I'm here to see him and to stay—if you'll have me," she said.

"Mademoiselle? Not madame?" he hissed, the spittle clearly striking her in the face.

"*Non.* Not madame," she answered quietly.

"So, you want to see your son *and* live here too? Do we have a choice?" He continued to block her way into the house. Then Thierry's impish face peeked from behind the farmer's legs, and he squealed with joy when he saw her. The farmer stood firm, but then swung the door open.

From the moment Marcelle entered the kitchen, she could tell her son had changed. His eight-year-old shyness now held a reticence with her. Yes, his eyes lit up as he embraced her, and he stood beside her not letting go of her hand, but something had been stolen from him. She set Gérard on the floor to scoop Thierry into her arms, but Thierry had grown so tall that she could not lift him off the floor. She started crying, sobbing really, as she was so relieved to find him. She pulled herself together. She was scaring him, and Gérard, too. The Amberts huddled on the other side of that drab kitchen, watching her and waiting. They seemed a stern sort, but Thierry was well fed and healthy. She could only be grateful.

Monsieur Ambert, having watched their reunion, finally spoke a single word, and Thierry immediately stood by his side.

Madame Ambert, guarded and resistant, reluctantly helped Marcelle with her bags. She spoke little; instead, anger seeped from every pore of her rigid body.

It was clear the Amberts had not wanted her to come. The two had been forced to feed the German soldiers on a regular basis and were also providing food for the *Maquis*, who hid out in the area. And then they were asked by the Vichy government to take Thierry into their home. With her arrival, it was two more mouths to feed, and they let her know without words she was an undue burden. She tried to show her appreciation for all they had done for Thierry, for her. But they ignored her, except to demand she work hard for their keep.

Many nights, after her boys lay down, she would cry herself to sleep. Here she was, one more time, in a position of not being wanted, and one more time, trying to justify her existence. But as she looked down at her dear Gérard suckling from a bottle or her sweet Thierry snuggled near her, it became easier to think about their future. She was twenty-four years old, and she had to believe that this war would not last forever and André would soon be at her side.

❧

Within a few hours, Sophie drove through the very village of Evaux-les-Bain they had been speaking of. Both women viewed the city with disdain as Marcelle's wartime journal had clearly spelled out how poorly the people had treated her.

"I'm surprised my mother chose to be buried here after all she experienced," Sophie said as she turned onto a narrow highway along a winding mountain ridge.

"She must have come to accept those earlier times as a reaction to war," Kate said. In silence, the two continued on to Thierry's farm.

CHAPTER TWENTY

A *R*eturn to the *E*xodus

*F*INALLY, THEY PULLED INTO Thierry's farmyard. The old stone farmhouse looked forlorn in the soft purple light of late afternoon. Sophie honked the horn wildly to signal her arrival, but only the geese acknowledged her presence by flapping their wings and resounding with an equally obnoxious racket. She laughed out loud, turned off the car, and jumped out. Just as the aroma of freshly baked bread assaulted them as they stepped from the car, the kitchen door swung open and out stepped Jeannine, Thierry's wife. A shy grin stole across her face as she brushed blonde straggles of hair back from her brow. Sophie, always the most demonstrative of her family, grabbed her in a hug and kissed both cheeks.

"How are you, dear sister?" she asked Jeannine. "And where is my brother?" She eagerly peered over her sister-in-law's shoulder and into the house, awaiting her brother to barrel out the door.

"He went into Fontanières. He thought he would be back before you arrived. One too many cups of coffee at the café, I would imagine. Not to worry, come in! Come in and we'll have our own coffee!"

As Kate was introduced to Jeannine, Sophie said, "Kate, this is my dear sister, Jeannine. She is the best person who ever came into my brother's life. The very best!" Jeannine's broad face lit up, and then she blushed.

Embarrassed, Jeannine quickly embraced Kate, then spun around and led them into the house and directly to the kitchen. The redolence of cinnamon and freshly baked bread now hit them full force. Both Sophie and Kate grabbed their stomachs as they moaned with delight.

"Oh, Jeannine, it smells soooooo good in here!" Sophie said, taking her scarf from about her neck and unbuttoning her jacket.

Again a smile crept across Jeannine's face. She went directly to the coffee pot and began filling it with well water and measuring out the coffee before turning to chat with Sophie. They conversed easily in French, catching up on each other's activities and family tales. Kate wandered around the room imagining what life was like for this family. She remembered Sophie telling her that the farm had been passed down through generations in Jeannine's family. As she tried to judge the age of the house, her eyes scanned the stucco walls and then up and over the cracks that etched themselves across the ceiling. The floorboards were well worn and uneven, but the room was spotless. A table covering appeared to once have been dotted in light blue and yellow flowers but was now almost completely white from hard scrubbing. A bouquet of sunflowers sat prominently in a pale green canning jar in the center. Sophie pulled out a chair and invited Kate to sit down. Once the coffee finished perking, Jeannine set cinnamon pastries and steaming mugs of coffee before them and joined them.

"Jeannine, how long have you lived here?" Kate asked.

"I was born in this house in 1937 and grew up here." She shrugged and took a bite of the cinnamon twist. "This farm was the family home of my great-grandfather. My grandfather and father both were born here and lived on this farm until they died.

"Probably right smack on this table," Sophie said as she slapped the tabletop. "That's how I came into this world."

Both Jeannine and Kate's eyes popped open, but neither chose to comment on Sophie's observation. Jeannine continued talking.

"Because my parents didn't have sons, I was expected to take on that role. I worked on the farm and walked three kilometers every day to school. In the winter months it was difficult because we didn't have many warm clothes. And none for special occasions."

"Sounds like hard work," Kate said.

Jeannine shrugged again. "It's simply part of farm life, but it's an existence that I know and love." Just then, the front door opened and slammed shut as the thudding steps of Sophie's brother echoed throughout the house. "Especially sharing life with Thierry," Jeannine said as her husband burst into the kitchen.

"Thierry! Thierry!" squealed Sophie as she leapt up from the table and wrapped her arms around her brother. His arms folded her to his chest and he stood there holding her fast, then gently gave her *poutous*, or kisses, on the top of her head.

"Thierry," Sophie said, finally separating herself from his embrace, "I want you to meet my dear friend Kate." Kate stood up from the table and walked around to shake his hand. He, too, pulled her to him and gave her *poutous* on both cheeks. Kate had expected a shy, quiet man, but Thierry's exuberance filled the room. She returned to her seat opposite Jeannine, but her eyes stayed on Thierry. *Here is the child, the man,* she thought, *Marcelle spent her life trying to love and protect, but always from a distance. Here is the child Marcelle walked away from—just like I did from Lisa.* Kate knew so much about him—maybe too much. She squirmed in her seat. She felt uncomfortable that she held an unfair advantage of which she did not wish to betray. Thierry stripped off his canvas coat, and pulled up the chair next to his wife and across from Sophie.

His face was deeply tanned and weathered. He was stocky; his shoulders were somewhat stooped, and once he sat down, he talked with his hands moving in small turns and swirls. Just like Sophie had said. Once he doffed his hat, the thick dark hair Sophie had raved about appeared to have given way to a grey-streaked crown. But it was his eyes that caught Kate's attention: they were the same as his mother's.

"Here, Thierry," Jeannine said, standing up to grab another cup. "Join us. Kate is asking us questions about life on our farm."

Sophie reached out her hands and took Thierry's into her own. She murmured a few words of Occitan to him and smiled broadly, and he picked up a cinnamon twist and inhaled it.

"Tell Kate about the festivals," Sophie insisted.

"In the fall, like now, there was always a harvest," Jeannine said, looking over at her husband. "When I was a child, this was one community activity my family enjoyed. It was the annual harvesting of the wheat. Usually a battery of people would travel from one farm to another. The men would all work together, and the women would prepare the food for all of the harvesters."

"Sounds like work, and little pleasure, but at least you were with friends," Kate said.

"Ah, but she's failing to mention," Thierry interrupted, "that we usually had some kind of music, a band of sorts that played, and we would have dances right in the farmyard." He cast an adoring smile at his wife.

"Isn't that how you two met?" Sophie asked slyly, catching the look and laughing. Jeannine reddened.

Thierry broke in. "I started working in the fields when I was twelve. And I started dancing at age fifteen—I still love to dance. I remember I used to have a bicycle, and I would ride many kilometers to get to the dances. Sometimes, I would return from the dance at 5:00 or 7:00 AM the following morning." He pulled his hand through his hair, and a slow grin enveloped his face. "The farmer I worked for," he said, "did not give me credit for dancing the whole night, so, as tired as I was, I had to work hard all the following day." He groaned, and Sophie giggled with delight.

"Tell Kate about the time of the big storm, Thierry," Sophie prompted.

"Well," he chuckled and tipped back on his chair, "as I recall, it was the summer of my fifteenth birthday, and it was the day of one of our biggest summer festivals in the region. Everyone from kilometers around had been excited for weeks anticipating this one particular dance. There was to be an exceptionally good band performing on that night. At a previous dance, I had attracted the eye of a good-looking gal, who I hoped would be in attendance at this festival. I was especially looking forward to it." Again, his eyes lovingly found his wife's. Jeannine blushed once again.

"Kate," Sophie interrupted, "Thierry was not always good with words when he was younger, but I have been told he could sweep the women off their feet with his elegance on the dance floor, especially in the waltz. Right, Jeannine?" She smiled at Jeannine.

Thierry licked the cinnamon glaze off his fingers. "After I got off work that afternoon, I went down to the pond, pulled off my work clothes and boots, then scrubbed myself raw. Then I put on my best dancing clothes and best shoes—well, my only shoes—and headed out. I got on my bike, my only mode of transportation, and rode those dusty, dry roads thirty-five kilometers to the dance. Oh, I flew down those roads, as I could hardly wait.

"By the time I arrived, the barnyard was already filled with pickup trucks and cars, and people were everywhere! Lighted lanterns swung from the trees, and tables were loaded with more food than I had ever seen. Laughter rang out, and everyone was talking, eating, drinking, and having a great time. I quickly put my bike into the barn for safekeeping and walked out to join the crowd. I headed for the food; I was so hungry. I hadn't eaten all day and I could just taste . . . But, before I could down a drink or grab a snack, the band began to play—as if they had been awaiting my arrival." He winked at Sophie.

"Well," said Thierry, with a bit of bluster, "when the band began to play, they played some popular songs along with some waltzes. I had mastered the waltz. Don't ask me where or how I learned, but I had." Question marks formed on three sets of eyebrows, but he plowed on.

"*C'est un secret?*" Sophie asked slyly, cocking her head to the side. She sent a mischievous wink across to her brother.

"*Non,*" he answered simply. "*Non!*" He had no idea what his sister was implying. "I could see that lovely young lady across the farmyard who I was hoping to impress, and I was making the rounds with some of the other gals, dancing with this one and then that one, all in order to work up my courage to ask Jeannine. I was biding my time, as the night was young and I had the entire evening to make my move. I had thought it all out ahead of time while riding over on my bicycle." Thierry turned in his chair, smiled at his wife, and reached over to take her hand.

"After a few sets of dances, the owner of the farm and his hands began to set off a string of fireworks. I looked around for Jeannine but could only see her silhouette in the glow of the red, blue, and gold flashes of light. As I was working my way around the edge of the crowd, a bolt of lightning suddenly joined in with the fireworks and the sky lit up, as if electrified. At first, all were in awe, but then panic struck, and everyone dashed to the barn for cover. Even before I was able to get inside, the sky opened up and rain and hail came down in torrents. The wind ripped at the trees, and the lanterns, which had been so festive a few moments before, were shredded in front of our eyes. The food table went flying, and the band grabbed their instruments and they, too, raced to the barn to get out of the rain.

"When the storm was finally over, most people were soaked and they rushed to their cars and trucks to leave. I went in search of my bicycle. It was then I found it had been trampled in everyone's rush for the barn." His fingers played a little tattoo with his spoon as he talked. "The front wheel was bent at right angles. Mangled! After attempting to straighten it, all I found I could do was drag it all the way home—thirty-five kilometers." He sighed. "And all for the love of dancing . . . and my dear Jeannine." He looked up, his eyes filling with mirth. "And to top it off, after walking all of those miles, I also lost the heel of my shoe. My best good shoe."

"Your only shoes," Jeannine corrected.

Thierry grinned. "And it was weeks before I had money to replace it," he said as his body rocked back and forth as he began to laugh silently. He closed his eyes tightly and tittered until a light chuckle broke loose. Surprisingly, tears began to flow down his cheeks as he held his sides with laughter. Now, loud chortles erupted from Sophie and Jeannine, and Kate found herself caught up in the contagion.

"And after all of that," Sophie guffawed, "you didn't even get a dance with your true love."

"*C'est vrai,*" he said, wiping tears from his face. "*C'est vrai.*"

After the laughter faded, Kate asked, "Do you still go to dances?"

"Yes," said Jeannine, "we do still go to dances, just not as often."

"And I still know how to waltz," Thierry put in with an air of bravado.

⁕

That evening, after the four of them returned from dinner at a local café, Jeannine and Kate begged forgiveness and headed off to bed, giving Sophie time alone with her brother.

"Even though I called you often from the road, Thierry, I haven't brought up the subject of *Maman's* letters."

Thierry nodded his head in understanding.

"So, what did you think? I didn't read but a couple of them, so . . ."

"Soph, I should have thanked you. I'm sorry I didn't bring it up on the phone either, but it took me a while to get through them."

"I know, Thierry. But I've been concerned—concerned that you understood *Maman*'s intentions." Sophie stuck a sugar cube into her tiny eau-de-vie glass, letting the liqueur fill the crystalline cells.

Thierry scratched his head. "Probably you were concerned I *misunderstood* her intentions."

"Well, that thought crossed my mind," Sophie said as she sucked on the sugar cube. She winced. "Whoo! This is powerful stuff!" Her eyes watered.

Thierry grinned and sipped his straight. "I suppose I read all of *Maman*'s letters that first night, but it was too overwhelming." His head dropped. "What I remember being told when I was young and what *Maman* was writing—at first, it just didn't make sense." He looked across the room at Sophie, his vision slightly blurred.

"You know, Soph, I've been angry with *Maman* most my life," he continued, "yet I've always loved her. But to realize that she had loved me and wanted me with her all those years—well, I had no idea!" A sudden sob caught in his throat. Sophie started to get up, but he waved her to stay seated.

"I thought all these years she had abandoned me. *Mon Dieu!* If it hadn't been for Jeannine, I don't know what I would have been thinking." He slurped his eau-de-vie. "She helped me put the letters together in order of dates written, and then I could see a pattern. We figured it must have been Madame Ambert, the farm lady, who was keeping me from leaving."

"Was that her handwriting on the outside of the envelopes?"

"Mm-hmmh! I realized that Madame Ambert was trying to get *Maman* to send more money for my care. She was already receiving a government stipend to keep me, but from *Maman's* letters, I learned Madame Ambert must have tried to convince her that I would kill myself if I was forced to leave. Sophie, I didn't even know *Maman* had written." Tears spilled down his weather-worn cheeks and splashed onto his old leather jacket. He dropped his head close to his cupped hands. Sophie crossed the room and slid onto the sofa next to him. She reached over and stroked his dark curly hair. Little tufts of white hair jutted out from his ears, and when he raised his head, she could see how much he looked like their mother. Like never before.

Sophie took a sip of her now sickeningly sweet eau-de-vie. She blanched. "Where did you get this stuff?" she said, her nose crinkled with distain. She felt like she was breathing fire.

"Papa," was Thierry's answer. "This was one of his last bottles. It's got to be over twenty years old by now," he said as he tipped the glass up again.

Sophie burst into fits of laughter. It seemed every relative she visited had one more of Papa's last bottles of eau-de-vie. Obviously, no one had been drinking it.

"It's older than that, but, Thierry, time has not been kind to it, has it?" she giggled once again. "After I first read a couple of the letters *Maman* wrote to you, it was if a whole series of answers—like cogs in a wheel—lined up in order to make our past lives make sense. Maybe for the first time. I never realized before, forty-some years ago now, that we had come to take you home with us. But, unfortunately, we returned to Ste. Barbe without you. There are so many details I don't recall. Probably, I didn't understand much of what was going on, but I still don't know why all of those letters were returned to *Maman* or why they were kept. But the fact that they were found in Papa's personal box . . . well, I dare not guess. He certainly had his own little secrets."

She looked over at him and caught his smile slipping. Tears again began to bloom in Thierry's eyes, but he brushed them away.

He sat facing Sophie as he gathered his words. First he started, stopped, then finally blurted out, "But I had to wait until she died to find out she loved me. When she first moved to Fontenières, I was so angry with her, and I know I didn't treat her well. But I never understood—until now—why she chose to retire here. I thought it was all because of my children, not me . . ." The lines in his face furrowed as sadness replaced the tears in his eyes.

"Thierry, there were a great many things we didn't know about *Maman*—or Papa for that matter. But one thing that was never a mystery to me was that our mother loved you deeply."

The following morning, after a hearty breakfast worthy of farmhands—freshly-baked bread, fried eggs, bacon, and *saucissons* —Thierry led Sophie and Kate out the back door and into his garden. With great pride he showed them a garden that was bounded on the edges with sunflowers and enclosed with heavy mesh fencing. He pointed out where he would plant his sweet peas and lettuce in the spring and showed Kate where he planned to place his radishes, squash, potatoes, and corn. "Future raspberries and blackberries will grow here, along with some table grapes," he promised.

Kate stepped out of the enclosure, where birds fought for attention in the almost-bare cherry trees and hens searched near their feet for a succulent worm or two.

"Let me show you where I'm going to build my house," Sophie called to Kate. They walked to the edge of the property, and from this point, they had an unobstructed view from the top of a long hillside, which dropped into a beautiful, copper-colored valley below them.

"When Thierry gives me permission, I'm going to buy this parcel of land next to his and build right over there so I can always have this view. Isn't it bea-u-ti-ful?" she beamed, looking over her shoulder at her brother. His look of chagrin told all.

"Sophie, you know I can't divide this property. It's not mine to sell, and Jeannine won't divide the . . ."

"Oooooh, Thierry," Sophie cajoled, "You know I was only teasing you. But you know how much I love this view. You are so lucky," she cooed. Thierry shuffled toward her, then said, "Instead, let me show you our rabbits." He began steering Kate toward a pen where he gathered up a floppy-eared rabbit from the hutch.

"This one has been a family pet for years now. He's most fortunate, as we will never eat him. But, his brothers? Now, that's another story," he laughed.

The three walked around the farmhouse, out to the barns to look at the equipment, and back into one of the outbuildings, while Thierry proudly told Kate the history of the property.

"Because the farm has been deeded to Jeannine from her side of the family (she is known as the *cultivateur*), I will never receive any income from the farm. But I am very comfortable with this position and I am very grateful to her.

"Why, Thierry, that's just what your wife said about being here with you," Sophie said.

Just then, a horn honked in the farmyard, and Thierry stuck his head out of the doorway to catch Jeannine pulling out of the driveway.

"An errand to finish before Christian and Julien arrive today," she called out.

Eventually, the three wandered back into the warmth of the kitchen, where they found a fresh pot of coffee waiting. While Sophie poured the coffee, Kate and Thierry sank down at the table, as if they had put in a hard day's work.

"What do you remember of the exodus of Paris, Thierry?" Sophie asked. "Do you remember that time at all?" It was asked with gentleness and sincerity, but it was such a bold question, something totally out of the blue. She sat down across from him.

Thierry sat stark still, staring at his fingernails, giving thought to the question before him. His head bent forward as a glint from the light above the kitchen table reflected in his hair. His dark blue work shirt, that had seen years of wear, stretched across his shoulders. Kate held her breath. It was such an invasion of this private man. Surely, Sophie knew what she was doing. She loved and adored her brother.

Kate turned toward Sophie, who began talking softly to Thierry in Occitan. Sophie reached across the table. His reddened hands did not yield to her touch but remained tightly folded on the tablecloth.

Not understanding what was being said, Kate's mind worried through the question before him. Like moving from one prayer bead to another, her mind paused, reflected, and moved on. What would be the impact? She didn't have long to wait. He shoved back his coffee mug and laid his head on his arms and began to sob. His back shook with years of pent up emotion, and the tears flooded without restraint. Sophie stood up and moved around the table and wrapped her arms around him. Cradling him tightly to her small body, she held him until his tears slowed. Minutes passed. Sixty-one years had come and gone since the exodus, and yet the ripe emotion of memory had broken free as if it had happened yesterday.

He mumbled something, wiping his cheeks. He glanced quickly at Kate and then back at his hands. He took a light blue handkerchief from his pocket and blew his nose long and loud.

Sophie whispered to him again, mentioning Kate. He then sat up, tucked his handkerchief back into his pocket, and cleared his throat. Kate had no idea what Sophie had said, but Thierry's trust in Sophie was evident. His eyes acknowledged Kate, but he began haltingly, "Yes, I remember the exodus. Mostly I remember the bombing that went on before the exodus—before *Maman* left for Bordeaux."

Carole Bumpus

"What do you remember, Thierry?" Sophie asked softly. She was met with silence. "Thierry, I don't mean to pry, but Kate and I have spent many days on the road trying to track down *Maman's* story, and what you and *Maman* experienced during the war would be greatly beneficial." She waited.

Thierry struggled to control his emotions, but his mind was swirling with the detritus of his past. Having spent most of his adult years putting those nightmares behind him, he was not eager to bring them to the surface again. When he thought of his mother—when he thought of having a mother—those memories in Paris were the only ones that eked out on their own. The only ones he emotionally embraced. But now it felt Sophie was invading them. Because he had faith in her, he managed to face his sister head-on. "I was staying at the nurses' home—you know, the home for the children for the Citröen employees? It was in the suburbs of Paris, far from where *Maman* was working. I'll never forget the shrill scream of the bombs as they first hit and everyone was so shocked and scared." When he took a sip of coffee, his large claw of a hand shook.

Then, a timid smile flitted across his face. "At first, I remember my friends, and I thought it was fun, or funny. . ." his smile then fell, "until we saw everyone running and crying. After that first attack, our nurses raced with us children across the street into the underground *Métro*. I remember crying for *Maman*; I was so afraid I would never see her again."

Looking across the table at her brother, Sophie could see the terror in his eyes—the terror from so many years ago that still haunted him today. Sophie clutched her heart, as she felt pain for this beloved brother across from her. Again, she reached across the table for her brother's hands; this time they yielded to her touch.

"You were so young, Thierry. Only four at the time, and you had every reason to be frightened," Sophie soothed.

"I suppose so. As it was, I was only able to spend weekends

with *Maman,* but after the bombing raids began, that came to a stop, too. I'll never forget coming up from the shelter—we were all holding hands, and the air was filled with smoke and dust. I could barely breathe, and we were all coughing . . ." He began coughing loudly, as if smelling the smoke once again. His handkerchief came out and he mopped his mouth but continued on. "I dropped the hand of my partner to cover my mouth, and when I looked up, I couldn't see him—any of them. I panicked and started to cry out, but then I stumbled and fell in the street. When I got to my feet, I realized that I had fallen over . . ." Tears began to stream once again down his face. He silently shook in his seat, barely able to control himself.

"It was a leg, Sophie," he hoarsely whispered. His face contorted, and in that one moment, all the grief of his childhood was etched in his expression. "A child didn't make it into the shelter in time." He stared into space and gulped in air as if his throat was constricting once again.

Kate got up and went to get a glass of water for him. She, too, thought she was going to be sick. *Why have we forced this poor man to relive this? I know better than this,* she chastised herself. *I know damn well you don't rip an old wound apart and expect it to easily cleanse itself from years of pain.* Kate leaned over the sink, as she felt light-headed. *I should have stopped Sophie from asking those questions. No mystery is worth . . .* She turned back to the two remaining at the table. *What is she saying?* Kate's knees went weak. She couldn't hear their words, but it was the first time she wanted to scream, *What the hell's going on?*

But Thierry was sitting up now. He was speaking more calmly and without tears. *What is he saying?* Kate returned with the water and placed it before him.

". . . and when *Maman* came to me and told me that she was being sent to Bordeaux with her job, we all knew what to expect."

"What do you mean?" Sophie asked.

"We were all told by our mothers to remain there until they could send for us. I don't remember being afraid, because that was the only place we knew and all my friends were with me. I don't recall that our lives changed much during that time. I know that I turned five while Maman was gone, but I didn't realize it at the time. She told me later when she returned, and then we celebrated. I think she was only gone about a month.

"At the time of the Exodus," he said, once again wiping his nose, "the Germans had begun marching in from the North while everyone else evacuated to the West; to the South. Even our French government fled," he fairly spit out. Even though he would have been too young to understand what that meant at the time, the words carried the venom of second-hand knowledge, second-hand rage.

"While Maman was gone, the Germans began their occupation of the city, so the bombing raids stopped. We must have felt safer after that. And we did as we had always done: play in the playroom and wait for visits from our mothers." His words were matter-of-fact.

"Do you remember when Gérard was born? Did he stay at the same nurses' home with you?" Sophie asked.

He paused to think. "I think I had turned seven when he was born. It was in the late summer of 1942. I don't think he came to live with us immediately, as *Maman* was still nursing him . . ." He thought for a moment. "I don't remember ever having a conversation with *Maman* about it then, or later. I don't exactly know what went on. But I do recall being proud that I was a big brother. I loved Gérard right away."

"Did you meet Gérard's father?" Sophie asked.

Thierry tapped his fingers on his forehead. "I did, but I don't remember his surname . . . I should, but I don't. Gérard asked me that same question not long before he . . ." he said, his voice dropping in tenor. "I wasn't much help to him either, I'm afraid."

He shook his head. *If I had been able to tell Gérard, I would have—I should have,* Thierry thought. Guilt of having failed his brother gripped his gut. He felt if he had remembered him, then maybe he could have saved Gérard. Like all members of the family, collective guilt was woven into the fabric of their makeup.

"I remember Gérard's father was a kind man—a man who was as gentle to *Maman,* as he was to me. He was tall, and his blond hair would flop down into his eyes when he bent down to talk with me. He thought I was bright. He was the only one who said so, and I remember talking with him, my hand in his, as we walked along the Seine. *Maman,* of course, was at our sides carrying the baby. Gérard." He stopped and paused for a long moment. "You know, Sophie, that was the only time I recall feeling I was part of *Maman's* family . . ." Tears filled his eyes. "It was the one moment I carried with me when I was parenting my own children. Hand-in-hand, walking, sharing the day . . ." He stopped and blinked. Sophie patted his hands and smoothed the cuffs of his sleeves.

"And then it started all over again . . ."

"What started all over again?" Kate asked.

"In 1943, the Allies were the ones bombing Paris." He hesitated, and then lifted his chin. "At first, I was terrified of those raids. Fearful for my mother, fearful for my baby brother, but," a mischievous smile swept across his face, "this time I was older, and I would get up on the edge of my bed with the other boys, and we would peek out of the holes we made in the black-out sheets. It was a great game. We could see if the planes were coming—see them before we had to go to the shelters. The first one to see the planes and dive under the bed was the winner! That was the only power we had in our lives. To know when they were coming . . . But, oh," Thierry grabbed his head, "there were many nightmares. I guess it was around this time that all the children of Paris of a certain age—I was still seven then—were put on trains bound for the free zone.

"Was that any better? Were you any safer?" Kate asked him.

Thierry shrugged. "When I had to leave *Maman* behind, I felt even worse. I was more frightened to leave than I was of the bombing raids. This was the first time I had gone on a train without *Maman*. Once I got on the train by myself, I didn't know if I would ever see *Maman* or Gérard again." A sob caught in his throat. "I was with one of the nurses and some of my friends, but none of us knew where we were headed or what we would find when we arrived."

"Do you remember *Maman* putting you on the train?" Sophie asked. "She wrote about it, by the way. She loved you so much. Did you know that?"

As if not hearing her, Thierry answered the question at hand.

"Oh, I remember. *Maman* was crying so hard, and I was crying."

He stopped and wiped his eyes with his handkerchief, then took a swallow of water. "To this day, when I smell the acrid odor of coal smoke, I feel like retching."

"Coal smoke? From the train?" Kate questioned.

Thierry nodded.

"What do you remember about your train ride?" Sophie asked him.

"Very little, other than that smell. It was horrible. The ride was very long and there were lots of Germans on board with us. I suppose, in the end, I was so relieved to get off the train that . . . that I've never left!" he said with a thump on the table. Or was it resignation?

"Other than a few sorties to Algeria and Ste. Barbe, I've rarely left home." Just then, they heard the crunch of car tires on the gravel outside. Jeannine had returned, and Thierry jumped up to help with her packages. Kate sat at the table, allowing Thierry's last words to linger in the room. He had told them so much more, but was it worth the price? She laid her hand on Sophie's arm as Sophie sat staring off into space.

"Are you all right, Sophie?"

"Oh, but, of course, Kate. I was just trying to imagine what my brother's life must have been like—the pain and sorrow he must have endured because he thought he was abandoned."

"Just like your mother, Sophie. Just like your mother," Kate put in.

Sophie nodded her head, then gave that some thought. "Ah well, he is such a tender soul. I was just trying to help break open some of his memories so they would no longer have a hold on him. And maybe to get him to understand how much our *Maman* loved him. I didn't get to all of that yet, but we did talk about some of it last night. So," Sophie swiveled toward Kate, "how did I do, Madame Psychologist?"

"Well, dear friend, you certainly made a valiant effort, that's for sure. You'll need to check in with him later though, because these memories may still have a hold. If you need some help, I'll be here."

Just then, Jeannine and Thierry came into the kitchen carrying packages of cheese and some bottles of local wine.

"We can provide only so much from our farm," Jeannine laughed. She was in good spirits, and her laugh came easily. "Have you heard anything from Christian or Julien? Have they called to tell us when they'll arrive? I can't wait."

"No," Thierry said, "I imagine they're not far away." He put the wine bottles on the kitchen counter and unwrapped the cheeses before placing them into the refrigerator.

"Can we help, Jeannine?" Sophie asked her.

"Not right away. I just need to get a few things done before the others come, so if you two need some time to yourselves, now is probably the time."

Kate and Sophie put on their jackets and headed out the back door. The wind had picked up, but the sun was warm. Two weathered chairs sat on the knoll overlooking the valley below. Sophie sat down and Kate pulled the other up close.

"Sometimes," Sophie said, "I try to imagine what Thierry's experience was like growing up without our mother. I knew *Maman* was always there for me—always nearby, always a comfort—but Thierry never knew our mother in that way. That saddens me a great deal."

"I've thought about that with Lisa, too," Kate said. "She never knew me as a mother—I'm not saying that I was the best parent, but she never got to know me the way my other children do. And it saddens me to think of all I missed out on with her, like her many firsts—her first tooth, first words, first steps, first date, first teenage angst . . . And I can imagine your mother felt the same way about Thierry.

"I'm looking forward to building my relationship with Lisa, but nothing can ever make up for the loss of history we could have had together.

$\mathcal{T}$he $\mathcal{M}$ysteries $\mathcal{A}$re $\mathcal{R}$esolved ... or $\mathcal{A}$re $\mathcal{T}$hey?

$\mathcal{A}$

$\mathcal{T}$HE SOUND OF A CAR entering the gravel driveway was followed by the sound of a second car doing the same. Both Julien and Christian—coming from opposite points in France—arrived at the same time. Thierry bolted out of the house to welcome them both. "How did you two manage to arrive at the same time?" he asked excitedly. He kissed Julien on both cheeks, but he grabbed his son and held him close. Their bond had been strong from the beginning.

Jeannine and Sophie tumbled out the front door after Thierry. Jeannine embraced Julien, but she, too, grabbed her son and held him tight.

Sophie was clearly happy to see Julien and gave him big *bisous*. When she had left his house—how many days ago?—they had parted on uncomfortable terms, and she felt she owed him an explanation of her behavior.

"And, Christian, I'm so happy to see you, too," Sophie chirped, as she hooked her arm through his and led him into his father's kitchen. "I'm sorry we couldn't meet up in Brittany, but I appreciate you meeting us here."

"No problem," Christian said, after he kissed his Aunt Sophie. "I appreciate all you've helped me accomplish," he said, as he tapped a thick folder. As a tall young man in his thirties with light brown hair and a slight build, he was a masculine version of his mother. Kate had waited in the kitchen and walked over to Christian as Sophie introduced them. His smile was genuinely warm. Over the course of the past few weeks, they had been working together to sort through the family mysteries, but this was their first meeting.

Shortly, they all assembled at the family table for *déjeuner*. Jeannine had prepared a roast chicken along with new potatoes and home-canned green beans from their larder. Wine flowed freely as everyone caught up on old news, and in no time at all, they were enticed by Jeannine's apple tarts. When Jeannine got up from the table to prepare a fresh pot of coffee, everyone had time to stretch, before they each headed back to the table.

"Do you want to join us?" Christian kindly asked Kate. "The family conclave is about to begin."

"Thank you, but I'm going to take my cup and sit out in the sunshine to read. This is your family's time. If you need me for anything, just holler. Sophie, I'll be out by the garden," she called over her shoulder as she went out the door.

Sophie nodded to her as she went to the other side of the table and sat next to Christian. Julien pulled a chair up on the end next to Thierry, while Jeannine and Thierry took their normal places.

"All right, Christian, what did you find out for us?" Sophie said, without further ado.

Christian riffled through a sheaf of papers, spread them out on the table, and then straightened them again.

"What is all this?" Thierry asked. Chords in his neck had tensed. Julien, who was seated next to him, placed his elbows on the table next to his. "I'm here for you, Brother," he said quietly. Thierry, surprised at Julien's comment, opened his mouth, and then closed it. He turned toward his son.

Christian pulled out another piece of paper, laid it on the top, and said, "Papa, before *Grand-mère* passed away, she gave me the name of your real father, my grandfather. I had wanted to find out about him." Christian kept his eyes down. "Your father's name is Ambrose Yieux. And I located him at the Yieux dairy farm—the very same farm where *Grand-mère* had worked when she was young. The farm is outside of St. Brieuc in Brittany. It seems the family is still there," Christian said, afraid to witness his father's reaction.

"I asked *Grand-mère* if she had heard from him after you were born." Christian stopped and finally looked up. Out of the corner of his eye, he saw his Aunt Sophie and Uncle Julien smile. He was grateful they were there. His mother, too, sat immobile, but nodded for him to continue.

Thierry, on the other hand, kept his head low. His large rough hands clutched and released his cup as he observed his own reflection, waiting, waiting for the rest of Christian's story. His head was throbbing.

Christian gulped his coffee, burning his tongue in the process, but moved quickly on. "*Grand-mère* said your father had actually sent her money on a number of occasions, along with an apology. She never saw him after . . . the incident, and then after four month's later when she found she was pregnant, his mother forced her to leave the farm. And she never heard from him again once the War began in '39. She told me she felt sorry for him because he never got to know you." Christian paused, his eyes flashing up from his papers to catch any reaction from his father. Thierry sat stony faced; only one muscle twitched in his neck.

"Now, Papa, I took it upon myself to go to St. Brieuc and have a look for myself." Christian was staring down at his papers again, but both his hands and voice were shaking. He could hear his mother's quick intake of breath.

"I didn't know if I would find Ambrose Yieux, but . . . well, Papa, I found him." Christian's eyes flashed up to meet his father's. He couldn't determine in that split second if he saw anger or fear, but he continued on. "Papa, he was sitting right there in the same dairy where he had been all those years ago. He is now the owner." He paused. "It's not a large dairy; only a few milk cows and a small store attached to the barn. Two young fellows—I assume they were grandsons, like me—were hanging out in the store, but I think they were running the operation for him," Christian stopped, attempting to catch his breath.

"I talked to them, but I didn't tell them who I was." Christian took another deep breath. He was feeling light-headed. "Things were a mess. You couldn't find anything in there if you tried. I'm not certain if, or how, they expected to stay in business." He drew in another deep breath and cast his eyes anxiously toward his father. *Mon Dieu,* Christian thought, *am I killing him with my words?*

Finally, Thierry stirred. The words he uttered were low, almost inaudible. Julien looked up from his coffee cup and repeated his brother's question for Christian: "Did you meet my father?"

Christian wiped his hand across his brow and let out his breath. "I did, Papa," he wheezed. "I did meet him. The old man is in his mid-eighties now and appeared to be in bad health. He was sitting by the fire in a worn-down rocking chair with a tattered quilt wrapped tightly over him. I was sure it was him, though, because his resemblance to you, Papa, was uncanny."

"What did he look like, Christian?" Sophie softly prodded.

"Well, he had a similar facial structure, like the same shape of nose, eyes, and ears as Papa. Because he was covered by the quilt, I can't be certain, but it appeared he had the same body type. His hair was different, though, as he was slightly bald with a fringe of pure white hair wrapped over his ears. Not like the full head of hair that you, Papa, must have gotten from *Grand-mère*." He shrugged and ran his hands through his own hair. "If he wasn't my grandfather, then at least I'd be willing to bet we are related."

"Did you talk to him? Did you tell him your name?" asked Jeannine.

"I did talk to him, and I did introduce myself," he stammered. "I don't know if it was the right thing to do, but I just wanted to see if there was a reaction to our last name, Pourrette."

Thierry's head rose up as he turned to face his son. His eyes were open with expectation. "Was there a reaction?"

"Well, let me tell you, Papa, he didn't have much strength. He was stooped over, smoking, and coughing most of the time. I sat down next to him and told him my name. His head lifted immediately, but when I looked into his eyes, both were covered with cataracts. I have no idea if he could see me, but he definitely reacted to my voice. When he began to talk, it was clear from his babbling that he was locked in the past and probably had dementia. I didn't know what to do then. I asked him a couple of questions about the farm, and he extended his sinewy arm out of the blanket and waved it wildly about, but I had no idea what he was saying." Christian scratched his head. "Plus, I think it was a different dialect. More Welsh than I was used to hearing. I'm sorry, Papa."

"Oh, Christian, how difficult that must have been for you," Sophie said. "I know you were trying to do the right thing in finding him."

"But was I, Aunt Sophie? Papa?" Tears formed in his eyes as he looked at his father for confirmation of a job well done.

Thierry, too, was blinking back tears. No words were forthcoming.

"Papa," Christian pleaded, "I just tried to remember what *Grand-mère* used to tell me. She said she was always happy that you were her son. And even over the years, her love for you never changed. She told me that over and over again."

"Yes, Thierry," Sophie said softly, "*Maman* told me many times that you gave her life purpose and direction when she was young and even during the war. She was never sorry that you were her son. She was always proud of you and loved you dearly."

"And after the war?" His voice, almost a whisper, hung in the air above them.

"Oh, Thierry," Sophie said, "like I told you earlier, all the time we lived in Ste. Barbe, she longed for you to be with us. I hope that some day you can believe that."

"Thierry, Sophie's telling you the truth. There was never a day that went by when we were young that *Maman* wouldn't mention how much she missed you. And that was long before we had ever met you," Julien said.

Jeannine stood up to get the coffee pot. She quietly filled the cups, and as she passed Thierry, she tenderly touched his shoulder. "I knew that was the case, too," Jeannine said, as she returned to the stove. "Marcelle told us many times over the years, especially after she moved here to Fontanières, how much she had wanted you, Thierry, at her side when you were a child."

"But," Sophie put in, "I know it has been difficult for you, Thierry, to accept . . . even after I found those letters, which were proof of her love." She looked at him and reached across the table for his hands. "I can never understand how you must feel: to have spent all of your childhood shuffled from one place to another and rarely with your own mother . . ." She puffed out her lips and blew out a breath of air. "No wonder you found it difficult to believe. But it's true. Like I said, I hope you can find some inner peace knowing that you were loved—by three wonderful women."

"Three?" echoed Thierry, Jeannine, Julien, and Christian. "Three?"

"Yes, of course. First, there was *Maman*, then your lovely wife,

Jeannine, and most naturally, ME!!" she hooted. She broke into laughter, jumped up from her seat, and ran to the other side of the table to wrap her arms about her brother. She squeezed him to her.

Thierry's face and ears reddened, but he smiled shyly. "Thank you. And, thank you, too, Christian, for finding out this information. It is more than I've ever known in my entire life. All these years, I've wondered and wondered . . ." He looked down at his cup and paused. "So, our last name should have been Yieux?" He looked at Julien, then back at Christian, as he slowly pronounced the name—Yi-ee-uuux. He said it again, "Yi-ee-uuux! Hmmh! I think I'll stick with the name I have. Pourrette! How about you, Christian?"

Christian exhaled and nodded his head enthusiastically.

Julien popped in with a laugh. "I can't change your name in the address book, anyway. That's the only name I have for you. You're stuck."

Both Thierry and Julien started to get up, but Christian reached across the table to stop them.

"I know this is a lot, but there's more, Papa and Uncle Julien. There's more, and this includes your history, too, Uncle." He thumbed through his pages again and turned up a couple sheets of paper. "*Grand-mère* also asked me to look up the name of *her* father to see if I could find anything. I located the documents, and Sophie and Kate located letters and a diary that suggest that his name was Raymond Pourrette—that is where we got our own surname." He spread several Xerox copies across the tablecloth, facing his father and Julien. At the top of the page in bold print read: *Ascendance Pourrette, Marcelle.* There, before the family, were not only dates, but thumb-print-sized black-and-white photos of their descendants. Some names the family was aware of, but others they had never known:

Pourrette, Raymond

Born – 12/27/1893 – Paris

Died – 9/30/1970 – Paris

There he was! The man known as Pourrette! Three generations had wondered about this man and had only dreamed of finding a connection. This man, whose surname Marcelle, Thierry, and Gérard and their families carried, looked up at them from the miniature photograph. The tiny image, only ten centimeters square, was of a handsome young man with dark hair and a well-trimmed mustache wearing a WWI uniform and glancing over his left shoulder at them.

"And here is our grandmother's name and record," Sophie said:

Tetiau, Honorine

Born – 7/27/1898 – Vannes

Died – 8/14/1936 – Cherbourg

༄༙྾

The dates loomed up in their faces as they calculated the ages for each. Honorine, their grandmother, had died young, at the age of thirty-eight-years-old, the same age as Christian. Raymond had died in Paris at the age of seventy-eight.

"So why did our mother never know who he was?" Thierry asked perplexed but slightly angry. "Why didn't he make contact with her, especially when she was living in Paris? Or with me? I was born there." Pain crept into his voice, which cracked slightly when he tried to control his emotions. "Both my father *and* my grandfather wouldn't have anything to do with me. What more do you have, Christian?" He shoved back from the table but, again, his son convinced him to sit down.

"There is more, Papa. Not all is bleak. There are more details here that might help explain some of your questions." He turned the page, and there in bold, black ink was the date of Honorine and Raymond's wedding: *5/9/1916 – Vannes.*

"1916? Is that what it says?" Sophie asked, pulling the pages around so she could see for herself. "Then, here is the evidence, for certain—our mother was born legitimately. She was born two years *after* they were married," she declared, triumphantly." She looked over at her brothers and for a split second thinks of mentioning the possibility of their mother being someone elses, when Thierry suddenly stood up shoving his chair back. It slapped the wooden floor with a bang. Not able to sit still any longer, he strode out of the back door, past Kate, and into the garden. Jeannine followed silently at his heels. Sophie sat staring at the papers before her. Kate looked up from reading and smiled as the two entered the yard. After a quick assessment of Thierry's face, she stole quietly back into the kitchen. Seeing Sophie still seated, she asked, "Is everyone all right, Sophie? Christian? Julien? Have you found out some news?"

"*Oui*, Kate. Christian here has presented us with our first maternal family tree." She slid the pages across the table toward Kate.

"Oh, my," Kate said, "look at this beauty!" She pointed at the small image of Honorine. The lovely young face was cradled in a black fur wrap, and her dark bobbed hair circled her head in soft wisps and tails. Her mouth was full and carefully sculpted into a hint of a smile as she looked shyly at the camera.

"She looks so much like you, Sophie," Kate said. "This sweet coquette . . . she looks like you."

"Wasn't that what Raymond called Honorine, our grandmother? Seems like I remember that," Sophie said, tapping her chin, not really hearing what Kate had observed.

Christian and Julien both leaned over the table to take another look. "Kate's right. That is you, Aunt Sophie."

Julien placed the photo squarely in front of his sister, "You still look like this, you little coquette," he said sweetly.

Sophie took another look and a glimpse of recognition flashed through her own eyes. "Well, maybe in days past . . ." she said, with a slow smile.

$\mathscr{J}$ules's $\mathscr{P}$ast $\mathscr{C}$omes to $\mathscr{L}$ight

"$\mathscr{J}$ULIEN," SOPHIE ASKED her brother, once she cornered him outside the next morning, "You wanted to talk with me?"

He was holding a steaming cup of coffee while sitting on the lawn chair overlooking the valley. The sunlight had not climbed high enough in the sky to fall on the eastern side of the valley where he sat, but the rest of the hills were brilliant with shimmering lights reflected off the valley of dew. Sophie inched her chair closer, then slipped into the seat.

"About what?" he said, blowing the steam off the lip of the cup.

"Yesterday, you said you had something to tell me—something about Papa." She elbowed him in the side. "I know I didn't dream it."

"No. No, you didn't dream it, Sophie," Julien smiled. "I'm hoping to help your nightmares or bad dreams go away."

"Well, thank you, but I . . ." Sophie began, but Julien interrupted.

"First of all, Sophie, I'm sorry I gave you such a hard time a few weeks back. I know you were going through a difficult time and needed my help for—what did you call it?"

"Research?" Sophie answered.

"*Oui.* You wanted to know about our father's past, and I was resistant. Frankly, I didn't want to be dragged down that path." He sipped his coffee as he looked over the rim at his sister. "I was hoping to keep the blinders on. At the time, I couldn't fathom what we would gain from the past, especially after all this time. But, Soph, when you told me about your nightmares, I realized something needed to be done."

"Now you're sounding like the policeman I've known you to be," Sophie said. "I'm sorry, Julien. I know I was throwing a lot your way, and, of course, we were still reeling from *Maman's* death." She cradled her cup in her hands, warming them. "Since then, I've discovered some answers."

"Oh?" Julien looked startled. "You have? You found out what you needed to know? You mean I made a fool of myself by knocking on all those doors in Pont-a-Meuse and asking questions for nothing?"

"Really? You did that for me?" Sophie tried to imagine the scene of Julien marching up and down the streets of that dilapidated little town and grinned. Then her expression turned serious. "Remember the piece of paper I found in *Maman's* attic? The one showing the date I was supposed to have been in the hospital in Ste. Barbe?"

"Yes."

"I found out that the date in question of my hospital stay coincided with . . ." she blinked; her lip quivered, "a stillborn birth." Sophie gulped. "I didn't even know I could get pregnant. But it seems somehow I did. I think that event was the cause of my nightmares all these years."

"Stillborn? Stillborn? So, your nightmares were about . . . about the hospital, after all?"

"For all these years I've been afraid Papa had done something terrible to me that I didn't want to remember."

"But it wasn't Papa?" Julien's face relaxed with relief.

"No, it was that old *escargot*," Sophie said with a grimace. "Once Kate and I put those pieces together, the nightmares disappeared."

"Oh, Sophie, I'm so happy for you."

"So tell me, what propelled you to walk the streets of Pont-à-Meuse?" Sophie asked. "There are only a few streets in that village, so it probably took you fifteen minutes."

Julien shifted in his chair. "It was our talk about Papa's funeral, and the floral spray that arrived from someone claiming to be Papa's child. Remember?"

Sophie nodded. She reached down, plucked a sprig of long grass from the lawn, and lifted it up to her nose to inhale its natural scent. She needed to smell something untainted by the past.

"Well," continued Julien, "I went in search of one or all of our possible siblings and to investigate that second cousin of Papa's, Clarissa."

"*Mon Dieu!* What did you find out? What was she like?"

"At first, I only found people who remembered the family. I wasn't certain of the last name, but for some reason I remembered Papa taking me to the cousin's house when I was young."

"I do, too. I'll never forget the smell. I told Papa I never wanted to go back again."

"Same for me. I can still picture that old rundown house that needed painting. The front porch sagged so low that the stairs, which were cracked, were easy for me to climb. And there were dogs—many, many dogs!"

"Oh, and the dogs were into everything. It was a horrible little place, wasn't it? Well, did you find it? Did you find them?"

"I didn't find Clarissa. She died not long after Papa, as it turns out. Died of syphilis, I was told."

"Who did you get that information from?" Sophie asked with

an uncharacteristic sneer. "Obviously not one of her own."

"Actually, she *was* one of her own, but she wasn't very proud of her mother. I found her at a tavern on the corner down the street from where the house used to be. It's been torn down now."

"How did you find her?" Sophie dropped the grass to the ground, picked up her cold coffee, and hung on tight.

"I went detecting," he said with a laugh, "and she was perched at the bar when I went in. And I asked about the old house down the lane." Julien leaned back in his chair and described the scene for Sophie.

The ramshackle tavern stood at the corner of Pont and LeDeau, in the old river section of town. Teetering on its moorings, one half of the building listed toward the river while the other half struggled to stay dry. It must have been a century-old wrestling match, but the building remained somewhat intact. Julien hesitated outside the bar, then after sizing up the thickness of the door, swung it open, hard. He lost hold of the handle, and the door slammed against the wall with a loud crash, surprising the occupants within. Sheepishly, Julien smiled, closed the door, and strode toward the bar. The bartender resembled a skeletal version of his own father. Possibly a long-lost uncle, Julien surmised. He nodded his head in apology and sat down at the bar. The room held tight to the odors of the past century: one hundred years of stench from spilled beer, the filth from clouds of cigarette smoke, and the reek of greasy food.

Julien ordered a beer. It was midmorning and it was certainly not his practice to drink beer at that hour, but he was on a mission. He settled on a barstool in the center of the five rickety stools available. A handful of patrons eyed him suspiciously before dropping their eyes to their cigarettes and beer, a light haze billowing above them. They resumed whatever conversation he had stopped with his raucous entry. One scrawny-looking woman nodded in Julien's direction. The dim blue beer sign over the bar reflected the pale blue pallor of her skin. She had the sickly appearance of a late-stage alcoholic. Lifting a red-checked apron to her mouth, she wiped her lips dry. Julien was thinking *waitress*, but he couldn't imagine anyone eating here. He didn't have long to ponder the thought because she slid off the stool and headed over to him. She smiled a semi-toothless smile, a smile of poverty.

"I know who you are," she announced as she arrived at his side. "You're that Zabél boy, aren't ya? *C'est va?* How are you?"

Julien nodded but stared into his beer. He had come in search of answers to his father's licentious past, but he was feeling anxious. As a retired police detective, this would have been a snap. But he had never delved into his own past, and this was awkward. He gulped down part of his beer.

"Yes, I am. I'm Julien. And what would your name be, madame?" he replied.

"Madame? Madame?" Her raspy voice rose so the others could hear. "Did you gents hear that? He called me 'madame.'" She grinned and brushed a strand of wiry hair from her face and answered, "I'm Amelie Brouard. So, what brings you slumming into our parts, Ju-li-en," she slurred.

"I'm here to find the family who lived in that old house down the way—the one by the river. I remember it as a boy, but well," he hesitated, "it appears to have been torn down. Do you know anything about it?"

"You don't remember me, do you?" Amelie said, as she slipped like an eel onto the stool beside him.

Julien turned to face her and realized that she was not as old as the bad lighting had led him to believe. He peered into her dark blue eyes and recognized . . . *Mon Dieu, is she one of my siblings?*

"All right, all right, I can see that you don't remember me. I was a couple of years behind you in school. Graduated in '67. You graduated from Ste. Barbe in '65, right? Married that perky little gal named . . ."

"Michela. Yes. We have three grown kids now. How about you?"

"Oh, I married, but never had children of my own. I married Hervé Brouard. You remember him? He was in your class."

Julien sat on the stool feeling foolish. His graduating class was small, so why couldn't he remember Hervé Brouard? It hadn't been that many years ago—only what, thirty-something?

"I'm sorry; I've had a brain injury," he lied, "so I don't recall all my past. That's why I'm here. To fill in some of the blanks." He watched her face soften and knew that his lie had touched her. He felt terrible, but she seemed eager to help out. She slid closer.

"Well, that explains it. I'm so sorry. My maiden name was Beaulieu. You knew the Beaulieus. Really well, I would figure. Or, at least your father did. The Beaulieus are the ones who lived in that disaster of an old house you referred to," she said, as she waved her hand over her right shoulder. "Yes, that's where I grew up. Thought I had escaped from here once I married Hervé, but then he was in a mining accident. You know about mining life— your Papa was quite the miner."

"How is it that you knew my father?" He kept his knees under the bar, as he could feel them knocking together; his nerves were shot—and his lies weren't helping.

Amelie studied his face, but her eyes were not focusing all that well. She gave him the benefit of the doubt. "I would have thought the Beaulieu name was indelibly inscribed on your brain, Julien. I would have thought our name was one that was batted about your house like the swatting of a live wasp! Always trying to strike it to the floor, but somehow just missing, as it would always rise again. Do you know what I mean?" she said, as she leaned against him. The smell of her greasy hair made him gag. He shifted away and coughed.

"I'm not certain," Julien said, hesitantly. "I know my father visited his cousin's house in Pont-à-Meuse over the course of many years, but I . . . I have to admit I never knew her last name."

"Now, that lights up my knickers to hear you didn't even

know our last name," she said, as she slammed her hand down on the bar. She signaled the bartender to pour her another beer and looked to Julien to pay for it. "But, then, we had so many names, come to think of it. Each one of us kids carried one name or another. Different fathers; same mother. Not even enough room on our mailbox for all the names!" Her words dripped with sarcasm. "But, then, you probably know that much. I'm not bitter; no, not one bit." She sat staring into the foam of the freshly drawn beer. She seemed mesmerized; she didn't move.

Julien cleared his throat and said, "I don't even know where to start, Amelie. I feel like I should apologize for my father, but we were victims as well." He couldn't believe he was having this conversation. He thought he had planned out what he would say, what he would ask, but this was not coming out like he had hoped.

She slurped her beer and said, "My oldest brother was Adrian —Adrian. Heard of him? He was born during World War II, in '43. He was named after my mother's first husband, who was killed during the war. Or, that's what she told everyone. My second brother, Christophe, was born in '44, just before the war ended. His father was a German who was passing through during the war. My mother may have married him, too. I don't know. No one ever knew. No one asks, no one tells. He had polio when he was a little bugger, and struggled all his life, but he was the best of our lot. Then, I came along, and I never knew who my father was. It didn't seem to matter, as none of my younger siblings—Raymond, Bella, and Robert—knew theirs either. We all just grabbed the Beaulieu last name and went with it."

"I hate to ask this, but were any of your brothers or sister my father's progeny?"

"Progeny? Progeny?" Her head bobbled on her thin neck. "Possibly. I don't really know. He did come over and hang out a lot. I know that he loved our mother—that much was clear—but she had a lot of men hanging around. She was once a beautiful woman—

long blonde hair," she said as she stroked her own stringy locks. "Bright blue eyes. I have her eyes," she said, as she faced Julien. Yes, they were blue; a piercing blue in the center of a sea of bloodshot red. If she had once been beautiful, he had no way of telling. Time had undoubtedly ravaged her. Amelie was still talking.

". . . trying to keep food on the table. I hate to think how she paid for our upkeep, but then . . . I guess you do what you have to do, right?" She smirked.

Julien nodded his head. What had she just said? "Amelie, do you think any of the last three were my father's, by chance? Were any of them close to my father?"

Amelie swilled down a slug of beer, burped, and then turned back toward Julien. "Wh—why do you ask?" she stammered.

"At my father's funeral, a floral arrangement arrived with a card which said something like, 'In loving memory of you, Papa.' My sister and I didn't know where the flowers had come from, but that was the first indication that we may have other siblings."

"That must have been a shock to the system," Amelie said as she slapped the bar and began to titter. Then she threw her head back and laughed outright.

Julien was immobilized, not knowing whether to join in on the joke or walk out. His face burned with embarrassment and some anger. How dare his father put him in such a position? Why did he, Julien, have to sort this out anyway? Then he remembered his sister, who had suffered for so many years. The least he could do was to bear up for a few minutes under this humiliation and see if he could find some answers.

Amelie blurted out a name. "Bella! It must have been Bella. She's the only one who would have felt that way about him. I don't know if he truly was her father, Julien, but she so wanted to have an identity. She died not long after our mother did. Always such a sorry one, she was. She could never accept who our mother was— what our mother was. She longed for a real family."

"How about you, Amelie? Did you long to be a part of a *real* family," Julien asked softly. In the back of his mind, he was wondering if he, too, had longed for a *real* family—one that ran smoothly, without rancor or anger, one without emotional upheaval or years of living with your stomach looped into knots.

Again, she turned to look into his eyes. She wasn't certain if he was making fun of her, but when she stared into those kind eyes of his, she could tell he wasn't. She was smart. He was reaching out to her. She had never allowed herself to think of being a part of a family. It just wasn't meant to be. Happiness was not just about being with someone or belonging to a family, was it? Oh, how would she know? She had only known a few years of bliss with her husband, and then when he was crushed in the mine, she tabled her feelings. She was numb to it all.

"*Non*, she answered quietly. "*Non*, I guess I knew from the beginning that was not my lot in life. But, that's not to say I haven't found happiness," she said firmly, slamming her beer mug down on the bar, spilling the remains.

"Can I buy you another?" Julien asked.

"*Non. Non.* I have to head home. I worked the night shift and I'm tired. Nice to see you," she said as she slid off the stool, grabbed her purse off the floor, and staggered out the door. She didn't turn around.

Julien sat there staring into his own mug. He didn't have the heart to finish it. Morning beer never held an appeal. He gave Amelie enough time to go her own way and then headed back to his car.

By the time Julien finished his story, Sophie's eyes were wide open with the shock. "Papa's daughter?" she whispered. "I'm not the only one?"

"Looks like he may have had one daughter by this cousin. Bella is a number of years younger than I am, but Amelie told me

that her halfsister was probably the only child she *thought* might
have been born to our father. She and the rest of the brood had
different last names, except for the last three, who had the same
last name as their mother." Beaulieu.

"Which was what? What last name did she have?" Sophie
asked. She was holding her breath and hoping it wasn't the same as
her old flirt, Christophe. Kate may have been right. That may have
been why her father was so enraged Christophe was her boyfriend
—especially if her father thought Christophe was *his* son or if he
thought Christophe was the father of her *own* child. Sophie
shuddered. Again, her mind raced through those back streets in
time searching for the answers from that lonely night so many
years ago. She could picture herself flying along that leaf-strewn
path, pedaling her bike as fast as she could to get to Pont-à-Meuse
to see Christophe. And the horror of finding her father's car
already there! Was her father seeing his other family? That was
the night that had no end.

"Her last name was Beaulieu. Did you know any Beaulieu kids
in school with us?"

Sophie blew out a deep breath. She wanted to flop on the
ground and roll down the hill. Christophe's last name was
Mulhollande. She would never forget that. She had written his
name over and over across her notebook as a teen. Mulhollande.
So, Christophe was not her father's son. She had *not* been in love
with someone who turned out to be a sibling! Sophie leaped out of
her chair and danced a jig around and around encircling her
brother. "Oh, life! It can be so sweet," she repeated over and over
again, as a baffled Julien gawked at her dance.

CHAPTER TWENTY-THREE

A Second Visit with Marie

HE NEXT DAY, Sophie and Kate took up an invitation from Marie Chirade to join her back at her home for *déjeuner*, and after an hour of conversation, Marie led the two into her kitchen for a meal of *tourte de viande*, pork and veal meat pie made with puff pastry. The rich aromas that had whetted their appetites over the past hour were exchanged for the savory flavors, which now filled their mouths with delight.

"Oh, Marie, this is divine!" Sophie blurted out. "I remember my mother preparing this many times when we were children, but I doubt that I've had it since. Did you teach her this recipe? Don't you just love this, Kate?" Sophie asked jubilantly without waiting for a response.

"When we were growing up, sometimes we didn't have the specified meat for this dish, so *Maman* would use leftover *lard maigre*," she turned to Kate, "which is lean grease. My father loved it, but I didn't. Too much fat, so this is superb!"

"Yes, Marie, it *is* delicious," Kate said. "Hopefully you will share your recipe. There is something distinctive about the herbs you've used, too," Kate commented to her host.

Marie had been sitting quietly with her plate half filled with the meat pie. Color had returned to her face since Sophie had last seen her, and Sophie thought she looked healthier. She was relieved.

"The herbs, Kate? Just a fluff of fine herbs I found growing wild—perhaps a bit of rosemary, thyme, parsley . . . I'm afraid I don't remember, as I can't seem to taste flavors the way I used too." She shrugged.

"Well, whatever you did, this is marvelous," Kate said. "Sophie and Marcelle introduced me to many new flavors in French traditional foods, but this is exceptional."

Sophie sat leisurely back in her chair while mopping up the bottom of her plate with a crust of bread, and she casually changed the subject, "You know, Sophie Marie . . ." She took a sip of wine before proceeding.

"In all the years of growing up with my father, he rarely talked about what he did in the *Maquis.* As kids, we were afraid to ask him about his past, but, can you explain to us what he did as a *Maquis?*" She patted her napkin again against her mouth and waited. This was not exactly the question she had in mind, but it was a good one to begin with.

Marie sipped the residue of wine left in her glass as she collected her thoughts. "*Certainement.* You see, some of the freedom fighters concentrated on politics," Marie continued, while slicing wedges of cheese, "and some focused on propaganda, while others helped the allies as they dropped supplies or troops. But there were a considerable number, known as the *Maquis,* who devoted their energies to sabotage and fighting. Your father, along with the rest of us, was attached to the latter. I think we were probably considered a ragtag bunch, but believe me—we felt our efforts helped to win the war. We were responsible for letting the allies know if the forests were clear of German mines, if the bridges were safe to cross, and if the Germans had been evacuated from the villages. We would ring the church bells to indicate that all was safe and then would watch as the allied soldiers passed through." Her back straightened as she placed a plate of cheese and sliced baguette before them.

"So, all of the guerrillas, insurgents, or "terrorists," as the Germans called them, of which the FFI (*Forces Françaises de l'Interieur*) were members, all came to be known as the *Maquis, right?*" asked Sophie.

"Exactly! I remember," said Marie, "when the hills near our home were suddenly filled with *Maquis* in the spring of '43. This must have been due to the forced German labor requirements when they could no longer get volunteers."

"That makes sense," Sophie said. "My father said something about running away from Ste. Barbe to avoid German Forced Labor." She picked up her knife and lanced a wedge of cheese.

"Marie," asked Sophie, "I remember my favorite uncle, Raymond, was sent to the Russian Front. I wondered why he was never bitter about that. He was so unlike my father."

Marie sat quietly for a moment. "I don't know if I'm out of line here, Sophie, but I felt your father was bitter *before* the war. He seemed to carry his anger and bitterness around with him like a badge." She looked cautiously at Sophie, who nodded for her to continue.

"Well, there were some young men who did not expect to return home after the war. I believe your father was one of these . . . until he met your mother, anyway."

Sophie picked up the cheese and started to nibble it. "Do you think my father loved my mother when they got together?"

"You asked me that the last time we saw each other." Marie leaned back. A long hesitation followed. "If he didn't love her, he certainly made a good show of it. I think they both were very much taken with each other, and with the war raging on, every moment became precious. Time and life are precious. Never underestimate how powerful that can be for two people alone in the world during wartime."

Marie paused, then said, "Plus, your mother had waited a long time for Gérard's father to show up, and, as I recall, your father had left Ste. Barbe because the woman he loved married another."

Sophie mulled over Marie's words. A memory flashed through her mind of the fights her parents had had; how the house would shudder as her father slammed out into the night; how her mother was left with tears streaming down her face and her back turned away from her frightened children. And the silence—the silence was thick enough to be cut with a saber. Maybe this was the information she was seeking from Marie—an understanding of her parents' relationship. The truth was she had always questioned her father's love for her mother. It had been a difficult marriage for sure, but as her parents were Catholic, there was no way out of it. Not for either one of them. Had her parents married because they both had lost the loves of their lives? Sophie shook her head to clear the memory.

"André! André! That was *Maman's* love," Sophie said, drumming her fingers on the table, "and the only time she saw André again after the war was when we traveled to Paris when I was around ten."

A look of guilt swept across Marie's face just as she started to bite into a slice of baguette. She laid it down on her plate. She dabbed at her lips and let out a deep sigh. "This, Sophie, has weighed on me for over fifty years."

The hackles on the back of Sophie's neck rose, and she felt a chill ripple through her body.

Before Marie spoke again, she closed her eyes, as she remembered that blustery day during the fall of '43. She had been walking to the farm to see Marcelle when a tall, handsome young man with deep blue eyes and wavy blonde hair was making a hasty exit from the farmhouse door. He had been knocked around, as red bruises were arising on his jaw. Marie had recognized him at once, as Marcelle had described him often. She had smiled and said *bonjour* to him and was just about to ask him about Marcelle when she saw Jules glowering at her from the farmhouse door. To this day, Marie did not know why, but she brushed past André and continued on to the farm. Jules, assuming she had witnessed their fight, grabbed Marie by the arm and threatened her if she should ever tell Marcelle of André's visit.

"Yes, he used his name," Marie said, as she recounted the memory that had haunted her over the decades. "Your father said that he would find me and go after my little boy. Oh, Sophie, up until this very day, I've never told anyone . . . but I've always felt I should have given your mother, my dearest friend, the very information that would have changed her life."

"Wait, that reminds me. When I was talking to my friend Mimi about André, she gave me a letter to give to you from *Maman*. I don't know if there is a connection, but . . . Now, where did I put that, Kate?" Sophie got up and went in search of her purse. In a matter of moments, she was back with the letter in hand. "I had almost forgotten."

Sophie placed the letter before Marie, along with her wire-rimmed glasses.

Marie's hands shook as she opened the letter. She took a moment to scan the pages and felt tears burn her eyes at the familiar sight of her friend's writing. Silently, she began to read:

To my dearest friend, Sophie Marie,

Over the course of many years, I gave you my journals for safe keeping with the hopes that, upon my death, you could personally give them to Sophie. With your opening of this letter, I know that you, dear friend, have honored my wishes, as has my daughter, and that she has followed through on this, my last and greatest wish—to find my father, Pourrette.

But, Marie, I owe you a debt of thanks and of gratitude—not just for your follow-through and your ability to accept my friendship (even in the midst of my turbulent marriage), but because of you, I was able to make one momentous decision during my marriage that I have never regretted: to return to the Auvergne. I should have told you long ago, but shame has kept me from explaining . . .

Sophie and Kate studied Marie as she read Marcelle's letter. The room was silent. When Marie finally looked up, her face was streaked with tears.

"Marie, what is it? What does she say?" Sophie asked, leaning forward.

"Your mother," Marie whispered. "She did see André once again. Not long before her move to Fontanières."

꧁ ꧂

The heavy metal door slammed shut behind her as Marcelle made her way from the main office down the narrow corridor of St. Aidan's Alcohol Treatment Center. With great effort, she had finally found her love. André resided here! In room 142, just down this hall. She knew his prognosis was not good, but she had come all the same.

She smoothed her best plaid dress down over her full hips, but her well-worn frock kept riding over her middle, suggesting years of babies and little else. Her hands flew reflexively up to pat her pillbox hat into place and to tuck any loose curls behind her ears. She was no longer the twenty-something she had been—what? Thirty years before? But, she also knew she had waited too long to go in search of him. In fact, as she looked cautiously around her, she wondered if she was already too late. She didn't know what she would do once she found André, but she was certain she could no longer continue the charade of a life she had been leading with Jules.

She was grateful for her good friend Jocelyne, who had driven her to Paris. Why, it had been Jocelyne and her husband who had brought the family to Paris one other time—the only other time Marcelle had seen André. As a loyal friend, she knew of Marcelle's deepest sorrows. Once Jocelyne pulled up to the treatment center, she waved her hand and said she would return in a couple of hours.

As Marcelle nervously walked down the claustrophobic corridor, she wondered if two hours would be too little or too much time. No other doors were open into the hallway, and the only sound she heard was the clack of her tattered shoes. The air was stagnant and filled with smoke, so she knew she was not alone. With no obvious flow of ventilation, the smell clung to every flat surface and seemed to seep into her skin as she walked.

She came to Room 142. Marcelle noted the name on the door: André Mathieux. *Right here,* she thought. *After all these years, I find him right here.* She dried the perspiration from her fingers on her dress, and she knocked. The noise reverberated down the hallway, unnerving her. She stepped back. Should she have called ahead? Did he already have a guest? Was he also married? How would he recognize her? What on earth was she doing?

"Entrez, s'il vous plaît," she heard a gravelly voice call out. This was followed by a raspy cough—the cough of an old man. Surely, this was the wrong André Mathieux. Her heart missed a beat as she thought to turn away from the door. But some force within her pushed the door open, and she stepped inside.

There before her lay a gaunt figure of a man; a man who took up only a fraction of the single bed, his frail frame a mere cocoon of its former self. But Marcelle knew instantaneously that this was André. Marcelle took another step forward, a smile enveloping her face.

Obviously André's liver was giving out, as the pallor of his skin was yellowed. His chin was covered in grey stubble, but his hair, now stringy and in need of a wash, was still a beautiful blonde. He began to cough again; his body racked with each jarring move. But once André wiped a kerchief across his face, Marcelle could see his brilliant blue eyes. Those magical blue eyes!

As André's vision cleared, he recognized her smile and beamed. Even though he was weak, he shifted onto one elbow to wave her into the room. "Why, it's you!" he exclaimed with a rasp. "I can't believe it. I'm so happy to see you, lovely Marcelle! I'm so . . . Is that really you, Marcelle, or a vision?" he asked, as she moved to his side.

"Oh, it's me all right. I came to find you. I couldn't wait any longer," she said, her body filling with the suppressed longing of years passed. "Finally, I found the only man I've ever loved," she blurted out, surprising herself with her own openness. She reached out to touch his hands, but instead she wrapped her arms around him, inhaling the sour smell of this dying man—her dying man. What did she care? She had finally found him.

Not believing her own audacity, Marcelle took off her hat, peeled off her dress, and slid into bed beside André. Tenderly, she kissed his face, his hair, and his lips, and the years of being apart slipped away. And although they would never make love again and his racking cough shook them where they lay, their memories took flight. Together they recalled only the sweet moments they had shared; the loving they had experienced; the gentleness they had known; and their gratitude for, even in these obvious last hours of André's life, the time to finally be together alone.

"I've longed for you Marcelle—every hour of every day—since I put you on the train so many years ago. I only wish I had come for you earlier in the Auvergne before you tired of waiting and got married." His smile slipped. "My timing was always off . . ."

"What do you mean, 'earlier'?" Marcelle exclaimed, her brown eyes flashing. She sat up. "What do you mean you came for me in the Auvergne? I never saw you! I waited and waited for you . . ." Her lips quivered as she tried to understand his words.

"I came as soon as I could, my darling. My wife passed away six months after you left, and I immediately joined the Résistance and made my way down to find you. I found the Ambert farm easily, as I carried all your letters with me, but, when I came to call . . ."

Again, André began hacking so hard Marcelle slid out of bed to pour a glass of water for him. When his coughing subsided, she gently wiped away the tears from his eyes and spittle from his chin. She asked softly, "You came for me after all?" She couldn't believe her ears; she wanted to hear him say those words over and over.

"Yes, I did, my love. I promised you I would come, but as it turns out, I was too late. A man met me at the door, and when I asked for you, he became extremely angry. He stepped outside the door, closed it behind him, and laid me out flat!" André said, as he rubbed his chin with the memory.

"I had no idea who he was, but after he threatened to kill me if I returned for you, he said he was your husband. He said, 'We've been married for some time and are both very happy.' It didn't seem so to me, but I had no choice. As I went limping down the road, I ran into a young woman. I almost knocked her down in my hurry to get away. She smiled at me and started to speak, but then she quickly moved on. Reluctantly, I made my way back here—to Paris. I'm so sorry, Marcelle! So sorry I was not there for you."

Marcelle struggled to make sense of the scene André had just painted, and then she said, "And I'm sorry we were not able to spend our lives together, too, André, for your observation was correct. My husband and I were never terribly happy." Life with Jules had become unbearable, as his capricious escapades with his cousin-lover had become more frequent and his malicious treatment of Marcelle more brutal. She gulped back the bile that had risen in her throat.

"Happiness, for me, came through my children and my memories of you," she said. For a moment she sat on the edge of the bed, her head in her hands, contemplating her decision to marry Jules. Oh, how that had gone so woefully wrong! She looked up to see tears streaming down André's grizzled face. She changed the subject.

"Your dear son, Gérard, will be happy that I have found you once again. He has longed to know you; longed to have his father's love," Marcelle said, sweetly.

"Of course, I've always wanted to see him, but now . . . I don't want him to see me like this, but do tell me, what is he like?" André pulled Marcelle back to him and cradled her in his arms. "I never remarried and never had another child, so I thought often of you both."

"He is so much like you that it is almost—almost, I tell you— like you have always been with me. And that has been a blessing. His eyes are the same brilliant blue, his hair the same shade of blonde. His eyes hold the same crinkle when he smiles." She turned to look into André's eyes. "His laughter is your laughter. His loves are of old classic books—like you used to teach—and he is a happy young man with a family living in the south of France. You'll be happy to know you are a grandfather three times over."

André's eyes brimmed anew with tears as he lay stroking Marcelle's hair. He was lulled by her low resonant voice, which melodiously wove the skeins of a life he had so often longed to be a part of. The hours fled quickly, and as Marcelle stood to dress and kiss him good-bye, he said, "Before you go, please look in the drawer over there." He pointed to the pine dresser on the other side of the room.

"Is there something you need?" she asked as she moved to the bureau.

"Open the top drawer, and on the right side, you'll see two letters—one for you, and one for our son, Gérard. I am not long for this world, and I had given instructions to have those mailed to you upon my death. But this is better. You are here. You must take them." Marcelle turned back to face him. "Pull out those letters and take them with you. They express the love I have been holding tight to all of these years—for both you and Gérard. Give Gérard his letter when you next see him. He needs to understand that this father loved him with all of his heart." Marcelle took the letters from the drawer, pressed them to her heart, and went to André to hold him one last time. Without speaking, the two knew this would be their last time together.

After Jocelyne dropped her at home, Marcelle was relieved and yet agitated that Jules had been unaware of her absence. He had obviously been with his lover. When he waltzed in the door later that night, Marcelle confronted him about his lies, of both omission and commission. She confronted him about André. Never once did she reveal how she had learned the truth, but she felt the truth was now on her side. For the first time in their marriage, she felt empowered.

"When you retire, Jules Zabél, we will be moving to the Auvergne. We are going to be living where I've always wanted to live, and that's near my son Thierry and my good friend Marie."

"Like hell we will," Jules said, as his cruel laughter shattered the air around her. "So you think your old lover came back for you, do you? That's old hat—old news! He was nothing but a coward! And that was a lifetime ago. So, tell me, you dirty whore, what makes you think I will ever leave Clarissa?"

He crossed the kitchen and came at her with such rage, she wasn't certain she would survive. "It was Marie who told you, right?" he yelled. Marcelle failed to grasp what he was saying.

"Sophie-Marie, you stupid bitch! Your so-called friend you want to live near? She's the one who told you André had come for you. Right?"

"What promises did you make to her, Jules? What did you say?"

Jules swaggered around the kitchen table as he recounted threatening to kill Marie's son if she told Marcelle of Andre's visit.

"That's what kept her quiet—until now!"

Mortified that her friend had been ensnared by Jules's cruelty, she pulled out the kitchen chair, sat down, and then murmured, "But Marie didn't tell me. Anyway, her son died years ago—in Algiers."

"Aha! I suppose now that her son is dead, she is no longer fearful of me," he spat. It took a few moments before Marcelle could sort out Jules's ravings. Then she remembered André's mention of having run into a young woman—that he almost knocked down. She realized that Marie had witnessed Jules's fight with André. He must have threatened Marie if she divulged the truth to her. Marcelle went limp. All those years ago, she had placed her dear friend in jeopardy.

I must have been pregnant with Sophie, she thought. *So there was nothing that could have been done—Jules and I were already married.* She sat up. This man could lie to her, but he could not hold her back any longer because she had something on him.

"Oh, but we will be moving to the Auvergne," she began rising up. "Because if you don't comply, I will expose you!"

"Expose me? Expose me?" he jeered. "What do I have to hide? *Tout du monde* knows of my affair with Clarissa. There is nothing to expose." His laughter again set the windows a-rattle.

"I'll expose your lies about where you were when your partner was crushed by a rock in the mine. I know the truth and have the proof to present to the authorities.

If or when I turn over those papers, you will not only lose your job but will be minus a pension. That's what I'll expose. You've crossed me for the last time," she said, shaking. She stood her ground.

My point, Marie, is that I was able to, for once in our entire marriage, convince Jules to move back to the place I had grown to love—because of our precious friendship and my dear son Thierry. And it was with the mention of your name that my life changed for the better. I truly do thank you . . .

Kate let out a low whistle after Marie had finished relating some of the contents of Marcelle's letter. "So that's how your mother moved back to the Auvergne."

"Finally, it makes sense," Sophie said, leaning back in her chair.

"But there's one part that's not true," Marie said, rising from her chair.

"What's not true, Marie?" Sophie stood up next to Marie.

"The day I saw André was *before* your parents married. In fact, I remember concealing my secret from your mother when she arrived on my doorstep the following morning. She came with the news that she and your father were getting married the following month. He had asked her just that morning. Oh, Sophie, she sounded so happy and, of course, your father was standing behind her, so I said nothing. How could I? I just hugged her to me." A sob slipped out, and Marie covered her mouth, her face stricken with grief.

"Oh, Marie," Sophie said, wrapping her arms around her, "you did what a good friend does. You could not have changed a thing at that point anyway."

"But I said nothing! All these years I said nothing to her, and I always regretted that." Tears slid down the narrow crevices around her mouth and fell onto Sophie's shoulder.

"As it turns out, Marie, Marcelle turned Jule's incendiary betrayal into a move of her own," Kate said. "She triumphed in the end."

Marie looked over at her. "I—I didn't realize." She took a deep breath and then let it out slowly.

"Marie, let me put your mind at ease," Sophie said, as she kept her arms around Marie's frail shoulders. "My father gave you no choice. And, from what I can tell, my mother was never the wiser about the timing of André's visit. So, that's a consolation. Only you and my father knew."

Letting go of Marie, Sophie turned and grabbed the teakettle to fill it with water. "Tea, Marie? May I prepare you some tea?" Through her mother's letter, she had learned so much, but there was still more to learn about her father. The thought made her nervous. All thoughts of her father made her nervous. Would she ever get over that?

"Yes, *chérie*, that would be lovely. Do you want dessert now?"

"Perhaps in a few minutes. Thank you. Were you at their wedding?" she asked as casually as she could muster.

"Yes, I was. I remember your mother saying that it seemed a frivolous thing to have a wedding under such circumstances," Marie said, sitting back down. "Not knowing from one day to the next if we would live or die, but that was how it was." She laughed out loud at the memory, shaking her head. The white ringlets on her head bobbed as if they had a life of their own, and the tension that had built up in her face relaxed.

"Honestly, your mother seemed very, very happy, Sophie. I believe your mother really did have feelings for your father, so they were married on January 6, 1944. It was the eve of Epiphany, or Twelfth Night."

Just then, the teapot surprised them all with an exceedingly loud whistle. They all jumped, but Sophie burst into laughter. Her fear of hearing any of these answers had built up so that laughter bubbled out in an explosion.

"Oh, my, yes," she said, as she tried to contain herself. "Tea? Where will I find your tea?" She fiddled in the cupboards for the tea bags. Marie waved her finger in the direction of a canister near the stove.

"It's odd that we regularly celebrated Twelfth Night together," Sophie said, "but I don't remember any mention of their anniversary." She paused to think. "What else do you remember about that day, Marie?" Sophie handed Marie and Kate cups of tea and started picking up the plates as she headed back to the sink. She found it easier to busy herself in Marie's kitchen, as it helped keep her mind off any unexpected details Marie might reveal. She glanced over her shoulder as Marie, who was looking a little weary, was starting to stand to join her. Sophie turned and placed both hands on Marie's shoulders and lovingly guided her back into place.

"It's our turn to help you, Marie," Kate said as she stood alongside Sophie.

Marie relaxed back into her chair, took a deep breath, and began again.

"Their wedding . . . I believe I was about as excited as they were, actually. I had convinced myself your mother would be happy, and I worked hard to make it a special occasion. It was a quiet little affair that we held at our farm. Their families were not in attendance, but of course, your brothers, Thierry and Gérard, were there, along with our son, Fréderic, and my husband, Jacques, plus me. Oh, and the Amberts. We kept it low-key, with no public celebration and just a quick trip to the church."

"And shortly after that, I came into the world!" Sophie proclaimed, turning from the sink. "Exactly nine months, minus two days. I was born right in the Ambert's farmhouse near the village of Mainsat." This was the part of the story she thought she knew best, but she needed confirmation from Marie. The soapsuds rose high in the sink, where she stood beside Kate washing the dishes. Steam lifted off her glasses as if they were on fire.

"Well, not exactly, Sophie," Marie said. Sophie spun around to face Marie, alarm registered on her face.

"Go sit back down, Sophie," Kate nudged her, "so you can hear your own story." Sophie slid back into her chair; her eyes were wide open with anxiety.

"Actually, you were born in an abandoned farmhouse which

was a *Maquis* hideaway called La Croix. It was five kilometers from our farm, so it was nothing for us to walk along that route several times a day.

Sophie laughed nervously, "But that's so strange *Maman* never mentioned that part."

"Once your parents were married, Madame Ambert no longer wanted the responsibility of having them around. That sounds harsh. Madame Ambert was an odd one."

"Did Thierry live with my parents in this little . . . hideaway?" asked Sophie.

"I believe the Amberts offered to keep Thierry with them. Thierry and your father didn't get along well, but we all thought it was nothing that time couldn't heal." She paused and looked at Sophie.

Marie stood up from her chair. "Can you excuse me for a moment?" She was stiff from sitting too long in one place and slowly ambled out of the kitchen and into the bathroom. Sophie stood and returned to Kate's side. She stared out of the kitchen window but saw nothing.

What had she been so fearful of learning? Was there something more that her mother wanted her to know about her own birth? Could she have been the daughter of another man? Always the questions. She had just found some solace with her father, but once again, her faith in the man she called Papa was slipping from her grip. She gulped.

As Kate finished washing the last of the plates, Sophie wiped them dry, hung up the dishtowel, and poured herself a cup of tea.

"Sorry! Would you like your tea warmed up, Kate?" Sophie asked as she sat down in her chair.

"No. I'm fine."

Marie returned to the kitchen and took Sophie and Kate gently by the elbows and steered them toward the living room. "My stuffed chair is much easier on my tired old bones," she said.

While Kate loaded their teacups onto a tray, Sophie walked Marie into the living room. Easing her into her chair, Sophie kindly lifted her tired feet onto the ottoman.

"Ah, this is lovely," Marie said, as Kate placed her cup within reach. Kate gave Sophie her cup and sat down on the sofa with Marie's dog between them.

"You know, Marie," Sophie said, as if not having been sidetracked, "I remember my mother telling me how dangerous the times were then. And then she would say, and I can repeat it like a mantra, 'And there I was, once again, pregnant. Your father was away at war, and I never knew if he would return to us. Then on a beautiful September day, the sky was so blue and the sun so warm, I woke up certain my time had come to give birth. I was alone and filled with trepidation, but I had become so very close to Sophie-Marie . . .'"

Sophie stopped suddenly. Her head snapped back. "That was the first time I heard your name. It was when *Maman* was telling me about my birth. All of those years ago, I knew your name," she wailed, "I was named after you, wasn't I?" Marie nodded her head, a smile caressing her face.

"I am so ashamed. I'm just now putting together the people my mother cherished most in her life." Sophie let out a moan. "What kind of daughter am I?"

Kate reached over and placed her hand on her friend's.

"Now, now, *ma pauvre fille*, don't you fret," Marie said. "Not until after our husbands had died were we able to open up to each other . . . and even now," she said, referring to Marcelle's letter. "Our husbands were never fond of talking about the war—your father especially—and *I* certainly didn't want to bring the subject up."

"So, Sophie, what more do you remember your mother telling you about your birth?" Kate asked.

"Right now, I'm questioning everything," Sophie replied, looking at Marie.

"Well, *ma chérie*, let me set your mind at ease. I remember arriving at La Croix and finding your mother in incredible pain. She was in labor with you and was having difficulty. A midwife was out of the question. I rushed out to get a message to the doctor. At that time, any movement, whether day or night, was suspect. Your parents were hidden away for a reason. Like I said, your mother had bravely opened up that tiny hovel for any *Maquis* in the area, which made your home all the more dangerous. I don't know how she did it, but she wanted Jules—your father—to be proud of her. I knew some of the freedom fighters in the area, so I had one of them send word to the doctor. The doctor, too, was a courageous man! He walked many kilometers around the German soldiers—along hidden footpaths to avoid the main roads. At that same time, our area was being threatened with bombs from the allies. Oh, Sophie, you picked a fine time to arrive." Sophie looked up with a sheepish grin.

"I returned to the kitchen, where your mother was crouching on the floor, writhing with pain. I'll never forget the horrified look on your Gérard's sweet little face. I pretended your mother was playing a game until the doctor came. It seemed like hours, but when he finally arrived, a place was made for your mother—right on the kitchen table. Guns, ammunition . . . all was swept off the table onto the floor and, in no time at all, you were there. You came kicking and screaming into the world, and yes, you were bright red, squalling up a storm, but, oh so beautiful. A prettier baby I never saw." A loving smile softened the lines in Marie's face as she looked at Sophie.

"It's funny how the birth of a baby is always a miraculous event, no matter the timing," Kate said, thinking of her Lisa.

"Thank you, Marie. I'm so glad my mother had you as a friend."

"My pleasure. Then, later that night, some of the *Maquis* found your father and told him you had been born. We all celebrated quietly, but we celebrated nonetheless."

"I suppose that's why I don't do anything quietly now," Sophie said with a grin. "Everything with me needs to be a wild celebration."

Sophie turned to Kate. "Do you remember asking me the importance of the family table in French family's life? I told you, in my case, it was where I was born!" She laughed and nestled back into the sofa, pulling an afghan over her legs. A sense of relief lifted from her now that she knew the stories somewhat matched. Whether she liked it or not, she was her father's daughter, and she found some relief in knowing just that. Even though he was a scoundrel, he was the scoundrel she knew. Kate settled back into the sofa to join her. Marie took a slow, easy sip of her tea, and her eyes smiled as she looked upon her guests. She set her cup back down.

After another hour of Marie relating her memories of Sophie's parents, she shrugged her shoulders and yawned. "I'm afraid, *mes chéries*, I have reached my emotional limit for one day. Truly, it's not that I don't want to answer all of your questions, Sophie, but . . ."

"Of course," Sophie said, standing up. "We must get going." Kate leapt to her feet and began picking up the cups before making for the kitchen.

～⊙～

As Sophie and Kate drove away from Marie's house, Marie made her way to her bedroom, where she slipped off her dress, hung it carefully in the closet, and prepared to lie down. She was exhausted . . . yet relieved beyond measure. After all these years of living with the guilt of having kept silent about André, Marcelle, her dearest friend, had managed to send a letter of forgiveness from the grave. She shook her head in wonder. After tucking her little dog near her legs, she pulled the comforter up to her chin. For the first time in over sixty years, when her thoughts rested on Marcelle, she had peace of mind.

CHAPTER TWENTY-FOUR

A Final Cup of Café

A

*T*HE TWO WOMEN WALKED casually side by side as they entered the cemetery, but they reverentially slowed as they edged into single file. The sleet had stopped, mercifully, and a small patch of blue sky breathed sunlight onto the glistening marble headstones. They moved toward their final destination: Marcelle's grave.

This was their last day together, the last day in the intimacy of more than a three-week tour of discovery that had come to an end. Days spent crossing France had yielded answers to many of Sophie's family mysteries and to Kate's life as well. And, as their friendship deepened, they too, had come to share their innermost secrets. Time in close proximity had given them the ability to unpack their reserves, peel off layers of denial, and begin to break down the barriers of their inner selves. But both knew that once Kate boarded her plane back to the U.S., those reserves were certain to be re-packed and placed high on a shelf of consciousness. Until then, vulnerability eked out of every pore for one last time.

"Here she is," Sophie called over her shoulder. "Here is my

mother's grave. My *maman*." She planted her feet in front of a massive dark-grey headstone as she clutched and re-clutched the brown paper bag she had brought with her. Carefully, she folded the top of the bag, smoothed it down, and promptly crushed it to her chest, the contents colliding precariously inside.

Kate sidled up next to her friend. The two stood respectfully looking at the black headstone before them. A silent moment of prayer passed between them, and then, as if a last gasp of air had been forced from a communal balloon, they exhaled in tandem.

"It's her birthday, today, you know," Sophie said, softly. "She would have turned eighty-three today. Happy Birthday, Maman. Happy Birthday to you."

"Oh, wow, I didn't realize today's date. I should have known . . ." Kate stammered.

"It's all right. But that is part of why we're here today. To celebrate with her. But, look at that marker," Sophie said, as she stepped forward. "It reads *Pourrette*; not *Zabél*, my family name. Until now, this stone, which marks the graves of both my parents, held a name of no known origins. With my mother's final imperative, my search for answers began here—right here—for my mother, my brothers, and their families."

"And you accomplished that, didn't you," Kate stated.

"Did I?" Sophie asked, putting the paper sack down and taking out her handkerchief to blow her nose.

"You left few stones unturned, no pun intended, and you found the answers you came for."

Sophie wadded the handkerchief up and stuffed it into her purse. She hesitated and then answered, "I suppose I will always have questions, but by solving some of the mysteries around *Maman*'s life, I admit I do feel more at peace. I feel I accomplished something special for my mother.

"Yes, you've done that. Now you know the connection to the Pourrette name."

"Yes . . . even if he may not be my grandfather in reality," Sophie said, wistfully. "But, Kate, I lay awake last night wondering about this. After all of our investigation, I wonder if it really matters. We've found out more than we've ever known before, but what does it change?"

Kate walked a few meters away from the headstone and returned to face Sophie. "Maybe nothing," she shrugged, "but knowledge can give you power. Thierry proved that the other day when he found out his biological father's surname. 'Yieux!' he said. 'Nope! I think I'll stick with the name I have. Pourrette!' Knowledge gave him the power to make and own that decision." Kate stood balancing on the edge of a paver then stepped off into the mud.

"Not long after I first met Lisa," Kate said, as her eyes wandered out of the graveyard and over the neighboring hills, "she got around to asking if I could help her find her real father. I felt uncomfortable about it, but it was the very least I could do . . ." Kate stopped and stared off into space.

"Anyway, once I located her father, I found he was actually open to talking with her. They had several pleasant phone conversations. But after he answered some family questions she had, she decided to opt out of their relationship. I'm not certain why, but she, at least, had the power to make the decision for herself—for the first time!"

"So, like Thierry, she didn't need to have any more information?"

"That's right. We often follow the adage, 'the truth will set us free.' In these two cases, it did, although the truth can also open old wounds or lead to even more questions. Is this what you were wondering about, Sophie?" Kate asked.

"Are you turning the tables?" Sophie laughed. "I would rather ask you what answers you've come away with. One of my goals was to bring you to France to help me out, which you've done a remarkable job of, by the way. Thank you very much. But did you find what you came for? And we know it wasn't just recipes."

Sophie turned to a short granite marker behind them, pulled out her handkerchief, and wiped the top of the stone dry. She patted it, suggesting Kate sit down beside her. She placed the brown paper bag on the ground at her feet.

"Well," Kate said, squirming around on the hard stone, "I came hoping to understand how your mother managed to deal with her losses, her sorrows, and her life with such grace. Her own life and those of two of her sons were defined by illegitimacy, so how did she manage to lift up her head and raise such a remarkable family? Do you think your mother thought of herself as a good mother?"

"I doubt it. As hard as she tried, she always felt she had shorted us children—especially Thierry and Gérard. I doubt she forgave herself for not doing more—alleviating the family sorrow or giving my brothers legitimacy. Actually, now that I think of it, that's probably the very reason she wanted me to find her father—to give our family an anchor; a sense of legitimacy, a true sense of identity." Sophie stood and stretched her back, unbuttoned her coat, then buttoned it back up and sat back down.

"Maybe that's what I've been searching for," said Kate.

"Legitimacy? Why you? Why not forgiveness? Let me ask you this, Kate. Has Lisa forgiven you for giving her up for adoption?"

"She has said as much, but I wonder . . . this is all so new. I guess I expect her to take it back or change her mind because forgiveness is a huge decision."

"Then how about you? Have you forgiven yourself for giving her up for adoption? You know in your head all the reasons it made sense all those years ago, but have you forgiven yourself yet?"

"Probably about as much as your mother did when she left Thierry behind. Maybe that's what my journey has been about—

finding out if and how your mother made peace with herself."

"Well, she didn't exactly leave a road map for you, did she. I'm sorry about that. In fact, much of what we discovered, she never knew about . . . like the packet of letters in the attic, her mother's diary, the fact that her parents were married . . . so much. Sad, isn't it?"

"But, on the other hand, maybe that is the road map, Sophie. Her outreach to Marie, to Mimi, to Christian, to her great aunt— all those actions were how she sought answers for her life and for her children. It was what she *did* that made it possible for us to discover the truth. Maybe if I continue to show my daughter I love her unconditionally, I'll find I can finally forgive myself."

"Kate, by embracing your daughter back into your life, you have empowered her, given her legitimacy, and shown her how to forgive. Maybe those are the steps my mother took."

"I suppose so," Kate thrummed her fingers against her chin. "I guess so," she said more emphatically than she felt. It would take time. Blessedly, she had time.

"Speaking of empowerment, that was one powerful letter your mother wrote to Marie," Kate said.

"I agree." Sophie stood again and walked toward the gravestone. Her finger carefully traced the letters of the name *Pourrette*. "I think that letter taught me more about how she became empowered than I had learned in my entire life about her. Finally, it became clear to me how she had dealt with my father and demanded respect."

"Maybe for the first time in her life! I believe when she discovered her love for André had been reciprocal, she felt legitimized."

"So," continued Sophie, "that's how she came to move back here to Auvergne. Again, it was by learning the truth, my mother was set free!"

"And that answers another question we had about your mother."

"Which one was that?" Sophie stooped down and patted the brown paper bag on the ground. She looked up at Kate.

"We wondered why she wanted to be buried here in Evaux-les-Bain," Kate said, sweeping her arm in an arc around her. "You know, since she had been so terribly mistreated during the war? She explained through her letter how much she loved being here—near Thierry and her good friend Sophie Marie."

"You're right. As much as she talked about her love for Brittany, this was the place she loved best. Right here!" Sophie exclaimed.

"So, what about you, Sophie? What answers have you found?"

"Oh, well . . ." Sophie paused for a long moment. When she picked up her thoughts, she said, "I still have *some* confusion. I guess understanding the origins of my depression has been liberating. And my relationship to my father has . . ."

Kate sat waiting. Finally, she asked, "So, how do you see your relationship to your father?" She turned to face Sophie.

Sophie sat mute again for several moments, and then she answered, "The man in my dreams *was* my father. You know, the man behind the gauze curtain?"

"Yes. What do you make of him now?"

"Remember when you and I discussed the nightmares? You thought the reason for his presence most likely was that he was there to protect me. I guess I would prefer to accept that concept. I prefer to think that, when all was said and done, he loved me and was there to protect me." Sophie paced back and forth on the grass, wearing a line of mud between the stepping-stones.

"We've learned a great deal on this trip about your father, Sophie . . ."

"Yes," Sophie interrupted, "and much of it has been uncomfortable, and quite frankly, vile. So maybe I'm fooling myself into believing . . . believing he could be there for me."

"Your father's life was one of stinging rejection and emotional anguish. What he spewed in your family's direction was the black feelings he must have harbored about himself. But in all of his bad days, I think he was there for you in the ways that he could be. I really think he tried to protect you. I don't question that he loved you in his own way, Sophie. The stories you've told me about the happier times . . . Why, life is not always all bad or all good."

Suddenly Kate's cell phone rang, which startled them both. She jumped up to pull the phone from her handbag and then turned back to Sophie. "It's Lisa," she said, whispering. She walked a few feet away.

"Mm hmm! Mm hmm! Yes. Yes. Oh, Lisa, how wonderful. It's all coming together for you, isn't it, honey. I couldn't be happier for you." Kate walked farther down a narrow path as her buoyant voice lifted over the headstones. Her daughter was reaching out to her. And for her, Kate was returning home.

Sophie smiled after Kate. Her body, which had felt like a coiled spring for the better part of her life, began to relax. For the first time in weeks, she had no headache. She began to circle around the tombstones again and returned to stand in front of her parents' grave. The cool wind warmed just at that moment, and her hair lifted as if in song. She reached her hand forward once again and caressed the name on the monument. There was no Zabél, no, just Pourrette! What an odyssey this name had taken her on. She breathed in deeply. Somehow, having *some* answers behind the name finally gave her peace. She sent up a prayer to her mother, along with another birthday wish and then one to both her parents. Remembered scriptural words came to her mind: *May the peace which passeth all understanding be in your heart, your mind, your . . .*

She suddenly stood stark still. She realized that, for whatever his reasons, her father *had* been protecting her. And that he had always loved her. She knew that deep down to her toes. She let out a deep sigh. This, she could accept. This, she would allow.

Anything beyond this . . . well, it wouldn't do. Kate was walking back toward her with a bounce in each step.

"She wants me to give her away at the wedding!" she called out. "Can you imagine that? Me! She asked me if I would consent to walk her down the aisle along with her adoptive mother. Just the three of us, walking side by side, together!" Her feet fairly danced along the edges of the path as she returned to Sophie's side. Her face was flush with excitement as she drew her hands through her hair.

"That's wonderful news," Sophie said, laughing. Her face, too, was resplendent, and she grabbed Kate in a hug.

"You look so serene, Sophie," Kate said, pulling back and looking into her friend's eyes.

"I am; I truly am!" She reached down and scooped up the paper bag. Raising it before her, she pulled out a large, somewhat cracked, blue ceramic coffee cup. She stepped forward and placed the cup on top of her mother's headstone and patted it with affection.

"There you go, *Maman*," she said with reverence. "Our final tradition. May you continue to savor your coffee throughout eternity!" She smiled and stepped back.

"Nice touch, Sophie. For her birthday, you've blessed her with a cup of redemption."

They both stepped back to gaze at the cup perched atop the tombstone. The breeze, which danced around them, caught hold of the water droplets high on the chestnut tree above them, and in moments, the cup began to fill.

"Now, that's magical," Sophie said with a laugh and a toss of her head.

"Think it's the magic of Dahut, or St. Anne?" Kate asked, as the two friends linked arms and sauntered back to the warmth of the car.

Acknowledgments

A

Having followed my passion for, lo, these twelve years to the book's completion, I first acknowledge my most loving, patient, and supportive husband, Winston, who never—rarely—blanched at the amount of time, money, and/or number of classes or conferences I took to reach publication. To my darling (adult) children, Beth, Adaire and Andrew, and sister, Melody, who never wavered in giving me support. I acknowledge those of my critique group, especially Lucy Murray, who actually waded through the manuscript twice when it was well beyond seven hundred pages. To April Eberhardt, who as an agent had faith in me and directed me to She Writes Press. And I acknowledge all those at She Writes Press, especially Brooke Warner, publisher; Caitlyn Levin, expediter extraordinaire; and Stephanie Staal, editor, (who, over the course of a year, whittled the stories down to only three). To Michael Morgenfeld, the excellent cartographer who lent his talent and expertise to my maps, in spite of having to add in fictitious places. And, last but not least, to John Shirley, who as a World War II veteran from the U.S. Army 3rd Infantry Division, gave me the opportunity to travel as a "war correspondent" for research throughout France with his liberating troops for the 65th Anniversary of the Southern landing of the Allies (in 2009). And to the many French men and women who opened their homes to me as they shared their favorite recipes, along with their war stories, over many, many glasses of wine.

$\mathscr{R}$eader's $\mathscr{G}$uide

QUESTIONS FOR DISCUSSION

1. What does this book's title, *A Cup of Redemption*, mean within the context of the story?

2. What does the final "cup" signify?

3. Marcelle calls her daughter Sophie back to France and makes a request of her from her deathbed: "Find my father!" Discuss the significance of this request to the family.

4. What did Marcelle sacrifice in order to survive Nazi-occupied Paris during World War II? What lasting impact did that sacrifice have on her?

5. Why did Marcelle leave André behind in Paris? How is finding him late in life important for her?

6. Marcelle's friend, Sophie-Marie Chirade, holds an important secret. Would it have mattered if she had revealed it during the war?

7. The three main characters—Marcelle, Sophie, and Kate—each have hidden a part of their pasts. How does this keep them apart, and how does it bind them together? What are the internal and external barriers to love for each one?

8. Sophie's nightmares have plagued her since her teen years. What drives her to find the cause of and resolution to those nightmares?

9. Sophie's brothers Theirry and Gérard each learn hidden truths about their fathers. Why are their responses so different?

10. Kate is ashamed of having given a child up for adoption. Is this past experience what drives her passion to know more about Marcelle?

11. When Kate runs to France to help Sophie, she is avoiding something. In the end Kate embraces the family complications around an unexpected wedding. Do you think she is ultimately able to accept the relationship her long-lost daughter offers?

12. Marcelle's husband is cruel, yet she remains in the marriage in hopes of giving her children a "family." Why is this so important to her? What strengths allow her to live with unhappiness and yet thrive?

13. Did you find this novel satisfying? What other stories regarding questions of birth or lost identity have you read? In those stories, were those who were separated ever reunited?

14. What understanding of women and families in times of war do you have after reading this book? How has your perspective about the people of France changed?

15. A shared cup of coffee or cooking for family and friends helps Marcelle, Sophie, and Kate each cope with past sorrows. Did you find the connections between women, food, and family in this story important?

$\mathscr{A}$bout the $\mathscr{A}$uthor

Photo credit: Bennington Photography

$\mathscr{C}$AROLE BUMPUS, a retired family therapist, writes a food/travel blog taken from excerpts of her interviews with French and Italian families, known as *Savoring the Olde Ways*. She has been published in both the U.S. and France for her articles on WWII veterans and has also been published in three short story anthologies: *Fault Zone: Words from the Edge, Fault Zone: Stepping up to the Edge* and *Fault Zone: Over the Edge. A Cup of Redemption,* her first historical novel, is loosely based on an elderly French woman's final request to find a father she never knew and the two women who, in their search, find they, too, are struggling with their own travails of wartime legitimacy.

SELECTED TITLES FROM SHE WRITES PRESS

She Writes Press is an independent publishing company
founded to serve women writers everywhere.
Visit us at www.shewritespress.com.

Bittersweet Manor by Tory McCagg. $16.95, 978-1-938314-56-8. A
chronicle of three generations of love, manipulation, entitlement,
and disappointed expectations in an upper-middle class New
England family.

The Belief in Angels by J. Dylan Yates. $16.95, 978-1-938314-64-3.
From the Majdonek death camp to a volatile hippie household on
the East Coast, this narrative of tragedy, survival, and hope spans
more than fifty years, from the 1920s to the 1970s.

The Sweetness by Sande Boritz Berger. $16.95, 978-1-63152-907-8.
A compelling and powerful story of two girls—cousins living on
separate continents—whose strikingly different lives are forever
changed when the Nazis invade Vilna, Lithuania.

Portrait of a Woman in White by Susan Winkler. $16.95,
978-1-938314-83-4. When the Nazis steal a Matisse portrait from
the eccentric, art-loving Rosenswigs, the Parisian family is thrust
into the tumult of war and separation, their fates intertwined with
that of their beloved portrait.

What Is Found, What Is Lost by Anne Leigh Parrish. $16.95,
978-1-938314-95-7. After her husband passes away, a series of
family crises forces Freddie, a woman raised on religion, to
confront long-held questions about her faith.

Fire & Water by Betsy Graziani Fasbinder. $16.95,
978-1-938314-14-8. Kate Murphy has always played by the rules—
but when she meets charismatic artist Jake Bloom, she's forced to
navigate the treacherous territory of passionate love, friendship,
and family devotion.

CPSIA information can be obtained at www.ICGtesting.com
Printed in the USA
BVOW03s0628060914

365123BV00002B/3/P